CREW

TIJAN

Edited: Jessica Royer Ocken
Proofread: Paige Smith, Kara Hildebrand, Chris O'Neil Parece, Amy English
Formatting: Elaine York, Allusion Graphics, LLC
www.allusiongraphics.com

CREW

For my readers.
For everyone who has a little Bren inside them.

CHAPTER ONE

YOU AREN'T SUPPOSED to want to die.

That isn't what society wants to hear. It's not supposed to be felt or thought. It's supposed to be ignored. But here I was, watching my crew beat the crap out of a guy, and all I wanted was to trade places with him.

I knew that sounded morbid. It was true, though, and not like the off-the-cuff comment when you bomb your history exam and it's "kill me now!" Or your boyfriend dumps you and "Gurrrrl, I just wanna dieeee! WTF?!"

No. I was talking about the *dark* kind of wanting to die, where it's in the back of your mind, where it's a little door you want to open and disappear through...

Some days it was hard to suppress and harder to ignore, so right now I wasn't doing either of those.

"You're not going to touch my sister again," Jordan growled before delivering probably his fourth punch. "Got it, *asshole*?"

It was my face getting bloodied. Not that guy's.

Jordan straightened to sneer at the guy lying at his feet.

Jordan Pitts.

He was the self-proclaimed leader of our crew. Note here: *self*-proclaimed. As in, he announced it one day. No one objected and off he went, embracing his cocky swagger and thinking he spoke for our group of four. The truth is he does, I guess, but only when we don't have a problem with what he's saying.

Our group isn't a dick-tatorship, whether he believes that or not.

Jordan bent down—with his long, six-foot-two self—grabbed a hold of the guy's shirt, and lifted him in the air. He shook him, growling again in his face, but the guy couldn't answer. His face was broken. Literally. Either Cross or Jordan had punched his cheek so hard it looked busted. His whole face was a mess of blood and bruises. I would've felt sorry except for two things: he'd tried to rape Jordan's sister, and when Jordan had asked him to report himself, he'd added a curse word and his middle finger, and spat on Jordan's shoes.

Apparently this guy didn't know the reputation of our crew, or Jordan himself.

Which made sense because Mallory Pitts just started attending a new private school at a neighboring town and that's where this guy met her. If he had known, he would've run the other way. You had to give the guy some props, though. Instead of lying, he was honest. He told Jordan exactly what he thought of that suggestion. And anyway, if he'd lied, we would've followed up, and when he didn't report himself, this whole beatdown would've happened anyway.

That was my crew.

Along with Jordan, there were two others besides myself—Cross Shaw and Zellman Greenly. My name is Bren Monroe, and even though I'm in the middle of this whole dark diatribe, and even though we look like the bad guys right now, things aren't always as they seem.

Jordan slammed the guy back down to the ground, then bent over him to issue more threats.

Cross stepped back, and I felt his gaze on me even before I looked up. Yes, there it was. The tawny hazel eyes that so many girls loved. We were family—and not that kind of family. But I'd have to be blind not to understand why so many girls at Roussou High salivated over him.

Six-one. Lean, but built. Cross had a strong, square jaw—one that would clench at times—and a face that was almost prettier than mine. He would've been gorgeous even if he was a girl, a fact I loved to tease him about. But teasing aside, Cross got the girls.

He could just show up somewhere, and ten would appear around him. He could nod at a girl, and she'd go to his side for the night, usually be down for anything he wanted.

Cross was the quiet, nice guy...except he wasn't really either of those at all. I mean, he was, but he wasn't. He was generally quiet, but he talked to me. And he was nice, but he could be lethal. Piss him off, and you'd never see him coming. He wasn't like Jordan with the growling and throwing people around. He'd come right up to you, and then you'd be waking up in the hospital a couple days later.

And while I loved Jordan and Zellman, they weren't Cross.

They weren't my best friend, the guy whose closet I crawled into so many nights when I needed a sanctuary from my own hell called home.

I met his eyes as he came toward me. His golden hair and tanned skin made him every pretty boy's nightmare. When would he wake up and realize he had more potential than all of us? He could go to New York and be a model, or go to Hollywood and be an actor. Why he stayed in Roussou was beyond me.

He wasn't messed up like the rest of us. He wasn't messed up like me.

"You got the look," he said, coming to stand next to me.

Yeah. I knew what he was referencing, but I didn't take the bait.

"Okay, fuckhead," Jordan announced. "We're going to leave you now, and if you think you'd like to turn any of us in, don't forget what we have on you. Got it? Nod your head, dickwad."

Jordan was the intellectual here. He was smart.

The guy made a gurgling sound and managed to move his head a bit.

It sufficed for Jordan, and he nodded. "Good." He turned, his long legs crossing the ground toward us.

I leaned against the bed of his truck, Cross still next to me, as Jordan opened the driver's side door.

Zellman had been standing nearby at the ready. That's what he tended to do—always lurking behind Jordan and waiting. Since

Jordan had come over to us now, so had Zellman. He launched himself up to the opened truck bed behind us.

I heard the cooler open, and he tossed a beer Jordan's way.

"Bren? Cross?" he called.

Cross shook his head.

I turned around to look at the guys. "I'm good. Thanks."

"You sure?" Zellman extended a beer.

"I am."

Jordan's eyes flicked upward—his response to a lot of the things I did. We had each other's backs, but to Jordan that meant doing everything he wanted. Sometimes we disagreed, and every time I didn't do what he did, he took that as disagreeing with him.

Family doesn't work that way.

I watched him, just for a moment.

One day we would battle.

One day it would be me against him.

One day his disapproval would make me snap, or one day he wouldn't *just* be a jerk because I wasn't doing what he wanted. He would go too far, and that would be the day I'd meet him halfway.

I already knew how the lines would shift in our group when that happened. Cross would back me up. Zellman would probably back Jordan. It'd be two against two. Even though I was the only girl in the group—one of only two girls in the entire system—I could handle my own, and I knew I would enjoy lighting into Jordan on that day. But that day wasn't today, and I hoped it would take a long time to come. I did care for Jordan like a brother, though he wasn't my actual blood.

"So." Jordan slammed the door shut again, the force rocking his truck for a second. He propped up a leg. "What's the plan for tonight?"

This was the last night before our senior year started.

Sunday night. People had been to church this morning, and we'd beaten someone bloody this evening. There was irony in there somewhere. I was just too tired to find it.

"Ryerson has a party tonight," Zellman offered. "I say we go." His shaggy curls bounced around as his blue eyes darted between us.

"Yeah?" Jordan's eyes lit up.

Zellman nodded. "I'm down to go. I think Sunday Barnes got new boobs this summer." He grinned. "I'm hoping to check 'em out personally."

Jordan laughed. "I'm good with that." He tipped his head back, finishing his beer, and then tossed the bottle into the trees behind us. "Bren, Cross, what about you guys?"

Cross would wait for me, so I said, "I'm good for the night."

"No party?"

"I'm gonna head home."

Jordan's disapproval settled in the air over us, but no one said a word.

"Think I'm down with you guys for the party," Cross added after a moment.

Zellman thrust a fist in the air. "Hell yeah. Take it." He offered his half-emptied beer.

Cross laughed, but shook his head. "I'll wait for the good liquor there. Ryerson always has something."

"Yeah! That's what it's about." Zellman finished his beer and reached into the cooler for a second. "Jordan?"

"I gotta drive." He glanced to me. "Ride home?"

I looked over to where the guy still lay on the ground. He hadn't moved.

I shook my head. "Think I'll walk. I can cut through the trees."

"You sure?"

Cross moved around us, clapping Jordan on the shoulder. "Let's go. Bren can take care of herself." He glanced back to me, circling around the front of the truck to get into the passenger side. He knew I wanted to be on my own tonight. He knew it because he could feel it. Just like I could almost hear his thoughts now.

She always has.

I finished in my own head, *Always will.*

Cross' statement seemed to settle the other guys, and Jordan started the truck. He circled around me, kicking up a cloud of dust, and zoomed back down the way we'd come. He saluted me with a finger as he passed by. Zellman had settled into the bed, sitting by the cooler, and he held up his beer as his goodbye.

I shook my head, the smallest hint of a smile tugging at my mouth, but that was all the reaction they got.

Once they were gone, it was just me, the bloodied guy, and the same dark quiet I'd felt earlier.

It came out of nowhere at times, swallowing me whole. Some days it would vanish just as quickly. Other times, like tonight, it lingered.

It used to scare me. I now missed it when it wasn't here, but I always knew it would move on. It was like a firefly slipping away into the night. When that happened, I was left with the feeling that I'd let something slip through my fingers.

This night, that firefly remained.

It warmed me.

CHAPTER TWO

THE DIRT CRUNCHED under my shoes as I headed for the guy.

He wasn't unconscious, like he'd been playing. At my approach, one eye opened, and I saw panic flare there. He tried to get away, but couldn't. His injuries were too much.

I sat next to him, fishing out my phone. "Stop." He was still trying to get away, but it was only adding to his injuries. "I'm not going to hurt you."

A gargled groan came from him.

I shook my head. "Trying to talk is useless. Save your energy." I waved my phone at him. "We're in the middle of nowhere."

Jordan liked to bring his victims to this part of town for that reason. It was a small alcove at the top of a hill. The street ended up here, and there were only trees surrounding us.

The guy quieted, watching me with that same panicked eye.

"I'm going to call for an ambulance. I'm going to give them your name, and then I'm going to sit here with you until they come. If you turn me in..." I let the threat hang between us.

Guilt flashed in his eyes. He knew what would happen.

I dialed 9-1-1 and sat with him.

This scene should've bothered me: a guy who could barely move and was bleeding out beside me. The silence in the woods around us. The fact that he was like this because of my group. But it didn't.

Now that the guys were gone, the firefly lingered beside me, keeping me company.

I closed my eyes, my insides matching the outside.

I felt one with the darkness.

7

No. This scene didn't bother me one bit.

I loved the silence. I welcomed the silence, and it wasn't interrupted until the shrill ambulance sirens cut through the air.

I let out a sigh, knowing the dark calm would go away now, and looked out over the hill. From the top, I could see the lights of the ambulance coming from miles away.

I'd have to move. They couldn't find me with him, but for now I waited.

The road wound all the way around the hill on its way up. Once the ambulance was just around the bend, I patted the guy on the leg.

"Okay, I'm off." I glanced back to him as I stood. "You're going to be fine." I dusted off my jeans. Some of the dirt seemed to land in his eye, and he blinked a few times, still watching me steadily. It seemed like he was asking me not to leave, but I shook my head.

"I can't stay. Just don't mess with another girl. Okay?"

I waited a beat. The ambulance was almost to us. I needed to go. Yet I bent down over him. I took out my knife and placed it against his throat. He went completely still.

"If I hear that you've touched another girl against her will..." I pressed the knife against his skin. "I'll come alone next time, and I won't leave you awake. Got it?"

He blinked. That's all he could do.

The lights began to turn toward where we were, so I moved into the darkness, slipping my knife back into my pocket.

The ambulance lit up the street where he lay, and as they parked, I stepped back into the trees. They hid me, even as I heard one of the paramedics curse.

"Fuck. Who did this?"

The other paramedic didn't answer, and as instructed, the guy didn't either. As one EMT began to talk to him, taking his vitals, the other opened the back to pull out a stretcher. It was only a few minutes later when they were gone again.

I stepped out and walked back to where he'd lain as the ambulance moved down the hill. Its lights disappeared into the darkness, and I was all alone.

There were shortcuts all through the woods, but I was content to walk down the middle of the road.

I just followed the white dashes.

CHAPTER THREE

I WALKED PAST the motorcycles on the front lawn, knowing the house would be unlocked.

What I didn't know was whether my brother would be home. It was Sunday night, his night off from the bar, but that didn't always mean he'd be here. He kept a random schedule, coming in and leaving at odd hours. I was usually okay if he was gone, but not because he was a bad guy. He was just an absent guy, had been most my life.

I stepped inside and quietly shut the door. I held my breath, waiting, listening. No lights were on, but I smelled smoke as it wafted past me on a breeze. The back patio door stood open. I crossed to the kitchen and stood at the sink. They weren't on the patio, but I saw the fire pit lit up, and a second later, Heather's voice drifted to me on another breeze.

"...can't blame her. She's a senior this year."

My brother's girlfriend, or his on-again-off-again-whatever-the-fuck-they-were-doing-childhood-sweethearts-girlfriend, sat forward in her lawn chair.

My brother, Channing, sat next to her, tipping his beer back as he spoke. "Give me a break. She should be home and you know it."

It was just the two of them.

They were talking about me. Even now, knowing that, I let some of the darkness sneak back in. When I felt it, it pushed all the other emotions away. I felt some peace, but I knew it'd come at a cost. There was always a cost. The darkness was there for a reason. I wasn't an idiot. I knew I was messed up, but I couldn't help it sometimes. Or like now, I welcomed it. The firefly had left me on the walk home. I loved feeling the buzz of its wing next to me again.

I turned and sat, my back against the cupboard beneath the kitchen sink.

Eyes closed.

Head down.

I listened to them.

A lawn chair creaked. A bottle clanked against another one. Then came the *swish* sound of another bottle being opened.

"She's my sister, Heather. You act like I shouldn't worry about her."

A frustrated sigh. "That's not my issue. I'm just saying, you're forgetting how we were at that age. We ran wild. The shit we did, fuck. You want your sister to act like some normal kid, and there's no way she can. Not with all that's happened to her. You need to be realistic."

"Thanks," he clipped out.

"Your mom died when she was so young, and your dad went to prison. Max died a few years ago. Give her time."

"It's been two years."

"She lost her parents, her half-brother, and she had to move out of the house she grew up in."

"Fucking bank. I offered to pay the rest of that mortgage. Asshole had a stick up his ass."

"Channing." Her voice was soft and soothing. "You can't blame yourself."

"Yeah." Glass shattered. "I could've been around more. I know that much."

It was the same conversation I always heard from them.

My brother blamed himself—for what I had no idea. I didn't blame him for his absence. Hell, half the time I was jealous of him. I wish I could've disappeared like he had when he was growing up. He spent most his time from eighth grade until he got his own house on someone else's couch. I would've done that too, if I could've. I'd been too young.

Heather half consoled him, but she was always frustrated too. I could hear it in her voice. It was in everything, actually, even the way she walked around the house. Some days I wished she would move in, but part of me was scared of the day it happened—because when that happened, something else would happen. I didn't know what, but I always felt it. I carried it around in my stomach.

The relationship between Heather and me was *half* because of that. We were half friends. We were half not-friends. We were half present, half not-present. Half haunted, half alive. Or wait, maybe that was just me? But Heather averted her eyes when we talked to each other sometimes, and she avoided having conversations with me in the first place. But other times, she was in my face, eyes blazing with fierce determination. I was never sure which Heather I would get, but I knew it wasn't me or her. It was the question of her relationship with Channing. I got it. I did. I could sympathize somewhat.

I generally avoided everything.

Heather was nice. She loved my brother, but I was in the way. They couldn't have a normal relationship because of me.

A part of me ached at the thought. Who was I to stand in their way? But this brought me back to the conversations they always had:

I would be out.

Channing would grumble.

Heather would comfort.

And when I overheard, I'd always wonder: why didn't they just let me go? Why did my brother keep trying to play the part of father/parent/big brother extraordinaire? It wasn't a role that suited him.

He was a legend.

He was a fighter.

He ran his own crew.

The domestic look was not something he wore well. I agreed with Heather on this part.

He hadn't been around when it was just my dad and me. Our half-brother was never around, or hardly. He was kept with his mother most our life. Channing started his own crew in high school—the whole reason the system was created. And when he graduated, he started working right away. He took over my dad's bar two years ago, and he made it better. He brought in our cousin, and they made it a success. And he'd been fighting at events the whole time. He talked about retiring, but I never knew if that was a wish, like he was wishing to become an adult? Or he was wishing he didn't have a teenage sister to take care of? Or he was wishing for his old life again?

Like that.

Maybe fighting was his way of coping? I didn't understand that either.

It wasn't like he and my dad had been close.

Channing was like our mom, and when she died, it was like he went with her. He left the family. I mean, I saw him around town and at parties sometimes—until he either kicked me out or had my guys and me kicked out. He said we were all too young.

Jordan was relieved when Channing stopped attending the same parties we did, and we had learned to avoid him at the bigger parties.

The Roussou scene was different than other towns.

People didn't leave. Or if they did, they weren't in the system, and those people—the Normals—didn't really exist to us anyway. In the crew system, we're all part of a big, fucked-up extended family, no matter the age.

"I'm going to get a refill." Heather's chair groaned. "You want more beer?"

That was my cue.

I stood and slipped down the hallway to my bedroom just as the patio screen door opened.

Then the refrigerator opened, lighting up the kitchen and dining room.

I grabbed my backpack and returned to the hallway. I paused, listening as Heather opened some bottles, pouring into a cup. I smelled rum. Bottles clinked together, and then the fridge door shut.

The inside of the house fell into darkness again.

The screen door opened and closed.

As I heard her footsteps going over the patio, down to the backyard, I slipped out the front door again.

CHAPTER
FOUR

I OPENED MY eyes at the sound of grass crunching.

When I looked up, Cross stood over me, but he wasn't watching me. He was looking at the reason I'd come out here.

He sighed, sitting next to me. "How'd I know you'd be here tonight?"

"You tracked my phone?" I sat up and grinned at him.

He chuckled, reaching for the whiskey in my hand. The cap was already off, and he took a drink, hissing through his teeth. "Fuck." He handed it back. "Why do you drink that shit?"

I smirked, taking a drink. Unlike him, I enjoyed the burn. "Why do you?"

"Because you do."

He said that like it made the most sense in the world.

I laughed, taking another drink before lifting my head. Below us, at the bottom of the hill and across the street, was my old home. I had no idea what time it was, but it was after dark and the house had been silent since I got to my spot. I hadn't expected otherwise.

I didn't know the people living there. They were new to Roussou, but I knew they were a young couple, maybe in their thirties, and they'd moved into my house when the bank sold it again. They had little kids, and they'd left some of the toys on the front lawn. I wanted to go down and put the toys away, place them on the porch and inside the toy chest there, but that was a bad idea. Talk about stalking. That was a line I couldn't cross, not yet anyway. Right now I just came to watch my old home.

"How was the party?" I asked.

Cross shrugged, hanging his arms over his knees with his hands looped together. "It was okay." He gave me a half-grin. "I'd rather hang, looking at your old house instead."

"That's total bullshit, and you know it." I handed him the whiskey.

He took it.

"You and Monica break up again?" She was his on-again, off-again girlfriend, but I knew they'd gotten back together on Friday. Seemed right they'd break up tonight, just in time for school to start tomorrow. The relationship was really one-sided anyway. Cross tended to sleep with whoever he wanted, though not a lot of girls talked about their time with him. Cross liked his secrecy, and I was one of the few privy to his freewheeling whoredom. Monica was the other. Cross had never kept it secret that if she wanted exclusive and steady, she needed to go somewhere else.

And how I knew so much about Cross' sex life was lost on me. We never seemed to talk about it.

He shrugged again, reaching for the whiskey and taking another drink. A second hiss, and he returned the bottle.

I took it, throwing my head back for a shot.

Goddamn.

The burn was still there. Good. It hadn't dulled yet.

"Bren."

I tensed, hearing the question in his tone. I heard reluctance too. Neither of us wanted to go where he was going with his next question.

"Why do you come here all the time?"

It wasn't all the time. Maybe two out of seven nights.

I focused on the whiskey. "You know why."

"No, I don't." He turned to watch me.

I hated when he did that. It was like I'd let part of the wall slip and he could read me.

I took two shots of whiskey this time. "I don't know."

I did, though.

I came to look for her, to see if she was moving around inside that house. I wanted a glimpse of her, even though I knew she was dead, even though I knew I was looking for a ghost. I still came.

I wanted to see her one last time.

"You're not supposed to lie to me."

I heard his disappointment and breathed in.

I let the air circulate through my lungs and then back out. One steady breath. Then I murmured, "You know why I come."

"For your mom?"

I frowned. Why did he have to say it? I didn't want to hear it. I just wanted to feel it.

I nodded.

"I figured." He took the whiskey from me again, drank, and handed it back. "I wanted you to say it. Just once."

My throat burned, but not from the alcohol. I wiped at the corner of my eye. "So, the party sucked then?"

"Yeah."

A small grin tugged at my lips. "Now who's the liar?"

He laughed and reached for the whiskey again. "Yeah. Maybe. Still rather be with you."

I nodded.

I was glad.

CHAPTER
FIVE

CROSS WAS WAITING in the parking lot for me the next morning. He was on the back of his truck, the tailgate down, a few others with him. They scattered when I parked and got out.

He jumped off, closing the back as I walked by. "Was your brother mad this morning?"

I grimaced, remembering.

We'd fallen asleep on the hill and woken up early in the morning, way too early. Cross gave me a ride home, and I'd hoped to sneak in, shower, dress, and slip out. It hadn't worked out that way.

"No."

I'd thought I was in the clear. Channing and Heather didn't always sleep with a fan on, but they had one going this morning. I crept in and saw Heather in bed with a lump behind her.

"Never mistake a body pillow for a person. I did that this morning," I told Cross as we walked across the lot and into the school.

Channing had been right behind me, and the quiet silence of the morning was finished.

"Where were you last night?" he'd demanded.

"Ssshhh!" I'd glanced back at him, but Heather was already rolling around. We'd woken her up.

"He let me leave without much of an explanation," I told Cross. "But I have to have dinner with him tonight."

"Doesn't he work tonight?"

"Yeah." We got to the school doors, and I used my back to open them. "Guess where we're going tonight?"

"You're kidding. Your brother is the opposite of a parent who'd want you to show up for home family meals. How's he going to do that? Between his guys, his woman, and his bar?"

I shrugged. I'd do my part, show up where or when I had to and let my brother figure out the rest. As long as I was in the clear, for once. I shook my head.

The hallway was full with people, but once we stepped inside, a nice clear path appeared for us. That's what happened for anyone in a crew. People thought we were gangs. We weren't. I hated gangs. If it was that situation, I wouldn't be in. So, no. We weren't gangs—there was no hazing ritual, and we weren't in until we decided to risk limb and life to get out. No one told me what to do, not unless I backed them up, and if it was a situation where I didn't want to back up my guys, that was a whole other problem that needed to be dealt with. We took care of our own, and unlike normal friendships, we went to bat for each other. Sometimes literally. That was the basic rule of being in a crew: you backed each other up. No matter what. Now, I couldn't say our case was the same for the others. Some were more official. They had auditions, a whole application process, but some just happened naturally.

Those were the best kind.

That's how we had come to be.

Jordan, Zellman, Cross, and me. We were known as the Wolves, though we didn't have an official name. There were no T-shirts or secret handshakes. Our crew had formed over several years because of a couple key events. The first was in sixth grade when Zellman was being bullied. Jordan had waded in. He'd thrown kids out of the way and given the bully a couple black eyes. Hence Zellman's loyalty to Jordan.

The next time was at the end of seventh grade.

A guy tried to creep up on me behind school one day. I fought back, but he had friends. What could've happened, I didn't like to think about.

Cross and I had been friends since Amy Pundrie called me fat in third grade, and Cross told her she was Amy *Pig*drie instead.

He'd kept calling her that until he got in trouble in fourth grade and was sent to the principal. He only whispered the name after that, and it got shortened to Amy Piggy. Once I hit puberty and realized what it meant to be a girl, I told him to knock it off with the weight-related name-calling. He hadn't uttered a word about it since, but he still gave her the side-eye sometimes.

Anyway, Cross had shown up the day the creeper was after me, and Jordan and Zellman had shown up too.

Cross took out the guys from the left.

Jordan and Zellman took out the guys from the right.

I returned the favor a few months later when a guy tried to knife Jordan in a fight. I showed up, grabbed the knife, and slammed it into his side. I wasn't one to throw punches, but people learned to be wary of me when I pulled out a knife. My throwing skills were decent, better than most normal people, but my talent lay in the slicing and dicing motion.

There were other crews that were bigger than ours, but we were the most feared. There was a reason for that.

"You already know your locker and schedule?" Cross asked.

I nodded, heading to my locker. "Unlike you, I showed up for registration last week. Fancy that, *me* being the good student."

A few girls were already looking at him. I was somewhat surprised he wasn't already gone, getting his dick wet, but it was the first day of the year. He wouldn't be leaving my side or Jordan and Zellman's, not unless he was forced away.

He groaned, resting his back against the locker beside mine. "Something tells me it won't last."

I grinned, turning the lock until the door opened. Then I pulled a piece of paper from my pocket. I stowed my bag inside and brandished the paper in the air. "Good thing I got your info too."

He snatched it. "Ah! I love you."

"What?" an irritated voice exclaimed behind us. "There's no crew coupling. Or at least there isn't in *yours*."

Cross and I shared a look as he turned around.

"Hey, twin sister."

Tasmin, who answered only to Taz, beamed up at him. Like Cross, she was naturally tan, with the same tawny hazel eyes and golden blonde hair. Even their lean builds were the same. Cross just had broad shoulders, while Taz was petite. Her hair fell to her waist, and today she'd braided one side along her skull, all the way to the ends.

She was gorgeous, just like her brother.

And while she wasn't in our crew, she was as close as possible. Cross was protective, keeping her away from the violence, and she also didn't like the system. She didn't understand it.

"Hey, twin brother!" She waved a finger between us. "Is this the reason I saw Monica crying at the end of the hall?"

He looked.

I sighed. "I knew it."

He turned back, frowning. "I never answered your question last night."

"So you two *were* together last night?" Taz's tone was accusing.

Cross cringed.

So did I. This was more attention than we needed. If you were in a crew, you got attention. Any, but especially ours. It was just a fact. Her voice rose and I cursed in my head, wondering who'd pick up on what she was saying and run wild with it. Wolves were infamous, but Cross was infamous in his own right. Me too, if I was being truthful and not hiding from it. Any girl who joined got noticed, and the fact I was in the Wolf Crew, which no one got into—this shit would be spread before the end of next hour.

I didn't like it, but I'd have to handle it. Still, this innuendo on Cross and me as a couple didn't rest easy on my shoulders.

"Hey, hey." I reached for her finger. She lowered it before I could grab it, and I rested against the neighboring locker. I raised an eyebrow. "It wasn't like that, and you know it."

She rolled her eyes. "I just think it's stupid. You two belong together. Now scoot!" She waved at her brother and nodded to the locker behind him. "That's my locker." She winked at me. "I pulled some Student Council strings and got us all together."

"Wait." He looked down at the paper I'd given him. "My locker is by yours?"

"You're smart," I deadpanned.

He rolled his eyes, but I could see a smile.

Taz nodded to where I was resting. "Right there."

A grin spread over Cross' face. "Nice. What about—"

"No. Those losers are in another hall."

Cross and I shared another look, but it was what it was. Taz made no secret of her hatred for Jordan, and her volume had increased over the last two years. Sometimes I wondered if her hate was covering something else. Was there something more going on between Taz and Jordan? I hadn't braved Taz's wrath enough to ask her, and when Cross shook his head at me, I knew he hadn't either.

After grabbing my notepad, I moved out of the way. My locker closed as both of theirs opened.

"This is awesome, Taz." Cross didn't have a bag with him, so he tossed his keys inside. "Thank you."

While her brother was empty-handed, Taz was not. She carried a bag overflowing with items, and she'd pulled a big pink cart behind her. Books were piled high on it, along with locker separators, anything someone would need for an office, and a small dry-erase board. She had cardboard cutouts for photographs and even some pink glittery stuff. I had no clue what she would do with those, but this was Taz. She would make the inside of her locker a masterpiece. I had no doubt.

"Are you kidding me?" She dropped her bag to the floor and began unloading the cart. "You guys are doing me a favor. If you're both here, the other girls will stay away." She glanced over her shoulder.

I followed her gaze, but I already knew who she was referring to. There were the usual girls who gawked at Cross, but she meant a whole other group. Though the hallway was busy, that other group had gathered across from us. I recognized a lot of girls from our grade congregating at Sunday Barnes' locker. Half of them were eyeing Cross.

They saw me, but kept eyeing him as if he were a piece of steak and they were starving. They didn't care I was here. I frowned at that.

If they saw me watching them, they'd usually look away. My presence alone would deter them. Not today. Today, I saw the hunger in their eyes. The girls were brazen as they watched Cross. Sunday was friends with Monica, but as I skimmed the group, I could see she wasn't there.

I shifted on my feet, rounding to face them more fully. I didn't like this. I didn't like that they were ignoring me, even though I didn't care that they were here for Cross. That never happened.

"Their notches have gone up," I mumbled to Cross. They were getting bolder.

He grunted, knowing exactly what I meant.

"Stop that!" Taz protested, her hands on her hips. "I'm the twin. I'm supposed to have the secret language with him. Not you."

I smiled.

Taz was my only female friend. I liked how feisty she could be, and she wasn't all fucked up like me. I knew there was pain inside her, but she was spunky. If I wasn't already best buds with Cross, I might've considered Taz my best friend.

Okay. If I was normal, she would've been my best friend.

I knew she had a special place in her heart for me too, and a second later her fight was already gone.

She groaned. "And you're smiling at me. Fuck, Bren. I'm like my brother. I can't stay mad at you for two seconds."

Cross laughed. Seeming to change his mind, he grabbed his keys, shut his locker, and snatched a pen from me. Moving around me, he kissed his sister on the forehead. "I'll see you guys later." He nodded to me, heading down to the other senior hallway.

She looked at me, her face reddening a bit. "He's going to check in with the other two, isn't he?"

I nodded. She knew it. I didn't know why she'd asked.

"We *are* in a crew together," I pointed out.

"Yeah." Her lips pressed together and resolve flashed in her eyes. "That's up after this year. Thank God."

I frowned at her, but didn't say anything. She went back to unloading the cart.

Taz was excited for graduation. She felt she'd get her brother back, and in a way, I understood. She'd confessed this to me a few times after too much wine. See? She wasn't like us even with her alcohol choice. She was classy, preferring martinis and wine. She'd long graduated from wine coolers. I didn't even know when she'd had those, but she claimed she had. I preferred the hard stuff, like whiskey or bourbon, or beer. Straight beer. Anything beer. Jordan had been known to get his own pony-keg at times.

But back to Taz. When she last got a little too tipsy, we'd been at a bonfire. We were all sitting on logs, and the guys had taken off, leaving Taz and me behind.

Staring into the fire, she'd started complaining about the group:

We took all of Cross' time.

We took him away.

He didn't even stay at the house much anymore.

Thank God we would graduate and disperse.

But not all crews broke up after graduation.

Taz was banking on it, but she was forgetting that sometimes that didn't happen. It all depended on the group. My brother had one of the longest running crews in Roussou. The only other one to challenge him had broken up a while ago. Their leader got sent to prison for assaulting some of Channing's friends from Fallen Crest. He was mum on the details, and I didn't push. If I wanted to know, I could've asked around to find out. I just hadn't cared.

I had a hard time imagining that our crew wouldn't last.

"Is it just the crew thing? Or is it personal?" I asked Taz tentatively.

Wide-eyed, she turned to me. "What?" I think she'd forgotten I was still here.

"Do you hate the group, or is it me?" I rested my shoulder against my locker, facing her.

"No!" Her mouth fell open, then closed. She shook her head. "No, no. I wouldn't want you to think that."

"So, it's Jordan and Zellman? Or the group as a whole?"

"Wh-what?" She blinked.

I figured it was the crew as a whole, but I wanted to push some buttons here. They were part of my identity, and while I had a soft spot for Taz, it dug inside me that she had such venom for us.

"It can't be Zellman," I mused. "He's a happy fly." Except in a fight. "Didn't you and Jordan work at the same place this summer?"

"Wha—huh?" She gaped at me.

"Taz!" a voice called suddenly.

And she just got saved from a couple more uncomfortable questions I'd planned to toss her way. I wanted to poke her a bit about Jordan. That'd have to wait, but I could already feel my desire to push back at her fading away.

Seeing that Sunday Barnes hadn't stayed at her locker, I knew my time with Taz was done for the morning.

Sunday approached, wearing her cheerleading uniform, with half her group in tow.

Smoothing a hand down her side, she perched her fist on her hip and smiled widely at us. "Taz, Mrs. Bellacheq said you left the squad this year. I was hoping to talk you into joining again."

Taz and I shared a glance. We both knew I was out, and we moved as one unit.

Taz stepped forward.

I fell back.

Call me unfriendly, but this was how I'd been all my life. I kept to my own, and my own consisted of my crew and Taz. That was it. I'd never played well with other girls, and I had no desire to talk to them. That wasn't a rule—I could talk to whoever I wanted—it was just my preference.

I'd begun to turn and head in the direction Cross had gone when Sunday raised her voice again.

"Bren!" Her voice hitched at the end, and she cleared her throat. Her smile got even wider. "Hey. Hi. You weren't at Alex's party last night."

I stopped, half-turned away from them.

Taz stepped in front of me. "Come on, Sunday. You know full well I left the squad. You've had practice for two weeks by now."

I glanced back, held Sunday's gaze for a moment, then turned and left.

Sunday Barnes tried to talk to me.

I frowned to myself as I moved through the second senior hallway. Other girls, no matter where they were on the social ladder, respected the system. They stayed away from us, but she'd violated that rule. Granted, it was an unspoken rule. There was nothing set in stone, but it bothered me.

What I'd noticed earlier was right. Something was changing this year. The girls seemed braver.

I was halfway down the hallway and could already hear Jordan's voice when a different one cut in. Someone grabbed my arm.

"You didn't show at my party last night!"

And all hell broke loose.

CHAPTER
SIX

WHEN THE HAND grabbed my arm, I reacted.

I reached back, took that hand, and flipped around so it twisted backwards. A guy yelled out in pain, but I wasn't listening. I was behind him, still holding onto his wrist, as I slammed him into the locker.

I heard yelling.

People were shoving.

I was only focused on the guy in front of me.

My knife out, I leaned in close, whispering into his ear, "You touch me again, and I'll slice your veins."

I eyed him as I made my threat. This wasn't just a random person who'd reached for me. It was Alex Ryerson, leader of the biggest crew at Roussou High School. He was a stout guy, muscular, but short, and I swear, his attitude was caked on to make up for his height. His round face had wide eyes—a little too close together and sunken in. He turned so he could see me. There was scruff on his face, probably hadn't shaved because of the party last night. I felt the stubble against my arm as I pressed into him a little harder.

Who he was didn't matter to me. *No one* grabbed me.

I felt hands reach for me, but then they were ripped away. As Alex stilled under my knife, I knew without looking that I had three guys backing me up.

"You touch me again, I'll make you bleed."

He growled, but jerked his head in a nod, "Yeah. Yeah. Sorry."

I waited. My heart slammed into my throat.

Then I heard a soft voice behind me. "Let him go, Bren."

That was Cross.

His hand touched me.

His hand, yes.

Someone else's, no.

"I'm sorry, Bren." Alex turned a bit more to see me better.

I blinked a few times.

Maybe he saw the crazy in me. Maybe he was nervous because my knife was still out. Whatever the reason, he was cautious as he began to straighten back up.

I kept my knife to his throat, but I moved back with him. Once we were both upright, I slipped it away. "Don't touch me like that."

"Yeah." He exhaled a deep breath. His chest lifted up, filling under his sleeveless shirt, and he held his hands up at hip-level. "I'm sorry."

"Come on!" A guy came forward, but Jordan slammed him back.

He was in the guy's face. "Come on what? You tell me."

"Hey, hey." Alex moved past me, keeping a wary eye on me as he went to his guys' side.

Jordan fell back, his own hands up.

Alex cleared his throat, his arms stretching between us and his guys. "We're good. Everything is good."

"Touch one of my crew again, and we'll have problems," Jordan threatened under his breath.

"Look..." Alex sent me a beseeching look. "I wasn't thinking. I was just going to give you crap for not being at my party last night. That's all."

"You touch your own like that?" Cross growled, right beside me.

His point was obvious: I wasn't a girl. I was crew.

Alex had forgotten that when he grabbed me.

"What is going on here?" a voice boomed from the end of the hallway.

Everyone stepped back. It would've been comical if I hadn't been part of it. Backs hit lockers again, but this time it was on purpose. Arms crossed over chests. A few people shoved their hands into their pockets. Everyone tried to look relaxed, like we were all hanging out. Even Jordan pretended to look at his nails, a faint grin on his face.

Principal Neeon shook his head.

He was tall, his bald head towering over most everyone except Jordan. They were the same height, but Principal Neeon outweighed him by a hundred pounds. If anyone could manage our school, a retired linebacker from the NFL fit the bill perfectly. It didn't hurt that his entire family were cops either.

His eyes narrowed on Jordan and Alex.

"Mr. Pitts."

Jordan's eyes lit up, like he'd just noticed our principal standing there. He straightened from the locker. "Oh hey, Mr. Neeon. How are you this fine morning?"

Mr. Neeon was unfazed. "Are you going to pretend an altercation didn't almost happen here?"

Jordan opened his mouth.

Mr. Neeon pointed to the right corner of the ceiling. "We had cameras put in over the summer."

Jordan's mouth closed with a snap.

"Surprise." Our principal's smile didn't reach his eyes. He raised his voice, booming again as he scanned the entire hallway. "That message is for everyone here. Roussou High School will not tolerate violence. Any violence! No violence." His eyes fell to me. "That goes for anybody, crew *or* Normals."

I didn't react. I didn't even blink.

Alex coughed, clearing his throat. "As an honorary member of Student Council, I think we need to make sure students' rights aren't being violated as well."

Principal Neeon turned, his hands going into his pockets. "An honorary member? Did you just nominate yourself?"

Alex grinned, a twinkle in his eyes. "I doubt they'll kick me off, and I'm serious, Mr. Neeon. We need to make sure our privacy and confidentiality are maintained."

The principal just stared.

Alex didn't buckle. He kept that cocky smirk on his face, and along with us, he was one who could. His group had around thirty members, ranging over all the grades, so he was protected. His older brother had established their crew, and when Drake graduated last year, Alex stepped into the leadership role.

It didn't always happen that way, but it had with their group. It was good as long as the previous leader okayed it, and he had. I would know. I'd dated him until he decided he was done with everything in Roussou. Every*one* too.

"Bathrooms and locker rooms are protected. There is no surveillance in those places, but everywhere else?" He stepped closer to Alex, towering over him. "You're damned right I put those cameras up."

Alex's twinkle looked a bit more forced. "Well, thank you for that respect of privacy."

"The times when you guys could walk around this school, literally shoving around your weight, is over, Mr. Ryerson. When you're on my grounds, there is no crew system."

"That's just—" Alex swallowed, his Adam's apple bobbing up and down. "Wonderful."

Principal Neeon looked at Jordan. "I am going to review those tapes, and if I find any violence on there, the appropriate persons will be penalized." His gaze fell to me. "Now!" He glanced back to Alex, his tone lighter. "Mr. Ryerson, if you could come with me to my office. There's someone here to see you."

"What?" Alex frowned. "I didn't do anything..." His voice trailed off as he gazed down the hallway where Principal Neeon had come from.

The rest of us looked too.

And there, standing unperturbed by the attention, was a guy.

His dark hair was rumpled. He had a bulldog-type face, with his mouth pulled close to his nose and his eyes set close to each other, but with a square jawline. He shouldn't have been good-looking, but with his broad shoulders and athletic build, he was. It was also in the defiant way his nostrils flared, his head rising as he looked at everyone staring at him.

There was something about him...

The way he stood there, a backpack thrown over one shoulder, his hand in his pocket. A familiar feeling tingled at the back of my neck.

When Alex said his name, it all clicked.

"Fuck, Race. What are you doing here?"

Race Ryerson.

This was Drake and Alex's cousin, the one I'd never met.

CHAPTER
SEVEN

"LANGUAGE, MR. RYERSON." Principal Neeon extended a hand toward Race. "And this is why I asked for your presence. I'll let, uh, your cousin give the explanation." He looked at Race. "You have your schedule?"

Race came over to us, nodding. "I do. Thank you, Mr. Neeon."

"Yes. Well..." Our principal scanned the group one last time. "I'll leave you to it then."

Alex didn't look like his cousin, or his brother either. While both of them were dark and somewhat rugged, in their own way, Alex's hair frayed at the ends. It fell to his shoulders, but he had it pulled back today.

Race's smirk never faltered, but a coolness came to his eyes as he looked from Jordan to Cross, then to me.

"Family emergency, cousin," he answered. His gaze left me as he turned to Alex. "You got yourself a roommate."

"What?" Alex straightened to his fullest height. "What happened?"

Race looked over his shoulder at everyone.

We were all listening. Not even hiding it.

"I'll tell you later, huh?"

"Oh. Oh yeah." Alex raked a hand through his hair. "That's cool." He looked at me. "Bren, I *am* sorry about grabbing you. I know better. I just forgot." He glanced at Cross. "You disappeared too."

Cross' arm came down around my shoulders. He raised his chin. "It was a crew thing last night."

Alex's gaze flickered to Jordan and Zellman. A slight question lingered there.

Jordan's eyebrows lowered as he nodded. "They had it covered." He jerked a thumb toward Zellman on his right side. "We were free to get wasted and laid." He held up a fist. "Thanks for that, man."

Alex snorted, hitting it with his own fist. "Yeah. Any time. That's why I throw those parties, so *you* can get laid, Pitts."

Jordan shrugged. "Seems a good enough reason in my mind."

Zellman started laughing. "It's the new theme for every party now: getting Jordan laid."

A warning bell sounded.

Most of the students began grabbing things, hurrying around us to their classes.

But not us. We stayed put.

"Anyway." Alex touched Race's arm and jerked his head to the side. "I gotta talk to some guys. You'll be okay? You know where you're going?"

"I'll be fine." Race's eyes were still fixed on me, blatantly staring.

Cross' arm tightened around my shoulder. "Can she help you with something?" It was in the tone of his voice that stopped Alex, had him turning back to look between us. There was a dangerous note in Cross' voice, low and lethal, and it sent those same tingles flaring down my spine. He didn't say it in an obvious way, where there was a challenge thrown down between them. Those same words spoken by anyone else might've come off sounding like they were insecure, or threatened. Not with Cross. Not when he spoke.

It was the opposite.

And as the new guy took in the casual way Cross stood next to me, the deliverance of those words, and the way even his cousin faltered, he knew Cross was someone not to cross. Pardon the pun.

"Guys," Alex murmured.

Jordan jostled forward to stand in front of me.

Race dipped his head toward his cousin. "I'm good."

"You sure?"

Race's gaze skirted from me, to Cross, to Jordan, and then he nodded again. He said in a sigh, "Yeah. I'm fine."

Alex nodded and began walking away. "Okay. I'll see you later then."

His cousin nodded. "Yeah."

Alex left the hallway, his guys following, though quite a few glanced over their shoulders, still watching us. It wasn't long until the rest of the hallway emptied, and it was just the four of us and Race Ryerson.

He looked around. "You guys don't go to class or something?"

Jordan ignored that, his eyebrows arching. "We're here because we're crew. You?"

"What?" A question formed in Race's dark eyes, followed by understanding. His eyes widened a bit. "That actually exists?" He looked between us, ending with me again.

"Fuck's sake." Even Zellman was fed up and moved to partially block me too. He was also blocking Cross, which didn't bode well.

Cross kicked, hitting the back of Zellman's knees. They jerked forward from reflex, and he rounded on Cross, laughing.

"Asshole."

Cross hit him on the shoulder. "Stop standing in front of me."

Zellman gestured to me. "I'm standing in front of her, but you know." He shrugged. "I don't want to piss her off at the same time."

I rolled my eyes. I didn't need protection.

"You should go," I told Race, moving around all of them.

He stared at me without answering. No blinking. Nothing. He just...stared.

Zellman growled, "Dude, move along. I don't care what your last name is."

A normal person would've scattered long ago.

But Race didn't move. He continued to stare long and hard at Zellman, then his gaze returned to me.

As those dark eyes met mine, I felt a stirring inside. I didn't like it.

I raised my head. "Do you have a problem with me?"

His cocky smirk came back, a soft chuckle slipping out.

The guys moved forward a step.

"Seriously, man?" Jordan glared down at him.

Still, Race didn't cower. "You're just like he said."

He. I knew who he meant the second he said it. My fucking ex-boyfriend. Drake.

"Who the fuck are you talking about?" Zellman demanded.

Jordan ignored him and moved forward, almost invading Race's personal space. "I will light you up, fucker. I don't care if Alex is your family. We've told you to move along."

Fuck this.

I stormed forward, nudging in front of Jordan so he had to step back to give me space. I got right in Race's face. I breathed out, softly, but I wasn't messing around. "You will stay away from me, because no matter what you think Drake told you, it was a lie." My back stiffened. This guy was creeping under my skin. "I was with Drake for six months. He didn't matter to me. Got that?"

Race stood above me, unmoved.

"You don't even know what he said."

I did. Or I thought I did, and if it was the secret Drake wasn't supposed to know, there'd be a problem.

"I don't care," I shot back.

The last bell rang.

Everyone was in class, everyone except us. And year after year, crews walked into their classes together. It was a tradition, one that I was sure Mr. Neeon hadn't thought to banish yet, but this year—for the first time since seventh grade—I went alone.

CHAPTER EIGHT

DRAKE KNEW A secret about me, a secret no one else knew.

It wasn't like we couldn't have secrets. I was in this with three other guys. It was ridiculous to think we all sat around in sweat lodges and shared our souls with each other. That was not what we did. It wasn't what I did, anyway. But this was a different situation now. The new guy had let it slip that there was a secret, and I knew Cross.

Jordan and Zellman would sit back and wait. They'd be patient, because if they tried to harass me, I'd pull my knife on them. I had authority issues, and they came out when people tried to make me do something, or say something, when I didn't want to. Putting it bluntly: they were scared of me. With reason.

Not Cross.

In every way, Cross was the exception to all the stupid rules I'd erected over the years, all the freaking walls I'd put in place. He would take a battering ram to anything between him and me, especially if he was convinced it was hurtful to me. I knew he was salivating at the chance for a go at me.

I walked alone to my first class.

That was a big fucking deal, but my head had been clouded over.

I hated the thought that Drake had told this guy something. I hated it, loathed it, it made my blood boil, and I was itching to hold my knife in my hand. I didn't give a shit if it was unfeminine of me, or unattractive. Those people who thought labels like that would make me act differently were morons. I didn't grow up living by other people's standards. I would not start now. Those types of people were never there for you. They didn't stick around after you were beaten to a bloody pulp and needed someone to call an ambulance for you. Those types were the first to scream, run, faint, or piss themselves. So no, this life was a hard one. You got tough in Roussou or you left. It was sink or swim, and yeah, the need to feel my knife in my hand so I didn't go apeshit was a coping mechanism for me.

A girl saw me feeling my knife and didn't blink twice at it. She turned and refocused on what the teacher was saying.

If only Cross would do the same thing, but I knew he wouldn't. And unlucky for me, he was in two of my classes. I felt the question burning in his mind.

It wasn't that I wanted to keep a secret from Cross... Well, I did. But not because it was him. I didn't want to tell anyone, but if I'd been willing to talk, it *would've* been to him.

No one knew my secret except Drake, and the circumstances where he'd found out had been beyond my control.

After fourth period, when the bell rang for our lunch, I knew my time was up.

A path opened in front of me, but not because of me this time. It was there for Cross, and he was bearing down on me. His eyes were smoldering, fierce, and his golden hair was pushed back. I knew the reason why; he'd been raking his hands through it the whole time. It wasn't real long, so for it to stay back showed me how frustrated he was with me.

I wasn't a girl who got scared, but if I had been, the sight of Cross heading my way, his head down and locked right on me, would've done the trick today.

Instead, I adjusted my books and met him at our lockers.

I turned my back to him as I opened my locker.

"Hey." Two hands hit the locker on either side of me. It was a short, quick slap as he trapped me in place. Like an exaggerated hello, but I got the message. He wasn't going to be ignored or avoided anymore.

I put my books into my locker and grabbed my keys and phone, closing it back up before facing him. He stood just behind me, close enough so I could feel the heat radiating from him, with his head down so our conversation would just be between us. Those same girls from this morning were gathering at Sunday's locker, and I heard their whispering. My eyes flicked over, more for a brief respite from Cross' silent demand, and they were there, eyes wide, watching us like goddamn spectators at the Coliseum.

As if we were gladiators squaring off for a fight.

Then again, maybe that's how we looked to them, to those who weren't us.

"Hey." Cross stepped close, almost touching me.

"Hey." I met his gaze, feeling seared from the contact. He was my best friend, and that meant he knew what was going on inside of me more than I did. It was uncomfortable at times, times like now. There was a reason I'd kept that secret a secret, for fuck's sake.

He let out a frustrated sound, raking his hands through his hair again before straightening. "Look." His hand fell, hitching on his jeans. "You gotta tell me, especially if it's something a Ryerson has over you."

I jerked my head in a nod. He was giving me time, but he was right. I would have to tell them, eventually.

"Lunch?"

I hated this. I hated keeping this secret from him, that night burning in my throat, but damn. It was better if he didn't know, if they all didn't know. I fell in step with him as we headed to the parking lot. Juniors and seniors got open lunch. We could leave to grab something, then come back.

A moment later, I wasn't surprised to find Jordan and Zellman behind us.

"What was he talking about?" Jordan asked immediately.

Zellman was on follow-up. "I didn't think you and Drake were that serious."

"We weren't." A knot formed in my stomach.

"You seemed affected by whatever Drake told him," Jordan countered. "There something we should know about?"

I stopped in front of my Jeep and turned around. A whole group of students had followed us to the parking lot.

From the whispering I'd heard, and the furtive glances sent our way all morning, I had no doubt word had spread fast about what happened before first period. I just didn't know if the interest was my altercation with Alex, Race's arrival, or the fact that we had a new guy in school.

I gestured to Sunday Barnes and some of her friends, who had stopped a few feet from us. They were waiting for something.

My eyes slid to Zellman. "Did you find out last night, Z?"

"What?" His eyebrows pulled together. He scratched his chin.

Jordan looked at the crowd and rolled his eyes. "Who cares. Look, we just need to know what's going on if we're going to have your back. Okay?" He gentled his tone. "Tell us what we need to know, when we need to know it."

Cross didn't say anything, but I felt his presence. He wouldn't push, not when they were with us, but the temporary moment of peace I'd gotten from him had a time limit. I could almost hear the clock ticking away, but I was glad for his support.

The knot in my stomach loosened, just a bit. "I will." I nodded toward the girls again. "That's not going to happen now."

The girls edged closer, and Z looked back and forth between us and them. An eager smile pulled at his mouth, and I sighed. "Go get 'em."

Zellman had been slouched. He shot upright. "Yeah?"

Jordan frowned. "You sure?" He didn't sound like he was in any hurry to leave.

I nodded. "Go. I'm sure." I waved at Zellman. "I'm sending you lots of luck if you still need to find out if they're real."

He began backing up, heading toward the girls. He winked. "I found out last night. They're not." Then he turned, throwing his arm around Sunday's shoulders. "Hey, boobs."

She tensed under his touch, and as her friends started laughing, she smacked his chest. He ducked his head, whispering something to her. He started to draw them away from us, toward his own truck. As they went, I could see Sunday's smile go rigid, then soften.

Jordan lingered. "You're positive you're okay if we take off with them?"

I glanced to Cross. He moved to lean against my Jeep, and I knew he wasn't going anywhere.

I nodded. "I'm sure. Go and flirt away."

Jordan began backing away too, and he gave a wave before he turned around and headed after them. A few of the girls were looking over their shoulders. I saw the hope in their eyes. When all of them except one kept watching, despite Jordan's approach, I knew who they were really waiting for.

I turned to my best friend. "You have a fan club."

Cross snorted, but didn't respond.

We watched as Jordan caught up to the group. One of the girls went up to him, and he lifted his arm, letting it fall over her shoulders. Her arm wrapped around his waist, and slowly, the entire group headed over to where Jordan's truck was parked, though a few girls still snuck glances back at Cross.

Another group of students walked right past us, interrupting the girls' view. I felt the break from their attention, and Cross turned to me.

He got right to the point. "Is it bad, what he knows?"

There it was. That punch again.

Feeling tears threatening, I scowled. I didn't fucking cry. Ever.

"Seriously?" I was more asking myself. I was mortified to be a girl.

As I started for the door of my Jeep, Cross blocked me. He held his hands up. "I just want to know how bad it is."

He was pushing, right after he'd told me he wouldn't.

I almost growled, shoving him back a step, the gesture so small no one could see because he was that close. "You know it is or I'd tell you."

I tried again to get into my vehicle.

His chin jutted out. "You liked Drake, but you weren't that serious. I know you better than anyone. I'm hoping that guy was bluffing and he doesn't know whatever it is you don't even want me to know, but what if he does? If it's that bad, maybe you should tell me sooner rather than later."

Fuck. That was my worst nightmare. Cross had put it into words.

He stepped close to me. "I racked my brain all morning, but I can't think of something you'd be okay with Drake knowing and not me."

I felt a knife in my lungs. "Cross, stop it." I started to shake my head.

"Bren." It was a soft and quiet command.

That almost broke me, coming from him. Anyone else, hell no. Cross, any day of the week.

"Stop." I put a warning in my voice. "I mean it."

We stood there. We were at an impasse.

His eyes narrowed. "What can it be? There's nothing I could know about you that would hurt..." His frown deepened, and he trailed off. "Unless it hurts someone else?"

I still didn't want to say, but he was making this hard. I squeezed my hands into fists. "Look, I will tell you, but give me time. Please? You're right. If he knows, you guys have to know. But not yet." I wasn't ready. It was plain and simple. It had been one of the worst nights of my life, and it didn't come easily to my lips.

He let out a sigh. "Fine." He moved aside, his hand brushing against mine, and I knew that was his apology for pushing me. That side of Cross didn't come out too often, and rarely toward me. His gesture meant a lot.

I unlocked the Jeep, but stopped as my hand closed around the handle. I looked back. Cross still stood at the end of my vehicle, his head down. He was deep in thought.

My heart tugged. I didn't like feeling like I'd let him down or hurt him. That was the last thing I wanted.

"I'm not proud of it," I called.

His head lifted. I'd just confirmed what he thought. We might not share our innermost feelings, but maybe he was right. Maybe this was something I should've told him and the others long ago. Still, the thought of saying the words, telling them what I'd done—it stuck in my throat.

"I'm going to skip."

"Yeah?" He frowned.

41

The unrest was too much in me. I was too on edge. "Yeah. Find me after school."

He nodded, our eyes holding for a second. If he didn't find me, I'd find him. It was how we worked.

I got inside my Jeep. I was already off to a stellar year.

CHAPTER NINE

I DROVE HOME after grabbing a burger.

Taz was the good student. Not me. And I was okay with that. Totally and completely okay with that. I was not the type of teenager to worry about SAT scores, college applications, or scholarships. I'd be happy if I graduated, and I knew I wasn't the only Monroe to go that route.

It was early afternoon, but I knew my brother would be at his bar.

He and my cousin had renamed it Tuesday Tits a year ago. It wasn't a strip club, but they certainly got the customers hoping for one. I overheard my brother's girlfriend talking about his branding, and though I didn't pay attention to that stuff, I did know the bar was doing well. Channing had bought it from our dad, and then Scratch bought in. These days Scratch did more of the day-to-day running of it, but my brother had the controlling share.

And why I was thinking about all this was beyond me.

I walked inside, tossing my keys on the kitchen counter.

Heather had her own bar and grill to run, so she never lingered at the house. If she did come over, it was just to see Channing. I was expecting an empty house, but then I heard, "I forgot you guys have open campus for lunch."

I whirled to see Heather coming in from the patio.

I slumped against the kitchen counter, a hand on my chest. "Announce yourself, would you?" As soon as the words left, I grimaced. I held up one of my hands. "Sorry. I thought everyone was gone."

Her eyes were tight as she pulled the screen door the rest of the way shut behind her. Holding up a pack of cigarettes and a lighter, she thrust them at me. "Take these. I almost broke."

Heather had been a smoker as long as I knew her, but she was trying to quit. She'd been trying to quit for the last year, though I knew she'd relapsed at moments.

I didn't say anything about it, just took the stuff and put it in a baggie before sliding that into my bag.

She collapsed into a chair at the table, watching me, a pained look etched over her face. Her shoulders lifted up and down. "You have half a day today?" Her hands drummed over the table.

I reached over for the bowl of candy we kept close and tossed a few at her. "Something like that."

She caught 'em with a flick of her wrist, pulling the wrapper off and tossing them into her mouth in almost the same motion. It was a practiced habit, for both of us.

Heather was one of the cool ones.

She'd grown up working in her dad's bar and grill, and she'd taken it over a few years back. She had a badass, no-nonsense attitude. And she looked pretty much the complete opposite of me. I had dark brown hair, usually just letting it hang down, and dark eyes. She looked a little like Cross and Taz, with this dirty-sexy blonde hair. She'd talked about dying it platinum blonde before the renaming party for Channing and Scratch's bar, but she never did. I thought it might be some kind of bad bedroom joke between her and Channing, but I never asked.

That was gross.

I could sometimes hear them having sex, which was enough to suppress my appetite. I used that as an excuse to take off, but I was usually itching to go anyway. For being the rabbits they were, most of the time they kept it quiet, but I wasn't stupid. I knew why they suddenly had a fan blaring at full force, or if Channing disappeared halfway through the night. He was either dealing with his own stuff or heading to Heather's.

When that happened, I was never far behind him—just not literally behind him. I'd head to Cross' place.

Heather sighed, adjusting in her seat. She was trying to calm down so she didn't fidget so much, but I could tell it was a struggle. I noticed her skin-tight jeans, ripped and faded around the knees.

"Cool jeans."

"What?" She looked down. "Oh yeah." She rested her hand on her leg, tapping there. "Wait." She looked over at my jeans, and her lip curled. "Gotcha."

We wore the same pair.

Different adult and I'd have a smart-ass thought, but this was Heather.

"How pissed was my brother this morning?" I asked.

She grimaced. "You want me to be honest or...not answer?"

I grabbed a water bottle from the fridge and let the door slam shut on its own. "That bad, huh?"

After we woke Heather up, Channing had started grilling me. He'd wanted to know where I'd been, who I was with, was I okay... He knew most of the answers. I was always with the guys. But he just kept going with the same questions our mother had drilled him with when he was in middle school.

Then came the questions about my phone. *Why couldn't I use it? Was it broken? Had I lost it?* The threats were third in line. If I didn't take his calls seriously, he was going to put a tracking app on my phone. He wasn't above stalking his own little sister. There'd be consequences if I didn't start checking in with him more.

I never admitted it, but part of me wondered how long it would take him to follow through with the threats. Shit. If I'd been my kid, I would've had the GPS app on my phone the first day. Or even worse, I'd have switched out the whole plan. I wouldn't have wasted my time with threats. I would've installed the apps before I gave me the phone. I was paying the bills, so I could have access to anything I wanted on there. Privacy be damned.

"Sorry I woke you up this morning," I told Heather, meeting her eyes.

I'd pulled their bedroom door shut, hoping she would go back to bed, but she hadn't. As Channing began his tirade in the hallway, the door had opened back up. She slipped by us to go make coffee and breakfast.

"It's more him than you," she said with a sigh. "He just goes off, and then I know he's not coming back to bed. It's safe to say your brother is feeling a bit more sympathy for your parents' situation back when he was in school."

Well, parent. And I didn't think he did. He and our dad were toxic. And it only got worse after Mom died. Bringing my bag of food and my water, I sat across from her at the table.

We didn't talk for a minute, until I noticed her watching my food, then my arms before a wistful expression softened her mouth. Her eyes darted to my bag, where I'd put her cigarettes.

The tapping started again after that.

I grinned. "Are you worried about me eating?"

The tapping stopped. Her eyebrows pulled together. "I'm that transparent?"

I nodded, unwrapping my burger.

She wasn't the first to be worried. It'd been a theme for me. I was thin—had been all my life. I just was. I didn't work at it. I didn't starve myself. I might forget to eat sometimes, but it wasn't intentional. Food was just not on my mind.

Being detached from myself meant from my stomach too. I had enough insight to know that much.

I shrugged, taking a big bite. "Mom used to worry too, when I was little." I swallowed. "Don't take it on. Channing knows this is just how I am. I'm not sick or anything."

"Still, you could do with a few more meals." She pulled her knee up to her chest, her foot resting on the chair. "I have a friend kind of like you, except she runs all the time. She told me once that she had an eating disorder, but it went away later."

I took a second bite and swallowed. "That the Olympic runner?"

Surprise pulled her eyebrows up. "Yeah. Sam. You know about her?"

I nodded, reaching for some fries. "I listen." I smiled. "Channing's proud of his Fallen Crest friends. They're big deals."

Unlike us. They were big deals. We weren't. The unspoken meaning hung between us.

Another town, another life and owning and running a bar would be an accomplishment, but I could see the thoughts in Heather's mind. There was a sadness in her eyes. Against an Olympic runner, whose husband was an NFL player, and the other dude who was in law school, I could tell Heather had a complex.

I held my burger in front of me. "I'm not stupid, but I know my path. Graduating is my big goal, and after that..." I shrugged, staring at the meat but feeling how quiet she'd gotten. "If I ran a successful business like you do with Manny's or Chan does with Tits, I'd be proud." A goddamn lump was in my throat. "I'd be damned proud." I looked up now, meeting her gaze. "I wouldn't let anyone take that from me."

Her lips parted, and she leaned forward. Her hand flattened on the table. "Bren, I wasn't thinking about—"

I stood, but I slid another fry from my container.

I knew she wasn't. Heather was good people.

I was just the one in the way.

Stuffing the fry into my mouth, I put the rest of them back in the bag. With my water in hand, I motioned with my head to the door. "Lunch is almost done. I'm going back."

Heather's hand fell to her lap. She looked down at it, not responding before gesturing toward the back door. "I'm parked out back. I should get going too."

She didn't move, but I did.

In just a moment I was back in my Jeep, pulling away from the curb.

I still wasn't going back to school, though I wasn't avoiding the new Ryerson, or well, everyone. I just didn't want to deal with people at the moment.

Surprise: I'm not a fan of people. They were like aliens to me. So I headed toward where I always went when I wanted to hole up.

I went to Cross' house.

He wouldn't be there, but neither would anyone else. And bonus, I knew where they kept the secret key.

CHAPTER
TEN

I SETTLED INTO Cross' room, though not in his bed or at his desk. I was in his closet.

I know it sounds creepy, but it's not. It's just our thing—or maybe it's more my thing. If I need to crash somewhere that's not my own bed, I like his closet. He usually crashes on my floor if he returns the favor. So me being in his closet wasn't weird—to us.

What *was* weird was hearing footsteps in the hall a few hours later and two voices entering his room.

"I don't think we should be in here."

I lifted my head, letting it rest against the closet wall. I couldn't place that voice.

"Sshhh! I want to just check it out."

I recognized that one: Sunday Barnes.

"Oh!" Sunday groaned. "Think we could get into his accounts?"

"Sunday, for real. We should go." The second voice again.

I still couldn't place her, but she was hesitant, her second statement more fearful than the first.

"Get over it, Mon. It's not our fault Taz let us roam free around here."

Monica? Cross' ex?

I remembered they were both on the cheerleading squad.

"This makes me nervous. Taz thinks we're going to the bathroom. You know Cross would be pissed if he knew we were in here."

"You said you wanted proof. That's what we're doing, looking for proof."

"Yeah, but—"

"But what?" Sunday snapped as Cross' desk chair squealed. "You think he's in love with Monroe."

Me? *Fuck.* I closed my eyes, an old wariness settling in my chest.

"He didn't say that—"

"But you see how close they are," Sunday countered. "He's in love with her. We all know it. We just have to prove it."

The floor creaked as someone crossed the room. The bed springs protested slightly.

"Look," Monica's voice was quieter. "I don't feel right about this anymore. She's crew. I mean, you have to be badass to just be in one, let alone *theirs.* I don't know. I don't want to mess with Bren."

"Why not?" I could almost hear the eye roll. Cross' computer booted up. "She messes with you all the time. If they're not together, she should let him date who he wants."

"She's never done anything."

"In front of you. Trust me. I know girls like that. They're all about pulling the strings behind your back."

Monica let out a small laugh. "You're projecting. That's what you do."

"Yeah. Maybe." Sunday agreed.

I heard fingers tapping on the keyboard, followed by "Fuck! It's password-protected even to get on the computer. I tried Bren's name. What else would he use as a password?"

The bed creaked again. "We're not going to find anything. Let's go."

"No way. We're here. Let's try a few more, okay?" More typing. "No. Wolves or Wolf Crew doesn't work. Come on. You've been with him forever. Think of some ideas—"

"What the fuck are you guys doing?" A third voice came from the doorway.

I knew that one, and I sat up straight, waiting for what Taz was going to say.

"Shit!"

The bedroom door banged into the closet behind my head.

She didn't disappoint.

"What the fuck?!" Taz's voice grew louder, and I could see the shadow from her shoes under the closet door. "Were you trying to hack into my brother's computer?"

"No, no."

Sunday snorted. "Yes."

Taz sucked in her breath.

I grinned faintly. I could hear how pissed she was. If she really got going, she was a terror. I'd witnessed a few verbal smackdowns between her and Cross.

"Look, it was my idea." Monica stepped closer. "He broke up with me again last night, and I know he spent it with her. I'm just so tired of being his second choice."

"So you needed to invade his privacy for payback?"

"What? No! No."

I angled my head closer to the door so I could see out through the small crack. Monica's head was blocked by the door's screw, but I could see where her hands were pressed to her chest, like she was praying.

"I just wanted proof that he loves her," she said. "I'm so sick of him denying it. I can *see* it. It's how they move together. Like they're the same person. It sucks. Do you have any idea?"

"Give me a break," Taz grumbled. "They're crew, and they're best friends. That's what they do."

"It's more with them. You know it."

Sunday stepped forward now. I could make out her hands on her hips. "I heard you this morning. You think it too. You said it yourself. They have their own language."

"And what? If you'd found something, what would you do with it?" Taz was incredulous. "Blackmail them? You think my brother would stand for that, or hell, Bren? Seriously? Do you really want to piss *her* off? You're an idiot."

Taz said, "There are no couples in crew."

Sunday said, "In theirs, maybe. But that could change and it's not the same for others."

"There's only one other female in the system."

Monica added, "Yeah! And she's dating one of her own group's members."

"I have a feeling the rule would change if something did happen between Bren and Cross, but are you even listening to yourself? It's Bren."

Sunday crossed her arms over her chest. "Whatever, Taz. Bren Monroe doesn't scare me."

My grin doubled. *Now* we were getting somewhere.

Taz snorted again. "She should. You can't bully her with whispers and rumors. You tell people she and my brother are together, they're either going to be like *duh*, or they're not going to give a shit."

"What can she do to me? Physically assault me? I'll have her arrested."

Taz stepped forward, her voice low. "Pat was working at the hospital last night. She called me because a guy came in with his jaw broken, three fractured ribs, and he can't even sit to take a shit right now. She asked him what happened, and you know what he told her?" She didn't wait. "He said he touched a Wolf girl."

"If he had touched Bren, he would've been sliced up." Sunday was laughing, but there was a thread of caution there now. I heard it.

"Pat talked to the cops later, and one mentioned that Jordan Pitts' little sister reported a sexual assault a few days ago. You think that's a coincidence?"

A soft "shit" came from Monica.

"Do you think they won't deal with you somehow if you're going after a member?" Taz paused, her voice soft, eerily soft. "You go after one, you go after all. You know the rules."

Sunday's closed arms jostled. "She'd have to know I was doing something and prove it. Come on." She sounded haughty, but her caution was morphing into fear. A nervous laugh left her. "It'd be rumors. She couldn't do anything to me."

"They've done worse for less," Taz snapped. "Stop whatever you're doing. Just stop. You'll regret it."

Sunday snorted. "How's she even going to know?"

"Trust me," Taz said. She edged closer to the closet. "You'll be surprised how quick she'll know."

"Only if you say something." She advanced a step toward Taz. "But you're not going to do that, right? You're not a narc. You wouldn't want *that* rumor to get around either. A member's sister is a narc?" She waited a beat. "Right, Taz?"

No one moved.

No one said a word.

Tense silence filled the room.

I waited. I could stand up. I could step out. I could make Sunday piss her pants, but I didn't. It wasn't fear that held me back. It was curiosity. I wanted to know how Taz would handle that threat, because on the list of them, that was a doozy. A damned doozy.

"You're going to regret this," Taz finally said.

"Hey!" a voice called from below. "Where are you guys?"

Sunday huffed out, "Whatever. My fight's not with you, Taz, but don't say anything. She knows, and I'll know it was you who squealed."

"I don't think—"

"Shut it, Mon. You already started this train. It left the station."

"Guys!" came another shout from below. "Where are you?! We have to start."

Sunday cursed, almost stomping from the room. "They can't handle being alone for five minutes? I'm cursed with the stupidest squad ever."

As she walked farther down the hallway, her stomping faded, then "What?! We were busy up there" carried back to the room.

A soft murmur followed in response, but I couldn't make it out.

"Taz?" Monica had stayed back. I still had a perfect view of her hands, hands she was wringing together in front of her. "Are you going to tell Bren?"

Taz was silent. A full ten seconds passed. Even I was affected by the silence. It was palpable. When she did speak, her voice was unnaturally soft. "I'm going to say this clearly. If you don't do anything, Bren won't do anything to you. Do you understand?"

"Yeah, but you're not going to say anything. Right?" She gestured toward the door. "You heard Sunday. If Bren finds out, she'll blame you. I don't want anything to happen to you."

Taz snorted. "Trust me. You don't need to worry about me. I can handle Sunday just fine on my own."

Monica let out a breath. "I suppose we should go down to the meeting. I'm glad you decided to join again."

They left together, but I heard Taz say, "Well, we'll see. I'm not going to let Sunday boss me around like last time."

They walked down the hallway, and I remained in the closet. When I stepped out, I'd have to take care of this Sunday problem. Nip it in the bud, get it done quickly. I didn't like to let things linger, and the whole Drake secret was one too many things hanging over my head already. But right now, I was tired.

I was seventeen, and I felt like I was nearing fifty-seven. Was that normal? Was life supposed to be this hard? This grueling day after day?

I liked Cross' closet. He didn't have that many clothes, and what he had was pushed to the back, so I barely felt them brushing against my feet. Four closed-in walls. Others might get claustrophobic, but not me. No one could sneak up on me in here. It was one of the only places I could sleep soundly. That's what I'd been doing when they came in, which meant school was out. If Cross wasn't here... I reached for my phone. He'd be looking for me somewhere else.

There were three texts from him.

Where r u?
Call me.
We're at Jordan's. Come over when you get this.

I was texting, **Heading over now** when the closet door suddenly opened. Only one person could've figured out I was in here, and because of that, I took my time finishing the text before looking up.

When I did, Taz stared down at me.

There was no surprise on her face. Her hair was pulled up into a ponytail, high on her head, and she had glitter on her cheeks. She'd morphed into one of them since I saw her at school. I was half-expecting her to be wearing a cheerleading uniform—they did that sometimes—but she was still in the same clothes.

Hitting send, I put my phone away and stood.

I glanced at the door to the room, but it was closed.

Taz stepped back, sitting on Cross' bed. "You heard all of that?" She pulled at her ponytail, her fingers flicking the end over and over.

"Yep."

She let out a resigned sigh, her hands falling to the bed. "What are you going to do?"

I raised an eyebrow. "Do you really want to know?"

"I'm being serious. What are you going to do?"

There was something more in her tone, something uneasy, something...

"You're not actually worried about it, are you?"

The guilt flared in her eyes before she hung her head.

"This has to do with Cross." I sat on his desk chair, connecting the dots in my head. "They came in here. They tried to hack into his computer, and you know I'm going to say something."

She didn't answer me. She didn't need to.

I went through the scenarios of what might happen if I told him, but only one stood out. "You're worried he's going to move out?"

This morning made a whole lot more sense now. That's what Cross would do *when* he found out his privacy had potentially been invaded. He wouldn't put a lock on his door. He wouldn't say something to his parents. He would move to my place, or more likely Jordan's, because Jordan's parents didn't mind that Zellman lived there half the time already.

Hearing a sniffle, I looked back at her.

Taz lifted her face with tears in her eyes. "Do you know what it's like to have your twin be closer to three other people than you?"

Not a twin, but a brother. Yes.

She kept going, her tears falling now. "I barely see him anymore. He's either partying with Jordan and Zellman, or off with you. You're his family, and he's eighteen. My parents can't keep him here. I feel like he's going to fade from my life." Her voice dropped to a hoarse whisper. "I'm going to be all alone."

Channing had always been gone.

He'd been out partying or fighting. I'd been home, just waiting, hoping he'd come back. When he did, there were fights, raised voices, threats. Doors slammed. Walls punched. But I remember one thing more than everything else.

"It was the worst when the door would shut."

"What?" She wiped at her eyes with the back of her hand.

"When Channing would leave, it was the door. I got to the point where I didn't care who was yelling or cursing, it was the silence after. He'd slam that door shut behind him and be gone. Days. Weeks sometimes. I hated hearing that damned door."

She looked at her hands, folded on her lap. "I forgot about your brother." She laughed sadly.

"Yeah."

She swallowed. "I'm sorry for unloading."

I shrugged. I didn't care about that, but I did feel bad because she knew what I had to do. There was no option here for me. "I gotta say something to Cross. You know I have to."

Her eyes slid away again, and her cheek pulled in like she was biting it.

I felt bad. I honestly did, but if Cross knew someone had invaded my privacy and tried to hack my phone, and he didn't tell me, I'd be livid.

"I'll get him to hang out here more often," I added. I wanted to say I wouldn't back him for moving out, but I couldn't promise that.

"Really?" She looked up at me.

It wasn't much. Nodding, I turned toward the door.

"What are you going to do about Sunday?" Taz asked.

I looked back. "Do you really care?"

She paused, then shook her head. "No. Not anymore."

I gave her a smile. "Don't worry. I'll make sure she sees me leaving. She'll know you didn't tell me."

"That's not—"

I was gone.

I liked Taz, but she shouldn't have asked me to keep something from Cross. She knew better. Something churned, twisted, tied up in a knot inside my stomach. I wasn't sure what it was, but I let my smile fade to a hardened grin as I walked downstairs.

I could hear voices in the kitchen as I turned and stopped in the doorway.

Sunday's squad was sitting around the table and spread throughout the kitchen. One by one, they looked up. One by one, they stopped talking, until no one said a word.

I waited until Sunday looked up.

"Guys, what—" She had a pitcher of orange juice in her hand. She'd just pulled it from the fridge. Monica stood at the counter, a vodka bottle in front of her.

Sunday's eyes widened.

I leaned against the doorframe, my eyes steady on her. "I heard everything." I pushed up and strolled over to her.

Her grip tightened on the pitcher.

"You think rumors and whispers behind my back are going to hurt me? You think you can come at me like I'm any other girl?" I shook my head, my hand coming up under her pitcher. Taking it, I dumped the contents over her head. She didn't move. She didn't say a word. She took it, and her gaze didn't break from mine at all.

"We don't fight like you do." I started for the door, saying over my shoulder, "And just remember, you declared war first."

CHAPTER
ELEVEN

"YOU DID WHAT?" Zellman's hands fisted in his shaggy hair as he gaped at me.

I'd just finished relaying the entire story, while both Jordan and Cross kept quiet. Zellman was anything but.

"She's not going to give it up to me anymore. I won't be able to see the V anymore. My times in that pussy are gone. Man, Bren. Really? She felt so good. Those boobs." He raised his hands, as if squeezing them in the air. "God. They felt so good. So firm." He groaned, slumping onto the couch in Jordan's warehouse/shed.

Jordan had talked his dad into letting him renovate so it was half a party shed, and half a place for us to hang out or live (if need be). There were couches, a bed in the office area, and a large screen mounted on the side wall. Another corner had been turned into a gym. A punching bag hung there with a whole bunch of weight-lifting equipment. There was a target on one wall for darts, or knives if I wanted to throw something sharper at it.

"Dude, lay off her," Jordan said, crossing to the fridge for another beer. "You're not in love with the girl. You were just telling us that."

"She gives good head." Zellman shook his head. "You know how rare that is? Not a lot of girls give good head. They're not properly taught."

"Stop." Cross winced. He nodded to me. "They were in my room?"

"Yeah."

"They think they know, but they don't," Zellman kept on. "They really don't."

I didn't explain how I'd overheard them. Cross didn't have to ask, and I wasn't sure the other two knew of my weird habit.

"Taz was the most upset."

At these words, a different feeling came over the storage shed. A more serious one.

"Yeah." Cross didn't say anything else.

I tried to judge how he was feeling, but he was locked down. He wasn't letting me in. His face was schooled, but his shoulders seemed rigid, stiffer than normal. He crossed the room, reaching for the fridge. That whole motion seemed normal, almost casual.

There it was.

He was too casual. Normal Cross would've been pissed. He would've pulled that door open with a bit more force than necessary. Not this Cross. A shiver went down my spine. He was furious.

He took out a beer for himself, palming a second one, and he offered it to me. "B?"

Definitely furious.

"Not right now."

Zellman came over and plopped onto the couch again. "So Taz is upset. What's she upset about? I know there's a whole serious thing happening now, but you guys are not giving enough credit to what I've lost. Good head is like an animal on the endangered list. You gotta groom that shit, protect it, look out for it, hope it grows to be more, but now..." He kicked up his feet, resting them on the coffee table between the couches, and took a long drink from his beer. "I'm going to have to start all over with someone new." He stopped to look at Jordan, but he didn't say anything.

"Yes," Jordan countered. "You cannot still sneak around with Sunday. We're united."

Cross remained by the fridge, leaning into it. He pulled his foot up to rest against the wall behind him and stared off into the distance, lost in his head.

"So you poured orange juice on her?" Zellman asked.

I nodded, leaning back in my seat.

Jordan sat on the opposite couch from Zellman. "I'm kind of hoping that was caught on tape."

Zellman snickered. "Sunday must've been so pissed. She's got a mouth on her."

"We know!"

He paused, his eyebrows pulling together as he stared at us. "No. I meant she's got an attitude. She's a spitfire. That's what I like about her." He held his beer up in a salute to us. "But I can see where the misunderstanding happened."

I was tempted to throw something at him. I refrained, getting up instead. Cross opened the fridge and handed me a beer.

I went back to my chair.

"Okay, whatever." Jordan leaned forward. "We don't normally take on catty bitches, and that's what Sunday is, but we'll ice her out. She fucks with one of us; she fucks with all of us."

Zellman snickered.

We ignored him.

"We'll deal with her," Jordan continued. "But I think we have two other issues to deal with first." He turned to me. "You gotta tell us about this Race guy and what's the deal with Drake."

"You told me I could wait until I was ready. I'm not ready."

"The guy knows something about you. He had Alex asking about you today."

That damn lump was back in my throat. "What was he asking?"

"Just where you were. Why'd you leave? Things like that."

"Yeah." Zellman leaned forward, bobbing his head up and down. "He was real nosy about you."

I glanced to Cross, feeling his gaze. His eyes were locked on me, flaring up again. A part of me was relieved. The guarded wall had slipped. I could see him again.

"What are you going to do about Taz?"

Deflect. I would go there instead.

Zellman twisted around. "What? Taz?"

"Not yet. Hold your horses." Jordan waved a hand in the air. "Don't distract us from this." He gestured to me. "We have to know. What did Drake tell him? We *have* to know."

"I want to know about Cross and Taz." Zellman finished his beer, but he didn't stand up for another. "What's your stance on your sis dating members?"

Cross shot him a dark look. "Are you kidding me? You want to groom my sister to give you the right head?" He pushed up from the wall. "You know how sick that is?"

"Comic relief." Zellman shot his hands up in surrender, standing and backing away. "That's my job today. Comic relief, everyone. Cross. Comic relief."

Cross' eyes flicked to the ceiling. "Right. I'll keep that in mind." He finished his beer and headed for the side door, tossing the bottle in the trash.

Jordan straightened. "Where are you going?"

Cross stepped out. "Need to think."

He was going to watch my house. We might've started going there because of me, but it was just as much his spot now as mine.

Jordan looked at me. "Where's he going?"

I ignored that. "Taz is worried he'll move out."

Jordan and Zellman fell silent.

"She thinks he won't deal with the hassle of getting a lock for his room. He'll just move somewhere else."

"Damn," said Zellman.

"Where?" Jordan asked.

It was obvious. Jordan's family had money, unlike the rest of us. They didn't have a lot, but enough to give Jordan an entire building, and they had land. A large bonfire here didn't attract the cops' attention, and there were lots of fields and woods around for people to slip away and do whatever. Plus, they had a creek that wound through their land. It was a good swimming area. With all that space, a camper set up in the back could be missed by Jordan's parents for weeks, maybe even months, and that was if they didn't just agree to letting Cross use the extra bedroom in the shed. There was a loft set up over the office room that acted as the first bedroom. With an outside hose for a shower, this place could easily be lived in.

I snorted. "Where do you think?"

Zellman slapped a hand on the coffee table. "I am down with that. I'm here most of the time anyway. Having Cross live here? I say hell yes."

Jordan shot him a look. "It's not up to you."

I frowned.

So did Zellman. "What? You're saying you might not let him? Shit." He flung a hand up behind him. "He could pop up a tent back there, and your family wouldn't even know. We're here almost all the time."

Jordan stood, gripping his beer. "You're here almost all the time. Not Cross, a pretty boy my sister has a crush on. We just took down some fucker who tried to force himself on her. She's all mixed up in the head now. I don't want her to get any more confused." He walked to the open door, staring out at where Cross had gone.

"But he's in our group."

There was no question that Cross wouldn't do anything with Mallory. He knew better. We all did, but it was her. What she thought, felt, would feel—I got it. I understood both sides.

Jordan hung his head. "That's the problem."

We weren't going to figure it out, and I didn't want the tables to turn against me. The Drake/Race conversation had been shelved, though I knew it wouldn't stay there for long. Jordan could sense trouble coming, and he was going to push. He'd want to be prepared for whatever was coming our way. I understood, but that wasn't what I wanted.

I wanted to avoid the whole thing, for as long as I could anyway.

I stood, handing the rest of my beer to Zellman, and started for the door.

As I left, Jordan called, "You have to tell us. You know that, right?"

There was no hiding. I knew. He knew. We all knew.

I stopped and looked over. "I know."

He nodded. "Tell Cross he's welcome here, just can't let my sister know."

I looked back, nodding again.
Then I was gone.

CHAPTER TWELVE

OUR ROLES WERE reversed this time.

Cross was the one sitting on my hill, and he looked up at my approach. He had a ball cap on, pulled low, but I still saw his eyes. They were guarded again. I glanced back over my shoulder before either of us said a word.

The hill was only accessible by breaking off from a small walking path a couple hundred yards back. Behind me was covered with trees, and beyond that was the path and a gravel road where we had both parked.

Before I'd pulled onto the gravel road, I'd paused to notice a new construction sign in the field behind our hill.

"Hey." He sat up, resting his arms on his knees. "You see the sign back there?"

I clenched my jaw as I sat. "I should've brought alcohol."

He laughed and reached to his other side, pulling out a whiskey bottle. He set it down between us. "Good thing one of us was thinking."

I grunted, reaching for it and taking a sip. Fuck. That burned. I hissed, but Cross' hand was up waiting for it. I handed it over, and he did the same. He put it back between us, looping his arms around his knees, and he hunched forward.

"You here to talk me out of moving out?"

I shrugged, looping my arms over my knees too. "You know me. I'm down for whatever."

He continued to watch me. "But you feel bad for Taz."

Because I'd been her. I'd been the sister hoping her brother would come home one night, but now... "She'll get over it."

If Cross was really considering moving out, there was a reason for it. I wasn't going to question him, not yet. I'd wait for my turn to pounce.

He frowned. "I wasn't expecting that response."

"It's your decision, but do you really want to stay at Jordan's full time?"

He grinned. "Who said I was thinking about Jordan's place?"

I looked at him. An uneasy emotion began in my gut, filling me up until one of those damn knots was back in place. "Mine? My brother would go nuts."

He stretched his legs out and reached for a handful of rocks. He tossed a couple, which sank into the tall grass at the bottom of the hill. "I don't think your brother would notice, but if he did, I think he'd understand. If anyone understood, it'd be him. Besides, your brother loves me. What's the problem?"

I snorted.

Love was a stretch. More like Channing *put up* with Cross.

He was the least of his worries. Jordan was usually instigating a fight. Zellman was a laughing hyena—Channing's words, not mine. But Cross, he was steady. He was good. He was my best friend, and my brother knew things weren't romantic between us.

Cross was the only one Channing might be okay having live with us. That was a big *might* though.

"We could sneak you in," I said. "He might like it, actually. I'd be home more than I am now. He's always bitching about that."

Cross laughed. He began flinging the small rocks harder and harder. The last one hit the road, rolling into the middle. He was holding back. He could hurl 'em all the way to my old house's front lawn if he wanted.

"Want me to live in *your* closet?"

I laughed. "Why not? It's good enough for me."

We shared a grin. I used to curl up in bed with him. That changed around puberty. There were wet dreams, we both smelled, and we had awkward breath in the middle of the night. Cross never asked me to move, but I did. I'd gone through a phase where one zit meant the world was going to end. I liked to think I was more sane now.

But it never had to be the closet. It was *his* closet, his home, his room. It was him. I felt safe.

"Speaking of that, are you really going to take on Sunday Barnes?" he asked. "Isn't that below us?"

"She was planning the first attack. Rumors. Whispers. That sort of thing. You know, the coward way."

He sighed, tossed the last of the small rocks, and stood up. Offering a hand to me, he nodded toward town. "Come on. Let's go do something about her. I'm in the mood to stir shit up."

I took his hand, stood, and dusted off my jeans. "What do you have in mind?"

"I don't know." He put the whiskey bottle underneath a bush, then led the way back. "I'm improvising."

I trailed behind him, but right where we would've disappeared into the trees, I turned back. My old house remained in my view, and I could see the lights on inside. The mother walked past in an upstairs bedroom, one of the kids in her arms. She had her arms wrapped so lovingly around him. The little boy wore a towel, the yellow hood almost covering his head.

My throat swelled up. Why I had a problem breathing lately was beyond me. It was annoying.

"Bren?"

I swallowed, forcing whatever emotion had been rising away. "Coming."

This had started out as a normal evening for me. I'd been content.

I wasn't anymore.

Now I was ready to stir shit up too.

CHAPTER THIRTEEN

"YEAH?" CROSS WAS on the phone with his sister.

We'd returned to Jordan's, and all of us now stood around Cross' truck, waiting for the final word.

He bent his head down. "The girls left then?"

Taz was talking. We could hear her voice, but not what she was saying.

"They went to Manny's?" His eyes lifted to mine.

I could read his mind.

Fuck.

Heather ran Manny's. She was in charge of the grill while her brother ran the bar. It was a popular hangout for Normals. Anyone who went to Fallen Crest, our neighboring town, was trying to be uppity. Fallen Crest was rich. Millionaires lived there, and knowing Sunday had gone there with the other cheerleaders pissed me off.

Roussou was blue collar.

We were supposed to stay local.

We didn't get fancy college degrees, or if we did, it was a community college or technical school. I mean, yeah, there were some who left for those nice universities, but they rarely came back. They were usually not crew.

Heather was different. She lived there. She'd gone to school there, but Sunday—she was reaching above her station. My need to stir shit up went from a fun zone to a pissed-off zone.

"Okay. Thanks." Cross ended his call and looked at us. There was a dark gleam in his eyes. "Apparently, they've been hanging out in Fallen Crest all summer. Manny's is their new go-to."

A resounding silence showed our enthusiasm.

Jordan folded his arms over his chest. "Fuck that."

Even Zellman's eyes narrowed. "What the fuck they doing there? Sunday hoping to land some rich prick?"

Cross' top lip curled, but he looked only at me. "What do you want to do?"

We had to work fast.

We took Jordan's truck. As soon as he parked next to Sunday's car, Zellman jumped to the ground from the bed. He stuffed his hands into his pockets and moved slowly. He looked like he was out for a stroll.

Cross hopped out next to me and laughed. "He just needs a little bird to perch on his shoulder."

A second later, Zellman whistled as he headed inside Manny's.

"Let's go." Jordan stepped around us, using a machine to make quick work of the lug nuts.

I was the lookout, and I settled behind the car next to Sunday's, positioned so I could see through the window, but people coming out couldn't see me. I could hear Cross and Jordan working behind me.

They moved fast and efficiently. This wasn't the first car we'd done.

They set the jack in place, removed the hubcap. The lug nuts were loosened, and the car was jacked up. It wasn't long before I heard the first tire being taken off. Jordan put it aside as Cross grabbed a cinder block. The jack lowered the car, and they were on to the next tire.

The second and third tires went just as quickly. I waited until right before they got the fourth one off, then headed inside.

I was part signal, and part of the con too.

Cross and Jordan would finish up outside, storing Sunday's tires in the trees so we couldn't be labeled thieves. They always put them close to the vehicle, but they were still a bitch to find. If people knew us, knew our ways, they'd just go look for the tires. That only happened once—when we did this to my brother.

I laughed to myself, remembering that night.

Manny's was full, which didn't surprise me. There were Fallen Crest students in the front section. I was walking past the grill counter when Heather came out of her office. She stopped in the hallway, a bunch of papers in her hand, and frowned at me.

"Hey." Her frown faded, but I saw her wheels turning. Her forehead wrinkled. "I thought you were supposed to be at Channing's tonight."

Channing. Wha... *My* wheels started working, and I cursed.

She grinned, stuffing her papers into her pocket. "Totally forgot?" She gestured behind her. "I thought I saw Zellman a few minutes ago. Is your crew here?"

"No!" Too much. I coughed. "No. I came to pick him up."

She twisted around, looking into the back section. "Okay, but listen." Her hand came to my arm.

I looked down at it.

Why was Heather touching me? Like she was comforting me? This wasn't our normal interaction. She'd get uncomfortable, then I'd get more uncomfortable, and you never knew who would cut out first.

It was me this time.

I stepped away from her hand and pointed behind her. "I gotta go."

"Okay, but—"

I brushed past her.

"Call your brother, Bren! He'll worry otherwise."

It wasn't just annoyance rolling around in my gut. I stepped into the back room, and I felt my hands shaking a little.

What was that about?

"You disappeared today."

Race Ryerson stood in front of me, drink in hand.

God, I didn't like this guy. He was coming at me like he knew me, or like he wanted to know me.

He'd changed clothes since this morning. He wore lightweight black sweatpants and a black hoodie. The clothes molded to his form, showing off his arm muscles and broad chest. He had the hood pulled up too. It would've looked ridiculous on another guy, but it only added a mysterious appeal in his case. I skimmed the room and saw that it was working. A few girls were sneaking looks at him.

I gestured to his drink. "Your fake must be pretty good to get alcohol in here."

He looked down at it, then back at me, a faint grin on his mouth. "The soda came from the counter. Alex snuck the liquor in."

I heard Alex's laugh and Sunday's giggle, and I turned around.

Alex's group was here—not all of them, but a fair amount of the teenagers and a few who'd graduated with Drake. Some were playing pool. Others were throwing darts, and Alex was at the biggest table, his arms around two girls like he was holding court. I narrowed my eyes, scanning for Zellman, but I didn't see him.

"Since when do we hang out at Manny's?" I asked under my breath, not expecting a response. I had a feeling they came more than I thought.

"It was my idea."

I turned back to Race. His grin became more pronounced.

"Drake told me about this place, and since it's my first day here, Alex asked where I wanted to go." He looked behind me to Sunday and the other cheerleaders. "The rest found us."

"Hey, hey!"

Alex's voice no longer came from across the room.

I braced myself as Race looked behind me. An arm came down on my shoulder. I was jerked against Alex's side.

Stop...

I whispered that word to myself in my head.

Breathe.

I was in Heather's place. I could smell the booze on Alex's breath. I could feel the sweat, the heat from his body. Race looked completely sober, but Alex was not. He was weaving, half-using me for balance.

My instincts were to lash out.

No one touched me against my will—a point I'd reminded him of twelve hours earlier—but he was drunk. *And this is Heather's place. This is Heather's.* I couldn't cause a fight... Not here.

Race's smile dropped. His eyes sharpened in alarm. "Hey, cuz. Why don't you step back from her."

"What?"

I could feel Alex's body become rigid.

He hadn't noticed that mine already was.

"No—" he started to growl, but suddenly he was gone.

I saw it in slow motion.

Sunday stepped up next to us with a high-pitched giggle. Then it dropped low in my head and faded out. Everything moved at a slower pace. She looked behind me, her eyes widening, her laugh changing to a yell. Race lifted his head to look too, craning to see behind me. Alex tensed even more, stiffening up.

I could see another girl's hair lift in the air as she suddenly dropped in position to jump out of the way.

It all clicked in the back of my mind, and then suddenly—time snapped back into place, and everything was a big *whoosh*!

A hand clamped on Alex's shoulder and yanked him backward.

I began to pivot around, dropping down like the other girl had, but I wasn't running for safety. I needed to get my bearings.

Zellman was on top of Alex. I tried to lunge forward, but someone pulled me backwards. Alex's members came running from across the room. One jumped on top of the pool table.

All hell was breaking loose. Again.

More bodies ran into the room, and I was in the air, going backward.

Cross ran forward. He bent down, wrapped an arm around one of Alex's guys, and threw him onto the pool table. He took out the other guy on there at the same time.

I looked around to find Race in front of me. He was the one dragging me back. I put the brakes on, my feet skidding across the floor as I tried to stop.

But I couldn't.

As I moved, Channing's voice entered my head. *"Go with the movement. Use it to your advantage."*

So I did.

I turned around again, running with the momentum, and stepped up on the wall. My body followed, like I was going to run up it, but I threw my leg over. I flipped, and as I landed with one foot on the floor, my other leg snapped around, kicking Race smack across his face. It was a perfect side kick.

Channing would've been proud.

Race fell, and I didn't wait for his next move.

I sprinted forward into the writhing mass of bodies.

Everyone was punching, throwing, kicking.

Zellman and Alex were trading blows.

Jordan took on three of Alex's crew. Why they seemed to wait for their turn to trade blows with him was beyond me. They weren't the best fighters, which was good for us.

Cross fought three of his own. The two from the pool table had regrouped, and a third headed for Cross' backside.

I went for him, but he was moving too fast. I wouldn't be able to stop him, so I planted myself in front of him and bent forward, using the same momentum as before. I kicked up and connected right under his chin. He fell backward into Race, who was advancing on me again.

Race caught him, stopped, and looked at me, then at the guy. His eyes were wide and he looked furious as he reared back and punched the guy. The member fell to the floor, unconscious before he landed.

Race winced and started for me again.

I reached into my pocket and pulled out a knife. "Stop!"

He did, holding his hands up. "I was trying to protect you."

I could feel Cross behind me, moving and hitting. Our backs bumped up against each other, but neither of us reacted. As everyone else kept fighting around us, Race and I had a small pocket of civility. For now.

I brandished the knife. "I don't need your protection."

He rubbed at his jaw, eyes flashing. "Yeah. I'm getting that." He raised his hands again. "I'm not here to make waves against you."

Suddenly, Cross was shoved backward into me. I pitched forward, and Race shot his hands out like he was going to catch me, but I rolled to the side, coming right back to my feet. Race gave a frustrated groan, but he met the member who was raining down punches on Cross.

Race threw a right hook, spinning his body with the punch. It knocked the guy sideways, and his body got tangled up with a second.

Cross rolled to his feet, and we both stood with our knees bent, hands up, prepared for the next move. Seeing Race fighting for us, we looked at each other for a moment, but that was the extent of it.

A rush of new members came flooding in from the front of Manny's, and we turned to face them. In the mess, we formed a circle with our backs to each other. Cross. Me. Jordan. Zellman. And now Race. He was fighting on our side.

I didn't punch. I used my legs for most of my fighting. I wrapped my feet around one guy's head and fell to my back, using the action and gravity to throw him over me when I saw red and blue lights through the window.

I pushed to my feet. "POLICE!"

Everyone unified.

We all took off, pushing forward to spill out the side door. I took the shortcut, not caring how pissed Heather would be. She'd had another exit door installed last summer so the cooks could step outside for a fast break.

Dodging the dishwasher and two girls huddled in the corner, I shoved open the screen door. It didn't slam shut behind me. Cross, Zellman, and Jordan were on my tail until Cross took the lead.

He patted my arm. "Come on!" He was the fastest in our crew, and he led the way, running toward Heather's house behind Manny's. Jordan's car was parked in the alley behind her garage.

No words were spoken as we piled in. Jordan started the truck right away.

Cross, Zellman, and I scrambled into the back, and as Jordan peeled out, all of us lying flat. We didn't get far. Jordan hit the brakes, but then eased forward as we saw more police lights going past us.

We stayed like that the whole ride back to Jordan's.

I closed my eyes at one point, replaying the scene in my head.

Race had our backs in there. Why, I had no clue, but there were going to be problems for him now. He was a Normal, and he'd gone against his cousin. They'd either turn on him, or if Alex decided to make it a family issue, he'd be kicked out of the house.

It didn't sit right with me.

None of it.

CHAPTER
FOURTEEN

WE WENT TO Jordan's, but no one left the truck. He parked and got out, opening the back bed, and the three of us sat on the tailgate, our feet dangling. Jordan lounged against the side of his truck, his hands in his pockets. He looked like a guy leaning back, enjoying the weather, except his eyes were downcast, his forehead was wrinkled, and he frowned.

I raked a hand through my hair, feeling the frayed ends and trying to smooth some of it. After a minute I gave up, letting my hands rest on my lap.

Cross sat next to me. He gripped the edge of the truck, next to his legs. His knuckles were turning white.

Zellman was the only one nonplussed. He watched us, an expectant note in his eyes, like he was ready for whatever was next on the agenda.

"The dude fought with us."

Everyone looked at Jordan. He looked at me.

"Why'd he fight on our side?"

"I clipped him when I thought he was going at me."

Jordan shook his head. "That's not an answer, Bren. He want in your pants or something? Is this about Drake, whatever he said about you?"

"You're asking me like I have an answer."

He rolled his eyes. "It's not the time to be a smartass."

"She doesn't know. She hasn't talked to him except when you've seen her."

Jordan's gaze switched to Cross, but he didn't retort.

"We're supposed to believe the guy backed us up for no reason?" he said after a moment.

A set of headlights came down Jordan's driveway.

All of us formed a line, waiting.

The car turned past the main house and began coming up the slight hill to the shed. After a moment its headlights lit us up. We weren't able to make out the car, or who was driving it. We were almost blinded, but there was no reason to hide. If they'd come to Jordan's, we would fight.

As the vehicle parked, I could tell it was a truck. I reached into my pocket for my knife.

The lights stayed on, but both doors opened.

"Put the knife away, Bren! Now!"

Oh shit.

Jordan glanced at me. "Your brother?"

I felt Cross looking at me too, but I only grimaced and did as Channing said.

The knife went back into my pocket, and I waited, his gait a brisk and angry motion. As he moved out of the headlights, I could see his jaw clenched, his eyes irate, and the bottom of his neck reddening.

Now, I had to give my brother some credit here. He'd been a terror when he was younger, but he was older now and generally more laidback. Generally. Having said that, I knew he did get pissed, but the times I'd seen his neck red could be counted on one hand. I almost stepped back, but I held firm, not looking away.

The person with him fell back, and when I recognized Race, I got a good jolt. An apology flashed in his eyes before Channing started.

"Want to tell me what the fuck happened at Manny's?" My brother raked his hands through his hair. "Heather called me and said it all started with you. You guys trashed the place? What were you thinking?!"

"Hey!" Zellman stepped forward, his hands balled into fists and his shaggy hair standing up as if a bird was trying to build a nest in it. "Back off. Alex had no business touching her. He was told this morning to keep his hands off. He ignored that warning tonight."

The redness on Channing's neck faded, but his jaw remained clenched.

"That true?" he asked me.

I narrowed my eyes. *Fuck him.* He knew it was true.

Cross moved forward. "What's Heather going to do?"

Channing stared at me a moment longer before saying, "Nothing. Your crew started it. If someone presses charges, no judge is going to care that Ryerson touched Bren against her will. There's no justification for your response to that."

But there was in the system. Channing let out a small sigh and moved back a step. It was the break in tension we needed.

"I'm sorry, Bren."

I looked at my brother and saw he meant it. But my anger still burned. I could only clip my head in a tight nod.

He should know someone touching me against my will would set me off. But the sad part was, he didn't.

The new guy was watching me, a captive audience. I looked at him, but he didn't turn away. There was no shame in his gawking.

Panic rose in me.

I couldn't. I couldn't stand here, not with my brother and what he didn't know, and Race and what he shouldn't know.

"I gotta walk," I told them as I took off, shoving my hands into my pockets.

I wanted to slink down. I didn't.

They were all watching me, so I kept my head up and my shoulders back.

A moment later, I heard a second pair of feet on the ground behind me. Expecting Cross, I didn't say anything. He wouldn't press me, knowing I would talk when I wanted. We could walk in silence. Sometimes that's all I wanted.

But then it was Race who said quietly, "None of them know?"

I whirled to him, seeing red, and a second later, I had him backed against a tree, my knife at his throat.

I blinked a few times.

He was saying something...

I couldn't—what was I doing? I wasn't in control, but I didn't retract my knife. It was right there. If I leaned forward into it, it would break his skin.

My eyes locked with his.

He stood still. Calm. Waiting.

I was frozen in place, but then my hand began to twitch.

"What are you talking about?" I demanded.

"Who touched you against your will?"

God.

I shook my head, pulling my knife away from his neck. "You don't have the right to talk to me like that."

His mouth opened. He was going to argue, then he closed it. He nodded. "You're right. I don't. I don't know you."

Finally.

An invisible weight lifted off me.

"I feel like I do, though."

I shook my head, going over to a bench Jordan's dad had built for his mom. It was set to look over the entire lot, with a walking trail leading into the woods behind us. It wasn't the only path. They were all over. I took comfort in knowing I could slip away. I could take one path, then another, and another until I was gone.

"Drake spent the summer with my family, and he and I were inseparable," Race said. "He talked about you. A lot. He told me about Jordan, about Zellman. Alex has always been my cousin, but I've not been that close to him. My dad doesn't get along with Alex and Drake's dad. There's family fighting, so it was nice when Drake stayed with us. I'm an only kid. It was like I had a brother for a summer."

He moved to lean against a tree about ten feet from me—close enough for a private conversation, far enough that I had my own space.

"He never said anything about Cross. Seeing how close you two are, I have to imagine there was a reason."

What? I looked up at him. "What are you implying?"

He shrugged. "Nothing."

I snorted. "You'd suck at poker."

"Drake wouldn't tell me why you guys broke up."

Goddamn. I felt his accusation more than I heard it. He was a stranger. A stranger. He fought with us once. I should rile up. I should...do something, but I was tired. It felt like I had bursts of fight in me. I'd rail against whoever I needed to, whoever was trying to hurt me, push me around, use me, whatever. But then that burst of energy would leave me drained, and the age-old tiredness from life settled back into my bones.

I was starting to ache for some Cross time.

I returned my attention to Race. "If you're accusing me of being a cheating whore, my knife is coming out."

The heat was feigned in my voice. My fight was gone.

He laughed. "You're not then?"

"Drake dumped me. Whatever he said, however he talked about me, I was not some love of his life. When he graduated, he wanted nothing to do with me or his group. He left all of us."

"Yeah." Race frowned. "He didn't mention that."

"Makes you wonder. He left out the heavy subjects, but rattled on about me, Zellman, and Jordan. He didn't give two fucks about those two either. They were like ants to him." I stood from the bench. "Do yourself a favor. Don't read into anything he told you."

"I'm starting to get that."

Easy laughter traveled up to us, and I felt another kick in my chest. Channing was still standing with the guys. He could laugh with them, but he only yelled at me.

Maybe recently that had been my fault. I ignored him. I came and went as I pleased. I didn't ask him for anything. I didn't give him anything. We were like hostile strangers in the same house.

I was the aggravating little sister. He didn't understand why I did anything. I wouldn't open up when he asked. I didn't eat dinner when he invited me. Even when he was angry, I would just leave. And if he tried to block me in the hallway, I'd go to my room and slip out through the window.

Every room in the house had an escape route.

Sadly, he had no clue, and maybe that was the problem.

Channing never did anything to me. He didn't help me, but he didn't hurt me. He just wasn't there until two years ago, and even that was hit-and-miss most the time. And it wasn't that I wished he had been.

I was jealous.

He'd gotten what I wanted—and I had to turn my thoughts off on that. That was for another night, one accompanied by hard liquor. Lots of liquor.

Race coughed once, tugging at his collar. "Look, I don't know anything."

Shit. I'd forgotten he was here.

"What?" I went still. Did he mean... I held my breath a moment.

"Before, at school." He cringed. "I was bluffing. I knew you and Drake dated, and exes always know secrets. I was throwing something out there, just trying to push you guys off balance." He held his hands up. "I swear. Drake never told me any secret about you."

I was still wary of him. "Why'd you fight with us tonight?"

"Because my cousin was wrong."

I eyed him.

"I'm not crew, obviously, but I'm not a pussy. And I'm not a bad guy."

So he thought his cousin was. If he thought that after the first day, he was in for a rough ride this year. And the way he looked at me, it was always changing. Now I was a new puzzle. He was unlearning what he thought he knew, trying to find the place where the new pieces fit in.

I shook my head. "Do yourself a favor. Stop trying to figure me out."

He let out a rueful laugh. "Maybe I should." He glanced in the direction of the guys.

"Alex is going to kick you out of the house. And that's if he decides you going against him was a family issue, not a crew thing."

"And if he doesn't? If he decides it's a crew thing?"

"Then you're fucked. His entire group will turn on you. You'll become the number-one enemy at school."

He barked out a laugh. "This whole system—it's like nothing else matters. Your rules, your way, your lifestyle. That's it."

Exactly.

I offered an olive branch. "You need to decide where your loyalties lie. If you're not joining a group, you better get to your cousin ASAP and kiss his ass until you got no lips. Alex can be a somewhat decent guy on a good day, but if he thinks someone's looking down at him, he turns into a viper."

"What about you guys? You taking on new members?"

My chest grew tight. "We don't work like the Ryerson crew. There aren't applications or written rules for us."

"I'm not much of an ass-kisser, and I've got a feeling Alex isn't going to be my biggest fan here." The side of his mouth lifted. "Good thing I know how to fight."

Yes, he did.

He seemed to have real training, not the rough-scraping most of the guys used in fights.

I was glad to hear about the bluff, but why do that? Why mess with us on the first day, then back us up that same evening? Only time would tell. And with that last thought, he was officially no longer my concern.

I nodded to where my guys were. "I'm heading back."

CHAPTER
FIFTEEN

THE GUYS WERE still laughing with my brother when we got back, and everyone looked over as we approached.

Jordan extended a hand to Race. "Thanks for backing us up in there." A cocky grin appeared. "Even though we're the right choice, I know Alex is family to you."

"Yeah." Race shook his hand, glancing sideways at me. "Got a little advice on how to act moving forward."

Jordan nodded, settling back against his truck.

I felt Cross' gaze on me, but Channing spoke up, drawing my attention.

"Can I talk to you?" he asked me.

No. I sighed on the inside. "Yes."

Things were stifled between my brother and me. That was the best word to describe it. After Mom died, he hardly ever came home, choosing his friends instead. Then Dad went to prison. And because he'd fucked up the financials so much, on top of his crime, we lost the house. It came down to me going into the foster system or with Channing. We had no other blood family in the area, no one who would take me.

Things were still...distant, on my part too. We'd been little more than roommates the first year and a half. It'd only been the last six months that he'd started to want to know more about me and where I was.

This talk right now was not something I wanted to deal with. He was in no place to lecture me. He'd gotten into worse shit younger than me.

He nodded to the side, and I walked away from the group for a second time.

"I know I said it before, but Heather's not going to press charges," he assured me. "Because of that, though, she's responsible for all the damages. You and your guys need to help out, come in and clean, do a fundraiser for her or something to help with the repairs."

I nodded. "Yeah. I can see that."

It was a technicality that we'd started the fight. The real person who'd started it was Alex Ryerson. He'd cover the damages; he just didn't know it yet.

"We'll take care of it," I added. "Don't worry."

"And apologize to Heather."

I threw him a dark look. That was inevitable. "I know."

His eyes narrowed, then he rolled them, shaking his head. "You drive me insane sometimes."

I grunted. The feeling was mutual. "What else do you want, Channing? You could've yelled at me over the phone."

His eyes widened. "What? You mean you would've answered it? You would've given me the time of day suddenly? Versus all the other days when you ignore that I'm even a part of your life?" He shook his head. "Trust me, I would've preferred to call and not hitch a ride with some guy I don't know. I could have stayed back and tried to help Heather clean up *your* mess."

I threw my head back. "It wasn't *my* mess! Stop blaming me for everything that happens in your life!"

His eyes narrowed again, and a confused look flashed across his face. He rubbed a hand over his jaw. "Look. Just... I'm going to stay at Heather's tonight. Maybe instead of you guys doing the cleanup, I'll have my guys do it. You can owe me."

The place needed to be fixed immediately. Heather needed Manny's to be operating, so I understood what he was thinking. It'd take forever if Heather relied on us to fix it.

But owing my brother? I already hated owing him what I did: a place to stay, sometimes food, and any signature a guardian had to give for a minor. And now this? I didn't want more on that list, but fucking hell.

I shoved my hands into my pockets and hung my head. "Yeah. Whatever. Just let me know what I owe you."

"Dinners."

I lifted my head. "What?"

"Dinners. Every night."

Fuuuck. "You work sometimes."

"You show up wherever I'm at. If I'm at home, dinner there. If I'm at the bar, we can eat in the back or in my office. If I'm at Heather's, go there. Seven every night."

"Come on." My lips thinned. I glanced at the guys.

He caught my gaze. "Bring your friends. I don't give a shit. You're my sister. I get you for another year before you take off, and after that, I've got a feeling you'd rather I never see you again. So dinners. I get that from you now. That's what you owe me."

This wasn't a debt I could pawn off on Alex.

I gritted my teeth, but there were other emotions mixed with my frustration. They all swirled together inside, and like every day over the last ten years, I just let them be. It would cost too much to try and unwind them all and face them.

"Fine."

He nodded, patting me on the shoulder. "I'm not going to kid myself. I know you're not coming home tonight, so I'll see you tomorrow at seven. We'll have tacos."

Tacos. Lovely.

But it was. My stomach growled at the idea, and I remembered I hadn't eaten since my burger for lunch. I'd only finished half before bailing out on Heather too.

"Okay. Tomorrow." He stepped around me, patting me on the arm before calling, "Hey, new guy!" He lifted a hand to Race as he headed back to the group. "I need a ride back. You brought me here; you take me back."

"What?" Race glanced around. "I wasn't planning on going back..."

He trailed off as the guys started laughing.

I started after my brother and could see his head shaking, his shoulders rolled back. This wasn't my brother being a pain in my ass. He'd used his cocky voice, the one he used whenever he was around his crew. That brother was charismatic, a leader, authoritative. I saw what everyone else saw. Channing had such a powerful influence on everyone in Roussou. He had started the entire system, but he did more than that. He protected our town too. I didn't know the extent of it, because he didn't let me know, but I knew shady shit went down in and around Roussou. And I knew it was his group that handled that all. He was revered, with good reason, but he wasn't anyone else's big brother. No one else was his sister. He walked away from me, and it was as if he shed his "big brother" skin. He needed a ride home. He wasn't making any of us take him, for whatever reason. His target was Race, and whether the new guy knew it or not, he was going to do what my brother wanted.

Even I felt a trace of sympathy for the guy.

He had no idea that what Channing said went. Channing ruled. It was as simple as that.

Jordan laughed, clapping Race on the shoulder. "You're shit out of luck." He gestured to Channing. "You met the big brother tonight. He gets different treatment when he's in that role. He's not just Bren's brother."

"Who is he?"

Zellman began laughing, but Cross spoke over him, looking right at Channing. "He's the godfather. If he says you do something, you do it. Bren's the only one who can talk back to him. Because, you know, family."

Race's shoulders fell. "Okay." He nodded to my brother. "I'll take you back."

They moved toward Race's vehicle, and as they opened their doors, my guys went back to where I'd been standing. Except I was gone.

Cross had glanced at me, and I gave him the look. I'd mouthed, "I'm out" before stepping away.

I only needed to take one step back, and I was in the shadows. I didn't wait to see Cross' reaction. Not wanting to hash it out with the guys, I headed back through the walking paths. I knew how to criss and cross until I came out to the road a couple miles north of where Cross lived.

That firefly had come back. I felt its presence enveloping me like a warm blanket. There was no one else but me out here, and I tipped my head back, drinking in the night. The silence was peaceful. I used to yearn for it when my mother wasn't sick, when Dad was drinking. I hated Channing for leaving, but he'd been the smart one. I was the only one who heard her yelling, him yelling. I had to wait until something shattered, then there would be thumps, thuds, things crashing to the floor.

The cries came next, but not from me.

I was always either under my covers, silent tears rolling down my face, or slipping out the window. I took lessons from Channing early on. If he could leave, so could I. I was six when I'd first walked across town by myself to Cross' house.

But over time those sounds had faded at our house, and different sounds took over.

The beeping of whatever medical device she had in her room. The sound of her vomiting, moaning, groaning, weeping. And the sound of his cursing, the crinkle of the brown bags he'd use to carry booze into the house.

When she got sick, they stopped fighting. She suffered in her bedroom, and he drank in the basement.

But even those sounds eventually went away.

She went into the hospital...and there was nothing.

Absolute silence.

Dad didn't even stay in the basement anymore.

Channing was gone, and so was he. He went to his bar, or his friends' house. If I wasn't at the hospital with Mom, I was home alone. That was a silence I hated until it became a part of me.

I blended with it.

From time to time I felt that same silence again—the firefly type. It rose up in me, wrapping around me.

It kept me company for about a mile until a truck pulled up next to me.

I heard it coming, the engine rumbling and the light growing like a slow-glowing candle. It chased away the firefly, and as the window rolled down, I felt my insides stop bleeding too.

Cross slowed the truck to my pace, but he didn't say anything.

I didn't either.

I wanted to keep walking, and he let me for a little while—until my insides had completely dried up. It was time to rejoin the world, and with a small exhale, I reached for the door handle.

Cross nudged on the brakes and waited as I got inside. Like so many other nights, not a word was spoken. He lifted his foot from the brake, and we drove the rest of the way into town to pull up outside his house.

No lights were on, and the house was quiet as we walked in. We proceeded as we always did.

He went to the kitchen where he would grab two bottles of water for us. I went up the stairs and to his bedroom, going into his bathroom. Nudging the door closed, I got ready for bed, using the toothbrush I kept here.

When I was done, I opened the door.

He was sitting on the bed, a pair of boxer shorts and sleeping shirt folded up next to him. A bottle of water lay next to them, and as I stepped out into his bedroom, he stood, and we switched places.

The bathroom door closed behind him.

I dressed in the clothes he'd left out, and I had the closet door open when he returned. I could smell his toothpaste as he stepped past me to the bed.

"You want the bed?" he asked.

He knew better.

My eyes met his for a second, and then I reached over to his desk, where he'd placed three blankets and two pillows. I spread two blankets in the closet, then scooted down. One pillow went under my head, the other I hugged to my chest. I pulled the other blanket over me, but I knew I'd probably kick it off.

I curled into a ball, lying on my side.

My phone was off. I knew Cross would wake us up.

He stood there, watching me for a moment.

I thought he'd say something, but he didn't. He just stared at me, and a different feeling took root. An awareness. It was low in my belly, beginning to trickle up, almost tickling my insides.

All the while, Cross never looked away until slowly, he reached up and pulled his shirt off. His muscles rippled from the movement. For a second I saw every single one of his muscles outlined, all the way to the V dipping under his jeans. His eyes stayed on me as his hands dropped to his pants. He unbuckled them, letting them drop, and he kicked them to the side.

He'd taken his socks and shoes off in the bathroom, and now he stood in his boxer briefs. It wasn't anything I hadn't seen before, but there was a different feel to the room that night.

The tickle was still there, but it had softened. It almost felt like a tingle now.

I couldn't endure it any more, whatever it was, so I closed my eyes.

The lights went out. Cross turned his sleeping fan to the lowest setting, and without opening my eyes—for a reason even I didn't understand—I reached out and closed his closet door.

I barricaded myself in, and then I slept.

CHAPTER SIXTEEN

I WOKE EARLY.

Cross was in the bathroom, but I didn't have any clothes for school. I scribbled him a note, then took his keys and, after a quick stop in the family bathroom, I drove to my place. I showered and changed there, but hurried right back out the door. Channing's bedroom door was closed as I passed. I didn't want Cross to wait or risk a run-in with my brother. After picking up coffee, I went back to his place.

He was sitting on his porch, and after I parked, I slid into the passenger seat. He got behind the wheel. I indicated the coffee for him in the console. He grunted his thanks, but that was it. Neither of us was up for morning chatter. I saw the bags under his eyes. We'd only gotten a few hours of sleep.

He'd just shifted into drive when the front door opened. Taz walked out, her backpack over one shoulder and her own mug of coffee in hand. Her eyes widened as she saw us, but Cross was already pushing the accelerator.

Cursing, he hit the brakes, then cast a cursory look at me.

"If you're pausing on giving her a ride because of me, don't. I'm okay with her. You know that."

He didn't respond, but I didn't expect him to.

After waiting another beat, Taz took a breath, rolled her shoulders back, and walked over. She looked like a three year old, her mind made up to ask for something she already knew her parents would say no to, but she was coming anyway.

Cross rolled his window down. "You want a ride this morning?"

She stopped right outside my door. "Sunday was supposed to give me a ride this morning." She looked to me, then back to her brother. "I'm guessing she's not coming? She never texted me back."

She gave us both meaningful looks.

Cross relaxed into his seat. His arm hung loose over the steering wheel. "Look, if she doesn't show, that's between you and her. Don't get mad at us because you have shit taste in friends. You know she's a shitty person. Don't know why you're wasting your time."

She rolled her eyes, adjusting her backpack over her shoulder. She switched her coffee to the other hand. "Yeah, yeah. I know, but not all of us have an entire crew at our disposal."

"You need a ride or what?"

Her eyes grew a little frosty, matching her tone. She ignored her brother. "Pretty sure one of your friends has a certain taste for her too. And like I said, some of us are a bit limited in the friendship category."

Cross chuckled. "My point still stands. Zellman has no taste in women. He'd bang a door if it had a hole his prick wouldn't get a sliver from. You want a ride or not?"

She groaned, but nodded. "I can't take Mom's car. She took it this morning." She nodded to me, opening my door. "Slide over, B."

I did.

Then we were off, windows down.

We didn't even try at conversation. It was pointless. We all knew how Cross drove. He took the back roads around town, going as fast as he could. The radio was turned on once we hit the main street, Kansas blaring from the speakers.

Taz bobbed her head in rhythm with the music, starting to sing, and the tension from last night was gone. It felt right again with the three of us.

It didn't last. Once we parked at the school, the tension rose, along with the windows. I felt it on my shoulders as we got out, silent once again.

Taz climbed out of the truck. I slid out behind Cross, and we saw them right away.

Taz was already around the back when she realized I hadn't followed her.

"Bren?" She followed our gazes and asked, "Something happen I should know about?"

Alex Ryerson and ten of his group were heading our way. The girls who'd been standing with them fell back.

I rounded the back of Cross' truck as Alex stopped about ten yards away. We moved to stand in front of Taz.

"Guys?" she asked again, so quietly.

I reached behind me and gestured for her to move away.

She didn't.

Alex and his guys moved closer.

"What's going on, Bren?" Taz asked under her breath.

"Get Jordan and Zellman." I thought about it and added, "And Race Ryerson."

She started off, but turned back. "The new guy?"

"Just do it." I flicked my hand a little harder.

With a soft huff, she moved to the side and around us, keeping a good distance from Alex's crew as they spread out in a line in front of us, forming half a circle. It was only Cross and me. His truck was behind us, blocking any escape route. Eleven to two was steep odds, even for us. We were going to get real bloody real quick.

"What do you want, Alex?" Cross asked, his hands half in his pockets and half out.

"I got a good earful last night from my cousin," Alex said. He turned to me. "It was my second offense against you. Now, I'm not saying I don't want war. We outnumber your crew, but having said that, I *was* at fault. You guys were doing what you have to for a crew member. I get that. So..." He tipped his head. "I'm apologizing, Bren."

My insides clenched into a giant fist. What was this? I'd expected a fight.

"You apologized yesterday morning, then did the same thing twelve hours later. I'm thinking your apology is bullshit."

His eyes grew wary. "Okay. That's fair." He raised his chin. "What do you want instead? What can I do to show you I mean it?"

"What are you asking?"

"What do you want?"

I cocked my head to the side. "Are you messing with us?"

He lifted a shoulder, his hands tucked back into his pockets. "I'm assuming Jax didn't press charges. All those repairs are on her. That's gotta be expensive." He stopped, like he was mulling over his words. "I can pay for it," he offered.

His dad would pay for it. Not him.

If he'd offered last night, I would've taken him up on it. But not now.

"That ship's sailed, buddy. My brother's covering all the repairs." I narrowed my eyes and waited. That bombshell should hit him hard. It would hit anyone hard.

My relationship with Channing was what it was, but I hadn't exaggerated his standing in town.

At my words, Alex's cocky attitude vanished. His eyes widened, and he snapped to attention.

"Oh." He moved back a step.

Yeah.

Two of Alex's crew stepped up next to him. He leaned over, listening to what they said.

Jordan and Zellman broke through the crowd that had formed to watch. They stayed back on the sidewalk at a safe distance. Jordan kept skirting from Alex to Cross and me, but he kept quiet.

Before the crowd closed back up, I saw Race standing outside the school door. He was watching, waiting to see what would happen. There was no uncertainty in his posture. His head was high. His eyes were calm. He was ready—for what I didn't know. Alex's words came back to me. *"I got an earful from my cousin last night."*

What had Race said?

"Okay."

The two crew stepped away from Alex. He scanned the rest of mine with an intense look. "We'll go to your brother today. We'll request a meeting with him." He gestured to me. "You still can decide what I can do to make it up to you."

"I'm already repaying your debt to my brother," I told him. "It's a family thing. Trust me. He won't let you take my place."

"Still." His Adam's apple bobbed. "I'll go to him separately, and if you're repaying my debt already, then I really owe you."

I shared a look with Jordan. He'd deemed himself our leader. He could act like one now. But as if he'd read my mind, he shook his head as if to say "No, you got this."

I sighed. "I don't know, Alex. There's nothing I want from you."

His top lip curled into a slight smile. "Okay, but if there is, let me know. I'll hold up my end."

I stepped toward him, moving out ahead of my crew. Right now, I was the leader. "There will be retaliation if you don't."

"I know." His eyes held mine. He didn't waver or look away.

I moved back again. We'd see. "Fine." I didn't have a lot of faith in Alex, but you just never knew with him.

A full smile broke out. "Are we friends again, Bren?"

"Don't push it." I didn't hold back a small grin, letting him see it.

He nodded, giving a wave to the rest of the guys. "Jordan. Cross. Zellman."

"Alex." Jordan stepped toward me as word spread the fight everyone expected wasn't going to happen.

The crowd started to disperse. People began heading in.

Not us.

Jordan, Zellman, and Cross waited until enough people had moved away that we had privacy.

"What just happened?" Jordan asked.

"Ryerson took ownership," Cross said. "He came to offer his debt to Bren."

"For real?"

Cross nodded, his arm coming to rest around my shoulders. He patted the top of my arm. "She made him bend down and sniff his own shit. Almost literally. He's going to face Channing."

Jordan burst out laughing. "That's awesome. Shit. He's going to face Channing? He thinks we're scary; he'll have to strap on a diaper when he goes to that meeting." Jordan looked to me. "Alex will chicken out. I guarantee he'll push that meeting off as long as he can."

"You think he won't go?" I asked.

"He has to now. If he doesn't, he's a coward. No crew is a coward. That's one decree we all agree on, but I bet you he'll wait as long as possible." He shook his head, whistling. "We'll see what happens."

The second bell was about to ring, and the parking lot showed it. The only people still outside were Alex's crew, who were on their way in, our crew, and—I looked over again—Race. He lingered by the door, but when our eyes met, he nodded and headed inside too.

I'd taken two steps inside when a teacher said, "Bren Monroe, go to the office for skipping yesterday."

I stopped and let out a full-blown groan.

One day. I couldn't last one full day without getting in trouble. I swear.

CHAPTER SEVENTEEN

"BREN MONROE IS in my office."

Nikki Bagirianni, the school counselor, spoke more to herself than me as she looked up at Principal Neeon holding my arm. She put down the phone she'd just picked up at her secretary's desk, her office door open behind her.

"She skipped the second half of classes yesterday." Principal Neeon let go of my arm.

Why he had to hold it, I didn't know, but I shot him a look like he'd hurt me. I even rubbed where he'd held me.

"I told you I was sick yesterday."

Neeon leaned forward, his arms crossed over his chest. "Then have your brother send a note next time." He nodded to the counselor. "She's all yours for now."

For now. Meaning there was more to come.

Exciting.

Ms. Bagirianni —or Nikki as she usually had people call her— was known as The Badger by most of us. We were crew. If we didn't find ourselves in the counselor's office or Neeon's office, we were doing something wrong.

"Right." She straightened her silk shirt and smoothed her hands over her hair. It was up in a bun, and her motion pulled out some of the strands. She smiled at me, patting those loose strands back into place. "Yes. Bren Monroe. It's Tuesday. That seems right to me. The new year has officially begun."

Her hair still stuck out.

She nodded toward the open door behind her. "My office?"

Like I had a say in the matter.

She went in and sat behind her desk.

I took one of the two plush seats set up in the corner of her office. A large green plant sat on the table between them, and I reached out to touch it.

The plant was plastic.

She typed for a moment on her computer before turning the screen off.

I gestured to the plant. "It's new."

"Administration decided we need to be green and healthy and alive. So..." She made a face, positioning her chair so she faced me directly. She folded her hands over her lap. "There you go. That's my contribution."

"You should name him Gus."

Her head fell forward an inch. "Name my plant?"

"Yes."

"Gus?"

"Yes."

"Okay." She straightened her skirt, smoothing her hands over the edge. "I have a male plant named Gus. I feel like I should formally meet my own fake plant."

I picked it up, holding it out to her. "Here you go."

Her eyes went to mine. "Are you joking?"

Yes. I shrugged. "You're a counselor. Isn't doing crazy shit part of the job description?"

"Crazy shit?" She sucked in her breath, shaking her head. "Yes. This is it. I *am* back to work. Summer is over, and Bren Monroe is swearing in my office. It's a normal Tuesday like all the other years. And yeah." She glanced at her wrist. "That took two minutes. We're back in our old roles."

"You're the one who has a fake plant."

"Because I will kill a real one, and come on—I'm doing the best I can. I'm following the rules."

"You got mad at me for saying 'crazy shit.' You made me talk to an empty chair last year. Three times," I reminded her. "I had a fight with an empty chair. It was air, and I got pissed off."

She smiled. "Well, the chair talked back. I heard it too."

I started laughing. Then I stopped because I didn't laugh—with her especially.

"You can laugh. Even Gus thought that was funny." She gestured to the plant still in my hands.

"You should go on tour. Be a professional comedian. You could be famous."

She didn't even blink. "Lame attempt at getting me to quit my job. We'd still be doing this, even if I did hand in the towel."

I lifted my shoulder. "It was a long shot." I scratched behind my ear. "I know the whole premise is that I'm crazy and that's why I get sent here, but I only feel nuts when I'm actually *in* this office. Life makes perfect sense to me outside of this square box."

"Perfect sense?"

I nodded. I would back up what I said. She didn't know about the firefly.

"You lost your mother when you were eight. Your brother was basically nonexistent in your life. And your dad, who had an intense anger problem, went to prison two years ago. I have already heard about two incidents you were a catalyst for—two potentially violent incidents—and the rumor around school is that there was a huge crew fight at Manny's in Fallen Crest last night. No one had to tell me you were a part of that too. That's three incidences in two days, Bren."

She leaned back in her chair, waving her hand between us. "You and me, we've been doing this dance for a while. Two years, to be exact. You were mandated to come to sessions with me when your dad went in and you went to your brother's custody, but we'd already met a few times after your mom died. You have stonewalled me at every turn. Isn't it time you start talking? Three fights in two days. That's a lot of pain to hold on to. You have to be exhausted."

Not on a bad day.

Not on a good day.

I grinned at her. "It was one fight. The other two things didn't happen."

"That makes it better?"

"Yes," I shot back.

"Okay." She crossed one leg over the other. Leaning back and rolling her shoulders, she put on the counselor stare. She was now ready to try to read inside of me, pull out all my insides and make me examine them along with her.

Fuck that.

But I held my tongue as she said, "Round one."

I arched an eyebrow.

"What were you talking about with Alex Ryerson in the parking lot this morning?"

"We were finalizing our friendship handshake."

"You're lying."

I grinned. "Do you want a friendship handshake too? You can't have the same one as Alex. He'll get jealous."

She rolled her eyes, and re-folded her hands on her lap. "Round two."

We were playing Twenty Questions?

She narrowed her eyes. "You skipped the second half of your classes yesterday. Why?"

My grin faded, but I shrugged and leaned back in my chair. "I got sick."

"It was the first day. It's one of the easiest days of the year. What student skips the first day?" She rolled her eyes at her own question.

"I told you, I was sick."

"You might as well be honest with me."

I gritted my teeth. "I was sick."

Her eyes fixed on me again. "You didn't answer the other question. Here's a new one. Are you still dating Drake Ryerson?"

That wasn't her question. She knew that answer.

"What does my love life have to do with this? Drake's in college."

She tugged at her skirt. "So you're not together?"

I didn't answer. She didn't need to know that stuff. She already knew too much.

She frowned, her head tilted to the side, but she let it go. "I've heard his cousin transferred here, and I also heard he's taken an interest in you. Is that right?"

I leaned forward and deadpanned, "I've missed talking to you." Not a flicker of emotion. I didn't blink. "So much."

She didn't either. "I heard he was talking to your crew yesterday morning." She watched me intently. "He looks a lot like Drake."

"Drake's prettier." I didn't look away. "The new guy helped me write a poem for you. It's from all of us, my crew and him."

"Do you like him?" She broke eye contact now, glancing down to her lap before looking back up.

I cocked my head to the side. "I titled the poem 'The Badger Named Gus'."

She paused, smiling faintly, and nodded. "Okay. That was funny. Round three." She wiggled her eyebrows at me. "I know you live for this, so don't even pretend you're tired."

I made a face. "Who's pretending? I'm happy I'm not fighting with an empty chair. My life's complete. I met Gus."

"No kidding. I met Gus too. I had no clue who he was. I just thought he was a regular fake plant like all the others."

"Nope." I shook my head. "Gus is a troubled fake plant. That's why you bought him. You were drawn to him. Gus pulled you in."

"Gus is a fucking manipulator then." She glanced at the door, but no one was out there. "I'm not supposed to curse, but it's Tuesday and Bren Monroe is here, so I'm taking advantage."

"I'm going to tell on you."

"And I'll tell them you're a fucking liar." She smiled. "And yeah, I'll say the F word because here's a secret: We're all adults. We all swear."

"And yet you don't want me to curse."

"Because here's another secret that most everyone knows except you: You're not an adult!"

I felt slapped by that one.

"What's going on here?" I gestured between us. "I thought we were joking—"

"You were being a smartass."

"I thought we had this camaraderie—"

"You were making fun of my professionalism."

"I thought we were getting past the surface walls and going to start braiding each other's hair."

"When I want a haircut, I'll ask you." Her eyes moved to my pocket. "I know where you keep your knife."

That one shut me up. I wasn't supposed to have it in my pocket. I always did, though.

She waited, but when I kept quiet, she tried again.

"Have we done the dance where you push me away, and I counter with my sarcastic wit because that's the only common ground I can get with you? Can we cut through the bullshit now?"

I rubbed at my neck. "I don't know. I'm still hurting from your comments."

She cursed softly, but she was grinning. "You and me. This isn't our first rodeo. You're a pro at evading adults and pissing them off so they go away. I get it. People leave you."

I looked away. I didn't want to hear about my mom, my dad, my brother, even Max. Or hell, Scratch too. None of them. My throat started to feel raw, the insides were peeling away.

"Your brother called me."

I almost jerked, but I caught myself. I held still in the chair. I showed no reaction.

"I'm only a few years older than your brother, so when I got a call from Channing Monroe, you can imagine how floored I was. My heart started pumping. My palms got sweaty. I mean, Channing Monroe." She raised her hands in the air, pantomiming a large crowd. "Even I'm not immune to him, but what struck me wasn't that he was calling. Parents, guardians, I get those calls all day long. They talk *at* me. They don't want to hear what I have to say, not the truth." She paused again. "But Channing Monroe, who created the Roussou crew system, called to really talk about his sister. He wasn't calling to talk at me, but to me. There's a difference, and I knew things must be bad if he was reaching out."

I thought I was looking outside. I couldn't tell. The window grew blurry.

"He told me you're not staying at home. You're not even going home most days. And he said he didn't know what to do, but he was worried. He didn't say anything about fighting, about skipping school, about swearing. I know. I know. You're crew royalty. It's almost expected of you, but I'm not here to bust your ass about those things. This is the beginning of year three for you and me. I want to help you, Bren. You can't keep me away any longer. I'm not going to allow it, and I don't want to waste your time. I have one year left to help you, so I'm breaking all the rules. Counselors aren't supposed to lead the tone. We're not supposed to argue with our clients, curse at them, curse *with* them, be sarcastic back—or fuck, be sarcastic first. I'm not supposed to corner you or make you feel attacked, but this is how you operate. Your crew is aptly named. You're a wolf. You snarl. You bite. You fight back. That's how you operate in life and with others. So fine. I'll meet you where you are, but here's one thing that's not going to happen: You will not make me give up on you. Got it? I am not going anywhere."

I checked the clock. That was blurry too, but I could make out that I'd been in here for thirty minutes already.

Why was everything so goddamn blurry?

"Now." Her voice quieted. "Tell me about Race Ryerson."

"Why?" It hurt to talk.

"Because I want to know *something* about you. I really want to talk about your brother. I really, really want to talk to you about Cross Shaw."

My gaze snapped to hers.

She held up a hand. "But I know both those topics will have you walking out of this office in two seconds flat, so give me something. Anything. The new guy looks like your ex, and he's related to your ex. You must have *some* feeling about that."

My nostrils flared. "Are you serious?"

"Yes and no." She held her hands toward me a moment before letting them fall back on her lap. "Tell me about him. And if not him, tell me something. I need to know something, anything, about your life."

Wha—my head was spinning. I heard her imploring tone. It sounded genuine, but this was a waste of time. I would either graduate or not. If I didn't, I'd figure it out. My brother had.

When the bell rang, I stood up. "First period's done."

CHAPTER EIGHTEEN

"GODDAMN!"

The last class had let out for the day, and I could see Zellman and Jordan at their lockers through the crowd of students in the hall. I hadn't really talked to any of my crew during the day, not more than a few words in class or between classes. At lunch I sat with Taz outside at a table. I didn't know where Cross had been. He slipped in late to two of the classes I had with him, and he slept through the third.

Zellman grabbed his bag and stuffed it back into the locker. He slammed the door, then kicked it.

"Stay closed, motherfucker!"

Jordan laughed.

"You told that inanimate object," I said as I approached. "It knows who's boss now."

"Second day of school, and already I got too much shit in my locker." Zellman nodded at me, stuffing his hands into his pockets.

"Hey." Jordan lifted his chin in greeting, leaning against his neighbor's locker. "Heard you got sent to the counselor's office this morning. How was that?"

I shrugged. "How it always is. A waste of time. I feel like I'm finally back to school now."

Zellman grinned at me. Then his locker popped open again.

"OH MY FUCKING GOD!" He slammed it shut and began beating on it. "STAY." Kick. "SHUT." Punch. "YOU." A second punch. "MOTHER." His elbow, a heel kick added. "FUCKER!" He braced himself on both sides of his locker and bent over.

I moved forward. Jordan straightened, and we both began to reach for him.

I thought he'd go for the head butt, but after a moment he seemed to think better of it. He used his fists like he was doing a boxing speed drill.

"Fucking locker!" He gave it one last kick.

It sprang open again, clipping his foot in the process.

"AHHH!"

"Mr. Greenley!"

The students in the hallway parted, and Principal Neeon strode forward. How we'd missed him coming, I had no idea. He stopped right in front of us, folding his arms over his chest. The movement lifted his suit jacket. I was impressed he was still wearing his tie.

"You are damaging school property. You need to stop." He spoke clearly, as if we were children. He turned to me. "And Miss Monroe. Why do I have a feeling we're off to a very bad start for the year?"

"You didn't have to take me to The Badger."

"It was either her office or mine. Did I get it wrong?"

Zellman cut in, pointing to his locker. "It won't close, Mr. N."

"It's Neeon, not N. And it's because you have too much stuff inside."

"It's my locker. I have my necessities in there."

"Well, some of your necessities need to be moved elsewhere."

Zellman glowered, grumbling, "That doesn't help." His head popped up. "Can I have another locker? There's gotta be an empty spare somewhere."

"No."

"Come on, Mr. N—eeon. Mr. Neeon."

"What's going on?"

I looked over my shoulder. Cross had appeared, his hair a little messed.

I gestured to Zellman's locker. "It won't close. Z's trying to commit murder on it, and Mr. N's not having it."

"I am not Mr. N." He straightened to his full six-feet and three inches and looked down his nose at us, literally. Except Jordan. "It is Neeon. You will call me either Mr. Neeon, or Principal Neeon, or just principal. You got that, Miss Monroe?" He included Zellman in his withering look.

I shrugged. "How about Mr. P? P for principal?" I read the big NO coming and amended it. "Prince? That's not a bad name. You like the color purple, Mr. N?"

"I went over your name choices—"

Race spoke up as he joined the group. "I'd take Prince, because if you don't jump on it, they'll shorten it to Prick."

Principal Neeon opened his mouth, but just let out a large gust of air. "Fine. I'll go with Mr. N." He pointed to Zellman. "Stop beating on your locker." He turned to me. "And you, stop skipping classes. You have one year left. I'd like you to graduate."

Zellman smiled, lighting up his face. "You don't have to worry about Bren. Don't you know by now, Mr. N? She's brilliant. She got Bs last year and skipped almost all of her classes."

"Zellman!"

Jordan let out a frustrated sigh, smacking the back of Zellman's head with his palm. Mr. Neeon looked at me, but he looked back at Zellman when he heard him yelp. By then he only saw Zellman rubbing the back of his head and Jordan yawning, scratching the back of his neck.

"Man, my neck is itching. There's not a case of fleas in the school, is there?"

Our principal pinched his nose, closing his eyes a moment. "I am pretending I didn't hear that, because if I did, and it was a true complaint, I would have to allocate money from the budget to test for fleas in this school. So..." He held his hands up, palms facing us. "I am backing away." He did.

"Hey!"

He bumped into Monica and Sunday.

"Sorry, ladies."

He was gone after that.

Zellman waited until Principal Neeon was almost to the end of the hallway before kicking his locker shut again.

It stayed this time.

Race shook his head. "No one can say you guys aren't interesting. That's for sure."

Monica and Sunday took a step forward, easy grins on their faces.

Jordan narrowed his eyes, the amusement over Zellman's locker fiasco gone. "You looking to join, Race? Is that why you're hanging around us every chance you get?"

Monica and Sunday retreated backwards.

Race's eyes narrowed. "I helped you guys last night."

"We didn't ask for it."

"Didn't need it either," Zellman added.

Race didn't seem to care. "You think Alex apologized out of the goodness of his heart? Or I'm sorry—would you rather have waged a full-blown crew war?"

"Alex knew he was wrong," Jordan said.

"You think he came to that conclusion on his own?" Race stepped closer, lowering his voice. "You think he's that smart?"

He had a point.

Cross, Jordan, and Zellman knew it too.

"Look." Jordan moved to face Race directly. "What do you want? You're around the crew a lot. Either you want in—and if you do, that shit doesn't happen overnight—or there's another reason." He glanced to me. "I figure we got something else you want."

Uh, what?

I froze a moment, looking from Jordan to Race. There were no elaborations or denials, and a full boost of heat warmed my body. I felt everyone's gaze on me—Cross especially—but no one said anything.

So I did. I shook my head. "No. I already dated one Ryerson."

Race spoke as if I hadn't said a word. "Maybe. I can't deny that could be part of it."

I closed my eyes, sucking in some air.

What was this guy doing? Was he for real?

I *felt* Cross' gaze on me, but I couldn't bring myself to look at him. I didn't want to see whatever was there—disappointment, or something worse. An image of how he'd looked at me last night, before he took his shirt off, flashed in my memory. That tickling/tingling was coming back.

I held my hands up. "I'm out." I jerked my head in Race's direction. "He's fucking with you all."

I pushed past Cross, then past Monica and Sunday, who seemed entranced where they stood behind us.

I could feel myself breaking out in hives. I didn't want a Drake 2.0 situation.

Taz must've seen me leaving, and I was shoving through the doors to the parking lot when I heard her voice behind me.

"Hey! Bren! Hey."

I was going to ignore her, then remembered Cross had driven us to school that morning.

"You move fast. Wow." Taz was a little out of breath when she caught up to me. Bracing a hand on my arm, she waited until her breathing evened out, then gave me a rueful look. "I was head cheerleader last year, and now I can't catch up to you walking down the hallway." She placed her hand on her hip. "My, how the mighty have fallen."

"You were the head cheerleader?"

"No." She waved in the air, twirling her wrist. "I added it for dramatic effect. Thought it sounded funnier." She waited, watching me.

I wasn't laughing.

"Huh. I must've been wrong."

I pointed to Cross' truck. "I need a ride home."

"Oh." She jerked a thumb over her shoulder. "I'm sure Cross will be coming in a bit."

Not the point. I went through the names I could call to give me a ride. Channing. Heather.

So, yeah.

The real question: wait for Cross? Or walk on my own? Normally, a walk was fine, but I wasn't feeling it with the heat today. The sun was blaring too much, so I had no choice.

I plopped down on the curb, and Taz sat with me. The last of lingering students headed past us, but there'd be another wave coming out in twenty minutes as the athletes went to the football field, tennis courts, track, and volleyball courts.

"Um…" Taz hugged her bag on her lap. "I have to prepare you for something."

"What?" I looked over. "Don't you have practice too? Didn't you join the squad again?"

"What?" She frowned at me. "Oh. No. I was just helping them out with some things yesterday. You know, because I was one of the managers last year, but no. Nope. I'm not on the squad anymore." She crossed her arms, or tried. The bag got in her way.

I eyed her bag. "You have a slight hoarding problem."

She looked down. "Huh?"

The bag was bulging. She'd brought more stuff to her locker the first day than Zellman could stuff into his locker.

"I'm just saying. It's starting early," I told her.

"What's starting early?"

"You need a hoarder's prevention treatment plan." I winced, hearing myself. I'd started it as a joke, but now I'd channeled The Badger. Lame.

"Oh." Taz laughed, waving me off. "I get that from our mom. Cross gets the other gene from our dad. He hates having anything extra. If he could do without his bed and desk in his room, he would." She raised her hands, trying to reach around her bag again. She failed. Again. Finally she leaned back, her hands propping her up from behind her. "But back to the cheerleading squad. They'd like me to join. Sunday wants to be the bully, but not do any of the actual work. I'm not going to take her crap this year. Some of the girls want me to join to help contain her, but they're on their own. They gotta stand on their own two feet. They can do it. They'll have a good base."

I eyed her with a sideways glance. And she said Cross and I had our own language.

"Yeah." She gave a quick shake of her head. "No way, but um...okay. So, speaking of Sunday..."

She looked like she was preparing for a formal interview. "Sunday is going to approach you today to apologize, and Monica is going to ask if there's anything going on with you and Cross." She grimaced, waiting for my reaction. "Can you not..." Her face pinked and her lips mashed together. "...beat them up when they do?"

I grinned. "So much for not taking her crap."

Her face went from pink to red. "This is different. That's different. I'm trying to prevent a full-out war. There'll only be one victim in all of that. Me." She pointed to herself, shaking her head. "You'll be protected by your guys, and Sunday will hide behind the squad. Me. I'm in the middle. So, for me... Don't?"

When she put it like that, I felt bad about the orange juice. "You don't want me to beat them up?"

"No!" She twirled her hands in the air. "Or pour things on them? Sunday doesn't know the tire thing was you, but if you do it again, she'll figure it out. She thought some criminals from Frisco must've been at Manny's."

And the irony of all was that she's from Roussou, thinking that.

Taz sat back up, picking at the end of her shirt. "They're trying to be real with you. Because that's how you like it. Real. No fake shit. They're scared, but they're going to try it your way."

It should have bothered me to hear people were scared to talk to me.

It didn't. I felt satisfaction. It was a perfected coping mechanism—scare 'em right away and not have to deal with them later. I felt myself smiling. Maybe Z was right. I *was* brilliant.

I started laughing.

Taz had been talking. "What? What's funny?"

"Nothing. I was laughing at myself. And I'll be nice, as long as they're nice." And as long as Taz didn't get hurt in the middle.

"They will be." She bobbed her head up and down. "I promise." Her shoulders relaxed. "I was so nervous to ask you about that, but I think Sunday forgot how fierce you can be. Dumping the orange juice on her, then starting a whole crew brawl in front of her—that helped her remember. I think she got lax this summer, because she didn't see you. She forgot she's not number one on the female alpha list, if you know what I mean. I mean, she is on the cheerleading squad, but outside of the crew system, there are other girls more popular than her—like Tabatha Sweets. But Sunday's domain is the squad. Tabatha's is the whole school, not the crew part of the school."

The door opened behind us halfway through Taz's statement, and someone had stopped there. I waited for them to pass us by. When they didn't, I looked back.

It was Sunday, with Monica coming through the door behind her.

Taz turned too, jumping to her feet. "Sunday! I—"

"You can't cover what you just said. I heard you." Hurt flared in her eyes, and she looked at me. "I was coming to apologize to you. I had no clue you heard me, but it doesn't matter. Spreading rumors about you and being catty wouldn't have been right. I'm sorry I was even thinking about it."

I nodded. As problems went, she was the least of mine.

But she wasn't done.

She turned to Taz again. "I—what you said really hurt, Taz."

"Is it a lie?" I asked.

All three of their heads swiveled to look at me.

"Is it a lie? Or is it true?"

Taz looked down.

Monica's eyes widened, and her lips pressed together.

Sunday was fixed on me, her face resembling an owl. Big wide eyes. Small mouth, lips pressed together almost in a snarl.

That gave me the answer. "It hurts because it's true." I nodded toward Taz. "You can't get mad at her for being honest. You do shitty things to people. It's a fact. You're not doing shitty things to me because I scare you. That's the truth, right?"

No answer. Her neck was reddening, and the color was moving up. The girl was pissed, but she looked down, and a soft "Yes" came out.

"It *should* hurt, but be mad at yourself, not her."

"Sunday, I—" Taz began.

"Don't apologize." I was trying to be gentle here, but if Taz wanted to stop taking her shit, this was a time to stand up and base her feet. Or whatever she'd said. "You were being honest."

Steam could've been coming out of Sunday's ears.

Taz's eyebrows lifted. "But I wasn't sensitive. You can be honest, but you have to be sensitive." She said the last bit to her friend/enemy. "I'll be more sensitive. I'm sorry, Sunday."

For fuck's sake.

This was why I didn't have female friends, except for Taz. Either I didn't know how to be sensitive or I didn't speak that language. If that's how female friends had to be with each other, I didn't know if I'd ever have one.

I knew Taz would say she was being nice, but she looked like she was kissing Sunday's feet. And as the red coloring left her face and a smirk flared, I knew Sunday thought the same. In her head, in her group, she had won just now.

The door opened again, and Jordan, Zellman, and Cross came out.

I almost sagged in relief. The school gods must've heard me.

"And that's my cue to go," I announced.

The guys saw me as they went out to the parking lot, and they lingered a few feet away, waiting.

I started for them, then remembered what Taz had said, and I wheeled back around to Monica. "Taz said you wanted to ask about me and Cross."

I could feel him watching me.

"He's my best friend," I told her. "That's all that's going on, so it's up to you whether you're secure enough to handle that. That's your problem. Don't make it mine."

Taz let out a short laugh as I caught up to Cross and the guys.

Zellman glanced back at the girls as we headed to Cross' truck. "What's going on there?"

"They're clearing the air."

"You okay with them now?" Jordan asked, his finger waving from me to them. "Can we get with them again?"

I nodded. "For now, I guess."

Zellman's eyes got big, but he didn't say anything. He stuffed his hands in his pockets, hunching his shoulders forward. "So what's the plan for hanging out?" Zellman's cheeks bulged out. He was refraining himself. "Jordan's or somewhere else?"

Jordan's lips twitched, so did Cross's. We could all see the struggle. Z just got the green light to get some Boobs, but it was crew time right now apparently.

"I'm down for whatever," I said. "I just have to have dinner with my brother at seven, wherever he's at."

"Dinner with your brother?" Cross asked. "That's the debt Alex can't pay off?"

"Yep. Which sucks."

"We could dress him up to look like a girl," Zellman offered.

Alex was probably a hundred and fifty pounds heavier than me. "You're right. Channing would be fooled. Let's do it."

Zellman frowned. "I wasn't joking. You guys always laugh at my suggestions."

"The dinner just you and your brother?" Cross asked, eyeing Zellman.

So was I, but I replied, "You want to come? He said I could bring anyone with me."

"Fuck." Jordan's eyes flashed with anticipation. "Dinner with Channing Monroe. I know he's your brother, but man. That'd be awesome. I'm in."

"Great game plan." I pointed at them. "You guys talk so much, I won't have to. Best family dinner ever."

Cross grinned. "It is just for one night?"

"It's up for debate." It wasn't. But I needed a plan to get out of the others.

"What are we doing today?" Jordan asked.

Zellman shot his hand into the air. "I'm right here, and you're ignoring me."

I knew what he'd love. "How about cliff diving, Z? You up for it?"

He wavered. I saw the fight on his face, until he melted. "It's like you get me, Bren." He pressed a fist over his chest. "Right here."

That's what crew did.

CHAPTER NINETEEN

"BREN!"

Taz yelled my name after third period that Friday, hurrying through the crowd. I'd just left the bathroom, but I needed to stop at my locker before the next class.

"What's up?" I asked once she got to my side. She looked well rested, so I added, "I take it you didn't partake in the partying last night?"

She laughed, shaking her head.

After the early hiccup, the week had passed without any big events. I'd been a good sister. I'd had dinner with Channing every night. I took all the guys to that first dinner on Tuesday, but Channing had stopped it after that. He hadn't enjoyed the twenty-thousand questions Jordan and Zellman had asked him about the crew system and how he'd started it. So the last two dinners had been me, him, and a whole lot of awkward silence.

I think he was reconsidering letting me bring the guys again, but we were done with dinners until Sunday night. He'd amended our agreement, saying he understood if I had social or crew events happening this weekend. That was really code for him having things going on, but I wasn't going to look a gift horse in the mouth. I'd agreed wholeheartedly.

But because we'd still had our dinner last night, I'd heard about the huge party at Manny's. Channing had gotten the repairs done, and Heather had agreed to allow Roussou people back in. Yesterday was their first day back, and somehow it had become the first official party of the year. It moved to a field after Heather eventually kicked everyone out, and it lasted late.

I knew that much because Cross had crawled into my bedroom at five in the morning. I offered him the bed, but he only took a blanket and curled into a fetal position on the floor. He never woke when I got up for school, and I hadn't the heart to bother him. He was still sleeping when I left.

Half the crew people either hadn't come to school today or were hungover. Half couldn't see where they were walking. The bags under their eyes were like dumbbells, and a couple guys got jostled, then just went at it in the hallway. If Mr. N. was smart, he'd let 'em all sleep during detention.

Taz, on the other hand, had an extra bounce in her step.

She shook her head. "No." She moved her books to her other side, combing through her hair with her free hand. "Half the girls were there."

"Speaking of the girls—" I started toward my locker, but two got in the way. I braked, an irritated sound slipping out.

They looked up, a smart-ass retort ready, but it died when they saw me. One squeaked and the other put her head down and put on a burst of speed, darting out of my way.

Taz grinned, leaning against her locker as I opened mine. "That never gets old." She adjusted her books in her arms. "And okay. I have to ask you for a favor."

I grabbed my notepad and book, then shut the locker. "I don't do favors."

Her eyes cast to the ceiling. "I know that's not completely true. You'd step in front of a bullet for my brother, so this isn't that big a favor."

"He's crew." Those weren't favors.

I waited for a reaction from her. Sometimes she'd get all pissed at the reminder that Cross was crew or Cross was more special than her. I never knew for certain when it might happen, but she usually got all pissy right about now. If she'd join the crew, she'd have equal footing to him. Well. Not really. Cross was more important than everyone, but Taz would've moved up above Jordan and Zellman. Easily.

Her anger never came.

And *that* told me I was going to hate whatever this favor was.

"You know on Monday when I told you I hadn't joined the cheerleading squad..." She leaned forward, her eyes widening.

I didn't say anything. I waited.

"Okay." She blinked a few times, shaking her head. "Dramatic pause aside, instead of joining them, I actually got *them* to join a committee with me. It's the new thing we're doing with Ms. Bagirianni. She's our supervisor."

Nope.

No way.

I knew what she was going to ask. I heard the excitement in her voice, and it wasn't going to sway me.

"I'm not going to be a part of anything The Badger's doing."

"What? Why?"

"It's The Badger. The fact that you're willing to spend time with her alarms me. Greatly."

"Oh, come on. She's not that bad."

I lifted an eyebrow. "You've never been analyzed by her, that you know of."

She opened her mouth, then stopped. "Are you serious? You won't help me because the school counselor is involved?"

I snorted. "Do you not know me? Like, at all? Do you not know your brother?" He and the rest of our crew shared the same sentiment about The Badger.

She looked so frustrated, a pout forming on her face.

I patted her on the arm. "The answer to that is like you asking me if I'm crew. A big fat *duh, yes*. It's like cosmic karma. It's a rule in the universe. If The Badger is involved, I am not. Plain and simple, unless it's mandatory or court-ordered."

"That's—" Her mouth fell open again. "That's insane! I need your help. Really."

"Let me put it another way. The Badger is the police. I'm a criminal. The two don't mix. Ever."

I started for class, but Taz fell in step next to me. She adjusted her books again, then once more. I was tempted to grab them and hold them for her. She was making me antsy with all the adjusting going on.

"I really need your help," she said again. "We're doing a charity event, and we need to go around town to get sponsors. Half the businesses here are connected to crews. They won't sponsor us unless a crew person asks them."

I snorted. "As it should be."

I veered toward my classroom, but Taz picked up her pace. She got in front of me, holding her books up like a shield. "Stop. Please. Talk to me for a second."

People were filling in behind her, casting us curious looks.

Jordan was heading our way too, towering over everyone, and his gaze locked on mine. His eyebrows moved together, and he began to slow down.

"You're crew royalty," Taz pleaded. "And this event is a big deal to me. This charity is a big deal to me. If you come on board, Sunday and Monica—they'll shut up. I can feel how they think I'm a joke and I can't get it done. I'll get it done with your help." She softened her tone. "Please, Bren. You'd be helping me so much with this one thing."

This one thing wasn't going to be just one thing. I could feel it. It meant a meeting, which meant more meetings, and then more meetings. One afternoon would be dragged out to thirty, and she wasn't listening when I said it was like someone asking a criminal to socialize with a cop.

Shit would go down, and not for the good.

"I'm actually doing you a favor by saying no."

Jordan had stopped behind Taz. All three of us were now in the way in the middle of the hall, but no one said a word. There was enough room to go around, but not comfortably. A few people squeaked through on the other side of Jordan. Most went around on the far side, and a few cast us dirty looks. When they saw me watching them, they changed their tune. We weren't being fully considerate here, but this was a standoff.

"You'll do anything for my brother. Help me with this. Please."

I glanced up to Jordan, and he laughed silently, his shoulders going up and down.

"What do you think?" I asked him.

Taz whirled around, saw him laughing, and smacked his arm. "If I wanted your help, Pitts, I would've asked. You have no input here."

He rolled his eyes and smacked her hand away gently. "Bren will do whatever she wants. She asked me as a distraction."

He pointed to me, and to prove his point, I stepped backward into the classroom. I flashed Taz an apologetic smile. "I really am doing you a favor. You'll thank me later."

Her cheeks flushed, but she didn't say anything. It looked like she wanted to, but Jordan moved around her. As the bell rang, he turned around and slowly closed the door in her face. He shook his finger, still watching her through the window like he was tsking her.

She made a motion, and he began laughing again.

Dropping into the seat next to me, he pointed toward the door. "What was that about?"

I dropped my books on the table and leaned back. "She wants me to scare the other girls away."

His grin widened. "Why'd you say no to that?"

I smiled back, but the teacher had walked into the classroom, so we stopped talking.

The two football players in front of us turned around to talk to Jordan before class officially started, and two girls on his left began flirting with him.

I zoned out until I felt a soft punch on my arm.

"What?" I rubbed where he had hit.

Jordan was looking at me, and so were the football players. The two girls were pouting, but Jordan had his back to them, so they were effectively cut out of the conversation.

He rolled his eyes at me. "I didn't hurt you, but where were you last night?" He pointed a pen at me, then stuck it in his mouth and began chewing on it.

I frowned at him. This wasn't normal Jordan, but the two football players were listening. He was asking for their benefit.

He knew I'd had dinner with my brother, then stayed home, but I only said, "I did my own thing last night."

He gave me the slightest of winks.

That told me all I needed to know. One of the guys had asked him to ask me. He'd decided to play along instead of telling them it was none of their business.

"You missed an epic party." One of the guys leaned forward, his hand resting on the table just a few feet from my books.

I looked at it, then to Jordan, and he shrugged again.

"I'll catch the next one."

"Yeah. You better." His friend decided to join in. He was nodding and smiling. "It was awesome. Best party of the year." He and his buddy grinned at each other. "For now."

"Yeah," one of the guys grunted.

I shot Jordan a look.

He had covered his mouth. He kept silently laughing as the teacher stood to start the lesson. The two guys turned around, but I punched Jordan in the arm.

A girl gasped.

I knew people were watching.

Jordan still had his head down, and I leaned close to him. "Thanks for that."

He sat up, wiping a hand over his mouth. His laughter had subsided, slightly.

"Come on. They like you. It's cute."

Cute. I winced.

I did angry. I did hostile, violent. I did fucked-up.

I didn't do cute.

CHAPTER TWENTY

I WAS SITTING at a table in the library for study hall when Cross walked in. He pulled his hood down over his face.

Oh yeah. He was still hung over.

"Mr. Shaw." Mr. Penski's voice boomed across the library. "What are you doing in here?"

Cross slowed, raising his head so Penski could see his face better. A slight cocky swagger came out, and he held up a piece of paper. "I'm transferring seventh period, Mr. Penski."

"Uh-huh." A scoff of disbelief. Mr. Penski took the piece of paper. His frown moved from Cross to me. "If there's trouble..."

He let the threat go unsaid, but Cross nodded and headed my way.

He sat across from me, glancing over his shoulder.

Mr. Penski and the librarian were both watching.

I understood why.

If something happened to one of us, the other would jump in to help. It could get messy, and it had at times. The recent brawl at Manny's was evidence of that, but this was study hall. And we were in the library. Chances of anything happening were slim to none.

"You switched?" I asked. He'd come to school fifth period, showing up during lunch.

"Ryerson's been cocking off in Latin this week. Getting worse than it was before. Figured it was better if I wasn't in there."

"Really?"

He surveyed the room and saw the Ryerson cousin. His top lip curved. "I didn't know this one was in here."

Race had been watching us, but hearing Cross, he picked up his stuff and came over to our table. He sat next to me, facing Cross.

"You talking about me?"

Cross shot back, "Yeah." His hazel eyes darkened; they almost looked brown.

The chances of something happening were going up, and judging by the others watching, they knew it too. I caught the same looks I saw every time a crew scuffle broke out. People should start carrying popcorn with them.

"Say it to my face then."

I had to give props to Race. He wasn't flinching.

Cross seemed pissed, and this side of him was scary, dangerously scary.

"Your cousin is getting a big fucking mouth, and I'm not enjoying it." Cross leaned back, raising his chin. "We going to have the same problem with you?"

Race's lips pressed together. "When are you going to get it?" He glanced at me. "Anyway I thought he was being fine. He's been good all week."

Cross narrowed his eyes.

"Cross," I started, dropping my voice. Too many people were trying to eavesdrop. "I—"

"We can talk later," he said to Race. "Your cousin was going on about how his crew is the biggest and baddest. You seem to have put yourself in the middle for whatever reason, but if Alex keeps saying the shit he's saying, there's going to be a crew war. You ready for that?"

Race's mouth opened an inch. He was surprised, but I wasn't. Sadly.

This was Alex being Alex.

Yes, he'd apologized after the one fight, but his head had been swelling steadily since then. I wasn't surprised to hear any of this.

Normal Alex was cocky all the time.

He liked to start fights.

He seemed to have developed amnesia after his apology. He'd stayed away from me, but the guy who'd seemed like a leader was nowhere to be found now.

"Is there a problem here?"

Mr. Penski had materialized at our table.

Cross leaned back. He kicked his feet out and shook his head. "Nah. We're fine." He and Race shared a look. "Just getting on the same page, that's all."

Mr. Penski swung his gaze to Alex's cousin.

"Yeah." He gestured to Cross. "What he said. Same page. We're besties now."

"Mmmm-hmmm. I'm sure you are." Our teacher held his pen in the air. "I won't tolerate any crew business—not this year, not anymore. This is a zero-violence area." He ambled back to the librarian's desk, his hands out like he was talking to himself.

Cross shook his head. "They talk like we ran the school before. It was never like that."

"The cameras are new," I pointed out.

He glanced over. "Still, though. We could never fight in a class. Why are they so anti-crew this year? It's like it's their new theme."

"Maybe it is," Race said.

We turned to him.

He held his hands up like he was surrendering. "My stupid cousin aside, maybe Principal Neeon went to a summer seminar? Bullying is a big deal now. He could've gotten that twisted so he thinks crews are the bullies. Or they're treating you like you're gangs."

Cross snorted. "We're not gangs. There's no blood in and blood out bullshit. The most illegal crap we do is drinking. We protect our own above anything else—that's the only similarity. That's what a crew does." His gaze went to a table where a few jocks were sitting. I recognized one as the football player who'd been talking to Jordan in class before. "If anyone's going to bully, it's them."

"You're stereotyping." Race grinned.

Cross shrugged. "I stand by what I said. We're not the bullies."
He nodded to me. "Can you imagine the target that'd be on our
backs if we were?" Then his smile fell away. "But Alex is starting
to shoot his mouth off. He could be a problem for all crews if he
doesn't rein it in."

"You don't think he can handle being their leader?" I looked
at Race, but spoke to Cross, "You think maybe he could talk to
Drake?"

"About what?" Race asked. "I'm not crew. He won't talk to me
about that, not unless I join theirs."

Cross narrowed his eyes, tilting his head toward me. "Jordan
will push you on this. Do *you* want to talk to Drake? The guy's
right." He nodded at Race. "Drake won't talk to him unless he's in
the crew."

I wanted to growl. Cross had gentled his tone because he
knew this was the only course of action. If Alex kept popping off, I
might have to reach out.

I didn't want that. I didn't want to deal with Drake again.

But I nodded. "If I have to, I will."

Race nudged my arm with the back of his hand. "I could go
with you."

I didn't respond, but shared a look with Cross. He knew I
wouldn't want him there. If I wanted anyone with me, it'd be Cross.
But it was a moot point. Drake wouldn't talk if Race was there. If
anyone should go, it should be my brother. Channing could scare
Drake into talking, but that meant I'd have to spend more time
than I already was with the new brother-extraordinaire persona.

Thumbs down to that.

I lifted a shoulder in response to Race's suggestion.

After that we got down to business—we actually studied.
For all the trouble we caused, we weren't bad students. Usually.
Or Cross wasn't. And judging by Race's notes, he seemed like a
good student too. And it wasn't that I was a bad student, just not
super motivated. Twenty minutes in, they were both reading, and
I was watching the other students—the good ones according to the
school's staff and administration. I wasn't a part of the normal

universe, but from where I sat, I had a feeling they were just like us. Maybe worse in some ways too.

Cross was right. My gaze switched to the jock table. I remembered walking to a basketball game and seeing some of those guys stuff two freshman into lockers.

If my crew had done that, there would've been a reason. And it wouldn't have been *those* two guys that got stuffed. They'd been the nerd types. I had a hard time imagining either of them doing anything that would cause us to go after them.

"You okay?" Cross had been watching me.

Race lifted his head too.

At Cross' question, Sunday and Monica looked over. I saw the envy flash in their eyes and sighed.

No. I'd never trade places.

If that's what it meant to be normal or a good student, I didn't want it. They didn't have the loyalty I got every day.

When Cross asked if I was okay, he meant it. He wasn't asking so he could mock me later—something I'd heard Sunday do plenty of times.

I nodded to Cross. "We should hang out with your sister more often."

His head moved back an inch. "Where'd that come from?"

Race looked over to where my attention had been focused.

"She asked for my help," I told him. "I think I might actually do it."

I watched Sunday and Monica again. They bent their heads together, whispering.

Cross narrowed his eyes. "Are you serious? The Badger thing?"

"Yeah."

Fuck. I'd end up in jail. Somehow.

123

CHAPTER TWENTY-ONE

"MY DAD CAN be one of the sponsors," Race offered.

I was headed to the parking lot after study hall, and he had fallen in step with me.

"What are you talking about?" I asked.

"My dad's kinda wealthy. He owns a Harley-Davidson store, and it does well. It does really well."

"How do you even know about the sponsorship stuff, though?"

He ducked his head, a little sheepishly. "One of the girls already asked me. I'm assuming Alex told someone about my dad. He and my mom are divorcing. That's why we're here, and there's an underground fighting ring here. I wanted to get involved with that."

His dad was rich. That meant he was rich, and he was going to fight like my brother?

I shouldn't like this guy, but for some ungodly reason, he was starting to grow on me. Like an annoying itch.

I stopped in the middle of the parking lot. "Are you offering your help because you want to get to my brother?"

"Wha-what?"

"Channing Monroe. He's a big fighter—"

"No, I know." He shook his head, rubbing a hand over his jaw. "No. No, not at all. I just—I don't know. I wanted to help. Besides, when Cross' twin sister asks a crew girl for help with her charity event, word spreads fast." His eyes slid to the right as we passed some of Sunday's friends. "They sit behind me in chemistry, and trust me, they're not quiet. Just tell me the amount you need, and I'll email him." He added, "He'll do anything I want. He thinks I can talk my mom into going back to him."

"Yo!"

Jordan was moving fast behind us. He swooped in, and before Race could look behind him, Jordan's arm was around his shoulders, pulling him forward. He forced Race to move with him.

Zellman and Cross trailed behind him, and both sliding me looks as they passed.

Jordan had a bug up his ass. I didn't know what was going on, but I sighed and fell in line.

Jordan half-walked, half-dragged Race to the opposite end of the lot. Once we were tucked on the other side of his truck, he let him go.

Race shoved him away, scooting backward. Alarm filtered over his face, his eyebrows pinching together. "What's going on?"

Jordan bent down a little, so he was almost looking Race in the eye. He wagged his finger between Race and me, making a tsking sound. "Is this a thing? The two of you?"

I flung my arms in the air. "Again?!"

"Yes, again." Jordan's smile had an edge to it. His arm went around Race's neck before he could move out of the way. Race struggled, so Jordan tightened his arm. If he'd bent over again, it would've been a chokehold. "I called him out on Tuesday, and he didn't deny it. You did, Bren, but not him. He never denied a thing, and now he's sniffing around your pants again." He turned to Race, jostling him a little. "I'd really like to know why." He cast a look at Cross, adding, "I don't think I'm the only one."

Cross met my gaze, but his eyes were shielded. He wasn't letting me in.

I gritted my teeth.

I wasn't some helpless, hapless little girl. I didn't need this big-brother act Jordan was doing. He could watch Race. He could be suspicious of him, and hell, he could even give him crap. One time. Not a second time. And not when we were almost in front of an audience. We were hidden by his big truck, but people always watched us. People would've noticed Jordan's fast walk over here, how he'd had his arm around Race.

I was betting we had five minutes before Alex showed up.

Cross stepped up next to me, his arm brushing against mine. He lowered his head, but his eyes were locked on Race. "Jordan, you know why Race is in town? Why he's here in the first place?"

Fuck.

I recognized that tone. It was low and chilling. It was the same he'd been using in the library, and I realized now he'd just checked his attitude. He'd been waiting for this. And that fucker, he must've planned this during that time.

Jordan frowned, becoming still. "No. Why?"

I waited, wondering how he knew about the divorce.

Race started to smirk.

Jordan saw his reaction and looked back at Cross. His eyes narrowed, and he tilted his head.

Cross gestured to Race. "He's here for the underground fighting ring."

Jordan went a whole new level of still.

People from all over came to Roussou to fight, and to watch, and those who were serious about the ring were good fighters. Crew members could fight. We'd had our fair share of tussles, and we could handle ourselves, but underground ring fighting was a whole different situation.

Those guys were out for blood.

If someone fought there and stuck around, they could do serious damage outside of the ring as well. There were no official rules. They *could* fight outside the ring, and Jordan finally started to put two and two together.

He let go of Race and drew away from him. "You're a fighter?"

There was dark amusement in Race's eyes, and he nodded before skimming a look over Cross and me. His top lip curved, just a bit. "I am."

"You good?"

There was some hesitation, but then Race nodded. "I am."

It was almost karmic for Jordan to be nervous now, but a part of me felt for him. Jordan was pushing Race's buttons because he was the new guy, but also because of me. Mostly, however, I think Jordan was doing it because he could.

I started to feel better about this confrontation until Cross stepped forward.

Both his hands were in his sweatshirt pockets, and his shoulders were stiff and taut. Race could fight. I'd seen enough to know it was true, but the one guy who could go toe to toe with him was Cross.

Race's quiet confidence was nothing compared to the air that radiated off Cross.

He was dangerous.

And when Race's chest rose and stayed, I knew he was feeling it too.

Cross was also still furious, but I hadn't figured out the reason—that is until he started speaking.

It was quiet, and the hairs on the back of my neck stood up.

Whether Race realized it or not, he was treading dangerous ground with Cross.

The rest of us stood back and let him talk. We'd learned to shut up when Cross had something to say, when he was in *this* mood. He didn't strike, unless there was a reason. And there was always a good reason when he did.

"I'm saying that because I see you." He took another step forward. As he did, Jordan backed out, so it was now Race facing us with only Cross in front of him. It was almost a conversation between the two of them, but knowing Cross, he did this to send another message. He didn't need us to back him up. He didn't need us to help him. He could stand on his own just fine and Race swallowed, seeming to get it.

His throat moving up and down. "I get it."

"No." Cross shook his head briskly. "You don't get it. You're around us, a lot. You're around Bren, a lot. You're putting your nose in our business. You're standing up to your cousin for us? We didn't ask you for that. It's to the point now where we have to acknowledge you and the 'help' you're giving us, but that's not how we work. You want to be crew, you straight up say it. We decide then. Not you. You don't worm your way in with us. You don't get to try to weasel your way in." He straightened up, but his hands

CREW

remained in his sweatshirt pockets. With his hood still on, he was the image of a bad boy facing off against a threat.

Shivers snaked their way down my spine, turning into a throb in my stomach. That throb was moving lower, and I flattened my hand against my stomach. I hadn't felt this before, with anyone.

I moved to the side so I could see Cross' face. I almost couldn't look away. He was entrancing, the way his chin jutted up defiantly and his nostrils flared, how he looked down his nose at Race.

He was pushing back a foe, one maybe we hadn't seen before. Cross was right. Race had been slinking his way in, and as if feeling my thoughts, he looked my way.

He shook his head. "I didn't—I offered to help because I want to help. There's no agenda. I mean it."

"Bullshit."

Race focused on Cross again. "I mean it. I don't want anything from you guys. My parents are divorcing. That's the real reason we're here. The fighting ring is a bonus. It's a way to piss off my dad, to be completely honest. But I do like fighting, and yeah, I mean..." His eyes cast down. He rolled his shoulders back. "God. I don't know. Maybe I did have an agenda. Drake told me to stick close to you guys if I wanted protection. I don't want to join my cousin's crew. They're not the good ones. I've heard them. I've been around them. They're turning into the bad crew." He stopped again, licking his lips, his throat moving up and down. "Shit. You're right. I was trying to weasel my way in." A fleeting panic pulled at his face. "I'm sorry. I am. I know that's how you guys are. I didn't—I wasn't thinking it through. Drake said you guys were the ones to be friends with."

Cross snorted. "Drake was fucking with you." His eyes slid my way again. "He knows we don't bring in strays. He wanted to mess with us."

Us.

I swallowed over a knot.

Me.

My ex wanted to mess with me, and I remembered all his sniping comments about Cross.

128

He wanted to mess with me and Cross.

I swore. "I'm going to rip his balls off."

Jordan and Zellman laughed.

A faint grin showed at the corner of Cross' mouth. Some of the air lightened too, but he didn't say anything.

"I..." Race looked between us, eyes lingering on me and Cross. He moved back a step, his head lowered, almost in submission. "I wondered, but I didn't..."

Cross snapped his gaze back to him, sharpening once more.

"Wondered?" he bit out.

That was enough. I stepped forward, my hand touching Cross' arm lightly. We didn't need to have untruths dredged up, not yet, not when I wasn't ready to think about that either.

I cleared my throat. "If you're serious about the charity thing—"

"I am." His head lifted. "I really am. Tell me the amount, and I'll call my dad."

"That's for Taz, right?" Jordan spoke up.

"Yeah."

"Then come on, moneybags." He stepped forward, his arm coming around Race's shoulder again, but this time it was casual, like they truly were friends. He patted Race on the arm. "Let's you and me go and find the female Shaw. I'll help out with this charity thing."

He wasn't giving Race an option. He started walking him right back out, just a little more respectfully than the way he'd dragged him back here, and he winked at me as they went by.

Zellman watched them go, his hand twisting some of his curls before he turned to us. "Jordan's got a thing for your sis. I'm announcing it now before it becomes a problem." He held his hands up. "And don't go all dark Cross on me now. I won't take it like that guy. I'll just pop you in the face."

And he would. He'd get beaten up by Cross in the end, but to him it would be worth it.

I grinned, but I was relieved when that lightened the mood even more. Cross started asking questions, but Zellman wasn't answering.

He kept shaking his head, saying, "You have to ask Jordan," until Jordan himself came back. Alone.

Jordan gestured over his shoulder. "I left the new guy with Taz. She was cornered by the cheerleaders." He nodded at Zellman. "Sunday wants to know if you want to hook up tonight."

Zellman grunted. "Am I in a crew?" He stopped, squinting at me. "Are you still fighting with her? I thought that ended after the tire thing."

"What?"

"Never mind." He gave Jordan a thumbs-up. "I'm up, on, and in for whatever's going down tonight that has to with Sunday and being all sexual." He was starting to bounce up and down.

I grimaced at that thought, but remembered the other conversation from study hall. Sharing a look with Cross, I said, "Uh, guys?" I bobbed my head at Cross. "You want to loop them in on what else is going on with Ryerson? The bad one."

Jordan and Zellman snapped to attention.

This was crew business, and after Cross relayed Alex's latest antics, Jordan cursed.

"You serious? He's fucking proclaiming they're the biggest and baddest?"

Cross nodded, and then we all grew silent.

We weren't saying a word, but I knew what was going on.

We were the Wolf Crew. We were four, and we were fierce. We didn't need the numbers other crews took on, but what helped us all gel sometimes didn't make up for the fact that there were only four of us. If it came down to a war, we'd strap on and step up to the line, and we'd be smart about it. But prevention was always the first step.

Which meant someone had to talk to Alex. He was a hothead, and the best person to talk to him was Drake, which meant I was right back where I'd been earlier.

Me talking to him.

"Fuck."

Jordan sighed. "You know it's the best option."

But still.

I shook my head, shoving my hands into my pockets. "This fucking sucks."

Cross stepped close, his shoulder grazing mine. "I'll go with you."

"Ah." Jordan clipped his head from right to left. "No. Hell no. Not to be a prick here, but that would not be good. We all know how much Drake Ryerson hates you, so I agree with Bren."

"You do?" *I don't have to go?*

"You should take your brother."

Oh. Double fuck.

"And we should go now, before anything gets worse."

Look at Jordan, being our leader.

I grimaced, but gave in. "Fine."

Jordan and Zellman went to Jordan's truck, and Cross and I went to my Jeep.

CHAPTER TWENTY-TWO

TUESDAY TITS WAS pretty much the exact opposite of Manny's. The name itself should've given that away. As we drove up to my brother's bar, a line of motorcycles were parked outside the front door. We pulled into the back alley and found a whole second line of motorcycles parked there too.

Tuesday Tits catered to a rough crowd—not just my brother's crew, though they fit in, but a biker gang that frequented Roussou. As we stepped inside, a bunch of guys wearing leather cuts were drinking and playing pool. A few lounged at tables, talking.

The conversations lulled and all eyes came to us.

They seemed to sense fresh meat.

"How's it going, Bren?" the bartender asked.

It was just a formality. He didn't want to know.

The bartender was one of Channing's crew members. He wanted the regular customers to know we were hands-off.

I tipped my head up in greeting, pausing just inside the back door. "He around?"

He nodded toward the back hallway. "In his office."

Jordan and Zellman moved around me, heading to one of the empty pool tables. They knew the policy too. Unless they knew the bikers, they couldn't talk to them. Extra attention was not helpful, and Jordan's mouth—that would've drawn extra attention.

My brother's office door opened, and he stepped out. "I hear my sister's name?"

"Yeah." I headed for him with Cross behind me. "Hey."

He frowned at me, then at Jordan and Zellman. "I don't want you guys here."

"I know, but I'm here for a reason."

"Why?"

"I have to go see Drake, crew business."

"Crew business? From what I'm told, he's not crew anymore."

"Yeah. That's the problem."

Channing kept looking behind me to where Jordan and Zellman stood. I followed, seeing the reason for his concern. Some of the bikers had congregated nearby. Sometimes this wasn't a bad thing. Most bikers were fine, but these weren't. They were from a one-percenter MC. If they targeted Jordan and Zellman to hustle—or as hustlers—there'd be problems. The biker clubs were fiercer than us. There was no line they wouldn't cross. We co-existed. That was about it, and even that line was shaky.

But this was one of those areas Channing handled for Roussou while the rest were kept in the dark.

"Your ex goes to school six hours from here," Channing said. "I don't want you driving there."

"What?" I turned back to look at him. "Come on. Are you serious?"

"Chad had to take off. He's in the same town." Chad was another of Channing's crew members. "He can find him and have the talk you need to have."

"No."

"Yes."

Channing went back to watching the bikers. Two of the guys approached Jordan and Zellman. The bartender had paused, looking from them to Channing. He was waiting for a signal. Another door opened from the hallway, and Congo, another member of Channing's crew, came down.

He stopped right next to Channing.

Congo might've been short, but he was muscular, and he wasn't someone to mess with. He was like a bald mini bodybuilder.

"Yes, Bren," Channing repeated, cursing under his breath as he moved around me.

The bikers were now talking to Jordan, holding out a beer and gesturing to the pool table.

My brother started for them, then turned around and flung a hand toward me. "Get her out of here. Now." Then he was back to closing in fast on the pool table.

I looked over in time to see his crew member lock the register.

Congo started forward, a metal bar in his hand. Where he'd gotten that, I had no clue. He didn't have it when he walked down the hallway.

"Shit." Cross moved closer to me. "Maybe you should go?"

I threw him an incredulous look. This was my crew, and my brother. I wasn't moving.

I reached for my knife, tucked against my body under my shirt. I didn't pull it out. My hand was there, just in case.

"Hey, fellas." Channing walked up and threw an arm around Jordan's shoulders. He was an inch shorter than, but he yanked him down like he was going to put him in a headlock. He maneuvered him back behind the table, taking his pool stick at the same time. "If you'll excuse me," he said to the bikers. "I gotta kick these minors out of here." He shoved Jordan toward us. "You heard it, kid. Beat it."

Jordan took a couple steps, frowning at us and then my brother.

Zellman stayed right next to him.

"We were going to play a game of pool." One of the bikers picked up the pool cue Zellman had left behind. He had a scar that went down the entire side of his face. "They look like they have cash to burn. You don't mind, do you?"

Channing stood directly between us and them, but more of the bikers had started to take notice. A few moved closer. My brother held his hands up. His voice came out smooth and almost cheerful, but his jaw clenched.

"I got a fine recently for underage kids. Sorry, guys. You're going to have to play somewhere else."

The biker with the pool cue pointed it at Jordan. "How about it? You guys want to go somewhere else to play?"

Channing's shoulders tightened. "Somewhere in Frisco then."

Not Manny's.

Not in Roussou.

That was my brother's message.

I waited to see their reaction, but Chan didn't. He turned his back, and as soon as he did, his whole nonchalant façade dropped. His mouth set in a furious line.

Jordan took a step backward, seeing it.

Channing would beat his ass if he didn't leave.

Jordan cleared his throat. "Nah. Maybe next time. I think we got what we wanted." He looked at me. "Right? You're off the hook tonight?"

He widened his eyes dramatically.

I got his message too. "Oh yeah." I smiled at my brother. "I'll see you on Monday?"

I didn't wait for Channing's response. With Cross, Jordan, and Zellman behind me, I hurried out of there, veering right in the alley, past a couple more of Channing's crew members and my cousin, Scratch. I recognized Moose. He was bald like Congo, but tall, with tattoos all over his head and neck. I didn't recognize the other guy.

Scratch went right for me, not breaking stride. "Hey, little cousin!"

I had two seconds before he caught me in his arms and half-bounced me in the air.

Channing was a fighting machine, and he kept his body toned, but Scratch was almost as tough. He was the same age as Channing. They'd grown up together like brothers, except Scratch had been in the foster system. Well, to be more accurate, he'd spent his life everywhere, bouncing from his mom's house to ours, then to other people's. He and our half-brother had a similar upbringing, but Max was barely allowed to see us. His biological mom hated us, hated Roussou, hated our dad. It'd been a contentious life and because of it I barely knew Max. But for both he and our cousin, how they grew up had been for the best.

I knew Scratch said it helped mold him into who he was today.

"Hey, Scratch." I couldn't encourage him. If I did, he'd keep jostling me around. He liked to pick on me. I endured it as long as

I could so he'd feel loved, but usually it wasn't long before he got a good elbow to the stomach, neck, or junk. If he picked on me too much, the junk shot came quick and had some extra oomph to it.

He heard the warning in my voice and dropped me onto my feet almost right away. His hands went to my shoulders.

"What are you doing here? What are you up to?"

Moose and the other guy waited next to him.

"You getting in trouble already?" Moose asked.

Feeling Scratch's fingers tighten on my shoulder, I moved to dislodge his hold. He stepped back like it'd been his decision to release me.

He gave me a half-smirk. "Should we expect your brother to be in a mood?"

Moose laughed. The other one remained impassive.

Cross moved forward, falling in line next to me.

Moose greeted, "Cross."

"Moose."

My cousin and the silent guy nodded to him. Cross returned the greeting.

"He should be fine," I told Scratch. "It was crew stuff."

Moose and the other guy's gaze sharpened.

"Crew stuff?" Moose echoed.

"You're in trouble?" Scratch asked.

I shook my head. "No. Ask him. It's nothing big."

Moose and the other guy shared a look, then headed for the bar. My cousin stayed, frowning at me.

"What's going on?" His eyes narrowed.

"Talk to my brother."

"I *am* your brother."

Yeah. Yeah, he was. Sometimes I forgot he considered himself like a brother to me. He'd been around even less than Channing, but he was right. In some weird way, they'd both tried to look after me when they could, or when they remembered.

It got confusing to me sometimes.

I held up my keys. "It's crew stuff. Channing will tell you."

Scratch looked at Cross. "You're watching out for her?"

Cross rubbed a hand over his face. "I'm watching out for her as much as she'll let me. Let's put it that way."

"Are we going or what?" Jordan asked. Zellman waited with him.

Cross waved them on. "We'll be behind you. Go."

With a wave out the window, Jordan peeled out. Cross and I moved toward my Jeep.

Scratch had opened the door to the bar, but he turned again. "Be safe, little Monroe," he hollered. "Got that?"

I held up an arm in an absentminded wave, getting inside the car. "See you later, Scratch. Give my brother hell for me."

He grinned at us again. "I don't have to. You do that enough!"

I had the keys in the ignition when a familiar Taurus pulled up behind us.

CHAPTER TWENTY-THREE

"WHAT THE FUCK?" Cross leaned forward, peering ahead.

It was Taz. We watched as she got out, opened the back door, and pulled out a pink tote filled with papers and other items.

"What is she *doing*?" I groaned.

"Are those stuffed animals?"

Cross was asking me. I had no clue. I shrugged, and as if we had rehearsed our move, we both reached for our door handle at the same time. We got out on opposite sides of my Jeep just as she walked past. Seeing us, Taz jumped and shrieked, and half of the tote's contents fell to the ground.

"AGH!" She glared at us for a heartbeat before bending down to scoop up the things. "What are you doing here?! I almost had a heart attack. Announce yourself. Let me know when you're in..." Her hand thrust out, but then she looked, and her voice faded. "When you're in your Jeep."

A paper rolled past Cross, and he stepped on it to stop it. Before he grabbed it, he glared back at his sister. "Unlike you, we have reason to be here. What are *you* doing?"

She sent us a scathing look before she finished grabbing the rest of her stuff. There were books, two stuffed animals, lots of papers. I saw a yearbook and a pom-pom. She grabbed a fistful of the papers and gestured to Tuesday Tits' back door.

"I was going in there to get a sponsor—one that's never been gotten before."

Cross glowered, thrusting one of his hands toward the sign on the door. Tuesday Tits' Back Entrance. A black hole had been scribbled underneath, with arrows scratched in the wood, pointing to it.

"The name alone should tell you you're not allowed here!" He was half-shouting.

"This is for the thing you asked me to help with? That charity thing? Did Jordan not take Race Ryerson over to you? He should've given you enough money. That's what he said."

She paused. Her mouth fell open, then snapped shut. She raised a hand, smoothing down some of her hair. "Yes. I mean, yes he did, and that's more than enough money. Yeah." She left the tote on the ground and stood upright again, smoothing out her clothes. "Have you—I mean, I might've thought maybe I could get more, you know?"

I could only lift my eyebrows at that.

She was here, at my brother's bar—his very rough and very dangerous bar—to get more.

Cross groaned, his head falling back, and I could see him rolling his eyes. "Are you fucking kidding me?" He grasped his hair, holding on a second. "Oh my God, Taz. This is so fucking dangerous for you to come here—"

"And alone," I added.

His voice raised. "And alone! You CAME ALONE!"

I gestured to the back door. "Look, whatever you're doing, it'll have to be handled later. You can't go in there."

"What?" Her mouth fell open. "Why not?"

Because it was dangerous, like Cross had just yelled at her, but at the moment it *really* was. Channing would be yelling at me the same way if he came out and saw we were still here.

"We have to go, Taz. I mean it."

"But." She looked at all her stuff, at the animals (why the hell she had animals was beyond me), the yearbooks, and groaned. "I had a plan. It was a whole big thing. There was a presentation. I had props. I was going to play a song on the radio. I had it all worked out."

She sniffled, still gazing at her stuff.

Ah. Shiiit.

Cross and I looked at each other.

This wasn't really about getting a donation. I mean, it was, but there was more going on here. More with her, more with—I was guessing—Sunday Barnes and all the girls Taz was trying to impress. And if I dared wonder, maybe some of it was about us too.

I was going to regret this. I knew that, but I still heard myself saying, "Look, if you still need a donation from Tuesday Tits, I'll get it for you."

She looked up, her eyes wide and hopeful.

"But not now." I held my hand up. "And no one, I mean no one, can know I got it for you."

Cross glanced sideways at me.

I caught the small grin. He was wondering how their donation would even be approved. Those sponsored ads have huge posters printed out. Tuesday Tits? Not really a brand an educational place would embrace.

But that was a different problem for another day.

She looked ready to argue, so I added, "A rough crowd hangs out here."

"But... Okay. Fine." She bent back down to get everything scooped up and stood up with the tote in her arms. "I still would like help with sponsors. Race's dad is a big sponsor, but he admitted at the end that we might not be able to count on him."

What a shocker.

All this talk of sponsors and what that led to, for an event, with ads—it wasn't what I was used to.

She was talking like one of those girls, like a Sunday or a Monica, or... I had to admit, like a Taz. Because she was one of them, whether she was trying to forge her own path or not. She was normal. I was the outsider to that kind of life.

Jordan's truck roared up behind us, and Taz groaned. "Are you serious? Do they have to be here for this?"

I didn't trust Taz.

Even if I got her to leave now, if I didn't come through with the donation, I had a feeling she would come on her own—and that might be worse than things were in there now.

"Hold on." I pulled out my phone and leaned back in my seat, dialing the bar.

A moment later I heard, "Tuesday Tits! Tonight is $2 Friday Night Titquila Shots."

It was Moose this time. "Moose."

"Bren? You still here?" He didn't let me answer. "You want your big bro again?"

"No. Uh, can I talk to Scratch instead?"

"Hold on."

The line was quiet, then I heard a beep and my cousin's voice came over. "You forget something?"

"Hey." Taz was watching me intently, so I turned around. "Cross' sister showed up. She's asking for donations—"

"Sponsors," Taz corrected.

"Sponsors for some charity thing. I don't trust her to let me ask Channing later. I think she'll try again on her own."

"Hey!"

I ignored her. "I was wondering if you guys wanted to give some money, and if you do, can you come outside right now so we can get this done?"

"Oh." He paused a beat. "You know, we've never done that, except for a bike rally or something. Yeah, I'd be interested in that. It's for charity?"

"It's for charity, right?" I asked Taz.

She nodded. "The children's hospital."

Cross started laughing.

I frowned. "We have a children's hospital?" The hospital we did have was crap. Most didn't even consider Roussou to have a hospital. Sane people went to the one in Fallen Crest.

She hit her brother on the shoulder. "Yes. Well, it's two hours away and in a different town, but yes."

I spoke into the phone. "The children's hospital that's a couple hours away."

"Yeah, I heard you. I'm heading out right now." I heard a thud, then the line went flat.

"He's coming out."

Taz's eyes widened, and the excitement was building. She rolled back and forth on her heels.

It wasn't long until my cousin appeared. He'd been wearing a muscle shirt going in, but he'd put on a short-sleeved Tuesday Tits T-shirt. Both Channing and Scratch wore whatever they wanted to work. Sometimes they looked professional. Other times they looked like regular customers, and sometimes they looked like the type of customers who never went home. He'd combed his hair back too, but his eyes were twinkling at us, and I knew some of this was for Taz's benefit.

She was gawking, checking out Scratch's tattoos. He and my brother were both covered in them.

"Long time no see!" Scratch winked at me. He leaned in and whispered, "There's shit going down inside. You need to get out of here five minutes ago."

I nodded, murmuring back, "We will."

He looked at me for another moment, making sure I knew he was serious, then turned. He had Taz eating out of his hand within seconds. She was almost giggling and blushing. Cross looked ready to lose his lunch a couple times, and so did Jordan, who'd gotten out of his truck and come to stand next to me. His arms were folded over his chest, and they stayed like that until Scratch pulled out his checkbook.

Jordan grunted, touching my shoulder lightly. "We saw some different bikers headed here when we came back." And as if on command, a couple bikes roared past the alley, followed by a couple more. Then three more.

"I know."

My chest had tightened with the first warning. It was hard to breathe now.

Scratch straightened, check in hand. When a few of the bikers came to the alley, looking down at us, Scratch shoved it into my hand. "Time to go, Bren."

"Wait. What about a receipt?"

"Get her the fuck away from here," Scratch said under his breath.

Jordan moved ahead of Taz, saying, "We'll give it to him later."

"But, my car—"

"We'll come back for it later." His hands found her shoulders, and he began walking her backward, all the way to his truck.

The bikers watched us. They didn't approach.

Cross and I were almost to my Jeep, but I paused a few feet away. "You need backup?"

Scratch waved us on. "Just go. Your brother usually gets it handled. We'll be fine."

Cross glanced to me, but I did as my cousin instructed. We drove to the end of the block and circled around with Jordan's truck behind us. Zellman had jumped into the cab, and I could see Taz's hands in the air. The pink tote sat on her lap. A stuffed flamingo sat on top, and she had to keep moving to see around it.

Half the bikers were still outside. Another four joined them.

Cross said quietly, "That's an entire motorcycle club."

My mouth was dry. "I know."

"Scratch said they'd be okay?"

I didn't know what to say. So far my brother and cousin hadn't needed to wade in against an MC, but this group usually came to party or relax. They were on edge today.

I didn't have a good feeling.

I turned left on the road, away from them. And when we got to the main street through Roussou, I turned right.

We were going to Manny's.

CHAPTER TWENTY-FOUR

CROSS GOT ON THE phone, relaying the plan to Jordan and Zellman.

Though, to be honest, there wasn't much of a plan. I was just going to see Heather. If Channing was in trouble, besides myself and his crew, she was the only other person I knew to reach out to. I didn't know what she could do, but she might at least know what to do or not to do. I trusted her. If she said not to be worried, I wouldn't, but I had a bad enough feeling in my gut to go the extra mile and ask her opinion.

Heather's house was behind Manny's, so I parked in the back. Jordan pulled in behind me, and as everyone got out, I said to Cross, "Grab your sister and take her into Manny's. See if Heather is there."

"I need to get my car," I heard Taz saying. "What if those bikers trash it? Mom will be so mad, Cross."

I headed up to the front porch of Heather's house and knocked once on the screen. Sometimes Heather's brother was here, sometimes he wasn't. I didn't hear anyone inside, but the front door was open, and the screen door wasn't locked. I rattled on it again.

"Heather! Are you in there?"

A door slammed shut behind me, and I whirled.

It was Brandon, Heather's brother, holding a trash bag and standing at the back door of Manny's.

"She's in here," he yelled. "What's going on?" Brandon was older than Heather and Channing, but he still looked young. He was probably close to his thirties.

"I just gotta ask her something."

"Okay." He waved over his shoulder, dropping the trash at the same time. "You want me to send her out?" He frowned, staring at me a little harder. "Is this about crew stuff?"

Brandon wasn't crew. Neither was Heather, but they knew enough to be wary.

"Just something I have to ask her. That's all."

Brandon nodded. "Wait five minutes. Every ten minutes she gets all pissy and explodes." He lifted both his shoulders up in a helpless gesture. "All the sugar is making her extra cranky."

"I heard that!" came from inside.

He rolled his eyes and opened the door behind him again. "I know. I meant for you to hear that."

Heather came out as her brother went inside, her blonde hair pulled up into a messy bun, with the bottom half braided. Reaching for her pocket, she cursed and plopped down on one of the lounge chairs around a bonfire pit. She threw a leg up on the pit, exposing a good amount of her skin through the tears in her jeans as she lounged back.

Zellman groaned. "Goddamn."

"Really?" I stared at him. "She's practically my sister-in-law."

That was Heather. As long as I could remember, exuded this sexiness, whether she meant to or not. It was just her.

He just shook his head. "Goddamn."

"Bren." Heather patted her pockets again, then groaned herself. She motioned me over. "Your friend is accosting my brother right now. Should I know the reason?"

I went over, but didn't sit across from her. Heather still made me uncomfortable.

"Just wait. She's going to ask you too."

Heather grunted before tapping the armrest on her chair. "Okay. So. What's up? It's not normal for you to come look for me. Willingly."

Jordan and Zellman sat down. Both chuckled at what she said.

I shot them a look. They shut up.

Then I sat down. "An MC showed up at Tuesday Tits—like, the whole group. They didn't look like they were there just to party."

"Shit." She stood up, her hands patting her pockets again as she went inside. "I'll be right back."

Jordan was watching her go. "What's with the hand stuff?"

"She quit smoking. It's been a lifetime habit."

"Ah." He nodded, knowingly. "I had an uncle who smoked all his life, until he was in his sixties."

"What happened?" Zellman asked.

Jordan didn't blink. "He got Parkinson's and burned the house down trying to light a cigarette."

"Man. I'm sorry. He quit after that?"

"Nah. He died." Jordan added, "From the fire."

Zellman and I stared at him, but there were no words. Then we all heard Taz's voice inside. Maybe it was the catalyst or maybe it was because I heard Heather snipe at her to "chill," but for whatever reason, I felt calmer.

Heather wasn't like Channing.

If I needed to know something for his safety, she would tell me. That was one thing—she never minced words. She didn't seem to feel I needed protecting and shielding. She knew I had a crew, and it was a good crew. She would tell me if we needed to do something, so that issue moved more to the back of my mind.

It wasn't long until Heather came back. She waved her phone at me before sitting back down.

"It sounds like they have it under control. There was a little hiccup, but I have someone who's going to call me if I need to be worried. So, I guess stay tuned?" Her grin was lopsided. "Sorry. I know you were worried."

"I just need to know if we have to go in to help them. That's all."

She shook her head, pulling her eyebrows together. "No. That'd make Chan even more worried. He'd call more of his guys, but I'll let you know what's going on."

Hearing Taz again, I gestured inside. "My friend wants you to sponsor something for a charity event."

"Right. She said something when I went in."

"Are you going to?"

Heather reached down and straightened back up, her old smoker's can in hand. She bit down on her lip, gazing a bit too adoringly at it. She murmured, distracted, "Are you asking on her behalf? Or are you asking for the sponsorship too?"

"On her behalf."

"That's funny," Heather said, lifting her head. "She opened with a line that if I sponsored an ad, I'd be helping you out."

"Are you serious?"

"Her exact words were, 'You're dating Channing Monroe, and his sister needs your help.'"

"I—" I sighed.

Jordan snorted in laughter. "That sounds like Taz."

Zellman kept looking at Heather's exposed leg. I was almost sure I saw a drop of drool at the corner of his mouth.

Cross came outside then, letting the screen door bang shut behind him. He had a burger in one hand and a small bag of fries in the other. He handed the fries to me. "That's for you." Digging into his pocket, he pulled out two packets of ketchup and handed those over too.

"What? We're eating here?" Jordan asked. He looked at me. "We're eating now?"

I glanced at Heather. She seemed relaxed, though she was looking at that can almost the same way Zellman was looking at her. I shrugged. Why not? Taz was still inside.

"I'm okay with that."

"Score."

Jordan jumped up. Zellman didn't, still distracted.

"Dude." Jordan hit his shoulder with the back of his hand.

"Huh?" Zellman blinked a few times. "Oh, hey, Cross." He zoomed in. "Wait! You got food? We're eating here?" And it was inevitable; his gaze drifted back down to Heather's leg.

"Boy," she growled, her hand tightening around the smoker's can. "If you don't stop ogling me, I'm going to hit you upside the head with this can. Got it?"

"Got it." He jerked back, as if slapped, then rushed inside after Jordan.

"Yesss." Cross dropped down in one of their abandoned chairs. He lounged back, kicking his feet to rest on the empty bonfire pit.

"Okay." Heather stood, handing the can to me. "I have to go work or do something. You'd think I'd be over this shit, but nooo. A bad fucking habit for life really means a bad fucking habit for life." Her eyes settled on me a moment as she headed for the door. "I'll let you know if they call again."

"Thank you."

"You're still worried?" Cross asked when the door closed behind her.

"He's my brother. I mean, that's normal. Right?"

Cross put his burger on the chair next to him. "He'll be fine." He looked over his shoulder to where Heather had gone. "If we're really needed, she'll tell us to go. You know that."

I knew he was right. Channing wouldn't want us involved, but Heather wasn't my sister. She'd send us in if she thought we needed to go, or she'd call in other guys to help back him up. Coming here just helped me know one other person was worried about him too—and shit, I just realized I was worried about my brother.

My brother.

I blinked a few times, straightening up in shock. "I'm worried about my brother." How'd that happen?

Cross bit into his burger, and he grinned at me around it. "I know. It's like we're in an alternate universe or something. How's it feel?"

"How's what feel?"

"Feeling a little normal." He swallowed his food, his eyes darkening, suddenly getting serious. "It's typical to be worried about family."

It wasn't in my world.

I scowled at him. "You're my family."

His tone quieted. "You know what I mean." He bit into his burger again.

I'd never offered to back up a crew with ours before. That was different too. Channing had stepped in to handle disputes between crews, but actually aligning my crew with his—it hadn't happened. But we were related. It made sense.

"You know," Cross said. "If our crew and his crew were connected, together we'd be bigger than the Ryerson crew."

I did the math. Channing's crew had twenty-six members. Our four brought that up to thirty, and some of his weren't active. They'd moved away, gotten old, and started families.

"Ryerson's would still be bigger, by a few."

"But we'd be the *baddest* of them all." He grinned, taking another bite of his burger.

There was that.

"Well, that hasn't happened." I could hear Jordan and Zellman coming back outside, and as they pushed the screen door open, I added, "I like how we are right now."

Cross grunted, and the conversation dropped.

Jordan and Zellman sat down across from us with bags full of food. As they devoured everything, Taz came out with a soda and a chicken sandwich balanced on top of her tote bag. She took the last empty seat between Cross and Jordan, but she paused before she did.

No one acted like they noticed, but everyone did.

I glanced at Cross. He met my gaze. More food for thought.

Taz placed her sandwich on her lap, then dug into her bag. "Thanks for coming with me. I got three big sponsors I know no one else will get. It's a big deal."

She handed over some papers, but I declined to look at them, putting a fry into my mouth instead.

"Yeah. And don't forget about Race's dad," I told her.

"I know." Taz's eyes rounded, like they had when my cousin came out. "Did you know his dad runs the Harley-Davidson dealership in Wakefield?"

"How do you know that?" Cross asked her.

She put the papers back in her bag and reached for her sandwich as she answered. "It's all over school. Sunday knew the first day he showed up." She was about to take a bite when she noticed the stares from everyone. "You guys didn't know?"

They looked at me instead.

"You did?" Jordan asked.

"I just knew his dad ran a Harley store." The dealership in Wakefield was big, really big.

"I'm getting sick of this kid. He's everywhere. I bet if I took a dump, he'd be in the shower," Jordan grumbled. He was looking at me.

"What?" I asked. "You know why he's here. He told us."

"Yeah, yeah." He kicked up his feet. Balling up his wrappers, he tossed them into the empty bonfire pit. His arms folded over his chest. "I don't know. I mean, yeah. I heard what he said. Drake messed with him, then the fighting ring and the divorce, but why do I have a feeling he's not going to go away?"

He kept looking at me, though he sounded like he was talking to himself.

I snagged another fry, but Jordan was still watching me intently. "What? I'm not his spokesperson."

His eyes narrowed. "I got a feeling he wished you were." His eyes skirted to Cross, taking on a speculative gleam. He lifted his chin towards us. "And what was he talking about before? About wondering, but not?"

Tension settled back over me, pressing down, but so did a ball of anger in my gut. The more Jordan pushed me, the more it rolled around, getting bigger and bigger with each circle.

Did he want to fight? Was that what he wanted?

Race wasn't an issue for us. I was getting sick of even hearing his name, not to mention the way Jordan was directing all this crap at me. Race had helped us. He wasn't an adversary. That might change in the future, but Jordan pushing me now had me ready to take up a cause I didn't care about in the first place.

"Ask him yourself!" I snarled.

And we were back to the old dynamic—where Jordan was pissed at me for something, and I was defiant. That ball was percolating, getting larger and larger.

"Or we stop talking about the guy." Cross tossed his burger wrapping into the bonfire too. "Hmm? How about that?"

Zellman's eyes shifted between Jordan and me, then went to Cross as he took another big bite of his burger. It was almost gone, and he reached for his bag of fries.

Jordan snorted. "Of course you'd take up for her. Why am I not shocked?"

Cross' eyes narrowed. "You got something to say to me?"

Taz's eyes were wide and round. I was surprised too. Cross had already said a lot against Race. Now he was piping in against Jordan? Where'd the silent and lethal guy go? He was becoming more confrontational.

"Okay." Taz waved her hands in a circle. "Not sure what's going on here, but I only need a few more sponsors in case Race's dad doesn't come through." A nervous laugh filtered from her. "Remember? That's what we're doing here. Not fighting."

I continued to stare at Jordan as I asked her, "How many more?"

"Three, and they're small packages. Your cousin, and the two Jaxes inside got the big ones."

I had ideas on a few more spots we could visit. I stood up. "Come on. I'll take you to the rest." I handed my fries to Cross. "I lost my appetite."

Taz stood too, her bag and sandwich in hand.

I squared my shoulders. "You got a stick up your ass when it comes to me," I told Jordan. "You better get right with the fact that I'm not going to always do what you want, and you better stop putting other shit on me, like this guy. He's not a problem. Stop making him mine." I looked at Cross. "You want to come?"

He inclined his head toward Jordan. Almost lazily, he gestured to him with his finger. "I'll get a ride."

I was ready to head off when his gaze transferred to me again. It lingered. I got the message. He'd stay and watch my back.

He held out his hand, grazing me as I slipped past.

I paused for a brief second.

I didn't look down. I didn't think I dared.

A need was captured in my throat, along with that tingling from earlier. Pushing forward, I headed to the Jeep, feeling my stomach starting to churn in anticipation, in excitement.

I didn't realize my lungs had ceased working until I got inside the car. A large amount of air expelled from me, and I had to sit there for a moment.

Taz said something and ran back.

My mind was whirling. I felt like my blood was buzzing.

I needed a minute to center myself, and when Taz came back, her tote bag in hand, I said, "I'll take you back to get your car when we're done."

"It's not a problem." She shut her door and put her seatbelt on, juggling her bag and sandwich. "I gave Cross the keys. They'll go get the car; then he'll take it home." She gestured over her shoulder as I turned my Jeep to go around Jordan's. "Does that happen often?"

"What?"

"The fighting."

I couldn't answer that. I didn't want to. "Sorry you had to witness it."

"Jordan might mean well deep down, but it's way far down, like seven layers of Dante's Inferno down. All those layers are his asshole layers." She settled back, unwrapping the last half of her sandwich. "If I joined your crew, all I'd be doing is fighting with him. I get it."

I turned onto the road, leaving Manny's behind, and glanced sideways to Taz. I had a feeling her way of "getting it" and mine were total opposites.

CHAPTER
TWENTY-FIVE

I TOOK TAZ TO a couple more crew businesses, but it wasn't until I was driving her back to her house that she mentioned a main sponsor.

"What do you mean?" I asked.

"The big, big one." She was waving her hands in the air again. I could see from the corner of my eye. "You know, when you go to events and you see the main sponsor? Race's dad could do that one."

"Why didn't you mention it before?"

She shrugged. "Because it's not mine to fill. It's Ms. Bagirianni's job, but I just texted her and asked if she'd found someone yet. She said no. You want me to read it out loud?"

I felt the blood drain from my face. "No way. I don't want to hear, see, or know about any personal texts from The Badger. There should be a rule where teachers and staff can't leave the school. When you enter, you deal with them there and only there. It's too much, thinking of all of them having their own lives."

"Man." She whistled. "She really got under your skin, huh?"

I fixed her with a look. "If you think The Badger hasn't psychoanalyzed you, you're dumb. Trust me. She analyzes everybody."

"I'm not insecure about what she might think of me."

"Ask for her thoughts on your relationship with Cross."

Taz's smug smile vanished.

"See? Not so secure now, huh?"

"That was mean of you."

Maybe. Well, yes, it was. "Sometimes I'm not so nice."

I pulled up to the curb by their house and put the Jeep in park, letting the engine idle. I'd only be going in there if Cross was home, and I already knew he wasn't. He'd texted before saying they were at Jordan's.

Taz looked down at her lap, at her bag sitting there, and she sighed. "I know you're not normal. Your friends are your crew, and I get it. I mean, I think I do. Kind of. But that was a cheap shot you just took. My relationship with Cross is—"

"Where you're vulnerable?" I asked. "Guess what? My whole life is where I'm vulnerable."

She held my gaze, then let out another quiet breath. "You think I took a cheap shot at you?"

I remained like a statue. Taz knew my relationship with The Badger was a sore subject. She got her feelings hurt? Tough. Welcome to life.

She looked down at her bag again. "Maybe I did."

I knew she was jealous of my relationship with her brother. I was jealous of how normal her life was. She took a dig at me, and I punched her back. And now she was feeling bad? She'd go inside, sit, and get a home-cooked meal with both of her parents.

She'd get over it.

I cleared my throat. "Let's just talk tomorrow, okay?"

"Okay." She slid out of my vehicle, her hand up in a wave. "Thanks, Bren."

I nodded.

I meant to go watch the house, or maybe finish that fight with Jordan, but instead of turning left, I went right.

I didn't know why.

I honestly didn't.

Maybe the whole stupid thing with Jordan was on my mind, and I wanted it done. I didn't want any more questions about him.

Maybe thinking of Taz with her parents made me think of what Race must be going through, or maybe in some weird way I wanted to make it up to Taz, wipe away the hurt I'd caused her.

Whatever the reason, I drove to the outskirts of Roussou and headed to the Ryerson's home. Alex's parents lived on the outside of town, so they had a bunch of land extending behind them. There was a pool, a pool house, and a couple storage sheds. They had a setup like Jordan's, but with a longer driveway.

I wasn't surprised to find Alex's crew lingering around the pool when I parked and got out. Half of them were in it. Some were drinking and talking. Some were dunking the others in the pool. A few girls were straddling some of the guys, their tongues down their throats. Amid all that as a backdrop, I pushed ahead.

Maybe this wasn't such a great idea, but I wanted to know so I could tell Taz. I was there for her, and I didn't have the guy's phone number.

I had Alex's. That thought just came to me, almost making me stop where I stood, but I was already here.

A guy next to Alex poked his arm, pointing to me.

And Alex saw me.

I couldn't back out now. It'd make me look scared, weak. Wolf Crew wasn't weak, so ignoring what my gut was telling me, and ignoring a whiff of rotten eggs, I started over to him.

I didn't go far. I stopped a few feet away from my Jeep.

Alex stood when he saw me, a beer in hand. His skin glistened, and he had drops pouring down his forehead. He was almost drenched, and I didn't need to get closer to know it wasn't from the pool.

"Your cousin here?"

A full smile spread over his face, maybe too quickly, too eager. Too unsettling. "How about a beer instead?"

I shook my head. "I'm looking for your cousin."

"Ah." He nodded, the smile fading. A different, meaner grin took its place. "I was wondering what brought Bren Monroe to my place." He made a show of looking behind me. "And without your crew too." He whistled. "You're living on the edge, Bren. I might reach out and...hug you."

I bared my teeth. "Not without my permission, you won't."

He laughed, tipping his head back. The sound was a little too maniacal. "There she is. You looked almost *tame* for a second, like a sweet little kitten, not the feral *puss* I know you are." He gestured with his beer back toward where I'd come from. "As for my cousin, he took off after school."

"What?"

His smile was fully gone now. A hard glint remained in his eyes, fusing with the haze there. "Let's say we had a difference of opinion about something. Yeah." He motioned again. "He took off. I don't have a clue where."

Race was gone? Like, gone gone?

"What about his mom?"

Alex's eyes sharpened. He lowered his beer. "You know about his mom? About why she's here?"

"Is she still here?"

He tilted his head to the side. "How do you know about his mom? Even my crew doesn't know why she's here."

"Is she still here?" I was pissed, suddenly really, really pissed. Race had made a big fucking deal about his dad's money for Taz's thing, and now he was gone? And I was here, stepping in the middle of another fucking crew when I shouldn't be?

"Yeah." He took a sip. Slow, methodical. "She's here."

I was ignoring all of the signs that I should get out of here. *Pretend they aren't there*, I told myself. *Pretend you don't know. Maybe nothing will happen?* I'd walked into a den of vipers, and I needed to back out of here before they struck. Everything in me was screaming to run, but I forced a nonchalant look on my face.

I had to.

I was close to being in survival mode here.

And thinking...Race had just changed his location. If his mom was here, he was still in Roussou.

"Okay." I started back to my Jeep. "Thanks, Alex."

He waited until I was just in front of it, then called after me, raising his voice, "You fucking him?"

I stopped, my back to him.

He did that on purpose, wanting the rest of his crew to hear him. It was a call to action. Get in gear, little kiddies. Time to stop playing. It's a different kind of playtime now.

When I turned around, I wasn't surprised to find most of them heading our way. I began counting, guessing there were twelve here, maybe a few still in the pool.

Fake it, Bren.

So I did. I raised my chin, meeting his gaze square. "That's none of your business, if I were."

His shoulders fell back and whatever sick excitement he was getting from this conversation went up a full notch.

Those odds were so damn bad. He was safe, surrounded by *his,* while mine were absent.

My lips parted.

Fuck you, crossed my mind.

He grinned at me, that gleam so wicked. "Not so cocky now, Monroe, are you?"

"Funny." I indicated his crew. "I came looking for someone who's not crew, and yours and mine aren't warring right now."

Alex's hotheadedness was back, but he'd picked up other habits too. Bad habits. Life-threatening habits, for myself and others.

This. Was. So. Not. Good.

"Don't do this," I rasped out.

"Do what?" He tipped his head back, finishing his beer, and tossed it off to the side. He used the back of his arm to wipe his mouth. "Call you out for being a slut?"

My head went low. "Taz needs sponsors for some committee. I'm here to help her out. That's all. Race said his dad would help."

He walked toward me with a slow swagger, his hips rotating smoothly. The guy was high and drunk, and he was either trying and failing at being seductive or he was just out and out okay with the potential-rapist vibes he was giving off. He was enjoying this.

That chilled me to the bone.

"I want to know where my turn went. You went from Drake to Race. Shouldn't I have gotten a ride in therrre fisd?" he slurred.

God, he reeked.

I was going to slice him.

CREW

My mind wanted to turn off. I knew what was going to happen. There was no out for me, which meant I had one option. Fight. Take as many of them with me as I could, but I had to think. I had to stay rational. I couldn't turn it off.

Not yet.

Still.

My mouth was so dry. My lips parted as I gulped air. I couldn't get enough. I felt my throat constricting.

That's the fear, Bren.

For whatever fucking reason, my brother's voice sounded in my head.

Even now, even in this situation, he was trying to tell me what to do.

I tried to summon my usual annoyance, but it wasn't there.

I listened to him. I had to.

Make every contact count. Be smart, but efficient. Stay strong. Clear head, Bren.

Then Cross' voice, *Find your exits. Count them. Then look ahead, decide on your first targets. Think about where you strike first.*

Cross' voice melded with Channing's. *Clear head. Fight smart.*

I didn't think when I grabbed my knife—that was automatic. But I scanned the group. I saw four gaps in the crowd, four exits. My keys were in my pocket.

I suddenly wished I had an automatic starter, but there was no need here in California. Well, except for right about fucking now.

I felt my knife in my hand. That handle fit so perfectly in my palm.

It calmed me, just a tiny bit.

"Think about what you're saying, Alex," I said softly. "Think hard."

He laughed, the sound making me nauseous.

"Trust me." He gripped himself through his jeans. "I'm hard. I've been hard for you for a *long* time."

I wanted to do more than slice him, but I counted everyone behind him. He had around twenty people here.

There was no way for me. There was no way.

I could slice a few, but he'd grab me before I got inside the Jeep. I'd have to run out to the land around his place. There were trees, but unlike Jordan's, there was a whole lot of open land.

They would hunt me down. It was a matter of time.

They would beat me. Maybe rape me. Maybe worse.

This was Roussou. The shimmer of danger wasn't an illusion. I had stepped right into the thick of it.

"My phone is on." I pulled it out with my free hand and dialed 9-1-1. "They're coming, and I know enough people who listen to the radio. My brother is probably being notified as I speak, so it'll be his crew coming too. Not just mine." I locked eyes with a few of his members. Some were hostile. Some were cautious. A couple seemed fearful. I stared hard at them. "Something happens to me, you know what will happen to you. Blood for blood."

I knew that would hit hard with some of Alex's crew. They didn't all look wasted.

One gulped. Another hardened his expression, but I still saw the fear there, just under the surface.

Everything I'd said was true.

I had called 9-1-1. They would ping my location. Someone would hear the dispatch, and my brother *would* get a call. He'd call his crew, then mine, and all of them would descend on this place.

I hoped whatever damage they did to me would be worth it, because I had my guys coming.

I looked at Alex again, holding my breath.

He snarled, his hands balling into fists. "Then let's stop wasting time."

CHAPTER TWENTY-SIX

ALEX LUNGED FOR ME.

Still holding the knife in my hand, I palmed it so it lay flat, reached behind me to grab the edge of the Jeep door, and flung myself backward. I kicked under Alex's head as my legs went up and over, and I rolled to my feet on the top of my Jeep. From there I kicked and swung with my knife until I was too surrounded. I felt some guys climbing up on the back of my Jeep, moving toward me, and as they reached for my legs, I embedded my knife in one of their arms. The guy screamed, falling back, and I fell on my hip, jutting my feet out again to kick at the other guy. I connected with his nose, hearing a crunching sound, but it was too late.

The other guy still had my knife in his arm, and I felt hands scoop me up from behind.

Someone pulled me off the car and then let go.

I fell to the ground, landing on my side on top of a rock.

I grunted from the pain, and though it blinded me for a moment, I reached underneath me and grabbed the rock.

"Enough!" I heard Alex roar.

Two guys reached down for me. I brought the rock up, smashing one in the head and bringing my elbow back into the other's face.

A fist hit me in the side, and I doubled over again.

I felt tears coating my face, tasted my blood mixing with them, but I wasn't stopping. I wouldn't, not until I was put down. If I could move, I could fight.

"Stay down, bitch!" Alex growled.

The group surged back at his words, leaving me alone.

I looked up, panting. Holding my side, I winced as I felt a rib broken. "You fucker."

He snarled again and lifted his arm. He was going to backhand me. I braced myself, ready to fall out of his way and punch that rock up into his side, but before I could, before he could—another roar came from the crowd.

Suddenly someone grabbed Alex, hurling him away from me.

I stood, panting, my vision blurred. I was close to passing out. I felt it coming.

I tried to focus on who had just arrived.

The person punched Alex hard, and when Alex lifted a hand to block a second punch, he grabbed Alex's arm and bent it at an ungodly angle. A blood-curdling scream ripped from Alex's throat, stopping everyone else in their tracks.

The guy didn't waste the opening. He rounded with a strong punch. Alex crumbled to the floor, and the guy turned to face the rest of the group. They closed in before I could see who it was, but I looked around. My crew wasn't here. I didn't see any of Channing's...

I looked again, blinking and trying to see. I almost fell, so I grabbed hold of my Jeep's door and hauled myself in. This guy was fighting all of them at once. I couldn't tell who was winning, but then four trucks sped down the driveway and veered right for us.

Zellman and Cross were in the back of Jordan's truck. Before he even came to a total stop, they launched themselves out and were on some of the Ryerson crew. Jordan wasn't far behind, literally lifting one of the guys up and throwing him to the ground.

Channing was in one of the other trucks, and he paused as he exited. He scanned the mess, saw me, and as his crew waded in, he came my way.

It hadn't been Channing who attacked Alex, or my crew.

In that moment I knew who it was, and I tried to stand again, but my knees gave out.

Channing scooped me up in time, putting me back in my Jeep. "Are you okay?"

I grunted, pushing him away. "I'll be fine." He didn't budge. I shoved at him again. "Go! They need help."

Channing grinned crookedly at me. "I think it's probably over alre—"

Another scream sounded, and the fighting stopped. People shuffled backward, clearing out and revealing Alex on the ground. My knife protruded from his leg, and he rocked back and forth, trying to pull it out.

Race stood over him, bloodied, sweating, and bruised. His shirt was ripped, and parts of his jeans had been torn away.

He knelt, ignoring everyone, and reached for the knife. He leaned close, saying something to his cousin. Alex sucked in a savage breath, freezing, and Race yanked my knife out. A sickening groan came from Alex as he seemed to wither into a little ball.

Wiping the blade off on his jeans, Race came over to Channing and me.

The crews started to separate. Alex's crew picked him up and carried him away. My guys came over, and Cross stepped right in front of me, ignoring Channing and whoever else was there. He scanned me up and down, looking for injuries. Jordan and Zellman were right next to us, doing the same.

"Shit, Bren." Jordan shook his head, looking harried. "You scared the goddamn life out of me."

"Our normal shit seems petty, huh?"

He laughed, broken. "Yeah. Petty is one word for it. You okay?"

I nodded, but hissed when Cross touched one of my ribs. It was a soft prod, but it was still a prod. It hurt like a motherfucker.

Cross didn't care. He was still assessing.

Most of Channing's crew had gone back to their vehicles, but they lingered there, waiting for instructions.

Channing turned to me, nodding to Race. "Who's that?"

"The guy who gave you a ride to Jordan's that one night."

Channing's eyebrow rose. "That's the same guy?"

Race stopped next to us. He held my knife out. "Lose this?"

"Thanks." I took it, putting it back into my pocket. It didn't feel right not having it there. "I came to find you."

"Someone texted me, saying you were here. I got here as fast as I could." He glanced at my crew, but none of the three were paying him any attention. All eyes were glued to me. He looked at my brother instead. "Hello again."

Channing narrowed his eyes at me before turning to Race. He tipped his head back. "You gave me a ride last week?"

"I did." Race turned to me. "Alex and I have a difference of opinion. I had to find a new place to live today."

Channing grunted again. "You're a good fighter. I saw some of your moves."

"Thank you." Race winced, and I saw that he was hurting. His face was a little pale. "That's part of the reason I moved here," he continued. "There's a good underground ring. You're the champ, right?"

My brother nodded. He'd been keeping a mask up, but now he let a real grin shine through. "I am." He paused. "For now. I recently retired." He nodded to Moose and Congo, who were heading over. "Everyone handled?"

Moose said, "Everyone's down."

Jordan nodded at me. "I know Cross is checking, but are you okay?"

"Everything except maybe a rib." As I spoke, Cross straightened in front of me. His hand came to where my rib was, but he didn't touch me. He wanted to, his hand hovering there, and with a small apology in his eyes, he lifted up my shirt for a better look.

I pushed it down. "I'll be fine."

He wasn't listening. He held my shirt up higher and frowned at what he saw. His eyes closed, and a second later, he stepped close, his forehead softly resting on my shoulder. I felt his tension leave his body then, and couldn't help myself. I closed my eyes, running a hand down his back.

Neither of us commented as he shuddered under that touch.

Jordan cleared his throat, his voice still rough. "We'll take you to the hospital. Cross will drive you." He motioned to Zellman. "We'll be right behind you."

"I can go with her—" Race offered, but my brother shook his head.

That wasn't protocol. Crew took care of their own. Channing was my brother, and maybe if this were more severe, he'd step in, but even he respected the crew rule on this.

He stepped around so he could see me. "I'll see you at home tonight. Call if you need anything."

"I'll be fine," I told him.

He walked away with his crew, but yelled over his shoulder, "Call me!"

Cross glanced sideways at me, but I didn't say anything. I only nodded, waving to Moose and Congo. I refused to acknowledge the small part in me that was feeling all happy, glad that my big, bad brother had come to my defense. I wasn't like that. That was too girly.

Which I wasn't.

I was badass.

I had my own knife.

Right.

It took everything I had to keep from showing my stupid grin. It would've given me away, so I moved farther into my Jeep.

Cross held his hand out to Race. "Thank you."

Race froze. The rest of us watched, and after a pause, he put his hand in Cross'. "Yeah." He blinked a few times, rapidly. "Of course."

Cross added, "I owe you." And that was it. Turning, he got behind the wheel.

I tried to gauge his thoughts, but he only clenched his jaw and finally pulled out after the others had gone. We were the last vehicle.

We kept up with everyone going back into town, but after a while, I noticed Cross was going slower and slower, until Jordan's truck's lights were almost specks in the distance. Then he let out a deep breath and swung the Jeep into someone's driveway. He slammed it into park and was across the seat in a heartbeat.

I didn't have time to process.

He stopped just before touching me. His hand flexed. He let out a harsh breath. "Goddamn." His touch was gentle as he cupped the side of my face.

"I'm okay." I winced as I said that.

He pulled his hand away, shaking his head. His eyes were hard and dark. "Someone called your brother, and he called us on his way. We almost beat him here. Holy fuck, Bren." He breathed out again, shakily. He rested his forehead gently to mine. "I lost about two years of my life, seeing you like that."

My throat swelled, and I blinked away some water in my eyes, because that's what it had to be.

"I'm okay." I was in pain, but I was okay. No one had sliced or diced me.

His eyes closed. He didn't move away.

This was Cross. He was my best friend. He was more family than Channing or Scratch. He was more than... I stopped thinking.

I closed my eyes and breathed out in relief too.

CHAPTER
TWENTY-SEVEN

THE ER NURSE saw us and harrumphed. "You guys again. This week is complete now that I've seen you guys—or handiwork from you guys."

Jordan and Zellman started laughing, but I caught the dark cloud on her face. She wasn't amused. When the doctor came in to examine me, she booted them all out. Cross didn't move from his seat.

"Gotta go," she told him.

He locked eyes with her. His jaw firmed. "I'm not going."

She looked at me.

"He's family," I said.

She turned back to him.

He smiled.

"He's your brother?" she asked, but she knew us. She knew the truth.

"He'll look away if I tell him to."

She sighed and went out the door. The doctor didn't blink an eye at Cross' presence. He did all the usual exams, checking out my cuts and the bruises already starting to form. He pressed a hand over my stomach, listened to my lungs. He asked if I was having problems breathing.

Everything hurt, but my breathing was fine.

There were no knife wounds anywhere. I'd just been hit.

Thirty minutes later, after debating whether an x-ray was even needed, I was released.

"Clean bill of health?" Jordan asked when Cross and I got back to the lobby.

I shot him a look.

He laughed, and Cross answered for me. "She's got some nice painkillers to take, but that's it."

I stretched out my arm. A nasty bruise was fully black already, taking the shape of a boot.

"Looks like Florida," Zellman said.

"Or a boot," I countered.

He grinned. "That too."

"Who kicked you?" Jordan asked.

I had to think about it. It seemed like so many had taken a shot at me. "Alex maybe? I don't know. He was there. A few others got me in the side. I didn't even know someone had gotten my arm until the doctor saw it."

They were silent, all three staring at me.

There were topics to discuss, big and bad topics, but I chose an easy one.

"Race got there before they could do a ton of damage, right?"

Jordan's eyes grew suspicious. "What's his deal, if he doesn't want in your pants?"

I glanced at Cross, remembering the feel of his touch as he'd cupped my face.

Feeling an upsurge of tenderness, I shrugged in response to Jordan's question. "He's not said anything, but I've gotten the vibe that he and Alex don't see eye to eye."

Jordan grunted, looking around.

We were drawing attention, standing in the lounge.

The room was quiet for some reason, and all eyes were on us.

Cross cleared his throat, indicating outside. "Talk out there."

One by one, we trailed behind him.

Cross had dropped me off at the entrance, and I followed him now to where he'd parked beside Jordan's truck. The lot wasn't too big, but both vehicles were in the back corner, so there would be a modicum of privacy unless someone was standing on the other side of the fence around the lot.

As if reading my mind, Zellman went over and scaled the fence. He grabbed the top and hoisted himself up to see over.

"Clear." He dropped back down, dusting off his pants. "We're good. No one back there."

Jordan sat on his truck bed as Zellman came to join him. He sat on the top, one foot resting on the bed by Jordan, and the other hanging off the back.

Cross looked at me in silent question, indicating the back of my Jeep.

I nodded, and he moved over, half-shielding me as I climbed up, and keeping a hand on my side. He seemed to stand point then, as if he was the leader.

Jordan picked up a stray stick and began breaking it into pieces. "So we need to decide a few things." Here were the heavy topics.

"You want us to wait for this conversation?" Cross asked me.

If we went to my house, Channing would be there. If we went to Jordan's, no one would be there, but I was longing for my bed. Here and now. It was better to get it done.

"Nah. I'm on the happy pills. Do it now before I get sober."

I grinned at him, and he smiled back, his eyes lingering a moment before turning to Zellman and Jordan. Shoving his hands into his pockets, he leaned against me, but gently. I was tempted to run my hand down his shoulder and arm. I had to press it against my side to keep from doing that.

Jordan began tossing parts of the stick to the ground absentmindedly.

"Okay. So. What all happened exactly?" he asked me.

I relayed everything.

"Fuck." Jordan glowered at the end. "Alex jumped you, but he got his ass kicked, and he pissed off your brother. So what's the payback?"

Cross crossed his arms over his chest. He spoke in a low voice, a hint of warning there. "He's going to get his ass kicked *again*. I don't care if I have to do it my goddamn self. I *am* kicking his ass."

"Chill out. You're not doing anything alone. You know we'll have your back," Jordan hissed. "I'm not saying to ignore it, but we do payback on the Ryerson leader, and what then? It's crew war. You guys ready for that?"

Cross was unnaturally still.

That told me plenty.

I craned my neck a little. The painkiller the nurse had given me was starting to kick in. I swear there was a little glow around Zellman where he was perched above everyone else, but I could make out the anger too.

Zellman was usually happy no matter what happened, so I had to do a double take. Nope. It was still there.

Noticing me, some of the anger fled, he said quietly, "He hurt you, Bren. He has to pay for it."

"Some would argue he already has," Jordan mused.

"What the hell?!" Cross growled, jumping away from the vehicle and shoving Jordan. It was fast and forceful. His shove pushed him almost to the ground. Jordan's head whipped back, his face twisting in anger, but Cross didn't care. He stood his ground, his hands in fists. "What? You got a problem with me, because I sure as hell have a problem with you. Say it one more damn time. One more damn time, Jordan."

"Say what?" Jordan's hand thrust through his hair.

"You fucking know."

They were silent.

Cross was waiting for Jordan's answer, and Jordan lowered his head after a second. He submitted, speaking quietly, his hand fisting in his hair. "Look. I'm just saying a crew war could mean more of us like Bren. I don't want that."

"He didn't get hurt by *our* hands. He hurt one of ours. *We* have to do the payback. You know that," Cross gritted out.

Jordan's head lowered another fraction of an inch. "Okay. Yeah. I get it."

"We have to, Jordan," I said. They all turned to me. "He's pushed it too much. He has to be hurt back. We can't let it go."

"Okay, but we have to be smart about it." Jordan looked at all of us. "We hit him hard, and just him."

"We can do political shit to lessen any blowback on us, but it *will* happen," Cross said. "There's no question of that." He looked at Jordan, then Zellman.

"So what about Race?" I asked.

All eyes went back to me.

I added, "I don't know what to say about him. Honestly, I went there for Taz."

"We need to figure out how to deal with him," Jordan agreed. "He's been helping us. If he really doesn't have an agenda with us, then what the fuck, man?"

Zellman snorted. "Everyone has an agenda. If it really was because Drake said to hang with us, and it's not Bren's cooch he wants, we gotta know this guy better."

"Don't talk about my vagina. Ever. And *never* refer to it as a cooch."

"Huh?" Zellman blinked in confusion, glancing at the guys. "What'd I say wrong?"

Jordan and Cross started laughing.

"New crew rule: no one talks about my vagina, unless you want me to start referring to your two-inch, soft, limp dicks." I growled. The happy pills weren't helping.

"Cooch isn't bad."

"Say it one more time, and I'll wait until you're drunk, then tattoo the words 3 Second Man on your ass."

"Dude. Just stop." Jordan shook his head at him, half-laughing still.

Zellman frowned, itching his head. "I will. Yeah, but cooch isn't bad. Is it?"

"Fucking A, Z!"

"Sorry. Sorry." He ducked his head, holding his hands up. "I'll stop. Sorry, B."

"So we're set?" Cross asked. "We deal with Race first, then figure out the best way of handling Alex?"

One by one, we all nodded.

"I want to be there," I said.

They turned to me again. I frowned a little. "Not that you'd purposely cut me out, but I'm injured, and I know you guys might question him without me because you think you don't want to bother me. But I'm there. I want to take part."

Cross looked at the others again. "We do it as a crew, or we don't do it at all."

We were about to thank Race, in our way.

CHAPTER TWENTY-EIGHT

CROSS TOOK ME HOME.

We made it to my room before Channing appeared. I was prepared for an interrogation, but surprisingly, none came. He just asked if I was okay. Albeit, he asked a bit gruffly, but he seemed appeased once I told him I was fine. He didn't question why I'd been at Alex's place or ask how the whole thing had happened, like a normal parent would.

Heather lingered in the doorway after Channing left, biting her lip, her hair in a braid. She kept looking me up and down, as if searching for any outward injury that hadn't been treated. She kept pausing at Cross' hand on my hip. He wasn't helping me stand or anything, but the touch was nice. I found myself leaning into him, into his hand, and he flexed it in response. He tugged me even tighter against him.

"Where are the other two?" Heather asked.

"They were tired," Cross said. "Went home."

Her smirk told us she didn't believe him. "Okay." She nodded in the direction Channing had gone. "He's not questioning you because it's your crew business, same as with him."

Heather was our go-between.

I wasn't sure if that was a good thing, but I nodded. I got it. "Thanks."

She raised an eyebrow. "No need to thank me. Just doing my duty as someone who cares about both of you—you know, trying to smooth out sibling fights before they happen."

"Is that what he does for you and Brandon?"

She laughed this time. "Yeah. Right. He makes it worse, views it as his personal reality show."

I felt a pinch at her words.

Channing was funny, and viewed as a charmer, but not with me. Never with me.

I wasn't worthy enough.

I firmed my jaw, swallowing thickly. As if sensing the storm in me, Cross' hand smoothed over my back. His fingers slipped under my shirt and rested on my skin.

"So," Heather continued, her eyes noting that touch before flicking back to my face. "A normal girl who had been in a beatdown would stay in bed, watch movies, and have a good, old-fashioned cry fest. I'm assuming you're heading right back out?"

The painkillers were making everything a bit fuzzy, but I nodded. "Yep."

She sighed. "Okay."

I waited.

This was where a parent or guardian figure would get angry. How dare I go back out, especially now. Where was I going? What would I be doing? When would I be back? Channing hadn't asked about the fight, so I wasn't sure if Heather would step into those shoes now.

She ran her fingers through the end of her hair. "Goddamn, I need a cigarette." She started to leave, but turned back and pointed at me. "Be fucking safe tonight. Okay? Be safe. And call your damn brother to let him know when you're getting home. He stresses me out too."

She went back in their bedroom, shutting the door with a bit more force than necessary.

I didn't move. I stared at the closed door.

I had a weird feeling inside me, churning around.

It didn't feel bad, or wrong. It just felt...different.

Cross chuckled, seeing the look on my face. "She cares."

Yes. "I thought she hated me."

"She's caught in the middle." His hand fell away from my back, and he went to the window. "Do you still want to do this tonight? Jordan and Z just got here."

"How'd you know they arrived?"

"My phone buzzed in my pocket." He smirked at me. "Took a gamble."

I started to laugh, but winced at the movement. Someone got a decent wallop in there. It'd hurt worse in the morning, once the painkillers wore off, so I nodded. Now was the time.

"Yeah." I went to my closet. I'd need dark clothes for this. "Better tonight while I'm a little loopy than tomorrow. Tomorrow's not going to be fun."

"Stay home."

I paused as I shifted through my shirts and looked at him.

"Take a sick day." He gestured to the doorway. "You heard Heather. She wants you to do that. Hell, she probably wants to dote on you. That's what parents do. Makes them feel good about themselves."

"Your parents do that?"

He hesitated. "They should—for Taz."

I frowned at him.

Cross knew my relationship with Channing was messed up, and I knew there were problems at his house, but I hadn't pushed for the details. Hearing him now, I wondered if I should.

"I'm sorry," I told him.

Cross' eyes met mine.

"For Taz, I mean. She'd enjoy that kind of treatment."

His Adam's apple shifted as he swallowed, and he cleared his throat. "Do you need help changing?"

"No. I'm stiff, but I'll manage."

I took my clothes into the bathroom and examined myself. I sucked in my breath. I was bruised everywhere. There were scrapes on my head, like someone had wrenched my hair back and left a mark. The bottom half of my chin was one giant bruise. It went from ear to ear. Then there was another at the corner of my eye. I felt over my ribs, just skimming. I had a bruise the size of a basketball on my side. There was a yellow lining around it.

No wonder Heather had wanted a cigarette. If she showed up looking like this, I would've been smoking too.

Nonetheless, I hadn't lied. I was stiff, but I was still able to move around. Everything would be painful as fuck in the morning. I made up my mind. Whether Heather or Channing wanted to dote or not, I'd take a skip day tomorrow.

But first things first.

I dressed, pulling on black pants and a black long-sleeved shirt with a hood. Getting the clothes on was slightly painful, a fact the pills were helping. I would've been crying if they weren't working, and I knew they were because I had to try three times to lace up my shoes. Finally, I gave in and slipped on an old pair that I didn't need to tie.

Cross was waiting on the edge of the bed. He'd changed too. I didn't ask where he'd gotten his clothes. He kept a drawer here.

"I'm ready."

He stood, but his gaze skimmed over me, darkening before he took my hand and led the way. A vein popped out from his neck. Hearing laughter in the backyard, he turned to go out the front.

We weren't really sneaking out, but it still felt that way.

As we hurried to Jordan's truck, the passenger door opened. Letting go of my hand, Cross jumped lithely and soundlessly into the back. He settled into the corner as Zellman got out of the front. He paused once, looked me over, and gave me a slight nod.

He jumped in the back too, going to the opposite corner, behind where Jordan was at the wheel.

I got into the cab, having to hold my breath until I was settled. *Fuck.* I hated being injured.

There was no music playing. Tonight, that felt right. It felt appropriate.

Jordan tapped a coffee drink in the console. "I got this for you, if you want it."

It was his way of saying he was sorry. "Thank you."

When he turned toward downtown Roussou, I glanced over.

"He's not at Alex's?" But as I asked, I knew that was true. Alex had told me himself.

"Called someone. He's at a hotel. I got the room number."

"His mom?"

"We're in luck. Apparently, she likes her martinis—at the Fallen Crest Country Club."

I laughed. "Why am I not surprised?"

"Our boy is alone, unless he's got company of the female persuasion." He winked at me as he turned the vehicle onto the main road. "That'd complicate things a bit, huh?"

I shot him a dark look. "Shut it."

I did not want that to be the next thing, where they teased me about Race in a sexual or romantic way. Good grief.

Then I reconsidered. We still had a few blocks to go. We were alone. Cross and Z couldn't interrupt, so throwing all caution to the wind, I braved it.

"Why do you keep insinuating he still wants in my pants? That should be over."

Jordan was quiet. His hand tightened on the steering wheel, and he inclined his head toward me with his eyes still on the road. "Are you serious?"

"Yeah."

His smirk grew. "You're actually asking me this? Don't you see it?"

"See what?"

He gestured back behind me. "He admitted it, somewhat. He hates Cross. He keeps hanging out with us, or trying after we keep trying to tell him to take a hike. He waded into a big fucking fight for you earlier. I mean, Bren. It's plain as day. How do you not see that? No guy is going to do all that shit unless he wants in a girl's pants, and even then, this guy's going above and beyond. I'd worry about you getting a stalker if the guy wouldn't have to deal with Cross first."

I was stunned. "Wha—how?"

The slight interest Race admitted earlier didn't seem that deep, not what Jordan was describing.

He snorted again. "Come on, Bren. You're not stupid. Or dense." He paused. When I didn't say anything, he laughed again. "For real? You really haven't noticed it?"

Now panic was rising in me. If he hated Cross, that meant...

TIJAN

No.

No way.

I frowned. "What are you talking about?"

But the touches had been increasing.

The looks too. Cross had always known me, but it was different lately. Lately it'd been like I needed his touch, and he answered me before I'd even asked.

The shivers. The tingles. The throbbing.

I had started to ache in places I never had for him.

My heart was pounding fast and loud, thumping against my ribcage, and I bit back a groan. The pills were starting to wane. That must've been it.

"He's jealous of how close you and Cross are."

Right. Because—

"You and Cross are tight. He's got your back. You have his."

Jordan slowed, coming to the main intersection. The light turned green, and he flipped on his left arrow. The hotel was a block up.

"Any guy who's going to look at you romantically is going to look at Cross sideways. If I didn't know better, I'd think you had something going on with him."

He slowed, coming to the hotel's parking lot.

"People outside of us don't understand," I told him. "That's how it is."

He pulled in, then drove to the end of the hotel. He parked in the very last slot. As he turned the engine off, he grinned at me. "Lucky for you, we'll get all that straightened out tonight." He wiggled his eyebrows and was out in a flash.

Cross and Zellman jumped out from the back.

I eased out, Jordan's words still with me.

Cross migrated closer. "You okay?"

My words were stuck in my throat, and those tingles shot through me, zapping all over. I didn't like this feeling—not knowing what to feel or how to feel, or even why I was feeling what I was.

"You guys coming?" Zellman bounced next to Jordan, going up and down on his heels.

177

We were about to make a move. Cross had questioned Race at school. That'd been his first shot to come clean. The Drake thing—I didn't know. I was with them. It didn't quite make sense. So this would be a second and more direct, more intimidating move.

The adrenaline was starting to build.

The anticipation of not knowing what we'd be walking into, knowing we couldn't control certain situations, knowing that in those moments we had to go with it—it was addicting. It made us feel reckless, but powerful. We were going in, and it was going to be one huge ride.

This. This was what set us apart. This made us stupid, but it made us dangerous too. And though we shouldn't—we knew we shouldn't—we loved it. We hungered for it.

Not fear.

Normal people feared this shit.

Not us. We lived for this shit, whether or not it was a good idea.

"Yeah." I nodded.

I saw the excitement stirring in Jordan and Zellman. Z's bouncing had upped, and Jordan began to swing his arms around in small circles.

Cross was different. He'd crouch down, his head bowed until we were ready to go. He'd push off then, and that's when we'd see the dangerous side of him, the side I loved knowing he had in him. It's intoxicating to have your best friend be that fierce about you, that protective, knowing he'd go to any lengths and you would for him too. It was goddamn addictive.

This was my crew. My guys. Mine.

We were the ones no one wanted to contend with. As we followed Jordan to the side door, I knew we were about to prove that again.

He took out a key card, winking at us. "Compliments of a friend."

Zellman grinned, but Cross kept his head down, standing right in front of me.

Two steps down the hallway, and we were at the room.

We could hear the television inside. It was low, but we could still hear it. We couldn't see any light from inside, and there'd been none from outside, so maybe a lamp could be on? Either way, we expected it to be dark. We had to. Prepare and expect the worse.

Jordan used the same keycard for the door.

He released the lock, and like so many other times, we all played our parts.

Jordan held the door open, and Cross went in first. He was our weapon, the real one. He was the fastest, the best fighter, our wolf. Jordan went next, the oversized muscle, and Zellman was third.

Third was usually my place, but not tonight. Tonight everything was different.

I shut the door behind me. We were all in. Cross was already bearing down on Race.

Race gave a small shout, but it wasn't that loud.

I saw him jump up. But as he swung, Cross dodged it.

Cross was ready. Race wasn't.

There were no odds in Race's favor.

Cross didn't hit him. That wasn't the point here. He tackled him instead, and Jordan was on him in the next second.

Zellman and I went to work. We put the deadbolt in place and turned on the bathroom lights with the fan. We turned up the television, but not enough to have the neighbors complaining.

The hotel room had a kitchenette, so we flipped the microwave on, heating up air. I spotted a fan in the corner by the bed. Moving around them, I turned that on too. Zellman had already pulled the curtains shut.

It was as loud as we were going to get.

Cross and Zellman pushed Race down on the bed, turning him around and yanking his arms up behind him. Jordan stood at the end, duct tape in hand. He wrapped it around Race's hands and then his feet.

We waited, but Race didn't yell. If he had, duct tape soon would've covered his mouth. The guys pulled him up into a sitting position in the middle of the bed. Cross and Zellman stood back, but they were ready on either side, prepared to jump in if Race tried to bolt.

"I'm not going to yell." Race eyed the roll of tape in Jordan's hands. "I know what will happen then."

With that confirmation, Jordan stepped aside.

"We just want to talk to you," I said from behind them. "We're not here to hurt you."

Cross grunted. "Unless we have to."

Race started to lift his head to scowl at Cross, but I stepped forward.

I was the speaker this time.

I was the visual too. We wanted Race to see all the bruises on me. We wanted him to see what his cousin had done and yet, only a few hours later, I was standing here.

We wanted him to see what I'd endured and we would still come after him.

The scowl was forgotten. Race stilled, seeing me, and he cursed. "Fuck."

Zellman jostled next to me. "Shut up and listen to her."

The shock dwindled. Race's features clouded with anger. He started to struggle, trying to get free. "My mom went to get ice. She'll be back—"

"Your mom is getting shit-faced in Fallen Crest. She'll probably sleep in some old rich dude's bed tonight," Jordan countered. He folded his arms over his chest, nodding to me. "Listen to what she's got to say, and then we can go. No harm, no foul here."

Race's glare didn't go anywhere, but I didn't expect it to.

"You told me you came here to fight and because your parents are getting a divorce," I began.

This wasn't new to the guys, and no one reacted. All wore stone-cold expressions.

Zellman added, "We don't believe you're trying to become our sidekick because Drake told you to do that. That's weak, man."

I kept going as if Z hadn't said a word. "You keep stepping in. All our fights, you're there helping. We don't trust Normals, and while we're grateful for what you did, we can't let it go anymore. We have to know the real reason for it."

"You doing all this cause you're sweet on Bren?" Jordan asked. "Is this all for pussy?"

"Fuck off!" I snapped at him.

He lifted a shoulder. He didn't seem like he was sorry.

"You think I'm doing this because I want in her pants?" Race asked.

"Why are you doing it?" Cross lifted his chin, his eyes blazing.

Race sat forward, his eyes glazed, like he wasn't even in the room at the moment. Then he lifted a shoulder like Jordan had done.

"God. Fine. You guys are like bloodhounds. You want to know why I'm helping you?" He glared at all of us. "It's because I fucking hate my cousin. Okay? Got that? I hate my cousin. I hate his crew. I hate my uncle and my aunt. I hate how it's their fault that my parents are getting a divorce. I hate everything about their fucking world, and I want to destroy it all."

I...hadn't expected that.

"You're doing this because of your parents?"

"My aunt had an affair with my dad—"

"Then why the fuck are you here?"

Race kept on like Jordan hadn't said a word. "—but my mom doesn't know. She knows my dad was cheating on her, and the last affair was the straw that broke the camel's back, you know? She used to find out who the women were, but not this last one. He kept her hidden."

"How'd you find out?"

Race turned to Zellman, his eyes narrowed. "Because I followed my dad, and I saw." His eyes flitted to me before finding a spot on the floor. It felt like he wasn't talking to us anymore. He was confessing, almost.

"Our dads are brothers and my mom has no idea it was her sister-in-law who destroyed her marriage. I haven't been able to bring myself to tell her. She's got no one—like, *no one* no one. Gram and Gramps died a year ago. They didn't leave any inheritance to my mom, and she's got no friends. She never kept in contact with our other relatives."

There was a beat of silence.

"Shit," Jordan said.

"Destroy your aunt by destroying her son, and that meant using us to do it." Cross' voice was soft. "Right?"

Race looked over and swallowed. "Yeah. I mean, all of the other stuff wasn't exactly a lie. Drake did stay with us for the summer. He talked about the crew system, how he hated it, how he left it because of his girlfriend." He glanced to me, but pressed on. "There was no real plan set before I got here. I saw how Alex has a thing for Bren."

What?

"And then I started kinda liking you guys. So yeah, I guess hurt my cousin, and that'll hurt his mom eventually. I can't go after her directly because how shitty is that, right? But fuck. I want to. I want to tell my mom everything—"

"Except you can't, because you'd be further hurting your mom." Jordan made an understanding sound. "I get it. I do."

I looked around. Zellman and Jordan both offered pitying looks. Cross was on lockdown, drilling holes into Race's skull with his eyes, and I couldn't believe I was hearing or seeing any of this.

"Are you fucking kidding me?"

Four sets of eyes lifted to me.

A guttural rumble ripped from my throat. I was beyond pissed. "Tell your fucking mom! She can do it alone if she has to. It's her decision. Not yours! You're making it worse."

"But—" Confusion clouded Race's face, his mouth pinching in.

I wasn't done. "And what about Drake? Explain. Now."

"Oh." He blinked, shaking his head. "Uh...yeah. What I said was true. Drake left the crew because of you. You didn't know?"

That growl was coming from me again. "Does it look like I knew?!" I snapped.

"Guess not. But yeah, Alex wanted you in the Ryerson crew. Drake told me how he kept bugging him, saying he needed to recruit you."

"Because he's got a thing for her?"

But I knew. That wasn't it.

"Because of my brother, right?"

It made sense. Alex wanted the biggest, baddest, fiercest crew.

Race nodded. "If your crew teams up with your brother's, you guys are the most powerful crew in Roussou. I mean, Channing's already is. They have fewer members than the Ryersons, but they're older. They're—"

"Channing protects this town. Yes. His crew is the most powerful."

My guys all glanced at me, but it was the truth. I was just stating the truth.

"That shit doesn't mean anything to us." Zellman sounded unsure, looking in Jordan's direction.

Race shook his head. "It mattered to Alex, and to Drake. Alex hated that Drake was dating you, but not making you switch crews."

"Our crew didn't form like that," Jordan said. "We don't recruit people."

"But his does," Race said. "We had a fight one night because he was pushing me to go after you. Said I could join up if I brought you with me. The little fuck doesn't get how much I'll do anything to go against *him*."

"That's why Drake quit? Because of me?"

He nodded. "That's why as soon as he graduated last year, Drake spent the summer with us. Alex is ambitious, but stupid. He wanted the crew to start doing illegal crap, like dealing."

"Dealing drugs?"

Race looked at Jordan. "I'm assuming you guys don't do that?"

Jordan looked offended. "We're not a gang. We're friends. We hang out, and we have each other's backs. That's all we do." He seemed to remember where we were, what we were doing. "And we do things like this. On occasion."

Zellman grunted, a half-grin showing.

"But it's not that far of a stretch," Race continued. "You know that. I know that. Why do you think the school staff hates you guys? They think you're bringing in drugs."

There had been gangs in Roussou, but they were pushed out when the crew system started. The biggest gang affiliation we had in town were the Red Demons, but they had an agreement with Chan's crew. I didn't know what it was, but I did know they weren't allowed to roam all around the town. The only place I saw them was at Tuesday Tits. That was it. Their base was somewhere else.

"We're not," I said.

Race turned to me. "Yeah." His voice softened. "Look, I thought about asking you out. I did. But..." His eyes flicked to Cross, then back to me. Race's shoulders lifted, and he straightened up as best he could. "I learned that wasn't going to happen."

I glanced to Cross too.

There was a flicker in the depths of his eyes, something dark, something deep, but then he shut it down. He signaled with a flick of his head to focus on Race again.

I did.

Race shook his head. "Yeah. Well, that's why Drake left."

"Just to be clear," Zellman said after a moment. He spread his arms out in a flat line. "This has nothing to do with Bren's vagina parts." He shot his hands up, his palms out. "And I say that in the most respectful way. You can talk about my dick if you want, B. But it has to be respectful, just like I did."

I rolled my eyes. "Suck my cock, Z."

Jordan barked out a laugh. Cross grinned.

Zellman was still—very, very still. He tilted his head to the side. "You're joking?"

"I'm joking," I assured him. "But I'm going to make you hurt later when I'm not hopped up on painkillers."

He shrugged. "That's fair. You warned me."

Jordan was still laughing, and he pointed to Race. "We're done, right? We got what we wanted? We know what we wanted to know."

"That's it?" Race asked.

"That's it." Jordan nodded.

I was relieved. We understood Race. We knew he wasn't going to hurt us down the road. That's all we needed. He was right. We were bloodhounds. Give us a half-truth and we'd pound you until we got it all. We weren't trying to be assholes, but living this life, living in Roussou, you learn not to trust kind deeds. Good Samaritans were the first to turn on you, a knife in your gut, smiling as you fell down.

Race held his hands up, and Jordan took out a pocket knife. He began cutting the tape away.

"You guys did all that just to ask me why I've been nice to you?" Race asked.

Cross moved to my side. "Truth comes out if people are scared."

When the last of the tape was cut from his wrists, Race leaned forward and pulled at the tape around his ankles. Jordan handed him the knife, and he cut it himself, handing it back when he was done.

Rubbing at his wrists, Race looked around the room. "What are you guys going to do then? About my cousin?"

The guys and I shared a look. Alex had gone after me, and now if he was dealing drugs? He'd gone from being our problem to being a problem for all crews.

The truth was, we'd probably tell my brother, see what he had to say. But for now, Jordan only said, "He'll be dealt with."

"I'm telling the truth." Race kept looking around at us. "I mean it."

"We know," I said.

Jordan left first.

Zellman was second.

I was going to wait, but Cross moved behind me. I stopped at the door.

Race's mouth was slightly open, like he couldn't believe what had just happened.

He wanted to be in. He wanted to know what we were going to do, but that's how this worked. Race wasn't crew.

Cross touched the small of my back. He leaned forward, dropping his voice. "He'll be fine."

And I felt what I'd started to become accustomed to feeling when he touched me.

I felt that same tingle again.

CHAPTER TWENTY-NINE

JORDAN DROPPED US off and Cross snuck inside with me. He slept on the floor of my room. He was gone when I woke this morning—my head pounding and my ribs sore—and I knew it hadn't been a ghost that turned my alarm clock off.

I had to bite my lip to keep from crying as I made my way to the bathroom. I hadn't wanted to take a painkiller again—I didn't like my foggy thoughts—but I needed it this morning. I was sore, and I hated that.

This confirmed my plan to stay home from school for the day, and I found Heather in the kitchen when I padded out of the bathroom. She was dressed, grabbing some coffee. When she saw me, she nearly dropped the coffee pot.

"You stayed home today!"

I paused, the fleeting thought that I was in trouble fading once she broke into a wide smile. She came over, her arms out, then seemed to remember why I was at home. She stopped herself, laughing sheepishly.

A tear slipped out, and she flicked it away.

"Channing's going to be so happy. It's like you're normal." She waved to the kitchen table. "Sit, sit. What do you want to eat? I'll make you something." She opened the fridge door, then shut it. "I'll buy you whatever you want."

I rubbed my eyes. They didn't want to open this morning. "I'll just have coffee."

"Just have coffee, says the seventeen year old." Heather shook her head as she picked up the pot and cleaned off the bottom. She poured me a cup, adding a little milk before bringing it over. "I know I'm officially old because I keep thinking no teenager should be drinking coffee like an adult." She grabbed her cup and slipped into one of the other chairs. "What am I saying, though? My father would still be horrified at *me*." She slapped a hand on the table. "Change of subject. What's your plan for the day?"

I gestured to the living room. "I'm going to be a lazy teenager today."

"Oh!" She silently clapped. "I used to be cool, believe it or not, so my past teenaged self is incredibly embarrassed by how I'm acting, but I almost feel proud of you." She pushed herself up from the table. "Okay. So what do you want? I'll grab your blanket. I'll get all the remote controls for you. Food. Drink. Kleenex, because you never know. Movies—no, we have the DVR. Your phone? Where's your phone?"

This wasn't the Heather I was used to dealing with. She was being motherly, which should've made me feel all sorts of edginess, but today wasn't normal. She was right. I was recuperating. Tomorrow I'd go back to being normal Bren.

"Weren't you going to work?"

"I was." She'd been looking around the kitchen, but now she stood up straight. "I have to call in your absence. For once, you're skipping with permission. I'll do that right now."

"Hey, Heather."

She started for the hallway, but stopped.

I said softly, "You're still cool."

Her mouth snapped shut. Her cheeks bulged out. She blinked rapidly, and then a small cry escaped her mouth. "Oh, Bren." She flicked a hand to her ear, blinking again, a whole bunch. "I'll, uh... I'll—Oh! I need to call."

I almost made her cry.

No. I did make her cry.

It was a weird feeling, not just knowing she cared, but feeling it.

After she kept getting things for me, I finally waved her off.

"Go to work." I had everything I needed around me—my phone, a blanket... I wasn't even sure if I would watch television. "I'm fine. Really."

"Are you sure?"

"Yes. I'm sure. Go."

She still wavered, but then grabbed her phone and purse. "Okay. I'm going to go. I'm going to call your brother. He'll check on you this afternoon, and Bren?" She paused in the doorway. "Please stay here tonight. Don't go out. Just for one night."

I stared at her a moment.

I was used to hard, smart-ass Heather Jax, not this one. I got a glimpse of what she'd be like as a mother, and feeling a lump form in my throat, I nodded. "I'll stay." My voice was a bit hoarse, but she didn't seem to notice.

"Okay." I heard the back door open, and she yelled, "And call if you need anything. Please."

Her car started a minute later. I breathed a little easier once she was gone. It was overwhelming when all of her attention was focused on me, but already I missed it.

It was a lot, but it was a *good* a lot.

And that felt weird too.

⸻

I heard someone coming, but I didn't move.

I had become one with the hill, the trees, the grasshoppers chirping. I felt like I was up above, staring down at myself. I was there, right next to my mom, and I could almost hear her laughing in my ear.

"What have you gotten yourself into now, Bren?"

She would've laughed. She would've shaken her head at me, but there would've been a twinge of concern and fear in her eyes. She would've worried she was to blame.

It was nighttime. I'd stayed home all day until the restlessness kicked in. Heather had called a couple times to check on me, and she'd been right. Channing had brought food for a late lunch, but he'd had to return to the bar. Jordan texted and asked if I needed anything. I was tempted to have them skip and hang out with me, but I didn't. I tried to be a good influence, for once.

When I said I was fine, Jordan replied that he and Zellman were going to kick it at his house after school. That was fine with me. It was in the back of my mind to join, but I'd told Heather I'd stay the day, and that's what I did. Cross texted a few times too, but he wasn't a big texter. I hadn't expected a lot. I hadn't heard from him since school let out, so a part of me already knew what the plan for the evening would be.

At eight, Channing texted that he was heading to Manny's. Heather had to stay for closing, so I knew what their hours would be. He'd stay till she closed, which would be late.

I took that as my cue.

I'd headed out, and I knew who was likely to be standing over me soon.

I opened my eyes now as a shadow fell across me, and there he was.

I smiled. "How'd I know you'd come?"

Cross grinned back. "You're my best friend." He sat next to me, drawing his knees up, his arms hanging over them.

"You okay?" His fingers touched my skin where my shirt had ridden up. He wasn't just asking about the Ryerson fight.

I jerked my head in a nod. My voice wasn't working. Things were changing with Cross and me.

He had touched me again, and I liked it.

I was starting to *need* him to touch me more. *What would happen if I didn't stop this?*

I tried to think of being with Cross, and then not. Of finding him with someone else. I tried to think how it'd feel if he walked away from me like Drake had. It had hurt with Drake—I couldn't lie about that—but it would be devastating with Cross.

Pure agony sliced through my chest. That couldn't happen. Ever.

"You're never going to leave, are you?" It wasn't like his answer would settle a future problem, but I couldn't help myself.

I waited for him to respond, and my skin began to burn under his hand. I wanted his fingers to move, explore. I wanted them to slip under my shirt, and I tried to think of a way to lift it for him without moving a muscle.

"What?" His eyebrows drew together. "Where'd that come from?"

"Are you?"

"No." He turned to face me. His eyes bore into mine. "No matter what happens, I'm not going anywhere."

I felt my throat tightening again, that same damned wetness forming in my eyes. I curved my pinkie around his.

"We're crew," he added. "We don't leave."

Oh. "Yeah," I managed. "We're crew."

"Seriously, are you okay?"

I nodded. "I'm okay."

My eyes went back to the house, a different sort of yearning burrowing a hole in my chest. I felt Cross' entire body soften, and he moved his arm to rest over my shoulder. His pinkie never unhooked from mine, and I lifted my hand to keep holding on.

He rested his head against the side of mine. "You never love the ones who are going to go."

"What do you mean?"

"That's why you dated Drake. You didn't care if he left."

I almost sucked in my breath. It was true. I hadn't realized until now. "That's why I liked him?"

"Lust is not exclusive to need and love. You lusted after him. You didn't need him."

A ball dropped from my throat to my stomach. He had no idea what he'd just said to me, and I didn't respond.

I shifted my body to rest back into him.

We'd sat like this so many times, but this time, Cross did something new.

He leaned back, his arms bracing behind him, and I almost fell into him. He caught me, easing me to lie on his chest, and wrapped his arm around my waist.

He was holding me.

And I let him.

We didn't talk for the rest of the night. We never moved either.

CHAPTER THIRTY

IT WAS DAWN when I walked back into my house, Cross right behind me.

I was going to get dressed, and then we'd go to his house so he could do the same before school. It felt right having this closeness with him again—not that we hadn't been close before, but there'd been a brief interval when we hadn't been himandme, just him and me.

I'd stepped into the hallway, turning toward my bedroom when I heard the floor creak behind me.

I stiffened, knowing it wasn't Cross. He was just coming through the screen door.

"Why do you do that?"

My brother.

My heart dropped. He sounded mad, and I turned to find that he was. Or he wasn't. He had bags under his eyes. He seemed to have aged in just the few hours since I last saw him.

He wore a ripped T-shirt and grey sleeping pants.

I took a beat to consider my options.

Technically, I'd fucked up. He had been the nice one, checking on me yesterday, giving me space after the Ryerson fight. And Heather had asked me not to leave, but as I sat in the house yesterday, it had hit me.

If I followed their rules, they would keep piling them on.

If I became the dutiful sister/daughter, their expectations would rise.

I knew the end, because it's the end most families had in mind for their children: he would want me to be normal.

I couldn't do normal. That meant leaving the crew, and all the things we did as a crew.

There was no option.

"Just because you got stuck with the guardianship doesn't mean you get to parent me," I told him. Pain sliced through me, but I raised my chin defiantly. "You never had that privilege, and you certainly lost it when you were absent from my life for five years."

"I've been here for the last two."

"Not really," I shot back. "You've been fighting. You've been managing a bar and a girlfriend." I was tempted to name the other thing I knew had happened between him and Heather, but that wasn't talked about. She'd never said it. He never had either. So I wouldn't, but I ached inside too.

Cross closed the door quietly, and Channing came forward. When he saw him, he shook his head.

"Fuck. Now I get it." He looked at me, sorrow in his eyes. "I get why Mom was so frustrated." He gestured to Cross. "It sucks being on the other side."

"Bullshit." I couldn't hold it in any longer. My voice rose. "You were gone, all the goddamn time—when she had to go to the hospital, when someone had to stay with her in there, when someone had to hold her hand, hold her hair back when she puked. Shit. Do you know how many blankets I got for her? How many times I cleaned her face, or moved her heating pad? Do you know I have vomit permanently burned into my nostrils? And that smell. Cancer has a smell. Did you know that?" *No.* I shook my head. "You were doing what I'm doing now. You were gone."

He rubbed his forehead. "Bren."

I shook my head. "You don't get to say sorry now. She's dead. I needed you then, not now. I'm good now."

"You're not good."

"Oh, yes, I am."

I was shaking. I didn't realize until Cross touched my arm to stop the trembling.

I strained forward, all of my muscles tense, rigid. I was ready to attack, or be attacked.

"I'm sorry, Bren." My brother's voice dropped to a murmur. "I really am."

"You missed my birthday."

"What?" He dropped his hands from his forehead, trying to figure out what I was talking about.

"My birthdays. You missed them. All of them."

His forehead wrinkled, and he cursed under his breath, "Shit."

"I turned thirteen, fourteen, fifteen. I invited you to all of them. You didn't come to one."

"God, Bren. I'm sor—"

"I'm aware," I cut him off. "Saying you're sorry and being sorry are two totally different things. I'm immune by now."

He stared at me, long and hard. I felt like I'd pulled off a layer and showed him the underside of me, and he wasn't sure if he liked it or not—if he liked me or not. Finally, his shoulders lowered.

"I've been thinking this is normal teenage stuff, but it's not, is it?"

I pressed my lips together. And even though everything in me suddenly hurt, my eyes were dry. I wouldn't shed a tear, not for him, not for—I swallowed over a lump—not for what happened.

"Bren." He moved toward me, reaching out.

I evaded him, backing away toward my room, but Cross moved in front of me. I blinked, and he appeared. He was protecting me against my own brother. No, that wasn't totally right. He was shielding me.

His back was to me, and he held his hands up. "Stop."

Channing did, looking between us before his head lowered.

He nodded. "Okay. Okay. I got it."

He turned back to the kitchen, but stopped a few feet away. I hadn't moved. Neither had Cross, and my brother looked between the two of us again. A soft sigh left him.

"I *am* sorry, Bren."

I looked away. My dry eyes weren't staying dry. I couldn't have that.

"I was stupid and selfish back then, and I was a prick. I know it. Trust me. I fucked up other relationships during that time too," he added, sounding haunted.

Goddamn him.

I didn't want to hear those words. I didn't want to hear how he seemed to be genuine.

Air hissed from my closed lips, and I swung into my room.

Goddamn! That fucker—now? NOW?! Why now? I shook my head. No, no. I wouldn't go there. It was bullshit. Everything was bullshit. This was the safest way to live.

I went into my bathroom, but I didn't close the door. I stood there, in front of the mirror, and held on to the counter.

Cross stood in the doorway. He didn't say anything, but he didn't need to.

I looked up, feeling like someone had taken a battering ram to my body. "Did you buy that bullshit?"

He looked at me, his eyes uncomfortably solemn. "Yeah."

I frowned, grimacing. A small knife went in me at his words. "You're supposed to be on my side."

"I am."

God. He sounded so calm, so steady, so real. He sounded like the foundation I needed to handle all this shit in my life. I wanted to rail. I wanted to do something to Channing—make him mad, push him away—but I couldn't. He wasn't pushing me. I wanted to sever what he'd just done by making the first advances toward something good.

I couldn't handle that, and I glared at Cross. "Say he's a dick. Say something."

"I don't need to say anything." Again, so strong. He followed that up with, "I'm here for whatever you decide, but you don't really want me to say those words, and you know it. Not deep down."

I hurt.

It wasn't the injuries this time, and that's why it hurt even worse.

I adjusted my grip on the counter. I felt the world swirling under me, like I had since I was eight years old, and I did what I always did. I held on and waited. Once the world stopped moving, I'd keep going.

This time, when it stopped I looked over at Cross. I felt stripped naked in front of him. He saw me.

He frowned, tilting his head. "What are you thinking?"

I swallowed. "I don't want to. That's the problem."

He stared, long and hard, and then he asked, "You feel like not talking today?"

I had to remember to hold on or I'd fall. The floor could dip out from underneath me at any moment. Everything was spinning.

I nodded, my neck stiff. "Please."

"Okay." He gestured to my body. "How are the bruises? Still sore?"

Numb right now. "Fine."

"You're such a liar."

I shrugged, just staring at him. I didn't dare look anywhere else.

"I'll call the guys. We can do a crew skip day."

That sounded heavenly. I tried to smile. I failed. "You know all the right moves to make a girl happy."

He barked out a laugh. "Doubtful. Something tells me I've got things to learn yet." We stared at each other again, and this time there was some extra heat. It was long, and slow, and smoldering, and I couldn't stop myself.

I stared right back, and somehow, in some magical and miraculous way, under the layers of shit inside of me, I felt something good happening.

It scared the crap out of me.

CHAPTER THIRTY-ONE

"WHAT HAPPENED TO YOU?"

The next day, when I finally went back to school, Taz cornered me at my locker. Well, her locker was there too, but she already had her books in hand, and she didn't make a move to open her locker. I turned around, gathering my things, and closed my locker.

"Good morning to you too."

She wasn't looking at me—her eyes cut to the side like she was *refusing* to look at me.

"You were supposed to make sure Race's dad did the sponsor ad, but that was days ago. You've been gone from school, and my brother skipped school yesterday too."

Jordan and Zellman as well, I added silently. We'd hung out in Jordan's storage shed the whole day. We played video games and watched movies. And we napped, which I was most happy about. The guys smoked. A few beers were consumed, but that was it. We each told our favorite crew memories, and my ribs had hurt from laughter.

It was one of the best days I'd had in a while.

"No one told you what happened?" I asked her.

She frowned and still didn't look at me. "No. What happened?"

"I went to find Race, but Alex Ryerson and his crew jumped me."

"WHAT?!" She finally looked up and saw me. She let out a shriek. "YOUR FACE! What happened?!"

"What I said. Ryerson and his crew jumped me." I'd used makeup this morning, and I covered a lot of it, but I hadn't been able to hide all of the bruises.

"Oh my God."

I nodded, hearing the first bell. "No one's said anything?"

"No. I mean..." She tightened her hold on her books, moving them to her hip as she reached to open her locker. Her eyes remained glued to my face, even as she swung open the door. It almost hit her, but she didn't seem fazed. "Man," she said under her breath. "Things *have* been tense. Cross wouldn't leave Jordan and Zellman's side, but he doesn't normally anyway, at least when you're not here. I've been busy with the charity planning. We're hoping to get everything done by the end of the month since we have early Homecoming this year."

"Yeah." I looked up as Race came around the corner. He kept going, but he glanced over. There was no reaction on his face, but I don't know what I was expecting. He'd been honest with us, and we'd shut him out.

"About that," I said. "I won't be able to ask him after all."

She shut her locker closed. "Why? What happened?"

Cross came down the hallway now, moving the opposite direction from Race.

"Nothing," I murmured, watching his progression. "You can ask him, but I won't be."

Cross saw me, but then he noticed Race. He straightened up, his face stoic as the two watched each other pass in silence. Neither broke stride.

"You just went pale," Taz said, a deep frown on her face. "What just happened? What is going on with you?"

"What?" I asked, but then Cross was here.

He opened his locker. "What are you guys talking about?"

"You!" Taz said.

Cross paused. "Me?"

"You didn't tell me what happened to Bren." Taz's tone was accusing. "She's my friend too, Cross."

"Oh." Realization flooded, and his old grin came back. He shrugged, grabbing some of his books. "It's crew business. You know we can't talk about it."

"That's not true. You guys tell me stuff."

"Some stuff," he corrected her, shutting his locker.

As soon as he stepped away, a protected pocket formed around him in the flurry of activity. Students gave him a wide berth, weaving around him, and it only got bigger when I stepped in next to him. We began to walk to our classes, and Taz got jostled as she walked on the outside. Students were darting around her, choosing her side rather than going near Cross.

As I broke off, heading to my class, Taz started arguing with him. I glanced back, automatically grinning, then realized Cross had been watching me. He had tuned his sister out, and I paused in the doorway.

Once again, I felt a stirring inside of me.

I didn't altogether like it, but I couldn't deny that it excited me. It scared me too, and most terrifying—I didn't want it to go away.

Cross' eyes darkened, narrowing until Taz stopped talking and looked at me. The spell, or whatever it was, broke, and I waved.

"See you later."

Cross nodded, the slight blaze I'd seen in his eyes vanishing.

He was back to normal, but as I walked into my first class, I knew I wasn't. I was most definitely not normal, and sliding into my desk, I had a feeling this was just the beginning. There'd be more changes to come.

"Miss Monroe!" Mr. Jenston boomed as he came into the room, holding his briefcase high. He plopped it down onto his desk and jerked his thumb to the door. "Don't even get comfortable. You're wanted in the office."

"What?" I sat forward. "For what?"

"Uh?" He pretended to think about it, his eyes moving to the ceiling. Like Taz, he wasn't looking at me. "I don't know. Maybe because you weren't excused for your absence yesterday? Or maybe it's your delinquent behavior? Take your pick. What sort of trouble did you get into on the way to school today? Did you stab anyone?" He scoffed. "Yet?"

The class quieted.

I heard a girl gasp behind me.

I leaned forward, rising to my feet.

"Take that back." Jordan stood just inside the door, his hands in fists as he glared at our teacher.

Mr. Jenston had been leaning over his desk, staring at his computer screen. Seeing Jordan, panic flashed in his eyes, and he snapped upright.

"Excuse me?" He tried to glower back, but his voice shook a little. He ran a hand down the front of his tie.

"You heard me." Jordan moved forward a step. "Take that back."

All eyes came to me, and I would've liked to feel some triumph at the fear in our teacher's eyes, but I didn't. He looked at my face now, and a shadow crossed over his, but it didn't matter. He couldn't take back his words or the way they were delivered.

I rocked in place, but I kept by my desk. "You disrespected me."

"Look—"

"Do it again," Jordan growled. "Disrespect her one more time."

Beads of sweat formed on our teacher's forehead.

"I'm not—"

Jordan moved in a flash, but so did I.

Jordan went for the teacher, and I went for him.

"Stop it." I shoved him back.

We couldn't touch a teacher. Everything would be at risk then. Not just us, or me, but everything. The whole crew system.

There were gasps behind us. Some guy said, "Holy shit." But other than that, silence.

A guy from the back row ran from the room. The door slammed shut behind him, and Jordan and I shared a look. We only had a few moments before school security would be here.

I turned around, slowly, to face Mr. Jenston.

He was scared. I understood, and a part of me—the part that wanted to be a good student, a good kid—ached at that. I never wanted a teacher to fear me, but I was not normal. I never could be.

CREW

Maybe one day they'd know why, but I hoped not.

"You know my name. You know my family," I said quietly. "And yet you still talk to me like that." I paused, making sure his eyes were on mine. I felt my knife against my skin. It was there to calm me, and a part of me wanted to pull it out. I didn't dare. This teacher wouldn't understand how it was my security blanket.

I spoke even more quietly, so only Mr. Jenston and Jordan could hear. "You dismissed me from this class, and you never once looked at me." I pointed to my face. "This is why I was gone. You treated me just now like I'm invisible, like I'm not worth a second look, or even a first look. My absence was excused, and I did nothing this morning except come to school. And when I got here, you attacked me. That's how *we* view it. When you talk to us like that, you attack *us*."

"That's no—that's not…"

He couldn't talk. His eyes cut to Jordan's, and Jordan stepped back. I felt him.

Mr. Jenston's head lowered. He pointed to the camera in the corner. "That's not going to show what just happened here, not accurately."

Dread traced up my spine.

"Look." Mr. Jenston coughed, tugging at his collar. He looked in pain, or humiliated. I was going with humiliation. Or so I hoped.

"I can speak up for you, but it will look like you're threatening me. They won't believe me. They'll enforce further action against you both, but mostly against you, Bren." The corners of his mouth softened. "They'll blame you, so the best way to stop anything else from happening is to get that video."

"What do we do?" Jordan asked over my shoulder.

CHAPTER THIRTY-TWO

WE RAN OUT of the classroom as Cross ran in.

We almost crashed. The guy who'd dashed from the room was right behind him.

Jordan's jaw went slack. "Thought you narced."

The guy shook his head, but ducked around us and went back into the room.

"What happened?" Cross stepped between us, grabbing my hand. "Roy said you might need help."

"We had a situation. It looks bad on the security tapes."

Cross let go. "Got it. Go." He nodded after Jordan, who was already down the hall.

"What are you going to do?"

"You tell him," Jordan said to me. "I'm going to start."

"We gotta get that tape before they see it," I explained. Cross settled next to me and moved to catch Jordan.

"What are you saying?" I could hear the secretary, Mrs. Cooke, asking as we opened the door to the office.

The security cameras were kept in a locked cupboard near her desk. No one was paid to watch them while they were rolling, so chances were good that no one would see the incident until they were notified of it. If it came down to us versus the teacher, the school would ask the other students in the classroom what had happened. They'd likely side with us. Most did. Narcs were pieces of shit. It was a universal rule.

Race sat in one seat in the office. Two other students sat across from him, a few seats down.

CREW

"I'm telling you, Marjorie," Jordan said, nodding seriously. "Call the security staff. There was a fight in one of the PE classes. I heard it myself."

"What?" She reached for her keys, fumbling through them and wheeling her chair over to the security cameras.

"You don't have time! Get the security staff." Jordan pointed down the hallway. "You know they're back there, taking their morning break. Go get them, Miss Marjorie. Get them! They need help."

Cross and I shared a look, holding back grins.

Marjorie Cooke was Mrs. Marjorie Cooke, but since his first day freshman year, Jordan had always called her Miss Marjorie. She melted every time.

Well," she said under her breath, patting her hair. She cleared her throat. "I don't know." She bit her lip, palming the keys.

"Fine." Jordan leaned back, stepping away from the desk, and shrugged. "But it's on you. Who knows who the Ryerson crew is beating up."

"Ryerson crew?!" She shot to her feet. "This is crew-related?"

"Of course it is. I wouldn't be here otherwise."

She went past me, and I stepped into her. My fingers grazed hers.

She started to snap at me, but when she saw who I was, she gave me a distracted smile. "Oh, Bren, honey. You don't look so good." Then she straightened her shirt, smoothing her collar.

"Go, Miss Marjorie!"

She gave Jordan a look before hurrying down the hallway. "You should've said this was crew-related from the beginning."

And as she hurried to the break room, I scurried behind her desk, holding her keys.

Jordan smirked down at me, folding his arms.

I found the right key and unlocked the cabinet as Jordan and Cross moved so they were blocking the view of Mrs. Cooke's desk, yet still standing casually, as if they were waiting for her to come back.

"Hurry," Jordan said.

I rewound the tape, effectively deleting our altercation. It would start recording again where I let it go, but we wouldn't be in it. After I was done, I stood up, satisfied.

"It's not totally erased."

Jordan and I looked over at Race. He had leaned forward, a set look on his face.

"You're helping again?" I asked.

Race looked between us before letting out some air and standing up. "Move back."

I did, and he came around the desk.

Race hit a bunch of buttons, ones I hadn't known were there, and a couple seconds later, all of the screens went blue. He backed up, closing the cupboard and relocking it. "You have to erase everything, otherwise there's a memory storage thing. It's gone now."

Jordan gave him a nod. "Thank you." He motioned to Cross and me. "Let's go."

"Coming." I started out behind him, but turned back.

Cross was right behind me, and we both looked back at Race.

He'd dropped the keys back on the desk and returned to his chair. His gaze flicked up to us, and this time, I felt like I saw the real guy in there. There was sadness.

He sat alone in that chair, and it seemed a metaphor for his life. He *was* alone.

Cross must've thought the same because he dipped his head in a nod. "Thanks, man."

Race dipped his head down, giving us a wave. "See you guys later."

Cross nodded back in acknowledgement, and we stepped out of the office just as a woman came in—Race's mom. I recognized her right away. She had his same round face, the same pinched nose, and eyes a little too close. But I saw her sadness too.

She went in behind us, and we heard her say, "Race, honey."

"Hey, Mom."

Cross touched my back, a silent urge to keep going.

The security guys would go to the fields. They'd find no one, figure it was nothing, and return to their break. No one would think anything. No one would say a word.

We'd be fine. Knowing that, some pressure lifted from my shoulders.

Then Cross said, "I know what Race said the other night, but he still likes you."

His words stopped me.

Maybe. Jordan had gone ahead, gone back to our class, so it was just Cross and me in that hall. For a moment, we had a pocket of privacy at school, and I felt emotions flare up in me that I needed to acknowledge.

There could've been a Race and me. In another year, another school, another time. But not today. Not this year. Not at this school. Not in this hallway.

Cross was worried about Race. I could see it in his eyes.

I should've stopped. I should've stopped him, stopped me, stopped everything.

But I didn't want to.

I looked him right in the face, and I didn't flinch when I said, "It doesn't matter now."

I stared at the guy I had feelings for.

CHAPTER
THIRTY-THREE

DINNER. 8 TONIGHT. PIZZERIA.

I stared at the text Channing sent me, but I couldn't believe it. I re-read it. Still there. I read it a third time. Nope. It wasn't changing. I even went letter by letter to make sure.

According to this text—if it was sent by my brother, if someone hadn't stolen his phone or one of his crew guys wasn't playing a prank—he wanted to meet me at one of the only normal hangouts in Roussou.

We had the springs not far away. And there was Manny's in Fallen Crest. After that, to each their own. We had Jordan's warehouse. The Ryerson crew hung out at Alex's house.

But the Pizzeria was the only local public option, and it was mostly filled up with team events or family dinners. The basement had a pool table, foosball, and an air hockey machine. There were a few other machines too. I think they had a dance-hop. Those weren't my scene.

I texted back. **Really?**

Really. Meet me there. Moose is coming.

I thumbed back, **What's my middle name?**

Rayna. **Loser. This is your brother. I'm not fucking around.**

Okay. So it was him.

I had to make sure.

Another buzz. **See you there. Invite whoever.**

That perked me up. I was almost smiling when I put my phone away.

Cross was waiting for me at our lockers, and seeing my face, he stepped backward. "Who are you? What have you done with my best friend?"

"Lame. Get a new line."

He laughed. "I will." He nodded to where I'd put my phone. "Your brother?"

"Yeah," I told him. "You want to come?"

Suspicion clouded his face. He tilted his head to the side. "You sure? Jordan and Z will be pissed if they aren't invited."

I shrugged. "So invite them."

"Yeah?"

I nodded. I'd been down with the whole "the more the merrier" attitude when it came to my brother's dinners. If he was asking for me to invite them, then hell to the yes. I wasn't going to pass that up. Besides, I was heading into foreign territory. I didn't hang out at the Pizzeria.

It could be the new cheerleading headquarters for all I knew.

That evening I discovered I was partially right.

We walked in after hanging out at Jordan's for most of the afternoon, and I saw Sunday Barnes, Monica, and a whole other table full of them. I recognized Tabatha Sweets. She was considered the top of the top on the popularity charts for the girls in our grade.

They took up the entire back section of the Pizzeria, with the other tables full of some of the popular athletes too. All were Normals.

I scanned for Taz, but she wasn't here.

Wait. Nope.

Her head popped up from the back table, and seeing us, her eyes widened.

"Bren? Cross?"

Jordan and Zellman were behind us so I moved aside. At her question, that entire section had quieted and turned to take us in.

"Oh, hell yeah." Zellman pushed past us, beelining for their table.

Sunday sat with her elbows on the table. Her hands shielded her eyes as she stared down at the tablecloth. Monica's head was pushed close to hers. They were whispering.

Z didn't care.

A small partition blocked off that section from the rest of the place, but he hopped right over it and came around their table, ignoring everyone else as he dropped into Taz's empty seat. He draped his arm around Sunday's shoulders and pushed his head in too, as if conspiring with the other two.

Sunday stiffened, but she didn't push him away. He only moved closer.

Monica backed away, watching them a moment before shrugging and turning to watch us with everyone else. A few of the athlete guys were frowning at Z.

I had to wonder how they always handled the guys. Until this year, Monica was usually around Cross. Sunday and Zellman had their thing. And I knew Jordan had slept with half those girls.

Cross had slept with the other half in between when he was seeing Monica, or whatever they had been doing.

Those guys would usually have ruled the school. But not in Roussou. The jocks/athletes/populars were almost second-class here, though they liked to walk around with the same swagger I'd seen from popular guys at other schools. They still had the cocky attitude, just nothing to back it up, at least against the crew guys.

I wondered if the Normals had their own social classes, with a hierarchy and rules? They must've.

Cross nudged me. "Where do you want to sit?"

The hostess had been asking me, her eyes darting between us as she bit her lip. She held three menus in her hands, tucked in front of her body, and they were shaking, just a little.

The girl was scared of us.

I felt bad for her, because she didn't look like one of the girls who was friends with the Sunday Barnes' of the world.

Wait...

I looked more closely at her. "You look familiar."

She blushed, tucking a strand of her almost-white hair behind her ear. She was thin almost the point of seeming frail. "I work at Manny's too. I'm A—"

"Ava." I wasn't around Manny's that much, but I was there enough to have seen her. Quite a bit. "You work here too?"

She nodded, rotating the menus so the one on top was in the back. She repeated the motion. She kept doing it as she answered, "Yes. I have bills, you know?" A shy smile. Her eyes skirted to Cross, and her face warmed before she looked down again. "Did you want to sit near the back section? With your friends?"

"No." *God, no.* "There are two more coming, so put us at a table where you can sit six or seven comfortably," I told her. "Actually, Moose counts as two. Make it eight people comfortably."

Cross gestured to an emptier section across the room. "How about over there?"

"Sure." Ava grabbed a few more menus and came out from behind the hostess stand. "Follow me."

She led us toward the table.

Jordan held up a hand. "Yo, Z. You coming?"

"Yeah, yeah." Z went right back to whispering to Sunday, who seemed to be melting with each word he said. She dissolved into a sighing mess before our eyes.

We were passing by their section when suddenly Tabatha Sweets stood up. Her chair scraped against the floor, and her hands found her hips. She lifted her head, an alluring smile on her face. Brushing her hair back, she called, "Hey. Can some of us come too?"

Jordan stopped in his tracks, staring right at her.

Unblinking, her gaze roamed from him to Cross, to me, narrowing slightly, and then past me to where Ava had stopped to see what was going on.

"What do you say?" she called again.

I didn't know Tabatha Sweets that well. I knew she was their leader, but that was about it. She led the first tier. I'd never heard rumors that she was mean, that she was a bully, that she was easy, that she was stuck-up. Nothing. She was just the top. That's how Taz always put it.

She smiled at Cross. "Hi, Cross."

He wasn't even looking at her. He was staring right at me, and he smirked, as if reading my mind.

I refused to let anything show, but I asked, "Jordan? Did you want to sit with them?"

My tone was casual, not friendly, but not stiff.

He flashed me a grin, shaking his head. "Nah. I'm good. But maybe another night, Sweets?" He gave her a smirk.

"Yeah." Her smile remained, but it tightened. "Maybe." Her eyes darted to Cross again. She didn't say anything else, but it looked like she wanted to.

Cross nodded to Ava. "Sorry about that. We'll follow you."

We sat in the corner.

A different server brought over water, then soda. We had just gotten our second round of drinks when a hush fell over the Pizzeria.

I didn't need to look up to know why.

My brother had arrived.

I kept my eyes glued to the menu, not needing to see the sick worship Channing always received. I'd read the same sentence ten times before Channing and Moose got to our table.

"Hey, guys." Channing moved around, taking the empty seat on my left. He faced the rest of the restaurant, his back to the window. Moose sat next to him.

I'd been right. He pushed back one of the extra chairs and moved his over to take all the space. His massive shoulders hunched forward, but not in a sheepish way. He was trying to get comfortable, if that was possible. Moose could've told me he ate ostrich eggs as a snack, and I would've believed him. (Though, I don't support that.)

"Bren." He gave me a friendly smile.

"Hi."

Channing had been watching me. I ignored him, and he sighed. "Really?" he asked under his breath.

Zellman chose now to make his entrance. He literally jumped into the seat beside Moose, leapfrogging over the back of the chair as he clamped a hand around Moose's bicep. "I think this is as big as my head. What's your secret?" Z's grin was lopsided. "Vegan organic egg whites for every single meal of your life and for a midnight snack?"

Moose barked out a laugh, grabbed Zellman, and pulled him in for a headlock. "Let's see if it is." He flexed, his bicep pushing against Z's face.

Jordan's eyes got big. "Dude. It is. Oh my God. Look. Side by side, it's the same size." He pulled his phone out and snapped a picture.

"No way." Z grabbed for it, showing Moose.

And that was just the start. Z wanted to see what else matched the size of Moose's bicep.

As they kept taking photos, I began to believe they were going to do a whole collage. Jordan insisted he didn't know what Pinterest was, but I didn't believe him.

"You guys come in here a lot?"

Channing surprised everyone with that question.

The bicep-comparison photo session was paused.

Jordan lowered his phone and shrugged. "I guess. I don't know. It's okay."

Z propped his elbows on the table, a rapt expression raising his eyebrows. "Why? Are you getting into the pizza business?"

But Channing just leaned back in his seat. "I don't know."

"Really?" Z leaned over the table.

"Dude. That'd be amazing." Jordan held up a fist to Z, who met it with his own.

"You serious?" Moose asked.

Channing put his hand on the back of my chair. I wasn't looking at him, but he sounded bemused. "Maybe. It'd be an interesting business idea, don't you think?"

Moose shook his head. "Scratch is going to go ape-shit."

"Why?" Channing let go of my chair and pulled up close to the table again. "It wouldn't compete with the bar."

"Because you're already hardly ever there. Scratch says he's been running the whole thing by himself."

I looked up at that. "Really?" I turned to my brother. "Don't take our cousin for granted. It's not fair if he's the only one handling the bar."

The guys got all quiet.

I knew why. Everyone probably did.

It was rare for Channing to be questioned.

And my brother wasn't disturbed. He shrugged, picking up a water. He grinned at me, winking. "You worried about me, Bren? Don't want me to isolate myself?"

I flushed. Asshole. He was taking a shot at me.

I twisted forward so fast, my chair scraped against the floor. "Never mind. Do what you want."

I grabbed my water too, sipping through the straw until half of it was gone.

Conversation died, and I knew it was my fault. I should've let the guys pepper Channing with questions. I should've just kept my mouth shut, but I hadn't. And now it was awkward.

"I'm sorry." Channing's words were soft.

I tensed, but didn't turn toward him.

"I didn't mean that how it came out," he added. "Scratch has been busting my balls for being too involved with things going on. That was the reason for the bad joke."

Moose snorted. "You should never joke, Chan. Ever. You're the worst funniest person I know."

"Worst funniest?" I could hear my brother smiling. "We doing this same joke? Let me say my part. 'You need to go to college, Moose. Get a real education.'"

"Ha! Says the guy who barely finished high school." Moose slapped a hand on the table.

"Agh!" The server had approached, her order pad in hand. She jerked at the sound, and the pad went flying. It landed in front of Zellman, who started cracking up.

CREW

"Oh. Oh my gosh!" She scrambled for it, but Z was already reading from it.

"Look, guys." He pointed at Jordan. "You're 'tl gy'." He pointed to himself. "I must be 'wrd gy." He twisted around in his chair. "Is that for *weird* or *word*? Because I'll own up to both. Or, no. Wait." He plucked the pencil from her hand and crossed out something on the pad, scribbling another word. "There. I'll be 'fny gy.' Funny guy. That's my role generally."

Jordan snorted, even Cross was grinning.

A softness zinged me and I said, "We know you have layers, Z. You just hide them better than everyone."

Everyone stilled around the table.

Jordan and Cross watched Z for his reaction. My brother and Moose fell silent.

Even Ava seemed to be waiting.

Then Z coughed, a look in his eyes mirroring what I'd felt. He ducked his head a bit, sneaking a look at me from under his eyelashes. "I'll write you as 'pfs girl'." His grin was sly. "Pretty fucking sexy."

I frowned. I'd expected a different response, but shrugged. It was what it was.

"Thanks, Z."

Seeing the girl's embarrassment, Zellman took pity and offered the pad back. "I'm just giving you a hard time. I don't mean anything by it. Really."

She reached out cautiously. When he didn't snatch the pad away, she took it, and her smile seemed less mortified. "Thank you."

We weren't all just tough, just about sex, just about fighting, just about being loyal to each other. There was more. We didn't show it often, but we could be kind too. Zellman had just proven that.

Pride bloomed in me, and as the girl started taking our orders, a lot less nervous now, Zellman caught my eye. He motioned towards his phone and I pulled mine out, seeing a text from him.

Pretty fucking smart.

I got choked up. Legit.

He gave me his half-grin, and I typed back, **thanx.**

For some reason, it didn't seem such a hardship to be here right now.

⁓

Channing asked as we were leaving dinner, "Going home? Want a ride?"

Cross spoke up, "I got her."

They shared a look before Channing nodded slowly. "Yeah. Okay."

He and Moose headed to his truck, while the rest of us hung back.

Jordan rubbed a hand over his jaw. "Uh. Yeah." He and Z glanced at each other. "We're, uh... We're going to head back in. Is that okay?"

Most of the Normals had still been there when we left— especially the girls. As the families headed home, their table had just gotten louder. I'd stopped by once after returning from the bathroom, and Taz had told me the girls were hanging around as long we did.

"They want the guys to come over," she'd explained.

So I wasn't surprised.

Cross nodded. "That's cool. We'll see you guys tomorrow."

"What are you two going to do?"

I had no plans, so I waited for Cross to say.

He shrugged. "We'll figure something out."

Jordan grinned. "It's just nine thirty. You guys could do homework. Study for tomorrow. Be good students."

Zellman laughed.

Cross smirked. "We're already good students."

"Speak for yourself." I shook my head.

Smart students, maybe. Good students, no. Well, for me. I was in agreement with Jordan on that one.

As soon as they went back inside, I went with Cross to his truck. I'd left my Jeep at the house.

Once we were going, he noted, "You were quiet tonight."

I yawned, slouching down in my seat, getting comfortable. "I'm fine."

"You sure?"

I nodded. I was. I didn't know why, but I was. Rolling my head toward him, I asked, "Where are we headed?"

"I thought maybe we'd go to our spot."

Oh.

"That sound okay with you?"

It wasn't the same as the pride I'd felt at dinner, but another warm sensation flooded me. I knew I was smiling, and I was staring, and I didn't care. Going to our spot would be the perfect ending to the night.

I said as much. "I think that sounds great."

We both fell silent until we'd settled in to watch over my old house.

As I curled down next to Cross, my eyes growing heavy, I couldn't help but think that tonight had been one of the best I'd had in a while.

CHAPTER THIRTY-FOUR

"WHAT ARE YOU doing with my cousin?"

Two days later, I was grabbing my books out of my locker when Alex came up behind me. Déjà vu hit me, hard.

I turned around. This couldn't be right.

He couldn't be asking me *that* question.

Nope. It was.

"Are you kidding me?" I growled, slamming my locker shut.

My response quieted the entire hallway. My needle that went from caring, to kinda caring, to beyond caring, to not giving a shit—it went straight from lying dormant all the way to *soo* not giving a shit. It didn't matter who watched this scene play out, because it was high-time something happened to Alex.

"You're in my face?!" I asked him. "After what your crew did?"

He glowered back at me, looking like he'd been forced to seek me out and wanted to be anywhere else. His forehead creased. "I got my ass kicked on two occasions now because of you. That has to count for something. My own cousin beat me up."

I closed my eyes and waited. I counted to five before I looked at him again.

"You're an idiot. Are you aware of that?"

Alex tipped his head back.

Yes. Apparently, *I* was the one irritating *him*. So silly of me.

I was starting to feel a little reckless. It'd been nagging me, for reasons I didn't understand. Maybe I'd been waiting to be called to the office after the teacher/security video thing earlier this week. Or maybe all the stuff with Cross had filled my head with confusing thoughts and more confusing feelings. Or maybe it was because I'd been watching this fucker walk around the school, and every day that he *thought* he got away with hurting me, he got more and more cocky.

"Alex, do you know what your problem is?" I didn't wait for him to respond. "Because you do have one, and that's why you're tangling with my crew. It's not actually me."

"Yeah, it is." He flicked a hand toward me, short and dismissive. "It's because you're in a crew, you're in *that* crew, and you're a female. I wouldn't have these problems if you were a guy."

I'd expected an idiotic response. I got an asinine one instead. Goddamn, he was pissing me off. Anger rolled over in my stomach, but I didn't move.

If I moved, I'd attack.

"You are the reason the term *victim-blaming* was created," I said slowly.

He frowned. "Huh?"

I couldn't. Not today.

Calm down, Bren. Calm down.

He gave me a look. "I know your crew is looking to work us over. I got that coming. I know that. I'm okay with it. I started both fights, so we get the payback. But my question stands. What are you doing with my cousin?"

"You're all caring and concerned now?"

Alex shrugged. "I can just tell. Something's off with him, and the only thing he's had a crab crawled up his ass about is you and your crew." He crossed his arms over his chest. "So what is it? What'd you do?"

I could only stare for a moment. Then I laughed. I cursed in my head. And I went back to laughing. I finished up by shaking my head. "Are you fucking *kidding* me?"

"I—"

I shot forward, shoving my face right in his. "You touch me without permission. You touch me a *second* time without permission. You and your crew jump me. Then you come up to me and ask what *I* did to *your* cousin?" My hand flexed. I wanted to shove him into the lockers so bad, but that'd be a fight. My ribs ached at the thought of it.

I looked him up and down. "Here's a solid piece of advice from me. Don't think for yourself. Find someone smart, and every time you have to make a decision or have to figure something out, ask them. Then go with what they say. Get a new brain, because you're on a bad path—for yourself and your crew." I wanted to say more, throw the drug business in there. But I kept quiet. I had to.

That was for later, much later.

His eyes went flat. "What'd you say?"

"You heard me."

"Say it again." His nostrils flared.

"I'll do better." My smile wasn't pretty. "You're a hothead. You didn't earn your spot. You inherited it, and you're pissing it away. If your crew doesn't check you, the rest of us will."

"Yeah?"

"Yeah." I narrowed my eyes.

He was in my face now. I stood my ground, willing myself not to lunge at him. I could slice him, get in a good nick on his side, and I didn't think my ribs would protest too much.

"Do we have a problem here?"

I cursed.

Principal Neeon's voice boomed from down the hallway. As soon as he spoke, everyone else in the hall stopped to look. Only a few had already been watching. Alex's crew was hanging back, shielding us from an audience. That was done now.

People pulled out their phones.

I guessed I had about a minute before someone from my crew showed up.

"No problem, sir." Alex turned to face Neeon as he got to us, pushing through the crowd.

"Why do I think that's total bullshit, along with the weird coincidence of our security videos losing an hour of footage the other day, the *exact* same day our guards were sent on a wild goose chase?" He stared at me.

I didn't react. I didn't do anything.

When we'd gone back to class that day, no one had said a thing. Mr. Jenston finished teaching the class like nothing happened.

When the last bell sounded and we filed out, it was the twilight zone—eerily silent and calm. Word had gotten around, and I got looks as I walked to my second class.

Cross told me after school that someone had said something by the end of the day. He'd walked past the office and saw staff bunched over the security video cabinet.

Hearing Principal Neeon's words now, I knew they were aware something had happened, but they didn't quite know what to look for. Good. Because there was *nothing* for them to find.

"Look, Mr. N, we were just talking," Alex said, motioning toward me. "You can't write us up for that."

"I could write you up for having an attitude." His jaw clenched.

I didn't know what Principal Neeon would or could do, but I sensed his desperation. There was rage in there too, just under the surface. I wondered, for the first time ever, if he'd get angry enough to go outside the system.

No.

I dismissed that idea. I was overreacting. He wouldn't do anything. He couldn't do anything... Unless... I noticed the phones pointing in our direction.

Sick dread pooled at the bottom of my stomach.

We hadn't been watching on Wednesday. Someone could've pulled out a phone. We could've been recorded. There could be evidence out there right now. It still might not show what had actually happened, but they wouldn't care. They never did.

"Come on, Mr. N." Alex tried again. "We're just chilling."

"Stop trying to bullshit me, Mr. Ryerson. I'm well aware of the confrontations between you and Miss Monroe lately." He pointed to the cameras in the corner. "Don't forget those are there. They're there for a reason—safety for the other students and for you all as well." His eyes lingered on me, falling to my ribs.

"What's going on?"

Jordan's voice now drew everyone's attention. He announced his presence as if he had the authority to be included in this conversation. It worked.

Both Principal Neeon and Alex shifted, creating an opening for Jordan to step forward. He did, with Zellman right next to him.

I glanced around and spotted Cross not far away—just behind Alex, leaning back against the locker on the other side of Taz's. It was the perfect attack position. He could jump and take Alex out if anything were to happen.

"You're not a part of this conversation, Pitts."

I almost laughed. Principal Neeon had allowed him in without realizing it.

Jordan's face was blank. "You're right, Mr. N. I'm not, but Bren is like family to me, so you know how it is." He reached up, placing his hand on Principal Neeon's shoulder. "I'm sure you'd be concerned if it were your daughter."

Oh no...

Everyone paused for a moment. Just a moment. One peaceful moment, and I closed my eyes because I knew when I opened them, all hell would start.

And it did.

I looked again just as Principal Neeon knocked Jordan's hand away. He reached for his shirt, and in one motion, he picked Jordan up and slammed him against the locker. "Are you threatening my daughter?"

I had to dive out of the way, saying a quick mental prayer that my ribs had healed fast.

Jordan's back crashed into the metal, and Principal Neeon raised him off his feet. "Are you kidding me, you punk kid?! Who do you think you are?" His face was right in front of Jordan's. "What are you going to do? Hurt my daughter? Huh? HUH?!"

"Hey. Whoa. Whoa." A strained laugh came from Jordan. He looked at Principal Neeon's hands for a moment. "I was asking if you'd be worried about your daughter in a situation like this." He bobbed his head toward me. "That's all."

I'd moved out of the way, but not far, and I could feel Cross right behind me. We were sticking close, in case Jordan needed our help.

"Hey, hey, hey!" Mr. Jenston tried to wade in through the sea of students gathered around us. Two of Ryerson's crew weren't moving. Mr. Jenston scowled, unable to get past them, and he finally took one and shoved him aside. His tie flapped back over his shoulder.

"Robert." He straightened his tie, smoothed a hand down his shirt, and patted Mr. N's arm. "Let's let go of the student."

"He threatened my daughter, Pat."

Mr. J frowned, shooting Jordan a look, but moved to face Principal Neeon. "Come on, Robert. Think about this. You're physically manhandling a student. You know you have to let him go."

"This little shit punk of a kid." The principal's hands tightened on Jordan's shirt, and he started to lean even closer. He shook his head. "You think you can do whatever you want? You went after one of us. Yeah. We heard the rumors. I don't give a shit if there's no evidence. You can't do that. You messed up real bad this week, you and your crew's slu—"

"Hey!"

I didn't know who said that, but it wasn't quick enough.

I heard. I knew what he'd been about call me.

It was enough.

I understood his fear. I even understood the anger. He was a father. But what the principal just said about me? Or almost said. That crossed the line.

That crossed my line.

I felt myself falling back. I was pulling back.

I recognized Jordan yelling. I felt Cross move so he was behind me. All around me, people were moving, shoving, yelling. But everything began to fade. I only saw red, and Principal Neeon was the center of my focus.

I wasn't a *slut*.

I wasn't his *slut*.

I wasn't my crew's *slut*.

I stopped thinking.

My brain shut down. And I moved without thinking.

I ducked, evaded, dodged, and then hit someone. I twisted an arm around.

Hands grabbed at me, but I was rabid.

I don't remember taking my knife out, but I did. I embedded it in someone's leg. They pawed at it, trying to yank it out. But I did that for them. I turned my back, switched the knife to my other hand, and slammed it back into that person.

I.

Wasn't.

A.

Slut.

I wanted to keep stabbing, but someone shoved me back after I pulled the knife out a second time. Arms wrapped around me, and I started to fight, but Cross' voice grunted into my ear.

"Stop. It's me. Stop."

I did, for a moment, but I still wanted to lunge forward. I still wanted to use my knife, to cut what they'd said about me out of existence.

I strained against Cross' hold, but he only tightened his arms.

"Get her out of here!" Jordan roared.

There was a swell of people, and Cross half-carried, half-dragged me away. They were all running the opposite way.

The farther we got from the crowd, the more reality hit me.

I'd stabbed someone. The icy cold feeling inside me tripled.

I groaned, turning in Cross' arms. At that very moment, his hold morphed. He went from restraining and dragging me to comforting me. His hand cradled the back of my head. He was still moving us away, but I began shaking.

I couldn't believe what I'd done. This meant jail.

"Hey, hey." They were the same words he'd used not long ago, but he spoke them in a totally different manner. "Come on. Keep it together for a bit longer. Just a bit longer, okay?" His head dipped close, and I felt his lips on my neck. Then he resumed his movements, hustling me out of there.

The outside air hit my back.

Cross let me go, but he caught my hand, continuing to pull me forward. We were going to his truck.

Once we got there, he opened the door and helped me in. He patted my leg, then shut the door. He was in on his side within a second, and we were pulling out of the lot.

He drove away as two cop cars turned toward the school. That's when I lost it.

CHAPTER THIRTY-FIVE

I'D STABBED THE PRINCIPAL.

Cross and I talked once my head was clearer. I didn't know how long that had taken. It felt like hours, but it might've just been one. Time had started to blur. My shakes, the damned wet shit all over my face, and the trembling had subsided.

Now we knew there was no other option. We had to make the smart move: We went to my brother.

Cross called Channing and asked him to come home. While we were waiting for him, Jordan and Zellman called from the police station. They'd been arrested, along with Alex Ryerson and five of his crew members. There'd been a free-for-all after I let loose.

Jordan dropped the bomb that both Principal Neeon and Mr. Jenston had been taken to the hospital. Then he dropped a second bomb: the principal was in police custody.

"Are you serious?" I leaned over Cross to speak into his phone.

"Swear to God," Jordan said. "I saw 'em put the handcuffs on him and everything. That fucker's going to get charged."

Cross frowned. "Is Zellman with you?"

"They have him in the same cell."

I leaned back, and Cross grabbed my hand. He didn't look at me, but he laced our fingers together.

I looked down at them, resting between us, and a feeling of "rightness" swept through me.

It grew stronger and stronger with each touch, but since I was being all honest with myself—it'd been there since the beginning.

Cross had been right. It had been just lust for Drake, not something more or something real. But this... Holding Cross' hand, I remembered all the times he'd been there for me, the nights I'd slept in his closet, how I always went to him.

There was no wrong when it came to us.

I looked up and saw him watching me, smiling faintly.

I smiled back at him and tried to focus on whatever Jordan was saying.

"...see, won't we?"

A motorcycle engine roared outside the window. I didn't have to look. Channing had arrived.

The front door banged open, and he stormed into the living room. Tearing off his sunglasses, he snapped, "Hang up."

"We're talking to Jordan," I told him. "He has information from the police station."

My brother's jaw clenched, but he held his tongue. He glared at me as he crossed the room and took the phone from Cross.

"Jordan?"

"Here."

I cringed. Jordan didn't need to sound so happy to talk to my brother.

"What's going on at that end?" Channing demanded.

"We're all arrested, but they haven't asked us any questions yet."

"Okay. Listen, I'm sending lawyers. Don't say anything. Got it? Tell Zellman the same. Any other crew involved?"

"Some of Ryerson's."

Channing looked at me. "There was a teacher involved?"

I swallowed over a lump and nodded.

Cross leaned forward, hiding our hands, but also to speak for me. "The principal and a teacher, Mr. Jenston."

Channing sucked in a breath, his hand rubbing slowly over his face. "Are you fucking serious? The principal?"

"They're asking about Bren now." Jordan's voice came from the phone. We could hear conversation and alarms sounding in the background.

"Fucking hell, Bren." Channing looked scared for the first time I'd ever seen. "What'd you do?"

I refused to hang my head. "I stabbed him."

Channing cursed under his breath, walking away for a moment. He stopped, facing the kitchen, his shoulders rigid.

"Twice," I added.

Cross glanced at me.

"I think I got his leg and then his chest."

"His chest?" Channing turned back, his eyes bleak. His hand still covered his chin, and he closed his eyes. "Fucking hell, Bren. You messed up this time. Big time."

Jordan spoke up from the phone again. "He's arrested, though."

"What?" Channing's eyes opened. "What'd you say?"

"I was telling Bren and Cross before. He's at the hospital, but he had cuffs on. He's in police custody. As he should be."

"Why do you say that?"

"He manhandled me," Jordan explained. "He shoved me into a locker, and he called Bren a slut. I mean, those can't be good things. Especially with him being the authority and all. You know what I mean?"

The bleakness in my brother's eyes lessened, and a touch of relief shone like the sun breaking through the clouds.

"Jordan, you might've just saved all you guys, and my sister. Thank you."

"I did? I mean, hell yeah!" Jordan paused a second. "How'd I do that?"

"Just don't say anything if they pull you into a room. Don't believe anything they say. Cops lie. You need to remember that, and I'm calling the lawyers right now. Hold firm and tell the others."

My chest felt so tight. My throat burned, and my stomach tossed, but I sat forward and looked right at my brother. I was a Monroe. We didn't hide. We fought.

I'd fight.

"What do I do?" I asked.

Channing sat down across from us, dialing his cell phone. As he put it up to his ear, his eyes fell on our hands. But he had no reaction, just began to speak after a moment.

"Yeah, hey. This is Channing Monroe. My sister and her friends are in some trouble. They've been arrested. Her friends—" The other person started talking, and Channing listened, adding a beat later, "Okay. We will."

He hung up, his eyes never leaving Cross' and my joined hands. Finally, he looked up at me.

"Tell me everything."

I took a deep breath. "Before I start about today, you should know something about Alex's crew..."

CHAPTER
THIRTY-SIX

THE NEXT FOUR months felt like I'd stepped into an alternate universe.

Channing's lawyer did a sort of plea deal-compromise for me, where he mostly paid off anyone who could've made my life worse than it was.

My charge was assault with a weapon, but I was still a juvenile. Channing's lawyer told me I could've been charged as an adult, but having the entire confrontation on tape—and because Mr. Neeon was the one abusing his authority—helped my case a lot.

Bottom line, I took a deal in juvenile court, and I got probation, community service, and I had to agree to talk to a counselor for a year. Principal Neeon was relieved of his job, and Channing paid his hospital bills.

On that note, either Channing's crew was making money, or the bar was doing better than I'd realized. I'd always thought we were poor... We weren't. Even Cross couldn't hide his surprise when all the financial terms ironed out.

I was also suspended from school, so I took incompletes for the first semester. I'd be starting again after holiday break, which ended this weekend. In the interim I had spent my mornings waiting tables at Manny's and the evenings doing dishes at Tuesday Tits. I wasn't permitted to walk into the main bar area. I had to enter through the back door, which opened right to the kitchen, and I was only allowed to work in the kitchen. If I had to use the restroom, Channing had a Porta Potty installed outside just for me.

It was disgusting, but he'd only shrugged. "Consider it part of your punishment."

But even with that, all in all, my brother hadn't been that hard on me.

He'd been upset, but his cursing had been minimal. He'd never called me names. He never threw anything, threatened to kick me out, or blackmailed me into doing anything I didn't want to. For a replacement dad, he was doing better than the real deal.

Most nights I was either at home with him or with the crew. And half that time, we were either at Manny's or the guys were in the Tuesday Tits kitchen with me. When Heather and Channing thought they were getting one employee, they really got four of us.

Cross was almost inseparable from me.

If he didn't pick me up, he always rolled in an hour or two after I got to my job. Today, for instance, I was finishing a case of glasses when he walked in, his hands in his pockets and a twinkle in his eye.

I paused before pulling another case through the washing machine. "You look happy."

"I am." He washed his hands, then came over and helped me put the dry glasses away. After I stacked glasses, he took them out front. Unlike myself, he could enter the bar area—because he had a dick. He wasn't the owner's little sister. Channing insisted I had special privileges because of that fact. I still didn't see it. I did not consider the Porta Potty special.

I was piling up a bunch of plates when Cross returned. Loud music followed him, then faded as the kitchen door shut again.

"Jordan and Z are coming in a bit," he announced.

He hopped on a stool near where I stood. He leaned back against the wall, and his legs could've touched me if he'd moved them over a little.

I tensed up.

That's all I'd been doing since I'd realized my feelings for Cross.

I annoyed myself.

This wasn't how I was.

I didn't get shy around guys, especially my best friend and crew member. I didn't get all tongue-tied. But these days I sure as hell didn't know what the fuck to do when Cross got close to me. All the hand holding, shared looks, and double entendres had taken their toll. But with the upheaval after the stabbing incident, Cross seemed to sense that I needed space. He'd stepped back into the best friend role.

"What are you doing for your community service again?" he asked.

I shrugged, pushing in the last rack of dishes. "I thought Manny's and this was it, but it's not. Heather and Channing started paying me, so I'm assuming the judge declined their request to have this count as community service. I gotta start doing it, whatever it is, within six months. Why?"

"Taz is still asking about the charity thing."

"Are you serious? Still? I thought that would've been done. She said end of September. That was months ago."

"She said they're doing one for the summer. She wants you to help with the planning." His eyes softened. "It's an idea. You're not stuck picking up trash or mowing lawns. Plus, you can push the whole thing where you're socializing with people who aren't your crew. They said that was a concern—that you only spend time with us and no one else."

Everyone else sucked. No one else mattered.

The machine beeped that it was done, and I opened it. "Maybe. I think Channing's lawyer has to ask the judge for approval, but I'll mention it."

He nodded. "She's been asking about you, you know."

"The judge?" I reached for the last rack, pulling it out.

I could feel Cross' eye roll behind me. "You know who."

Yeah. I did. A whole twisty thing happened with my stomach. What was that? Guilt? What should I feel guilty about with Taz?

I stood staring at the glasses, letting them air-dry a bit longer. "How's she been doing?"

"Worried about you." He reached over and hooked another stool with his toe, dragging it closer to prop his leg on.

"Make yourself comfortable."

He smirked. "Always." He grew serious again. "She wants to see you."

I already knew that. I'd been getting emails from her every other week. I got emails from Sunday Barnes too, and Monica even—awkward. But they weren't alone. Alex Ryerson had reached out, apologizing for the fiftieth time. That was an exaggeration, but he needed to keep after it. It wasn't his fault I'd stabbed Principal Neeon, but it had been the third time I'd felt accosted by him. Enough was enough. I didn't need to stab him too. A few of his crew had gotten in touch with me, not apologizing for him, but just saying hello. It was their way of asking how I was without it being awkward. It was the crew way.

I'd ignored everyone. I ignored Alex and his crew because I was still angry, and because Channing had said to leave them alone. They were going to be dealt with. I ignored everyone else because... I didn't know what to say. I didn't understand why Monica and Sunday were contacting me in the first place. They hated me. But Taz. Yeah, Taz.

I needed to go see her, but I couldn't make myself. Which was unlike me.

"Are you actually thinking about hanging out with Taz?" Cross leaned forward.

"What?" I scowled, starting to stack the glasses now. "That's stupid. No."

"Why's that stupid?"

I swung around to him. "Since when have you ever wanted me and your sister to be friends?"

Cross' smile faded, and he brought his leg down from the stool.

I held my breath, feeling the air in the room shift. It'd gone from comfortable to something more, something hot, something uncomfortable, something... I felt my stomach doing all sorts of flips once again.

"I've never not wanted you and Taz to be close."

I looked at him again, raising my eyebrows high—and ignoring all the weird shit inside me. "Cross, come on."

"Come on what?"

"Every time I'm at your house, you start glaring when your sister comes around. You've been doing it since we became friends." I shook my head. "You didn't like it when I hung out with her. You can't act differently now."

He leaned back so his head rested against the wall again. "Yeah. Maybe I did that."

There was no maybe. It was a definite yes. He did it.

"I was being selfish." His eyes held mine. "I just wanted you for myself, okay? I was an ass."

Whaaat?

My throat felt suddenly tight, and so did my chest. Was this the official talk? My stomach was doing backflips like a professional tumbler now.

A tingle went down my spine.

"Cross?" I didn't know what I was asking. Maybe for clarification? What the hell was going on? It'd been four months of friendliness, and now suddenly we were talking real talk?

He continued to hold my gaze. A stark need entered his eyes, and he sighed. "Fuck," he whispered. "I'm sorry, Bren."

I licked my lips. My mouth was so dry. "For what?"

"I've tried to be the best friend during this whole thing. I have."

Yeah. He'd done a *remarkable* job. Not what I wanted.

His voice was quiet, yet I didn't need to strain to hear him. I hung on his every word. "We close in together. That's what we do when one of us goes through something. You—you need a solid friend, but I can't do that anymore."

"You can't be my friend anymore?" I set down the glasses, putting the stack of them on the counter, and reached back to hold on instead. I felt my knees growing weak.

He shook his head, tentatively at first, as if he were asking my permission. Then, like he saw something he'd needed to see in my gaze, he began to stand up.

I swallowed, my hand gripping the counter.

He was coming over.

Oh, God...

He stopped right in front of me. Two inches separated us. I couldn't look away from him, but the longer I held his gaze, the less I felt able to stand. He was inside of me, making me feel all sorts of emotions I'd never felt before. He knew me, every inch, every cell, every thought.

I parted my lips, and his eyes darted to them, staying.

He brushed his hand over my cheek, tucking some of my hair behind my ear, leaving a tingle in its trail.

I let out a ragged breath.

Goddamn. That touch. It ricocheted through me, sparking need between my legs.

I started to reach for him, *needing* to touch him.

He saw my hand and moved in, letting it land on his chest. I could feel his heart racing. He was as affected as I was. And like that, it clicked. Surrender flooded me. Our bodies let out a release at the same time, like we were finally accepting what was between us.

"Bren," he whispered. His lips brushed over my cheek, getting closer and closer to my mouth, but he paused. He didn't touch his mouth to mine. He tucked my hair behind my ear again, resting there.

He was breathing heavy, just like me.

I splayed my fingers out, savoring the feel of his strength. He was so tight, so firm. I knew what he looked like under his shirt. We'd gone swimming so many times together. We'd hugged each other. We'd sat next to each other. We'd driven together, ridden together. We'd done everything together. We'd even slept together, but this—this was different.

This was a different touch, a different moment.

There was no going back now.

I could lose him.

That sent alarm bells through me, but it didn't matter. I felt drugged. I just needed him, and I lifted my eyes, meeting his again.

He'd been waiting.

I parted my lips.

I reached up, and he dipped down.

His lips touched mine, and everything in the world softened.

It was different—not the kiss, but the feeling. This was *finally*. This was something I hadn't known I'd been waiting for. I leaned into him, and he opened his mouth, applying more pressure.

Sensations exploded in me.

"Cross," I murmured, looking up with what I knew were dazed eyes. "What are we doing?"

He moved even closer, his eyes smoldering and serious. I fit against him like a glove, and his hand cupped the back of my neck.

"What we should've been doing for a long time," he said.

He came back down, and I stopped thinking.

My hands formed fists in his shirt.

This wasn't like Drake. Cross was in a league of his own—

"Bren! Cross!"

Jordan's voice came through the back screen door, and we had a second's notice before it opened. Cross ripped away from me and threw himself across the room as they came inside.

I could only stand there, like an idiot.

We'd just—

I met Cross' gaze as Jordan hollered, "Yo! Where's the love? No greetings?" He went around me, casting a curious look before pounding fists with Cross. "You okay, B?" He came back, holding his fist up to me.

My insides were in an uproar. "Yeah. I'm good." I met my fist to his.

Zellman came in and threw his arm around my shoulders. "Heya, P.F.S." He leaned into me, his skinny hip digging into mine. "Did Cross already fill you in?"

"What?"

Zellman frowned at me. "You're usually quicker on the uptake. You sure you're okay?" His eyes widened, and he jumped away from me. "Wait. Is your side okay? I thought you were all healed by now."

Get ahold of yourself.

I tried to shove away the feel of Cross' lips on mine, the press of his body against mine, how he'd felt with his hands in my hair. I tried. I was failing.

"It's fine. I'm fine. Just..." I had no clue what I was saying. "What's up?" I forced a bright sound to my voice. "I didn't eat today. What's going on?"

There was a sack of apples on the counter, and Jordan grabbed two, throwing one to me. He hopped up on the counter, gesturing with his apple toward Cross. "We were thinking of doing something nice for you."

"We?" I sent Cross a look, raising my eyebrow.

He coughed. "I mentioned you could do with a fun evening." He gestured back to Jordan. "They said they'd cover it."

"We did." Zellman was almost beaming next to me. He crossed his arms over his chest, and his skinny jeans slipped down a bit. "We thought of the best idea, and that's where we've been just now."

"Thinking of the idea?"

"What?" He scratched behind his ear. "No. Not that." He laughed. "But funny, though."

Jordan took a big bite from the apple. "We're going on a road trip!"

"Yeah, yeah." Zellman leaned forward. "And we cleared it with the Mom and Pops."

I felt the blood drain from my face. "Mom and Pops?"

Zellman's eyebrows bunched together. "You know, Heather." He indicated behind me, toward the bar. "And your brother. He knows we're coming to get you. He agreed with us."

"He did?"

My jaw was on the floor. I could've used it to sweep the floor.

Things were better with Channing. I didn't ignore him when he talked to me now. But we had a long way to go.

"He did." Zellman unfolded his arms and clapped me on the back. "Grab your tits! Let's go."

Jordan and Z headed back through the door. Only Cross registered the statement, and he waited until the door closed behind them. "If Alex Ryerson had said that, he'd be impaled with a knife already."

I laughed, but my pulse had started to speed up. It was Cross and me again. We were alone. In a room.

I was already hot and bothered.

"I've heard him say the same thing to you." That was Zellman's phrase when he wasn't thinking, was distracted by something else going on. "He doesn't register that I actually have tits."

Cross looked me up and down, lingering on my lips. "I've never had any trouble registering that." He started toward me, but halted abruptly. His eyes dropped to my tits. "Yeah. Too soon here." Walking backward, he winked as his back hit the screen door. "And just so we're clear, I'm intending to grab your tits someday. I've been intending for a long time."

He backed out and was off toward the guys.

A whole flurry of nerves, excitement, thrill, and fear plunged through me at breakneck speed. I took a moment for myself before I followed him out the door.

I'd known this side of Cross existed. He got the girls, and plenty of them—but being on the receiving end? Whoa.

I wasn't sure I was prepared for what we were apparently going to do, but then I imagined the graze of his lips over mine again, and I knew. The train had already left the station. There was no going back.

Outside, Cross tried to go to his truck, but Jordan wasn't having it.

He flung open the back door to his four-door pickup. "Come on." He jerked his head toward the back. "I switched vehicles so we could do this crew style. You know what I mean."

Which meant we were going all together.

Jordan got in, and Zellman lingered by the passenger door. When we did these trips, he usually sat in the back with either Cross or me. Sometimes I sat up front, but I usually sat in the back with Z. It was a hierarchy thing. Jordan drove because he thought he was the leader. Cross and I were on equal footing, though Cross might've been higher than me, but Zellman was the bottom. I didn't understand who'd made up the hierarchy, but that's how it was except no one cared much about it besides Jordan. However, on trips like this, Z always wanted to sit up front with Jordan.

Both Cross and I knew what he was going to ask as he pointed to the seat with his thumb. "Do you guys mind..."

"No," Cross spoke for us. "Go for it."

A huge smile broke out, and he hopped in, all gangly like.

"You okay with this trip?" Cross asked me before we got in.

I looked back over my shoulder. Channing hadn't come into the kitchen, and neither had Scratch, but I guessed they knew. Jordan said he'd gotten it cleared, and I trusted him. He wouldn't lie about something like that.

Then why did I feel weird? I studied Cross for a moment. This didn't feel like him.

It was... I twisted back around to look at Tuesday Tits.

It hit me like a lightbulb going on—I didn't want to let Channing down. I didn't want to skip out if I really wasn't supposed to go. As soon as I thought it, I started laughing. Relief flooded me, and I patted Cross on the arm.

"I'm good." I moved toward the truck.

"You sure?" Cross went to the door behind Jordan, still watching me round the truck.

I nodded, a stupid and happy smile on my face. Even that felt weird. What the fuck was going on with me? But I felt lighter.

I got inside and closed my eyes as I felt the pickup start forward.

Normal Bren would've ditched without a second thought, but this new Bren, she was starting to care. And that should've worried me. It probably would later, but for now...

I looked at Cross. He'd been watching me, a confused look pulling his eyebrows together.

For now, I was okay.

CHAPTER THIRTY-SEVEN

"CAN WE TALK about the elephant in the room?" Jordan asked.

He leaned forward to turn the music down. Radiohead had been filling the cab for the last hour and a half.

Cross and I shared a look.

"What elephant?" Cross grabbed the back of the seat in front of him and leaned forward. "What are you talking about?"

Jordan looked at us in the rearview mirror, focusing more on Cross. "I have to tell you something, and I'm wondering when's the best time."

Cross released their seat. He shifted a little closer to me, but he remained on his side. I stayed on mine.

My stomach was in knots.

What if we let people know about us and something happened to tear us apart? I didn't know what or how, but it could happen. Hell, just life itself could do it. If I was happy, really happy, I was bound to lose him.

That thought dried my throat.

That couldn't happen.

I didn't even have him, and I was preparing for when I'd lose him. There was something wrong in that, but I couldn't focus for a moment.

Cross' hand covered mine. "Hey."

I ripped my hand away from his. "Don't!" I hissed.

I gritted my teeth. *Shit.* There it was. He'd be hurt. He'd be angry. I'd offended him. But I looked up, and nothing like that was there.

Instead, he wore his slight grin, and he pointed to Jordan. "The leader is speaking to you."

"Shut up!" Jordan burst out. "You give me shit, but no one else is stepping up to the plate."

"But how could we?" Cross sat forward, resting his arm on the back of their seat. "You've got all the bases covered. There's no room. And how would we even step up? Mutiny?" Cross hit Zellman's shoulder with the back of his hand. "Would I have to recruit Z here? Maybe bribe him with a hundred bucks?"

"A hundred bucks? I'm more expensive than that." Zellman shook his head.

"A hundred strippers?" Cross asked.

"Yeah." Zellman bobbed his head, laughing. "I'd fold for a hundred strippers. Pussy heaven."

"Hold your tits, Z." Cross grinned.

Zellman tipped his head back, his grin widening. "Hold *their* tits, you mean?"

Jordan shook his head, grumbling, "You guys are stupid. You give me crap, but I have a role. I fulfill it."

"What role is that?" I asked. "Our mouthpiece?"

"Yeah," he shot back, watching me in the rearview mirror. "I step up. I defend you guys. You all are so damned quiet. Someone has to talk."

Z was still grinning, shaking his head.

"So you fill the silence?" I asked. "That's what you're saying?"

Jordan was half-grinning now too. "I know, I know. You guys step up. If I weren't around, you'd all be just fine, but stop giving me so much crap. I like to take charge. Sue me, but for real—I gotta say something here. You have to know."

Z turned sideways, resting his arm on the back of the seat. "You've been spending a lot of time together, you two."

I glanced at Cross. A foreboding expression pulled down his eyebrows. His mouth was in a flat line.

I nodded. "Yeah. Why?"

Jordan and Zellman shared a look now.

"So this is kind of about Ryerson." Jordan cleared his throat. "I didn't know if I should say anything, but he's dating someone. And—"

"Who?" I asked.

"Who?" Jordan parroted. "You fucking with me now? Race Ryerson. Douchebag's cousin."

"No. No." I waved my hand in the air. "I got confused." I was making a mess of this. I'd been so scared they were talking about Cross and me. He said Race was dating someone. "Who's he dating?"

He adjusted in his seat, sitting up a little straighter. "This is going to be awkward."

"What?" I was lost. "Why?"

Jordan looked from me to Cross in the rearview mirror, grimacing.

"Like Z said, Cross, you've been spending a lot of time with Bren lately. I mean, like, a lot."

"What are you getting at?" Cross asked. His hand clenched into a fist, but he kept it on the seat between us.

I itched to take it, to soothe that frustration out, but I couldn't. A rock had fully lodged in my chest. It was pressing against my sternum.

"I'm getting that you probably don't know what I'm going to say."

"What?" Cross demanded. "Get at your point, Jordan. I don't like being yanked around."

Z hissed, "Just tell them."

Jordan paused a beat. "Taz."

There was silence for another beat.

"What?!" Cross jerked forward.

"Race Ryerson is dating your sister. Taz."

I... Nope. I had no words or thoughts. I... Nope. I still didn't.

"That guy is with my sister? How do you know?"

"We saw 'em at the movies last night."

Zellman shifted again so his back was against his door. "They were holding hands when they left."

"We followed them to the country club in Fallen Crest," Jordan said. "He took her to dinner there."

Zellman nodded with every word Jordan said. "Yeah, like, literally wined and dined her, and he took her *there*. Of all places. The richest pricks' place in Fallen Crest." He nodded to Cross. "Might want to check her, make sure her head's not getting big if she's hanging at spots like that. Though I gotta say, if I were him, I'd go with Taz as a second option too. Who else is he going to tap? Monica's still hung up on Cross. B was his first choice, and I'm tapping Sunday. Taz is good quality. She's girlfriend material. I can see why he picked her."

"Could you stop using the word *tap* and my sister in the same sentence?" Cross' eyes narrowed. "He probably took her there because he knew none of our crew would be there."

"Sorry," Z said to Cross. "The dude's rich, isn't he?" he asked me. "His dad owns a Harley store?"

I shrugged. I didn't care. I was more worried about Cross. "You didn't know?"

"Every free moment I have, I'm with you, but she *has* been asking about you." He gave me a meaningful look, and I flashed back to our conversation at Tuesday Tits.

"Maybe it wasn't all about the charity thing."

"What charity thing?" Z's eyes darted between us.

"I don't know yet."

I could feel Jordan's attention. He'd dropped the bomb. He was waiting for it to detonate.

I glanced to Cross. It was his sister.

He clenched his jaw and sat back, looking out the window.

His silence was telling.

"Let's lay off it," I told Jordan. "How far till we get wherever we're going?"

He'd been studying Cross in the mirror, but looked at the clock on the dashboard. "I think another hour."

This ride wasn't going to get any better.

I pulled out my phone and headphones.

CHAPTER THIRTY-EIGHT

A LITTLE WHILE later, Jordan pulled into a fast food place. The guys had been complaining about being hungry and needing to piss. The two 20-ouncers that'd been filled up with coffee and soda hadn't helped either.

Jordan and Zellman hopped out right away, running inside.

Cross and I moved at a slower pace.

"You upset about Taz?" I asked him as we got out.

Resting his arms on the truck's back-end, he glanced down a moment. He shook his head, still looking at the ground. "I don't know. I don't know what I'm feeling."

I paused and waited for him.

He looked back up, a smile flashing for a moment as he stared at me. "Been distracted with you, honestly."

Those flutters started again, tickling me on the inside.

The lines around his mouth softened, and he reached forward, grabbing my arm. He tugged me over to him, but I glanced back at the building. Jordan and Zellman were at the counter, ordering. Pee breaks could wait, apparently.

Knowing they were distracted, at least for the moment, I succumbed.

I let Cross pull me toward the front of the pickup so we were hidden, and he wrapped his arms around me. My head rested against his chest, and he held me as I slid my arms around his waist.

We'd done this hug before, so many times, but this was different. This hold, this touch, what it stood for—it was all so very different.

The flutters were building again.

I felt his voice rumble through his chest. "We're going to have to have the talk. You know that, right?"

I nodded, my head moving against his chest. "I know."

He ran a hand up and down my arm. He leaned back against the truck and opened his legs a little wider. I scooted in closer and felt him resting his head against mine.

"We'll have to tell them too."

"Later," I responded. We'd deal with it then. I closed my eyes until we heard Zellman calling our names.

I stepped back and Cross moved around me.

"We're coming," he yelled.

"You want us to order your food?"

Cross turned to me, and I nodded. They knew what we liked.

"Yeah. Give us another minute," Cross yelled back.

"Will do! B, you want a soda?"

"Yeah!" I yelled. "Thanks, Z."

He waved at us distractedly before going back in.

I didn't return to Cross' arms, and he leaned back against the truck, eyeing me.

I frowned. "What?"

He jutted his chin toward me. "Why aren't you freaking? You'd usually be freaking right now."

I lifted a shoulder. "I don't know. Maybe I'm too tired?"

"Bullshit." He tilted his head to the side. "What's going on with you?"

"I don't know. Really."

"Bren."

"Really." I laughed. "I don't know. Something's different. Maybe it was me stabbing the principal, or maybe I don't know. I really don't."

But I felt good, better. I was going with that. Things didn't scare me as much. I felt better. Life wasn't as bleak, though it probably should've been if history was the best prediction of the future. I should be scared as hell.

"I didn't go to jail. That's it."

He laughed shortly. "I doubt it. You wouldn't have cared if you went in there."

I should've, but he was right. I wouldn't have four months ago. And that told me how much I *did* care now. "Yeah. Maybe."

"You haven't gone to watch the house since the incident either."

Ah.

There was the underlying reason he wanted to talk. Not about us, but about me.

Some of the flutters dissipated, and I bit my lip. "We're talking about that stuff now?"

"I envision a lot of kissing for us in the future, so yeah. Let's do this now. I'd ask you anyway. I mean, I might not say it outright, but I'd still ask."

"About kissing?"

His eyes darkened, but his mouth lifted. "You know what I mean. Do you think we should talk about it?"

About us, about me, about everything. He was asking about everything.

I had a different opinion. "Nope. I'm good."

"Bren." He reached for me.

I stepped back, evading him. "I like what we're doing. You're right. I would normally be running for the hills or looking for fights, but I'm not. I don't want to force anything." My voice dropped to a whisper. "I can't lose you."

"Why do you think you'd lose me?"

I didn't want to open old wounds and go back to where I'd been before I stabbed Principal Neeon. "Just... Don't push, okay? Not with that."

"Okay." He nodded. "I won't."

Some of the knots in my chest loosened.

"What the fuck are you two doing?" Jordan yelled from the fast food place.

Cross and I shared a grin, and he moved around me once more. "Talking about my sister. Chill out. We're coming."

Cross fell in step beside me. I felt us falling back into our old roles. We were beginning to be more, but he was my best friend first. That's what I needed at the moment.

"What town are we even in?" I asked as we went inside.

"I don't know," he said. "Jordan, where are we at?"

We headed for their booth.

I should've had my first clue when Jordan went unnaturally still at Cross' question.

I should've had my second clue when Jordan paled, and his eyes widened.

I should've had my third clue when his eyes didn't go to Cross, but to me.

But nope. I didn't catch any of those clues.

I'd been happy. I'd been distracted by how I *wasn't* unhappy, I *wasn't* in so much pain, I *was* starting to care about things.

None of that clicked until we reached the booth.

Jordan gulped, crumpling up his sandwich wrapper, and said, "Potomahmen."

Everything connected, in a slow and almost morbid way.

I was sucker-punched, by my own crew.

Because Potomahmen was the city that housed my dad's prison.

CHAPTER THIRTY-NINE

CROSS SWORE.

Zellman frowned.

And Jordan paled.

That was all I needed to see. Guilt. He did this on purpose.

A flame exploded in me.

I opened my mouth, but Cross beat me to it.

"You asshole," he clipped out. "You know she doesn't talk about her dad. Ever."

Zellman kept looking from us to Jordan. His mouth opened, then closed.

"Come on." Jordan scooted to the edge of the booth and held a hand out. "Look, I was just trying to do something nice for you. With all the shit that went down, I know you miss your mom a lot, and so I thought, *Why not bring her to her other parent?* That's all. I swear."

He was lying.

"You knew this would hurt me," I shot back. "That's why you did this. You didn't want to fight Alex for me, but we forced you to do that. Then all that happened with Principal Neeon because of me, and I know you were pissed about that too."

He didn't know about my old house, and I never talked about my mom. He would've had no clue that I missed her. My stomach rolled like a sideways tornado. It wouldn't stop twisting around.

"You're a liar."

I hadn't itched for my knife in months. The judge had said I couldn't have it, but I got a new one. I had it on me. I couldn't

CREW

go without it, no matter the consequences. That was one rule I couldn't follow, but I hadn't itched to use it.

Months.

I itched now.

I shook my head. "There's a reason I don't talk about him. There's a reason I don't see him. There's a *goddamn* reason I don't even let him into my nightmares."

"Come on." Cross took my arm and began pulling me toward the door.

"Where are you guys going?" Jordan stood, but he didn't come after us.

I almost wanted him to. I wanted to take him down. I wanted to fight—the need to embed my knife in him was strong. I could taste it. The smell of blood rose up in my nostrils, but that was a memory, one I thought had been long buried.

"We're leaving," Cross threw over his shoulder, half-dragging me out. Again.

"I drove you here! How are you going to leave?"

"I'll fucking think of something," Cross clipped back, opening the door and guiding me past him. He fell in step behind me, his hand firmly planted at the small of my back. He knew I wanted to fight.

"Let me go back in there."

"No." He moved around me, taking my hand. I couldn't break free from his hold even if I'd wanted to. He took me to the truck and reached into the open back. Finding the extra key Jordan always kept clipped there, hidden from sight, he opened the door. He grabbed some water, some cash from the stash in Jordan's console, and closed it back up.

He was putting the extra key back when we heard the bells ringing from the restaurant door.

Zellman came toward us, his hands stuffed in his pockets and his skinny shoulders slouched forward.

Cross moved ahead of me and rolled his shoulders back. "Stop, Z. He crossed the line, and you know it."

Zellman held his hands up, his palms toward us. "I know. I'm not here to defend him. I'm coming with you."

Cross and I shared a look.

"Are you sure?" I breathed.

He was choosing us.

He nodded, his hands going back to his pockets. "Yeah. I'm not going to defend him, but I don't think he really thought this through."

I growled. "You *just* defended him!"

"No. I didn't. I'm saying he's an idiot. I'm not saying he didn't have deeper reasons for this, but..." He paused, glancing back to the building. We could see Jordan standing in the entryway, watching us. He had a stark expression on his face, but he wasn't frowning. He wasn't smiling. He was just staring.

Zellman looked back to us. "I didn't know we were going to the prison. He lined up a cabin for us to party at tonight. That's all I thought we were doing, but he told me just now that he set everything up for you to see your dad tomorrow."

"I can't believe him." I twisted my hands together. It was the only way I could keep from grabbing my knife.

"Dude, stop," I heard Zellman say.

Jordan had come out from the fast food place. The wind was whipping his hair all around so a lock fell over his eyes, baring bleak anguish for a half second before he rammed his sunglasses back on. He looked harrowed, bags under his eyes, and in that second, his tan had a yellow tint to it. He was still pale underneath.

I registered all of that, and a part of my brain was telling me to slow down. Maybe he really was being a dumbass, but the other part held up the years of discord between us. He wanted me to do something, and I didn't, and he was always disappointed. Like he was my father. He wasn't. He was a friend. He was my equal. He was my crew. I didn't have to do what he wanted, and today was another example.

He wanted me to see my dad. Well, fuck him, because who was he hurting? Me.

Knives sliced through my chest. The betrayal was real.

CREW

"Bren, I didn't mean..." he called. "I wasn't thinking—"
"Goddamn right you weren't!" I started for him.
Forget feeling hurt. I was furious. That pushed the rest away.
Cross caught me, pulling me back.
I twisted my arm free. I wanted to fight. Fuck him. Honestly. Fuck him.

I pointed at him, using my middle finger. "You get on this kick, thinking you know best for us. You don't! You're a mouthpiece, Jordan. You're an enforcer. You're not the brains, and it's insulting to the rest of us when you assume you have to make decisions for us. You fuck things up. Your leadership role is intact because the rest of us *don't care*. But don't think you can throw my father in my face." I started to go for him again.

He backed up as Cross moved in front of me. Zellman moved to his side to form a wall between Jordan and me.

Jordan's face twisted, and he grabbed fistfuls of his hair. "I'm sorry. I didn't think it would be like this." He let go, his arms falling back down. "I really am so sorry. I only told your brother we were heading to a cabin for the weekend. I wish I'd mentioned more now. I—" He turned away for a moment. His hands found his hips. His shoulders lifted in a deep breath, then he turned back. He tore off his sunglasses, and I again saw the agony there. "I know how much you miss your mom," he said softly. "I know about the house."

"What?" The wind was knocked out of me.

"I was worried about you one night, so I tracked you down. I saw Cross' truck pulling onto a gravel road and couldn't figure out what the hell he was doing. Then I saw. I saw you, and I saw the house, and it made sense."

"You did what?" The words came out strangled, like a whispered cry.

He was hand-delivering my nightmare to me.

That place was sacred.

My place. My sanctuary. My haunt. It held good memories, bad memories, nightmares, but hopes. I had hoped for something better, until I was forced away. He had no idea, no idea what that house meant to me.

It was mine.

Not his.

I made the decision who went there. I did. Not him. Not my brother. Not even Cross. He knew because I chose to take him there. And that'd been it. No goddamn one else.

"You're going through something right now, and I just thought that if you couldn't have one parent, you could see the other. That's all I was thinking. I swear." His hands fell from his hips. "I know I'm a douchebag, but I'm trying to be better. I'm *trying*, Bren."

My insides felt like they were being ripped out, one organ at a time. "You fucked up, Jordan."

"I know."

"Bad."

He sighed. "I know." He hung his head. "I'm sorry, Bren."

I could feel Cross' gaze and looked over. There was a question in his eyes. He was asking what I wanted to do, but I only shrugged. I had no clue. My mind was already forgiving Jordan, but not my heart. God. It hurt to bring in air.

He'd stabbed me, just in the front.

"What do you want to do now?" Jordan asked. "I still have that cabin..." He let his sentence hang.

It was my decision. Stay or go.

If we stayed, I was giving in. I was letting Jordan off the hook. Yes, yes. He'd said the words. He apologized. He looked the part, but I still burned with rage against him.

I saw how Zellman was holding his breath, his cheeks actually rounded and puffed out, and how he was chewing his bottom lip.

The little boy inside him was alive and well.

His eyes skirted between me and Jordan. It was clear what he wanted to do.

No prison, but he wanted to party.

"When you become one of us, you have to agree to three oaths."

"Three?"

"Three. The first, will you treat us as family?"

"Yes." Without hesitation, without regret, without a doubt—
yes.

"Will you fight for us as you'd have us fight for you?"

Another yes—no question, thought, or fear.

"And the last, will you forgive as if we're one person?"

I had said yes.

That was the one ritual we had to be part of this crew. Each question had been chosen for a reason, and each answer had to be true. I'd meant it when I said yes to the last, and remembering that now, I cursed under my breath.

He hadn't asked for forgiveness. It wasn't put in words, but he wasn't the only one here. I wasn't either.

Zellman wanted everyone to make up, and he wanted to party. If I made us all go back now, I'd be hurting Z. His love for the group, his desire for everyone to be happy—I couldn't take that away from him, not for this.

I let out a sigh. "We can go to the cabin."

"Yeah?" Jordan's eyes went wide. He almost took a step backward.

I nodded, but just barely.

He let out a whoop and high-fived Zellman. "Holy fuck, Bren. Thank you." He started for me, but I shook my head. "No."

He lowered his arm, nodding instead. "Thank you, Bren. I mean it."

He headed for the truck with Zellman and yelled, "I meant what I said, B. I'll make it up to you. I will. I promise. I'll show you."

"Yeah."

I loved this crew, so much, maybe too much. If he took that away, I would kill him.

My love for the crew outweighed my distrust for him. That's all I had at the moment.

His head bobbed forward as he got in his truck. They could wait for hours. I didn't give a shit, because I was going to take my time getting back into that vehicle. Jordan knew it too. He turned the engine on, and just blasted the music. I could see him and Zellman talking to each other.

Cross was looking too, and after a few seconds, his hand came to rest on my hip. He asked in a low voice, "You okay?"

No. Not even close. "I don't trust him."

He glanced back inside. "Yeah, but we'll have to see his game to play."

When he looked at me, I saw the same mistrust lurking in his eyes.

I frowned. "What are you thinking?"

"If it's worth anything, I don't think he wants to oust you or anything." His hand flexed on my hip. "Not that it would work. We'd just splinter. He knows that."

"He's already our leader."

Cross gave me a half-grin. "Which you kinda stripped from him just now."

I hadn't. Wait—I hadn't meant to. "Nothing's official."

I crossed my arms over my chest. We hadn't had nominations or voted. Jordan could be the leader today, but Cross could be it tomorrow. It could evolve, and maybe it should. Maybe Jordan wouldn't have such a big ego then.

"We're crew," I added. "That's all we are."

"I know." Cross' hand fell away. "You're not getting any arguing from me."

They were still talking. We could hear laughter now. Their heads were bent together, looking at someone's phone.

I sighed. "Let's go to this cabin, then get home tomorrow."

I slid into the back seat, all the way over until I was right behind Jordan. Cross got in behind me, and as he shut the door, Jordan caught my gaze in the rearview mirror.

I saw the unease there. That gave me a small piece of satisfaction. He could sweat, knowing exactly where I was.

He could worry about *his* backside.

CHAPTER FORTY

"HEY." CROSS APPROACHED me in the cabin and handed me a beer. "Here."

I took it, leaning forward from my seat in the screened-in porch. My legs were up on a footrest. "Thanks."

He sat in the chair beside me, and we looked out to the bonfire where Jordan and Zellman were sitting, watching something on Jordan's phone.

"They're watching cat videos," Cross said, and I heard the laughter in his voice. "We're the fiercest in Roussou, and half our crew are giggling like schoolgirls over cat videos."

"The booze helps." I reached mine out without looking, and we clinked our bottles together.

"Jordan's downed ten beers on his own."

The cabin Jordan got for us was owned by one of his uncle's friends. It was small and quaint: two bedrooms, a small kitchen, and a living room with a patio that opened to an outdoor deck. The bonfire pit was right behind it, with a river behind that. As soon as we arrived, everyone went swimming. The guys did a lot of dunking and wrestling. I just swam. Jordan glanced at me once, and I caught a slight gleam there. He had considered dunking me, but I gave him a warning look. The gleam vanished, and he grabbed Zellman, throwing him over his shoulder instead.

Now, after a grilled steak dinner, it was a little after ten.

My anger had thawed a bit. I still felt it, but it wasn't so much on the surface. I glanced at my beer and knew the booze was helping. This was my sixth.

"Jordan doesn't understand."

"What?" I looked over at Cross.

He wasn't watching me, but focusing on Jordan right now. The bonfire cast his face into shadows, and I watched them play across his features. His cheekbones and jaw were more pronounced. His face more angular. It gave him a more mysterious aura—and alluring at the same time.

"He loves his dad. He almost worships him."

I looked back to study Jordan. Cross was right. Jordan spoke with pride whenever he talked about his father. He provided for the family. He'd bought their home and helped build the warehouse and so many of the other buildings around their estate.

Cross was right.

"But I don't talk about my dad." I never had, particularly not since he left.

"He might've assumed that's because you were missing him, not the other way around."

Cross' words mixed with the booze and the way Jordan suddenly sat up, laughing at those stupid cat videos—and it all clicked into place.

Cross was right, so fucking right.

"Shit." I sank down in my chair. "I was livid."

"Yeah."

"I wanted to cut him."

"I know."

I'd jumped to conclusions. "I owe him an apology."

"No, you don't."

"Yeah, I do." I looked to Cross. Our eyes met and held before he sat back in his chair, shadow covering the top half of his face again.

"You don't. I don't care if this was a mistake. You don't owe him an apology."

"Cross—"

He shot forward, his eyes flaring again. The bonfire outside and full moon cast him in enough light so I could see how fierce he felt. "You'll owe him. And he'll use that to hurt you."

"We're crew."

"Not in this situation. In this situation, you're you and he's him. His intentions might've been good this time, but we both know there's a power struggle. He was knocked down. He's equal to us now. That won't last. He'll go back up, and we'll let him because he cares more about power than we do. Don't give him leverage. Keep quiet on this." He added softly, "Trust me."

It felt wrong not to own up to my mistake, but I trusted Cross. So I nodded.

"Okay." I sat back in my chair, lifting my beer again.

Cross looked back out at them. "You're my best friend."

My mouth opened, but words didn't come right away. My chest tightened, and it wasn't the flutters in there this time. I was past that. It was straight-up flooding now. I was overloaded by feelings, but there was a thread of confusion too.

Cross didn't speak like this. This wasn't normal. This, like so much else lately, was new.

"In every situation, against every person, it's you. Your first loyalty is to the crew, but mine is to you. It's always been like that." He finally turned to look at me, and my mouth dried.

God. "Why are you saying this?"

My voice was a hoarse whisper. I felt raw.

"Because I can feel it coming. Your first instinct, like just now, will be to own up to something. My first instinct is to protect you, even if you don't want it."

He was warning me against something.

"What are you saying, Cross?" I leaned forward, feeling my insides twisting up. "Be straight with me."

"It's just a feeling right now. Something's going to happen." He turned back to Jordan and Zellman. "I don't know if they'll be on our side or against us, but you have to know…" He swung those piercing eyes my way. "Everything I do is for you."

I couldn't talk.

I was excited. I was terrified. I was confused. I was still angry, and I was aroused. Lust flowed through my veins, and that throbbing only intensified between my legs.

I breathed out, just wanting him.

He saw it, and his own want flared to the forefront. The hazel in his eyes had morphed into a molten green, with specks of smoldering brown lining the outside. I'd never seen his eyes like that, and I couldn't speak. If he asked me a question, if a fire lit behind us, I wouldn't have been able to move, much less yell for help.

Neither of us held back. We let the other see. There was no hiding.

We stared at each other, both needing, not touching. Neither of us moved. Neither reached out.

The cabin was small. There were crew rules. We couldn't be together, not here.

Not yet.

Cross closed his eyes first. When he spoke, his voice was a sensual caress in the darkness. "If they weren't here, if you were ready, I would take you inside. I would strip you naked. I would lay you down, and I would worship every goddamn inch of your body because that's just the beginning of what you deserve."

If they weren't here...

If I was ready...

"You don't want to hear all the things I'd let you do." My voice was a hoarse whisper.

I wasn't ready, but I was getting ready. I could feel it happening, and unlike all the other crap in my life—I didn't fear this change.

"One day, Bren," he breathed. "One day."

He stood, finishing his beer. "I have to get out of here because I'm starting not to care about where we are." As he went outside to join the others, his fingers grazed down the top of my leg, over my knee, and trailed all the way to just before my toes.

I shivered and tipped back my head, finishing my own beer.

I was fast starting not to care either.

CHAPTER
FORTY-ONE

"YOU STILL PISSED at me?"

It was four in the morning, and saying we were wasted was an understatement. We'd all gathered around the bonfire, though I didn't know how we were sitting upright. Well, Zellman was lying on the ground. His eyes were open, and his head was propped up. He stared at the fire like it was the rainbow to his marijuana high. If he could've made love to the flames, I'm sure he would've tried.

I looked across the fire to where Jordan sat. His eyes still seemed alert. That wasn't a surprise. He had more body mass, so he had a better tolerance—or that was my excuse for how my own sharpness had lessened.

I felt myself tipping over, but I caught myself. The log had been sturdy and sound when I first sat down. Who knew when it had decided to tip out from under me? I glanced around. No one seemed to have noticed.

"Bren."

"What?" I looked up.

Oh yeah. Jordan.

I frowned. He'd asked a question. I snapped my fingers. "Yes!"

"You're still pissed?"

"I remembered."

"What?"

"Huh?"

Cross' head moved back and forth between us as we spoke. He held a hand up now. "Stop. I'm confused."

"I am too." I lifted my beer. I could see two, but I knew I was only holding one.

"I asked if you were still pissed at me." Jordan was scowling. That wasn't good.

I looked to Cross. "He's asking if you're still pissed at him." I waved my beer toward Jordan. "Answer him." I leaned closer. "Am I holding two beers?"

"One." Cross turned to Jordan. "You're asking Bren?"

"What?" Jordan rubbed his forehead. "I'm not pissed at you, or Bren." His hand fell to his mouth, and his eyes widened. "I can't feel my lips."

I pointed the right beer at him. "Maybe *they're* pissed at you."

He wasn't paying attention. He began rubbing his lips together. "Am I doing something? I'm trying to move my mouth around."

Cross grunted. "You're drunk. You both are."

"You too." I pointed at him.

"No. I stopped after I left you on the porch."

The porch.

I gulped. The porch had been hot. Like, hella hot. Like, I didn't think I could walk through it without squeezing my legs together— that kind of hot. Cross got girls. I knew he always had, but if he talked like that to them... I felt a bit sick. Something squeezed in my chest. I think it was jealousy.

All those girls. Man. He'd been with a lot of them, and I'd been with Drake. Stupid Drake. Six-month Drake.

Drake acted all cool, but he was a fumbler in bed. Not the best there was. Well, I couldn't compare. It'd just been Drake for me. Stupid bumbling Drake.

I think I'm on repeat here.

What was I doing?

Oh yeah. Jealousy. Stupid girls.

Jordan is pissed at Cross.

I scowled across the fire. "Why are you mad at Cross?"

"Huh?"

Zellman began giggling. He rolled so his face was almost all the way into the ground. His giggles only got louder.

"Him too."

"No. Fuck," Jordan said. "Wait. I mean, no shit. Yeah. No shit. And I'm not pissed at you." He squinted at me. "I'm really fucking drunk. I love you guys." He looked around, his eyes glazed. He was mostly directing his statements to the fire now.

Zellman's laughter lessened, and he lifted his head, like he was doing a side-crunch. "Huh?"

Jordan clapped Zellman on the shoulder. He squeezed, then patted. Hunching forward, he gazed at Cross and me again. "They sent my sister away."

Wait. Huh?

The bonfire was spinning.

I heard Cross respond to Jordan.

Jordan said something about his sister, who didn't go to our school. Where did Mallory go? I knew, but I didn't at that moment.

Why couldn't I remember?

Jordan added, almost in a grunt, "You guys know she started at that prick school in Fallen Crest this year, but she's not handling the assault very well. They sent her away, like away away. She's not even staying at the house."

Mallory.

Away.

But I knew that. She started at Fallen Crest Academy this year.

Cross said, "You didn't mention her. I'm sorry, Jordan."

Another grunt from our non-leader. His jaw clenched and he flicked a hand over his cheek. "I know, but whatever. I had a reason for saying that. You guys." He focused on us again. "I know I can be an asshole sometimes."

There was a dig there, but I held my tongue. I refrained.

He'd been talking about Mallory. That was serious for Jordan.

Cross began snickering.

I scowled at him. "He's being all open with us. Stop."

Cross shook his head at me. "You've got no clue what he's talking about. He could be talking about unicorns for all you know."

Wait. Was he?

I turned to Jordan, my head tilting to the side.

Jordan rolled his eyes, waving his beer in the air. "Yeah, yeah. Laugh at my expense. I get it. I'm only *sometimes* an asshole? But yeah, I am. Sometimes I'm an asshole. Sometimes I'm a really fucking great guy. I mean, I love you guys." He threw his arms in the air. His beer went flying.

He didn't notice.

"I'll own my shit. I can be a hothead, and egotistical. I like to be the boss, but your words hurt, B. And I'm not throwing a pity party here. I know why they hurt. Because they're the truth, that's why. You're right. I'm not super smart." His voice cracked. "You and Cross are the smart ones. You two are the thinkers for us. Zellman is the glue. He holds us all together. So what am I? What do I do? Except have a big mouth. But maybe that's it. I'm the mouth guy. I'm the mouthpiece. I make up with my size too. Right? I push my way in. That's what I do. I can brawl with the best of them, and you two." He stopped again. Another breath. "You guys are some of the best fighters I've met. I'm honored to have you at my back." He coughed, clearing his throat. His hands balled into fists. He was looking at the ground now. "I just... I want to prove that I really didn't have any bad intentions. I mean, I love my dad. I hate that he travels so much for his job—and I'm sounding like a pussy right now. I don't care. But you guys were there for me with Mallory. She's my little sis, you know?" His voice sounded gruff. "That means something to me. That means a lot to me."

His fists pressed into the sides of his legs, and he lifted his head. Tears shimmered in his eyes. "I didn't even think you wouldn't want to see your dad. You never talk about him, Bren. Ever. You don't talk about anything. I mean, anything. I'm scared to ask you about anything, and I'm in your crew. People look at me like I should know, but I don't." He motioned to Cross. "He gets to know. Not us. I don't know. I love you, B. You're my sister, but in a crew way, you know? And yeah, I don't know. I've always wondered why you don't see your dad, or talk about him, but I got it now. I said it before, but I mean it. I'm sorry. I *really* am."

CREW

He looked right at me.

He meant it. I felt it. He was being genuine.

I found myself leaning forward, waiting for the rest of what he'd say.

"I just, I love you guys." He clamped down on Zellman's shoulder again.

That was profound.

Pretty fucking smart.

I grinned at Zellman. He was dreaming about the unicorn, I bet.

Cross looked guarded.

I was normally jaded and mistrusting, but what Cross said earlier today was right. It was different when it came to the crew. My love for the crew was pure. It might've been one of the only pure loves I felt, but it was there.

I let go of anything lingering toward Jordan. He was crew. He was family.

I'd let Cross shift through the rest.

"I love you too, Jordan."

His eyes gleamed, and his tears fell. "Really?"

I nodded. "Really. And if I didn't say it before, I'm sorry what happened to your sister."

"You don't have any idea how much that means to me. No idea." He wiped a hand over his nose, sniffing. "Thank you. I mean it. Thank you."

Zellman shot a hand up. "High-five, brother."

He reached just a little above Jordan's knee, and he slapped it.

Jordan looked at me again. I saw the gratefulness there, and I was glad I'd pushed my doubt away. But I purposely didn't look at Cross. I didn't want to see his reservations. In fact, I tried not to look until after the fire was dead. The sun was beginning to peek over the horizon, making the sky a dark purple.

Jordan squinted, groaning. "Shit. I'm not stupid drunk—I'm way past that. I am totally dumb drunk, and we gotta be out of here in four hours."

Zellman sat up, rubbing his eyes. He'd fallen asleep earlier and snored half the night. He looked a little more refreshed than the rest of us. That wasn't saying much. Scratching his cheek, he pulled up the hood from his sweatshirt so it fell over his forehead. He yawned once more before closing his eyes.

He was going to fall asleep sitting like that if we didn't move. Too late.

He started snoring again, his head back in his hood and his legs crossed over each other. He'd stay like that till someone pushed him over.

"I can't go to sleep," Jordan said. "If I do, I won't get up in four hours to drive back."

Cross stood up. "I'll drive. We can go now before we all fall asleep."

Jordan peered at him, his eyelids heavy. "You sure?"

"I'm sure. It's annoying how sober I am. Come on." Cross motioned again. "I'm good to drive. I just need coffee, lots of it."

We picked up the mess we'd made, which was a slow and painful process. Jordan wasn't the only one drunk. I was still seeing double, but Cross zipped around, all stealthy and sober-like. If I watched him too much, I was going to fall over from dizziness.

Once we got in the truck and got moving, Jordan and Zellman started snoring right away in the back. I curled up in the front passenger seat, waking when we stopped at a gas station. Cross was the only one to get out, and his return was marked more by the whiff of his coffee than his door opening and closing.

We all slept through the rest of the ride, except for him.

When we parked, Jordan and Zellman climbed out after me, heading inside.

"What are you doing?" I turned to them.

Jordan waved to the house. "We're sleeping here. Fuck waiting."

So that's what happened.

Cross turned off the truck, pocketed the keys, and we all went inside.

It was a little after eight by then. Both Channing and Heather met us in the hallway. Channing was shirtless, scratching his chest. His tattoos seemed more prominent this morning, for some reason. Heather had a sheet wrapped around her.

He looked us over. "What are you guys doing?"

Heather saw the others and turned around, disappearing back into the room.

Jordan and Zellman veered around my brother, heading for the basement. "We gotta sleep," Jordan called over his shoulder. "We'll crash down here."

"Sure..." Channing said as his bedroom door opened again.

Heather came back out wearing Channing's shirt, which hung over her, and shorts.

"They're going to crash here," Channing told her.

"Okay. Yeah." She patted his arm. "I'm going back to bed."

He ran a hand down the back of her head, smoothing her hair. She stepped close for a hug. He pressed a kiss to her forehead, and she vanished into their room. The fan turned on a second later.

Cross and I remained with Channing in the hallway.

"Aren't you going to crash downstairs too?" my brother asked Cross.

Cross raised his chin. "No."

That was it. Just no.

Channing raked a hand over his face. "Fuck. This is going to happen?"

We didn't say anything. After another few beats, it was apparent he wasn't going to either. He wasn't giving his blessing, but he also wasn't stopping us.

Cross nudged me with his hand on my hip. "Let's go."

There was an awkward air in the hallway, but once we were in my room, I breathed easier. I went right to the bathroom as I heard Cross turn the lock. I wasn't thinking about the guys and what they'd say. I slept in Cross' closet all the time—well, I doubted that would happen anymore, but it was the norm. They'd just assume Cross had slept in my closet or on the floor. They wouldn't question it.

I got ready for bed.

When I opened the door, Cross was leaning back on the bed, shirtless, wearing only his boxer briefs. Lust slammed into me. It ricocheted all over, making me speechless for a moment.

Holy shit. He was gorgeous.

I'd always thought he could be a model, but I hadn't let myself fully appreciate him. Until now. Until I couldn't stop myself from looking at his lean muscles, at the V at his hips. His six-pack was clearly defined, along with muscles I never knew a person could show. He was graced with genes normal people didn't have. The way there was a slight shadow from his cheekbones, the way his mouth was perfectly sculpted, perfectly rounded, the way his eyes watched my every move. The cut of his shoulder and his arm muscles—he seemed so perfect.

He seemed almost too perfect at times, and I nearly groaned.

I bit my lip to keep it in.

He let out a ragged breath, leaning forward to rest his elbows on his knees. His nostrils flared. "Stop looking at me like that." His voice was rough.

"Like what?" But I knew.

That throb was back, and it had intensified, filling my whole body with waves of pulsating need.

"You know what?" He stood, pushing up from the bed, and I fell back against the wall.

"Cross," I gulped.

"Bren." He advanced, and I appreciated the few inches he had on me.

Cross was taller. He was leaner. He was meaner, and goddamn, I had no idea how fucking hot he was until now, until I *could* indulge. Finally.

His hand slid around my neck, and he approached until our bodies were barely grazing. My hands went to his chest. I was almost panting.

"We can't—not yet," I told him. My hand slid down his chest, dipping into his waistband.

But I wanted to.

Dear God, I wanted to.

He closed his eyes, resting his forehead on mine. He cupped the sides of my face. His thumbs rubbed over my cheeks, softly, so tenderly. He breathed out, and it felt like a teasing caress.

I bit back a groan, trying to keep my hands from exploring more.

"We won't now, but we will. If you want." He lifted his head.

I saw the effort it took. Strained lines showed around his mouth, and he pressed his lips to my forehead.

I nodded. Holy hell, I would want. I would want so bad.

"One day." He dropped back down to my lips, holding there, and I couldn't stop myself.

I met his mouth with mine, and I felt like I was drowning.

I wrapped my arms around his neck. His mouth opened mine, demanding more. I gave it to him. I was willing to give him anything.

His tongue slid inside.

I met it with mine, enjoying the feel of him against me, but then he paused—one second, one brief moment—before crushing me to him. I could feel him, feel how he wanted to be inside, and he kept kissing me.

Even my fucking toes curled.

I was swept away, not thinking, only feeling.

He picked me up, and his mouth never left. His tongue slid against mine as he laid me onto the bed. My arms were wrapped around his neck, and my legs wound around his waist too. I wanted him in me, all the way in me. I began grinding against him. I wanted him to slide inside.

He kept kissing me, his hand trailing down to push under my tank top and cup my breast. His thumb rubbed over my nipple, and my head fell back. I groaned low in my throat.

This guy.

My best friend. My partner.

I had no words. There were only sensations. There was only pleasure pulsating through all of me.

He took that moment to ease up, lifting himself to the side so he curled against me. I turned my face toward his, and he leaned forward, his lips finding mine once again.

I sighed at the contact.

It felt so right, so natural, and it only made me hunger for more.

Why had I not realized?

"Why did we wait so long?"

His hand rubbed over my stomach before sliding down and slipping under my pajama shorts. He moved to kiss my throat.

"We waited because you weren't ready," he said softly.

"I was an idiot." My eyes popped open. "I said that out loud?"

He nodded, laughing as his fingers found my entrance. All laughter stopped immediately.

I groaned again. "Oh, fuck." I grabbed the back of his hair as his finger slid inside.

It felt so good, so damned good.

I bit my lip, wanting him to move, knowing it'd be torment once he did. I'd want them in me again and again. Then he began thrusting. He moved deeper and deeper, adding a second finger, and I arched my back.

His mouth found my throat, moving down. He moved my shirt out of the way, stretching it so his mouth could find my breast. His fingers kept going. I reached down, grabbing his wrist, but I didn't stop him. I couldn't. I just wanted more. I moved with him, and as his teeth and tongue found my nipple, I cried out. His mouth was on mine instantly, drowning out my cry, and I could only lie there, captive to what he was doing to me. It was a goddamn ride, until I neared the edge, and then I was over it, and I trembled. He kept kissing me, his fingers staying in me until my body stopped shaking.

"Cross," I moaned. I reached for him. I wanted him on me again, and he followed.

He moved over me, but he didn't go inside. Not yet.

I felt him there. He wanted to slip in, but as I panted, he rested his forehead on mine and grinned down. His eyes burned with need. Mine must've looked glazed. I was still trying to catch my breath. I felt frenzied and sweaty, all at the same time.

He ran a hand down my arm. "You okay?"

"You ask me now? After *that*?!" I grinned, and then his mouth caught mine again.

We kept kissing long enough for those fingers to move back inside me and bring me to a second climax. Long enough for me to reach for him and do the same.

I felt wrapped in a cocoon afterwards. I was warm. I was safe. His arms held me, only pulling away once. I was cold for a split second, but then he was back, holding me, and he pulled the blanket over us.

I slept after that.

CHAPTER
FORTY-TWO

CROSS WAS GONE when I woke. He left me a text saying he'd heard the guys getting up and slipped out to meet them. When I padded barefoot out to the kitchen, no one was there. It was four in the afternoon. That meant both Channing and Heather would be at their bars, and the guys would be wherever. It was a Saturday, so they were probably hanging out at Jordan's or waiting to find out where the party was tonight.

I called Channing.

"What's up?" he answered.

He wasn't in his office. I could hear conversation and music behind him.

"Do I have to work tonight?" I asked.

"Uh..."

He could use the help, and we both knew it. And if he didn't need me, Heather would. Manny's had only gotten more popular once Ryerson's crew started hanging out there on a regular basis. Or I should say, once Heather had allowed them back. She'd kicked all Roussou people out for a while. But when word got out about the brawl, it didn't deter anyone. It had the opposite effect. Girls from even Frisco were driving over. Bad boys could be addicting, and thinking of that, images of this morning flashed in my mind.

I grew heated all over, feeling Cross above me, inside of me.

"You know what?"

My brother's voice was like a cold shower. Instant air conditioner.

"Yeah?" I tightened my grip on the phone.

"You've been working every single day since your suspension. You're good with me. Take the night off and tomorrow too."

My mouth went dry from shock. "Are you sure?"

"Yeah. If you still want to earn a paycheck, we can talk about regular work hours, but you start school on Monday. Just don't fuck anything up, okay? Not right away."

"Yeah. No. I won't fuck up. I promise."

He laughed dryly from the other end of the phone. "Don't get crazy. I know how crews work."

"Yeah." Nervous laugh. "Right." Fuck. I felt like an idiot on the phone with my brother. What was happening to me? "And Heather is good too?"

"She's fine. She said Heather's brother offered you the same deal. If you want to work there, you could talk to them about hours."

I grunted. I loved Heather. I was thankful Brandon let me work behind the bar, but serving the Fallen Crest prissy crew was not my idea of fun. Still...

"Okay," I told him. "Let me start school, figure out my community service hours, and I'll decide then."

"Sounds very responsible of you."

I could hear the smirk over the phone. "Har har."

He chuckled. "Okay, seriously. Don't stab anyone."

"Will do, captain."

"And don't be a smartass."

"You're pushing it." I was teasing, and smiling. I didn't even recognize myself.

He barked out a laugh. "I gotta go. Do me one last big favor?"

"Yeah?"

"I want to know what you're doing for community service by the end of next week. You have to get on that. I mean it. Your time is running out. You have to get it in for court approval or you're in violation. They'll take you to juvie if you don't."

"Okay." Off to find Taz. "I'll start today."

"And I want you home at a decent time tonight."

"Decent?" That'd mean eleven or midnight in most families.

"Two in the morning," he said. "I want to know where you're going tonight. Got it?"

"Got it."

"Okay. Love you."

I repeated the phrase back to him, hung up, and considered my surroundings.

I could be lazy. I could read, watch a movie, go back to sleep. Or I could go to Jordan's, knowing the guys would be there. But I must've really embraced the responsible side of me, because I found myself heading back to my room. I showered, dressed in ripped jeans and a black tank top, and grabbed the keys to one of Channing's extra trucks. He had a few, but all of them were here. He must've taken a Harley to work today.

Before driving to Cross and Taz's house, I stopped at the gas station for coffee and a couple energy drinks. It wasn't long after that before I was pulling into their driveway.

Hearing laughter from the backyard, I walked in the front door without knocking. "Taz?"

It was cool inside. The patio doors were open and a breeze wafted in, mixing with the smell of tanning oil and chlorine from the pool. I heard a door slide open, then Taz called, "Yeah! I'll get rum."

The door shut again, and she grumbled, "You'd think the world was dying if they lost their buzz."

I started for the kitchen until I heard the door open behind her.

"That was a little louder than you might've meant," a male voice told her.

"What?" She sounded alarmed.

A low chuckle.

I recognized Race.

"I heard you," he said. "No one else."

Taz groaned. "Sunday would've chewed my head off." She laughed. "I must be more buzzed than I realized."

They couldn't see me, but I heard hands sliding on clothes, a soft sigh...aaaaannd they were making out. She moaned.

I shifted back on my heel. This was awkward.

To move and deal with this now? Or not move and still deal with this now? Okay. There was my answer. I was going to deal.

I coughed, my first signal to them.

Race heard. "What the—"

I walked around the last doorframe. "Hey there." I held up a hand and offered a stiff smile.

He seemed frozen, his hands on Taz's waist. His dark hair had grown a little. It was wet and sticking up. He wore red swimming trunks and nothing else. Taz had on a white wrap that was translucent enough for me to see her red bikini underneath. Her sunglasses were pushed up over her forehead, and her hair was pulled back into a French braid.

If I hadn't known them, I would've assumed they were a perfect couple like you see on Instagram. The matching bathing suits did the trick. Taz was always pretty, but her hair was longer now, or she had extensions in, and she seemed to have upped her sophistication level. She could compete against the likes of Sunday—or hell, even the bitches from Fallen Crest.

I stopped and took them in for a moment. "Wow, Taz. You look incredible." I meant what I said. Her makeup was on point. Her nails looked manicured, the red matching her bikini. I checked her feet. Pedicured. Same red color.

I'd never felt drab before—no, I wasn't going there. I still didn't, but I felt like maybe I should have. She was dressed to be taken seriously.

"Bren."

That's all she could say. Her hands fell slowly from Race's shoulders, but his remained cemented on her waist. He seemed more startled than she did.

I grinned at them, crossing to hoist myself up on the counter. "Close your mouth, Race."

His mouth clamped shut, but his eyes were still wide.

Taz's shoulders lifted as she drew in some air. She turned around and leaned against the kitchen counter, across from where I'd sat. She folded her arms over her chest, pulling her wrap closed with the motion.

"My brother told you about us?" she asked.

"Jordan. Cross didn't know either."

"That's right." Taz blinked a few times, like she was remembering something. "You guys were supposed to be gone all weekend, weren't you? Or coming back tonight?"

I shrugged. "We came back today." I nodded to them. "Congratulations are in order? I feel like you guys have joined Roussou's Hall of Fame for Coupledom." I glanced behind them to the pool, and it was what I had assumed. Sunday Barnes, Monica—all the popular Normals were out there.

"How's your cousin feel about all this?" I asked Race.

"His feelings don't factor into anything I do." Clearing his throat, he asked Taz, "Where's the alcohol? I'll take it out back if you two want to talk."

"Oh." Her frown only deepened, but she grabbed the rum and handed him a few extra wine coolers. "Someone will want these."

He gathered them to his chest, reaching for a few beers too. With a last nod to me, he went back outside, his eyes on Taz as he pulled the patio door closed behind him.

Once it was just the two of us, a whole different feeling settled between us.

It was awkward again, like things had been tipped off-balance.

"Listen, I—" She gestured toward the pool area.

I stopped her with a brisk shake of my head. "Race is a good guy. You're a good girl. You two are perfect for each other." I meant it. I let her hear how genuine I was, and I didn't look away.

She did, her head folding down. Her neck grew red. I heard a sniffle, then she reached up to wipe her eyes.

I hadn't expected that response.

Grasping the counter, I leaned forward. "Are you okay?"

She threw herself at me. Her head landed right in my boobs, and her arms wrapped tightly around me. Her voice came out muffled. "Thank you. I wanted to tell you about Race, but Sunday kept telling me he had a thing for you, and he told me that wasn't the case, but I didn't know and you were gone, but now you're back, and I'm totally rambling and I can't stop. I just can't stop"

"Stop." I put a hand on her forehead and pushed gently.

She leaned back, then laughed. "Thank you." Her arms were still around me, and she snuggled in, pressing her head back to my boobs.

Good thing I didn't have huge boobs, or this might've been more weird.

"I'm sorry for not being around."

I expected her to pull back.

She didn't. She tightened her hold, hugging me harder. "I'm just so glad you're okay." Deep breath. "Cross said you were, that you just needed time, but I didn't know, and you know my brother. He never tells me the real truth when it comes to you. I'm so glad, though. And oh my God, I like Race soo much. You have no idea. All the girls are jealous. If they can't get my brother, they want my boyfriend. I don't know how to handle it, and they're all out there, and I'm so glad you're back."

My hands went to her shoulders. I was ready to push her back so we could have a real conversation when she stepped away, wiping the tears from her face.

"The first semester kinda sucked because you weren't there. But it kinda didn't because there were no big crew brawls happening. Everyone was on good behavior, and then Race happened." A soft smile appeared on her face. She beamed. "Tabatha is so jealous."

"Tabatha?"

"Tabatha Sweets."

The name rolled off her tongue like she said it often. I was a bit impressed.

"You're really moving up in the Roussou world."

Her cheeks pinked, and she ducked her head in a slightly embarrassed way. Moving back to her counter, she secured her wrap, hugging herself.

"You weren't around, and Race wasn't hanging out with the guys. He wasn't hanging out with the Ryersons, so he got snatched up by her crowd." She waved to the pool. "They're all out there."

I nodded. It made sense, what happened in my absence. Taz was now friends—or frenemies—with Sunday Barnes and her group. She'd been alone too, in a way. She'd usually be with me, and often it had been the three of us—her, me, Cross.

Cross probably congregated with Jordan and Zellman last semester, leaving Taz by herself.

If Race got claimed by Tabatha's group, that meant... I cocked my head to the side.

"Race showed interest in you, didn't he?"

He'd been the one to bring her in, not Tabatha.

She looked down again, and her entire neck went beet red.

"I was so nervous. Tabatha had been throwing herself at him." She ran her hands down the front of her legs. Even now, it made her sweat. She laughed nervously. "I thought she was going to filet me alive."

Normally she would've. "Tabatha was nice to you?"

"Yeah. She's been super nice, actually. Sunday and Monica were starting to be bitches to me, more than normal, and Tab was the one to stop them."

Tab. Not Tabatha.

Tabatha Sweets had been after Cross for years too. She was smart. Hearing how it had all played out with his sister, a part of me wondered if she was biding her time, if maybe she was okay with missing out on Race if Taz was brought into the fold. Did she think she'd have better access to Cross? On a more personal level?

"Does Tabatha hang out here often?"

What was more personal than his home?

Taz's mouth tightened, and she shrugged. "Sometimes."

She grabbed a glass and started to walk past me.

"Hold." I shot a leg out from the counter, blocking her. "How often?"

I watched as her fingers tightened their grip on the cup. "I don't know."

"Taz." A low warning.

Another jerking shrug motion. "Maybe once or...three times a week."

"Fuck," I murmured.

"What?" She looked up at me now, holding that glass like it was shield. "She's a friend, Bren."

"She's using you."

There was no heat in my words. I wasn't pushing her to believe me, but the way I said it broke her.

She looked down. "Don't do this."

"You know she's using you."

Her head snapped back up. "I was alone! Do you get that?! I'm always alone except when you're around, and that's only *some* of the time. You've been gone for months. I had no one."

I could've said, "You have your brother," but I knew she didn't. I could've said she had the cheerleading squad, but she didn't, even when she was on it. We were back to the conversation we'd had at the beginning of the year. The crew had taken her brother, and that was even more obvious when I was absent.

I felt bad. I did.

"You could've gone crew." I knew that was stupid, though. That wasn't Taz.

"Right." She barked out an incredulous laugh. "Are you kidding me? Because I'm the fighting type. Yeah, I'm the girl who reaches for a knife or wades into a fight when guys are swinging fists. Are you kidding me?" She glared. "I'm not tough like that. You're one of two girls in a crew. You know I wouldn't be able to hack it. Even if I tried, something would happen. I wouldn't be able to back someone up, and that would be bad." She quieted. I heard the pain there. "No, Bren. I can't hack it, and you know that."

"I think it's something you can aspire toward?" I was teasing her, and she knew it.

She laughed again, sounding much more relaxed this time. "God, I've missed you."

Whatever anxiety or irritation I'd had after hearing about Tabatha faded. Taz had me with those four words, and I slid off the counter, my arms out. She stepped into them, her arms coming around my back.

"It was so boring without you in school."

I laughed, still leaning against the counter. "Right. With the Roussou royalty circling you and Race Ryerson trying to date you,

I'm sure it was super lame. So boring not having to worry about your friend fighting or stabbing principals."

"Well, you know what I mean. It was dull." She looked out to the pool again. "Somewhat." She turned back to me. "Crews are different. Crew life is...exciting, exhilarating, dangerous." She nodded toward her friends. "They're like that, but in a different way."

I pressed my lips together. My opinion of Normals—Taz and now Race being the exceptions—was a bit low. There was a lot of backstabbing and manipulation. We had politics, but we had loyalty in crews.

"Have fun with that," I told her.

"Bren..." She laughed and stepped to the side, hip-checking me. "Tabatha wants to hang out with you, but she's scared to death."

I smiled. "Really?"

"They're all terrified of the crews, but what'd she call you the other night?" She tapped her forehead. "Oh yeah. She said you were like a wolf. Your crew is aptly named. You're beautiful to look at, but lethal. She's right. It's a good metaphor for you."

I frowned. "Are you talking about me, or all crews?"

She thought about that. "You. Well, I mean, the conversation was about all crews, but she was really only talking about you."

And Cross.

"She's got a thing for your brother. You know that." I tried to gentle my tone, but it had to be addressed.

"Bren." She let out a soft puff of air. "You're judging."

I didn't care. People like Tabatha Sweets needed to be watched, your back never turned toward them.

But she wasn't going to hear me now. I could tell. I'd push it later.

I held my hands up. "Okay. Backing off, but if she hurts you, I'm going after her."

She hugged me again. "I'm glad you're back."

Another melting moment here. She might've not been Jordan or Zellman, but I'd back her like she was.

This girl was crew to me.

CHAPTER FORTY-THREE

TAZ PULLED AWAY a second later, frowning up at me. "Cross wouldn't tell me anything, but is everything sorted? I mean, with the stabbing..."

"Yeah, and that's why I'm here—" I caught the guarded flash in her eyes and amended. "It's *one* of the reasons I wanted to see you. I have to figure out my community service hours. Cross mentioned your charity thing might be approved."

Her eyes went wide, and a smile crept over her face. "Yes! Oh my gosh." She jumped back, clapping softly. "Yes, yes! I'd love that. I threw that out to Cross, but I didn't think he'd actually tell you, but yes. Ms. Bagirianni is the head of our committee. She'd be approved in a heartbeat by the judge. She's the one who mentioned it."

Shiiiiiit. I forgot about The Badger.

Despite all the cursing in my head, I knew I was stuck. They'd given me a list of places I could volunteer, but none held my interest. At least I'd be with Taz for this one, but The Badger?

Two guesses as to who'd end up being my counselor. A sinking feeling washed through me.

Taz was still talking, not knowing I'd slipped into the Fucks of all Fucks Fairyland. When I tuned back in, she was saying, "... call her, but I know it'll all work out. We have our first meeting Monday after school." She paused, an expectant look on her face. She had her phone out too. "Should I?"

"What?" I looked from her to the phone, and back again.

"Should I call her?"

"Why would you call her?" I was playing.

"Bren!"

"I'm kidding."

"Oh!" She laughed, then flicked her eyes upward. "But for real, do you want me to call her? I can do it now."

I wanted to say no, give myself more time to find another option, but I had to be realistic. I'd already wasted four months. I needed to get this done, and it'd take me a long time to fulfill the thousand hours, plus twenty counseling sessions.

My cheeks hurt because my smile was so forced. "Sure."

"Great! I'm on it. This will be so much fun."

I was going to regret this. I felt it in my bones. Way too much The Badger.

I nodded, my neck so damned stiff. "Yeah."

She picked up her glass again, gesturing outside with her phone. "I'm going to let Race know what I'm doing, and then I'll give her a call. Are you sticking—"

I gave her a pitying look.

She stopped herself. "No. Your crew isn't out there."

I stood up from the counter, nodding toward the front door. "I'm going to call the guy—"

"Bren Monroe!"

Tabatha Sweets had come inside.

Sunday and Monica were right behind her, both with differing expressions. Sunday's mouth hung open, but she recovered quickly, smoothing a hand down her hair. Monica looked less shocked and more snarly. She didn't hide her sneer.

I looked from them to Taz and asked, "You guys have a uniform protocol now?"

All wore the same sort of wraps, but in different colors. Tabatha wore blue. Monica had red. Sunday had black, and all with bikinis underneath. The only one not wearing high heels was Taz, and they all had hair extensions with their hair down.

Not one person looked like they'd gone swimming.

Tabatha laughed. "We just spend a lot of time together." She came forward as Sunday and Monica hung back by the table. She came right into the kitchen, making Taz move to the side so she could open the fridge. Refilling her glass with juice, she leaned against the spot Taz had vacated. "How are you?"

I should've expected this. She was circling the wagons, bringing Taz in. She had her new backup. I glanced at Sunday. She'd tried approaching me in the fall. That hadn't gone well. But Tabatha was bigger and badder. I'm not talking physically. Power. I was usually lost in the crew world, but I knew enough to know that Tabatha Sweets was the top of the top, for the Normal world.

"You're friends with Taz now, I hear."

Her fake smile fell flat. "I am. I'm trying to be anyway."

I shook my head. I was going to call a spade a spade. "No, you're trying to get to Cross. You've been trying for years."

I waited for the denial.

She lifted a shoulder. "If I wanted to use Taz to get to her brother, I would've done it freshman year." She looked over to Taz. "I'll be honest. Race liked you. That's part of the reason I reached out, and yeah..." She glanced at me. "Some of it might've been about Cross. Can you blame me? Your brother is the best-looking guy in school," she told Taz. "But we're friends because I do like you."

"Are you serious?" Taz's lips opened in surprise. "You *were* using me?"

"I've been over here how many times now?"

She waited.

"Like thirty?" Taz said.

"And how many times has your brother been here, much less talked to me?"

Taz considered it. "Maybe once?"

"Once. One time. And that was just seeing him walk inside, talk to you, grab something from his room, and leave again. I never talked to him. I didn't even try, right?"

"Right."

Taz was buying it. She was licking it up like cream left for a cat. She wanted to believe it, and wariness heightened my dislike for this girl. She was good, damned good.

She was going to be a problem.

Cockiness flared in Tabatha's eyes as she swung her gaze my way.

I stepped up to her, keeping my voice low, because she wasn't worth the extra energy. "You're going to want to hope Race doesn't leave."

Now her lips parted. Confusion pulled her eyebrows together.

"Because if he leaves, there goes Taz's anchor in your group. We'll find out then if you become that anchor instead."

"Bren, come on." Taz stepped to Tabatha's side.

I felt that itch to pull out my knife again. It was small, but it was there. This girl was going to weasel her way into my friend's heart.

That was *her* weapon of choice.

I only had one more thing to say. "If you hurt her, I will slice you."

I was willing to make an exception to my reformed ways. And I wanted Tabatha to see the truth, so I waited. One beat.

I meant it.

When her eyes widened, I added, "I'll get you in just the right spot so it won't completely heal. Every time the temperature changes, it'll ache. If it starts raining, it'll ache. When you get older, you'll throb when you wake up in the mornings. That pain will be me. You'll be haunted by me. You won't get rid of me for the rest of your life. Even when you get really old, I'll always be there. You'll have to take pills to try to erase me, but it won't last. I'll always come back. That's what I'll do, if you hurt her."

Tabatha looked at me in shock, her eyes wide and unmoving.

A pin could've dropped and be heard in that kitchen. No one made a sound.

I moved around her and walked to the front door.

She'd gotten my message. I wasn't like the rest of them.

CHAPTER
FORTY-FOUR

TWO DAYS LATER, I was just settling back into being a student again when I heard Jordan's voice over my shoulder.

"Did you threaten that Sweets chick?"

I rounded in surprise, not from the question, but from the person asking. Jordan fell against Taz's locker next to mine.

"Tabatha Sweets?" I asked.

"Yeah."

I scowled, throwing my book inside my locker. "How's that your business?"

"I'm your crew." He folded his arms over his chest. "And it's her pussy I'd like to get into this weekend."

"Bad idea."

"You didn't answer my question."

I stepped back, my other book in hand.

Jordan reached over me to shut my locker. Then we fell in step, heading to my next class.

As usual, a path cleared for us. But since I'd gotten back to school, there'd been *more* looks, *more* whispers, *more* attention. Some of my teachers weren't the friendliest, but I understood that. I would've felt the same in their shoes, and I kept my promise to Channing: I was the no-attitude girl. There were court-ordered rules I had to follow. One legit said I had to cut the crap. So I had, or I was trying.

Ms. Bagirianni had gotten my participation in her charity committee approved as community service hours. And as I'd anticipated, everything got rolled together, so she was my court-ordered counselor too. The first committee meeting had been yesterday after school, which went splendidly. I said nothing. I did nothing. I just sat. I was happy with the end result, but my counseling was supposed to start tomorrow morning. That would not play out the same way. I was already prepared for another power struggle between The Badger and myself.

"You know my answer." I shook my head. "Why are you even asking?"

He groaned, looking at the ceiling. "Are you kidding me? She's not going to fuck me now that one of my crew has scared the shit out of her."

I shrugged, veering toward the classroom. "She's been wanting to fuck one of our crew for years. I doubt I scared her away. She won't discriminate against you."

"Wait." He grabbed my arm. "She wants to fuck me?"

I could see Cross coming up behind him, and as I pulled my arm free, I nodded at him. "She wants to fuck *him*."

"What's up?" Cross lifted his head in greeting.

Jordan turned around. "Since when does Sweets want to fuck you?"

Cross started to laugh. His eyes slid to mine, narrowing slightly before looking back at Jordan. "Since she started fucking guys. I don't know. Forever."

"Did you fuck her?"

Cross looked at me again.

I only smiled. I was waiting for this answer too.

Saturday morning hadn't been our only time together. He'd slipped into my bed the last three nights, coming in through the window. He disappeared when we woke up. We just made sure that was before Channing was up too.

The nights were torturous and drawn out, but so damned good. How we hadn't had sex yet was beyond me. Cross' restraint was both infuriating and amazing.

"No." He pulled his eyes from mine and gave Jordan a dubious look. "I'd never get rid of her."

"But that's you. If I screw her, she won't feel the same about me. One good pound and I'd be in the clear." He clapped a hand on Cross' shoulder. "Thanks, man. I'm going for it this weekend." He looked at me, a plea already in his eyes.

I shook my head. "I'm not taking back my threat."

"I know." He sighed. "But can you try not to threaten her again? At least for this week. Give me a shot?"

I groaned, but nodded. "I'll try to refrain."

"Thanks, B!" He clapped me on the shoulder too before he took off for his class, an extra bounce in his step.

Cross watched him go. "He's like a giant five year old sometimes."

I laughed. "This week's going to suck. I can already feel it."

Cross held the door for me, following me into the class. We both moved toward the last rows of seats, dropping into the closest two.

"What do you mean?" he asked.

Tabatha chose that moment to enter the room. A couple football guys followed, along with Monica and another girl on the charity committee Taz had put together. Tabatha looked over, her gaze lingering on me before she slid into her seat. The guys sat closer to us, one of them holding out a fist to Cross.

"Hey, man."

Cross met it with his, nodding and leaning back. Our conversation was done. Normals could hear.

"Hey, Cross." Monica smiled, sliding into the seat behind Tabatha and parallel to him.

Cross looked at her, then to me, and didn't respond.

Tabatha's mouth fell open slightly.

Monica just shrugged. She ducked her head to whisper with Tabatha.

Cross noticed the exchange and turned to me with a questioning look. I shook my head. I'd tell him later.

He kicked his feet up on the book rest of the chair in front of him. The other student didn't seem to mind.

The teacher came in then, with a note in hand. She read it for a moment before looking around to find me. "Bren, you're to go to the office."

I sat up straight, tension filling my shoulders. "Why?"

She shook her head. "I don't know. The note just says to send you there."

My counseling session was tomorrow. I hadn't done anything wrong. The next charity committee meeting wasn't till Thursday. There was no reason for me to go there.

Except get in trouble.

I had to go. I knew it, but I couldn't make myself get up. My legs literally wouldn't work.

Feeling Cross' gaze on me, I rested my hands on my seat. My palms were flat, my fingers spread out. "I'm good. Thanks."

She dropped the note onto her desk. She seemed tired and distracted, her hair frazzled around her, but she looked at me curiously. "Excuse me?"

"I'm aware this looks ridiculous to you, but I haven't done anything wrong. If I go there, I'll just get in trouble. So, I'm not going to the office."

The tension I could feel in my shoulders filled the room. Everyone fell silent and waited.

Here I went again. Starting trouble, but I swear this wasn't intentional. I just couldn't move around the boulder in my stomach. And what I'd said was true—if I went, I'd be walking into trouble. I was never called down there for good things. Always bad. Always trouble.

Hell, maybe I should at least cause a little trouble. Maybe then I wouldn't feel like I was walking to my slaughter.

The teacher looked at Cross. "Are you going to back her up if I send her to detention?"

There was no hesitation. His chin rose. "You know I will."

She rolled her eyes, letting out an impatient sigh. "This is ridiculous. This whole crew system is stupid. She!" She pointed right at me, her words directed at Cross. "Is not going to go anywhere in life. You know that, right? She assaulted a member of this administration with a deadly weapon, and she's still here. She should be in prison, or at least expelled from this place." There was a wildness to her words. "Bren Monroe! Get out of my classroom."

At least now I felt like I'd earned it, and I was aware of how stupid that was.

She waved her hand in the air. "I don't care who your brother is or what lawyer he hired. If you lay one hand on me, I'll make sure you go to prison. You hear that?" She stabbed her finger against the desk.

I winced from the force, but she didn't flinch.

The room was so silent. Someone's phone buzzed, but no one moved to get it. I stood, grabbing my books. A second later, Cross' chair scraped as he stood too.

The teacher's hands flew in the air. "Are you kidding me? Cross, you have so much potential."

He didn't reply. He just looked at me.

Everyone watched us leave.

"You can't follow her to the grave or to prison," the teacher called. "You won't be able to share a cell, and I don't think you'll care about a coffin."

Her words struck deep.

It felt like my own knife had plunged into me. I didn't know it was going in until it was there, and the pain took my breath away.

I didn't move for a second, not until I felt Cross behind me. His hand touched the small of my back, and I jerked forward.

I debated where to go—to the office, to find out what trouble I was in, or back out the door with another "cut day" under my belt. It was my second goddamn day back, and I already wanted to run.

Cross stepped close, but his hand fell away. I knew students inside the class could see us, and I knew I looked weak. I couldn't help myself.

I felt beat down.

In that moment, *they* won.

"You might not even be in trouble."

I rolled my eyes. "When am I not in trouble?"

He grinned, and I felt my toes curl.

"When you haven't done anything wrong."

"I'm sure they made something up," I protested. "It's day two, and I'll be out of here."

TIJAN

"Come on, Bren." Cross' hand came to my back again, slipping under my shirt.

Warmth spread under his touch, and my body started to buzz. My eyelids grew heavy as I looked at him. I knew what he was doing. Even just the slight reminder of his touch had my need for him growing. After the last three nights, I was almost feverish just being near him.

"You're not making me want to go to the office."

He laughed softly, but moved away. "Let's just see what they want. If you're in trouble, you know I'm walking with you."

I gave in, going with him, but the teacher's words haunted me.

Cross, you have so much potential... You can't follow her to the grave.

She'd touched on what I'd always thought about Cross.

Why was he crew?

Why was he friends with us?

Why was he friends with me?

Why was he *with* me?

I snuck a look at him. The teacher was right. He could do better than us. He had a future. He could have a future now. He had the smarts, the looks, and he could do bigger and better things than all of us here.

He shouldn't be with you, a voice whispered to me from the back of my mind. It didn't speak up often, but it was saying something now.

I looked at him more fully.

He ignored my perusal, probably knowing what was going on in my head. But I realized that voice was right.

The firefly was coming back. I felt the beat of its wings, the steady growing of its dangerous warmth. It'd been so long since it kept me company, and I felt its impending arrival.

I *was* bringing him down. I *was* holding him back.

I was spiraling.

Cursing, Cross reached in front of me to open a closet door, and he pushed me inside. It was dark, and he didn't bother turning the light on.

285

This was perfect. The darkness. His mouth was on mine two seconds after he pushed me up against the door.

Oomph!

I had one second of notice, and then I was slammed with lust. It scorched me, doubling what it'd been moments ago. I felt like I was going to explode as I kissed him back.

"Cross," I moaned.

He only kissed me. He didn't stop, and I couldn't do anything except go along for the ride.

It felt so good, all of it. The way he held the side of my face. The way his lips pressed against mine, his chest against mine. How I felt his strength, his power, his determination as he drew in a breath. His lips never left mine.

"Whatever you're thinking—" He ripped his mouth away, but only to take a ragged breath before he moved back for more. "Stop. I don't want to hear it. I don't want to feel the ramifications, but I know you're slipping away."

I closed my eyes, though it didn't matter. There was darkness all around.

He was talking to that voice inside of me, and he was right. She was there. She reared her head again. She was the firefly coming to me in the dark. She beckoned, wanting me to follow her, and that was a different seduction altogether.

I could stop it. I could stop her, but sometimes it was hard. Sometimes she was the only one with me over the years, she'd been all I had at times.

"Cross." My hands found his waist. I could feel his stomach trembling under my touch.

"Bren." My name was a whisper. He kissed a trail down my jawline, over my throat, lingering where my shirt met my chest. I'd worn a tank top today, and I was thankful for how low the cleavage dipped.

It was now my favorite shirt.

I ran my hands up his chest, skimming over his arms, and slipped them under his sleeves. His biceps moved, shifting under my touch, like I had awakened them.

His hand slid to the back of my neck and he held me. He straightened. I could feel his lips against my forehead, but he waited.

God.

I didn't want to.

I liked her. Whenever she showed up, I was protected. I was shielded. She protected me from the pain, the hurt. I didn't want to give that up.

"Bren, please." Cross' lips dipped back down to mine. I felt his breath. "Don't go."

Don't go.

His words repeated in my head.

I felt a strength I didn't know I had, bolstered from somewhere, flowing through me. And like an unconscious flip of a switch, the firefly was leaving again.

He'd pushed her away.

I missed her as soon as I felt her go, because I was raw once again. I was exposed.

I dropped my head to his chest. Cross wrapped his arms around me and rocked me back and forth, his hand sweeping up and down my back.

"Thank you."

When we left that closet, we didn't hold hands.

We walked straight and tall to the office together.

CHAPTER
FORTY-FIVE

"YOU WANT ME to do what?"

The new principal, Ken Brohgers, stared back at me from across his desk. They made Cross go back to class. He'd glanced to me, and I nodded, thinking it'd be fine. They said I wasn't in trouble. That was the only reason I was okay with Cross going. There'd been too much bad shit associated with it in the past. They said I wasn't in trouble, and this meeting was "absolutely necessary." Only good things would come of it.

What a crock of bullshit.

Principal Brohgers was almost as opposite of Neeon as possible. Mr. N was tall, six- three, and Brohgers barely topped five three. That wasn't true. He just looked like that sitting behind his desk. He was probably five-five when he stood up, with a head full of frizzy hair that was losing its reddish tint so it was half white at the same time. His face started off as round, then finished with a long and pointed chin. He had thick bushy eyebrows that jutted out over his eyes, which were wide-set and narrow. In his older fifties, Ken Brohgers was a thin rail of a man.

Superintendent Miller sat next to him, and they shared a look.

"Your father's lawyer reached out to the school because he's a part of a mentoring program," Principal Brohgers said again. "They would like to include our school, but there are stipulations since you're a student here. Normally you would be someone we'd ask to have included in the program—"

"No!" My decision was made before he finished.

I knew these programs. Convicts were supposed to mentor troubled kids until they went straight. It wasn't happening. I didn't give a rat's ass if my father's lawyer or anyone else thought I was troubled. That was the pot calling the kettle black.

"You guys need my brother's permission to even be asking me this."

"Well..." They looked at each other again.

The superintendent leaned forward this time. "That's the purpose of this meeting. We'd like to approach your brother about the program itself."

"Why? I already said I'm not going to do it."

"No, no." Principal Brohgers cleared his throat. He scooted even closer to his desk and placed his arms on top. "We'd like to work with the crews, get all of them integrated with this program."

Horror lodged in my throat—one big ball I couldn't swallow or spit out. I had to suffer it.

"Are you kidding me?" That was a horrible idea.

"It's not a bad program—"

"Let me guess," I managed, still reeling inside. "You want to fix the crews, work with the older members and have them encourage younger members to go to this prison, get mentored by a convict, and learn how to be nice. Right? No more bad crews?"

They just stared at me.

I couldn't have been far off, so I stood up. If I didn't get out of here, I was going to say things that would get me suspended again. Or worse.

"I have to go." I started for the door.

"Wait!" Principal Brohgers stood as well, his hand extended as if he could physically stop me. "Don't go. Please. We want to work *with* you guys. We don't want to continue down this path."

I stopped and turned around. "What do you mean by 'this path'?"

Superintendent Miller scratched behind his ear, looking everywhere except at me.

"Bren."

I heard the appeasing voice that adults used when they were about to promise you daisies, yet hand you rotten weeds.

I wasn't going to like this, whatever it was.

CREW

He tugged at his collar. "Uh...we realize the crew system began because there was a need to uproot a power alliance at this school. While we can understand the attraction crews have for certain students, you have to understand our concern with them."

My mouth was dry. The flame was there, a small flicker.

"Certain students?" I echoed their words.

"Troubled students."

The flicker burst into a full-fledged fire. It was heating me up. I knew who they meant—kids like me, who had violent tendencies, who had no futures, who were going nowhere in life. Prison or six feet under. Those kids.

"That's who you think joins crews?" I asked. "Those kind of kids."

"Well, yeah." The principal gave me a blank look. He had no idea how wrong that statement was.

"I see."

The firefly returned. She flew in, bringing the darkness with her. I felt it rising, coating my insides, blanketing me. It molded with the fire. I closed my eyes a moment, letting her take over. Once she had, I couldn't be touched. They couldn't hurt me anymore.

I stood and began to leave.

"Bren."

I didn't know which one spoke. I didn't care.

I reached for the door handle, and I left.

I didn't turn back.

The bell must've rung. A line of students started to leave their classrooms.

"Bren?"

I walked right past Taz, then Tabatha and the others as they left their room. Students slowed, casting me looks of confusion, of irritation, of concern.

I ignored every single one.

I went to my locker. I got my bag and keys, and I left. I was in the parking lot when Cross shouted my name, hurrying behind me.

I didn't want to see him. He'd try to shake *her* hold on me. *She* protected me. He just wanted me to be open to more pain. I couldn't.

I held up a hand. "Don't, Cross. Not this time."

He caught up to me. "What happened?"

I kept walking. I had ten feet to go. Only ten. It seemed the length of a football field.

"Bren! Hey!"

That was Jordan. I had no doubt Zellman was with him. My crew had come for me, but I couldn't this time. They couldn't protect me from this like the darkness did. The darkness, that firefly, had another name, one I'd put out of my mind.

Things were better. Channing was acting like a real brother. He loved me.

My crew was with me. I was with Cross.

I should've been happy. I shouldn't have any need for her, but her hold was so strong. Her hooks were in, and they weren't letting go, not until it was safe again to come out. I opened the door of my Jeep and got inside.

"Bren, stop!"

Cross blocked me from shutting the door.

Jordan and Zellman stood behind him. But I only shoved him back and shut the door. I put my keys into the ignition. I turned. The engine came on, and I put it in reverse.

The passenger door opened.

"Get out!" I yelled.

Cross climbed in, shutting the door and glaring. "Not a fucking chance."

"Leave, Cross!" *She* cracked. *She* let emotion ring out in my voice. "You heard our teacher. You can be someone. You can do things. Why are you here?" I shook my head. "You shouldn't be. You shouldn't be anywhere near me."

"Stop it." His jaw clenched.

"Get out."

"No."

"Cross!"

"No."

He put his seatbelt on, and the doors in the back opened. Both Jordan and Zellman got inside.

Jordan leaned back. "Just drive, Bren. We're with you whether you want us or not."

I laughed hollowly, but I couldn't make them leave.

I really had no option. I was easing back when someone rapped on my side window.

I braked. It was Alex. I lowered the window.

"What do you want?" I asked.

"What happened in there?"

"Walk, Ryerson." A low warning came from Cross. He wasn't messing around.

I began putting the window back up, but Alex clamped a hand over it. I would've cut his fingers if I kept going. That was tempting, but Channing had said *later* for Alex.

I stopped my window. "Leave me alone."

"What happened in there?" He wasn't moving.

"It's none of your business—" Jordan began.

"I heard it had to do with the crews, not just yours. I want to know what it was about." He scrubbed a hand over his face, briskly. He sounded frustrated. "Bren, you need to tell me. If it's all crews, you have a duty."

I felt *her* rallying in me. She didn't want me to feel or think or care. She wanted me to be numb to the world.

But Alex was staring me in the face, and I was surrounded by my crew. Her hold was slipping. Feeling the darkness draw back down, I could almost see the firefly moving away.

"They want to fix us," I said quietly.

A vein stuck out from the side of Alex's neck. "Fix who? How?"

"Us. The troubled kids, the ones who are going to prison or underground. They want us to be better."

"Say what?"

Cross cursed under his breath.

"What the fuck?" Jordan roared. "That's what they said?"

"They want us to be mentored by convicts." And the real kicker... "My dad is one of the ones in the program."

"They want you to be in the program?" Cross asked.

"They wanted me to ask Channing to get all the crews involved."

"You serious? We're all troubled kids?" Alex barked.

That was the implication, yes. I let him figure it out.

He cursed, and I swore I saw an actual red glint in his eyes before he stepped away from my Jeep.

"Where are you going?" Cross called.

Jordan and Zellman had stood up in the back of my Jeep. They were quiet, watching whatever was going to unfold, but not Cross. He hopped out of my vehicle and darted in front of Alex, forcing him to stop.

"Think, Alex. Think first."

Alex tried to go around him.

Cross moved too, still blocking him.

"Fucking hell, Cross. Get back. I mean it."

That was enough for the rest of us. I slammed the Jeep into park and yanked the keys out. Jordan and Zellman scrambled out, coming up behind Alex. I was there a second later.

Cross put a hand up, holding us off.

"They're wrong, Alex," he coaxed. "We all know they're wrong. We're not worthless. We're not the bullies. All those words are attached to the word *troubled*. *We* get that. *They* don't. We're not *wrong*."

"They need to learn." Alex growled in his throat, starting around Cross again.

This time, I hurried forward to stand side by side with Cross, adding to his wall.

"Really, Bren?"

I nodded. "Listen to him. He's smarter than all of us."

Cross glanced at me as he continued. "Alex, they're the uneducated ones. They're adults who don't see grey. They only see black and white. You go in there and do what you're going to do, you're confirming their assumptions. They'll put us *all* in the wrong category. We're not wrong. We're not worthless."

"You're not!" Alex shot back, that vein sticking out again. "They love you. Everyone loves you. You're lethal as hell, but you get away with it because you're smart, and you look like a pretty boy. You don't get stereotyped like the rest of us."

"You think that matters to me?"

Now Cross was pissed. His eyes narrowed.

A shiver wound down my spine.

"You're talking to me like I'm not in the trenches with you," Cross said softly. He looked to Jordan, Zellman, and me. "Like I don't bleed when my crew bleeds."

"You know what I mean," Alex huffed.

Cross got in his face, forcing him to step back toward Jordan and Zellman.

"No, I don't," he said with a scary quiet that promised he was about to strike. "Why don't you spell it out for me? I want to make sure you didn't just insult me to my face."

Alex swallowed, taking note of his surroundings. We'd attracted a crowd as soon as I left, and now it seemed to have doubled. A new wave of awareness rippled through them. It wasn't a student-teacher fight like before. Word would spread that the Wolves were pushing around the Ryerson crew's leader.

"You know what I meant." Alex looked at the ground.

Cross didn't let up. "Then don't fuck up the rest of our crews," he hissed. "You want to watch something burn, you wait until we can't get in trouble for it. Going in there, starting whatever shit you want to start—that's going to have effects for all of us. Not just you. They're going to blame Bren for whatever you do."

"So what do you want me to do?" Alex didn't have it in him to stand down. But he was keeping it together. He was a bull being told not to leave the pen while the door was wide open. He was stomping on the ground, wanting to charge.

But he was listening.

"Wait."

One word. That's all Cross said.

"They insulted all of us," he added after a moment. "They'll be *educated* on their mistake. But wait until we figure it out."

"Wait for what?"

"For me!" Cross snapped. "You wait until I tell you the plan."

Alex nearly snarled, but he clamped his mouth shut and swung away from us. Shoving his hands into his pockets, he walked off.

It took a second of silence, but Cross glanced around. Everyone was staring at him.

"What?" he snarled. "What are you looking at?"

I'd always seen this side of Cross, but everyone else was seeing it now.

I looked to Jordan, and he lifted his head, pride raising his chin.

He said, "We're staring at our leader."

CHAPTER FORTY-SIX

AROUND A BONFIRE pit behind Manny's that night, we filled Channing in on everything. When I told him we needed to talk, he'd said the crowd would be less bloodthirsty in Fallen Crest than at his own bar.

"He called you troubled?" Channing asked, his nostrils flaring.

Cross, Jordan, and Zellman sat with me, and three of Channing's own crew had come: Chad, Moose, and Congo.

I nodded. The words weren't coming. I didn't feel like speaking.

"They want all crews to do this program?"

I stopped interacting. It burned a hole each time I had to remember.

Cross sat on top of a picnic table beside me. "All crews. That's what she said."

Channing frowned, not saying anything for a moment. He shared looks with the rest of his crew before he nodded. "Okay. Thank you."

"Wait." Jordan pushed up from the wall he'd been leaning against. "That's it? Just thank you?"

Channing lifted his hands. "What do you expect? We're not in high school anymore."

"But..." Jordan looked at Channing's crew. "You guys are, like, the godfathers of crews. You're the longest-running crew there is." He turned to my brother. "You created the system. You have to help us."

"Look." Channing stepped toward him. "It's an after-school program. There's not much we can do except maybe help you start

296

a petition so they don't only target crew kids. Other than that, I'll be honest. I'm not sure it's a bad idea. You guys would be talking to convicts. I think every teenager should go through that. The more information you get, the better."

"Even Dad?"

I couldn't believe I'd said that word, but as all eyes looked my way, I couldn't shrink now. I'd spoken. I had to own my words, though my hand trembled.

I tucked it under my leg.

"What'd you say?" Channing asked.

"You heard me. You want me to see Dad? Hear his words of wisdom?"

Channing's eyes narrowed. "I recall asking you to go with me to visit him not too long ago, so yeah. Go and hear what he has to say."

He started to turn away, his shoulders rigid and tight.

He was such a hypocrite. He hated him more than I did.

"Should we talk about that night? That's what he's going to say to me. He's going to talk about his regrets."

Channing's back got even tighter. His shoulders seemed to stretch out, widening his shirt.

I waited. I wanted him to say something. I wanted to hear him acknowledge that night.

I laughed. "Don't you want to hear a play-by-play of that night? I can tell you. I don't need to go see Dad to remember." Slowly I stood, though I kept my head down. I felt like I was talking to a sleeping cobra. I was wooing him, trying to engage him. It didn't matter that the cobra was my brother.

No one talked about the night our dad was arrested. No one. I never had, and I knew Channing hadn't. I didn't even know if Channing knew what had happened. This was the first time I'd brought it up. And I was using it to needle him. I wanted to get at him. I wanted him to feel some of the pain I would have to suffer if we didn't fight the mentoring program.

He looked back toward me as I stood waiting.

"Bren."

He wanted me to let him off the hook. I wasn't going to do that. I wanted that cobra to wake up. I didn't care if I would get bitten. I might have welcomed it.

"Were you told what happened that night? Are you able to imagine it?"

"Don't." He drew in oxygen, then letting it out just as quickly.

So he did know. Maybe?

I began remembering myself, speaking the memories out loud. "She died. She was gone, and you were gone too. It was me and him in the house."

Way too many fucking years, just him and me. Him. Me. His alcoholism.

"It was quiet when she was sick. Did you know that? It was eerily quiet. Then she died, and there was no sound. Not a peep. You were gone. He was gone. *She* was gone. It was just me, until…"

I hated this. I hated peeling back the layers, the memories, the numbness. It was all being stripped away. "Then he started coming back. So did the booze. The partying."

Channing's jaw clenched.

He knew what that was like. It was why he'd left in the first place.

"His friends started coming around too."

I would be in bed. I'd be trying to sleep.

I could hear their drunken laughter. They'd hoot. They'd holler. Their dirty jokes had them slapping hands. They sickened me. They sickened me now.

"That became the norm, Channing. Every night he brought friends home. He didn't care who they were, just as long as the house wasn't empty. He didn't want to feel her like I did."

Like I still did.

"Stop, Bren," Channing rasped, but wouldn't look at me.

He couldn't. He would see what had happened to me.

"At first he stayed up while they were there. He was responsible, making sure no one found out about me. That didn't last."

He started falling asleep.

That night his latest group of "friends" had woken me up with their noise. But they always stayed downstairs, so I didn't think too much of it. I'd just needed to go to the bathroom.

"I didn't have toilet paper," I said aloud.

If I had...

"I was going to use the bathroom in the hallway."

Stupid toilet paper.

"Bren." Channing's eyes had shut tight. He didn't want to hear this, but it was coming. It was time. Finally.

"Maybe I should've grabbed a robe. I don't know. Maybe if I'd stayed in my room..." If I'd had toilet paper. If I hadn't needed to use the bathroom outside of my room.

I felt *her* coming now. She wanted to protect me. She wanted to envelop me so I didn't feel what I was about to say, but I pushed her off. I wanted to go numb, but I couldn't. It wasn't right, not this time. Not yet.

My throat was scraped raw. "The cops made note of what I was wearing that night," I told him. "A sleeping tank top and boy shorts."

Like it was my fault.

Like it mattered what I had been wearing.

I still felt their silent accusations. It had been in their eyes, the way they looked at me, as I sat there covered in blood.

I had to get to the bad parts. I couldn't hold *her* off anymore. Inch by inch, I let her in, and I became so numb I couldn't feel my lips.

"I was in the hallway, on my way back. The cops told me later that when I flushed the toilet, that's how he knew someone was up there. He heard me."

I had reached for my bedroom's door handle. Three feet and I would've had the door locked. I would've been inside. I would've been safe.

"He came out of nowhere."

I never saw him. I felt him.

There was a shadow on the stairs, and then his hand was on my mouth. He dragged me back into their room.

God. I clamped my eyes shut. What if it'd happened in their room? What then? What would've been the ending?

"Bren?" Someone had called my name.

He'd paused, just inside their bedroom, and he must have changed his mind.

"He was going to rape me in Mom and Dad's room. Then he heard Dad, and he took me into my room instead."

He'd shut the door and whispered in my ear, "*You fucking tell him you're fine and you're going to bed, or I will kill you. You got that, cunt?*"

"He shook me as he threatened me."

Our dad had said that's how he knew I was lying. I never told him I was fine. It was a lie.

I didn't lie.

"I said what he told me to. I recited it word for word."

But I'd known what was by my bed, what I could grab.

"He said he was going to kill me." Even now, anger swelled inside me. I felt it pushing at the numbness.

"He waited until Dad bought my lie and we heard him leave."

I'd heard one agonizing footstep on the floor after another until they faded. I'd felt my humanity going with him.

"He threw me on the bed. He started ripping my clothes off. He was in a hurry. He fumbled for his condom—so thoughtful of him, right?"

I'd known where my knife was.

He'd gotten distracted for a second, and I reached for it, under the mattress.

"I stabbed him. I thrust that knife in as far as I could, as hard as I could—just like he wanted to rip inside me."

He'd knocked my hand away, but I fought him. I rolled too, punching his dick as hard as I could. As he doubled over to the floor, I was on him.

"I grabbed my knife and pulled it out."

I'd raised it above my head, straddling that asshole.

"Then Dad took it from me."

It had been time for his crime.

"I wanted to do it."

He'd taken the knife from me, and with a gentle hand, he'd ushered me to the side. He'd told me to leave.

"He tried to get me to leave. But I knew what he was going to do." I could feel tears in my eyes. I hated them. They were weakness. "He cut his throat, and I watched from the door."

He'd killed him so I wouldn't.

I waited a beat, then asked Channing, "Still think I'd benefit from hearing how I should be in prison and not him?"

My father went to prison for a crime I should've committed.

CHAPTER
FORTY-SEVEN

THE SILENCE WAS THICK.

Weak. Vulnerable. Exposed. I was all three of those, and I hated it.

I reached for my knife, and as soon as I felt it, everything off balance centered again.

"Were you going to kill him?" Channing asked.

I'd expected the question from Cross, so I looked over. He already knew.

I turned to my brother. "Yes."

He nodded once. He didn't say anything, but I caught a darkness in my brother, one that I saw in the mirror, one that scared me to my core at times.

It was the firefly, but there was a different glint to it in him. A murderous glint.

He reached out to touch my arm, but turned to his crew members. "We need to talk to the rest of the active crews, get them filled in on what's happening at the school."

My head reared back. "I thought you weren't going to get involved?"

He gave me a long look. "I changed my mind. We're stopping the whole goddamn fucking thing."

I didn't know what to say. "That's it? I tell you all that and now suddenly you're going to do something about the program?" Didn't he have anything else to say? About Dad? About that night?

Channing's eyes fell to my knife, which I tossed in the air and flicked my wrist around to catch.

"You have your knife out, Bren."

I flushed.

His hand gentled on my arm until he dropped it. A look so stark, so pained, so anguished looked at me that I froze. I found myself blinking back tears at the suddenness of it.

He stepped close, his hands coming to touch my shoulders, so delicately, so gently, as if I were a broken egg held together by one piece of tape. He dropped his voice, whispering, "We'll talk later. Trust me." He pulled me in, moving my knife out of the way, and then folded his arms around me. "God, Bren." He was shuddering.

I was—I was still frozen.

He pressed a kiss to my head. "I'm so fucking sorry."

He hugged me one more second before stepping away. As he did, he wiped his thumb under his eye, catching a wetness I'd only seen there twice before.

"You're going to stop the school thing?" Jordan straightened from where he'd been resting against Manny's back wall. Zellman and Cross came to my side.

My crew watched my brother like somehow he had the answers.

"We'll get it fixed," Channing said. "But you have to give us time. Okay?"

It was like the four adults were leaving to do adult things, and us children had been told to stay.

Channing and his guys disappeared around the building. My crew waited for my decision. If I wanted to talk, they knew I'd say something. If I wanted to fight, I'd say that too.

Cross stood right next to me, heat radiating off of him.

"We're with you," Jordan offered. "Whatever you want, B."

I wanted to forget.

"Anything but remembering," I told them.

Jordan snapped his fingers. "How about a good old-fashioned egging? I know a principal and superintendent who deserve some new decoration on their houses."

It was childish. It was something a sixth grader would do, but it wouldn't land us in jail. It was perfect.

"I'm in." I was *so* in.

We were heading to our vehicles when the side door burst open.

"Cross!" Taz ran down toward us, out of breath and red in the face. Her eyes were wide, almost frenzied. Tabatha and Sunday came right behind her, looking less panicked, but still concerned.

We all paused, waiting.

Taz grabbed Cross' arm, panting slightly. "It's Race. Alex's crew showed up at the house."

A fight between Alex and Race was trouble. The fact that he'd sought Race out at Cross' house was even more trouble. That made it crew business.

"Our place?" Cross asked. "You sure?"

She nodded, sucking in air. "They asked if you were home. When I said you weren't, he told Race he'd better step outside. Those were his exact words."

Jordan moved closer. "They could say it's family business."

But it was happening at Cross' house.

There could be ramifications if Cross didn't say something.

I touched his arm. "Let's go see what's happening. It's at your house."

Zellman agreed. "That's your home."

"Come on, guys!" Jordan threw a hand up. "We've already got big problems. This is a fight we can avoid."

But Cross started off, turning to walk backward. "Then don't come," he said.

He'd just thrown down the worst insult possible to a crew member.

Zellman and I went with Cross. Z jumped in the back. I got in the passenger side, and Cross was starting the engine when we felt the truck dip under someone's weight.

The window slid open and Jordan rolled his eyes. "Fine. I'm with you guys. Don't fucking insult me again."

Cross looked in the rearview mirror, meeting his gaze. He didn't reply, just put the truck in drive.

Taz tapped on the window, so he rolled it down.

"You're going to go?" she asked, her eyes still wide. Her breathing was shallow, and there were beads of sweat over her top lip.

Tabatha came to stand next to Taz. "The other guys are there." She pointed to Sunday. "Our friends."

Zellman snorted, resting his elbows on the truck's edge. He smiled at Sunday. "You have other friends I don't know about?"

She rolled her eyes. "You're hitting on me *now*?"

"I'd hit on you if we were in the middle of the apocalypse." He winked. "Make me a zombie, and I'll still try to boink you, then maybe eat you."

She laughed and pushed at his shoulder, shoving him backward. "I've learned my lesson, Z. I've moved on to older guys. They're more..." Her head cocked to the side. She pretended to think about it. "Longer lasting."

His grin went to a scowl. "Who? Who's longer lasting than me?"

She backed up, waving. "Almost anyone at this point."

Zellman frowned, but he was trying not to laugh.

"Can we ride with you?" Taz asked.

Cross paused, frowning.

"We got a ride here," she continued. "It'd just be easier if we could hop in."

He shrugged, gesturing to the back. "Hop in, but hold on, T. We go fast."

She nodded. All three girls scrambled toward the back. Zellman lowered the tailgate, and they climbed up. He pulled it closed again after swatting Sunday's ass. She tried to look annoyed but failed.

Once the three sat down and the guys positioned themselves at the end of the truck's bed, Cross started off.

Despite what he said, he did drive safer than usual, slowing down at turns and even stopping at an empty intersection because the light was red. The rest of the crew smirked at him as he pulled into the alley behind his house.

He noticed our looks and grimaced. "Don't fucking start."

Jordan laughed. "You're a good brother, Cross."

Cross walked ahead of him, extending a middle finger in the air.

I followed Cross, glancing back toward Jordan and Zellman.

The girls had fallen to the back. Tabatha and Sunday were whispering. I slowed, letting Jordan and Zellman go past me. I felt their curious looks, but I ignored them.

Tabatha looked smug, with her chest jutting out, as they approached me.

"You okay?" Taz drew up next to me.

It was her boyfriend we were here to save. "Shouldn't I be asking you that?"

"Yeah, but..." Her eyes ran over my face. "You look tired."

Tabatha laughed, linking her elbow with Taz's. "That's her nice way of saying you look like crap." She jiggled Taz a little, those smug eyes on me. "Be nice, Taz. Her guys are here to save the day. Remember?"

Oh.

No.

In an instant, my hand was around her throat, and I walked her back until I could shove her into the side of Cross' truck.

"He—whoa!"

"OH MY GOD!" Sunday screeched, and the guys came back to see what was happening.

Zellman grabbed Sunday's shoulders and began walking her into the house. She resisted at first, digging her heels in, but after he whispered in her ear, she began edging away with him. She kept looking back, biting her lip.

I waited, my hand around Tabatha's throat.

She wasn't fighting me. She was tense and still, watching me.

Taz twisted her hands in front of her. "Bren, don't. Please."

Everyone ignored her, and Cross stepped up on my left, followed by Jordan on my right. As they closed in, Taz was shut out. She could hear me, but she couldn't see my face.

"Cross," Tabatha pretended to croak at him.

I couldn't hide a grin. As soon as I'd gotten her against the truck, I'd loosened my hold dramatically. She could've stepped free. She was putting on a show.

Cross knew it too. "Yeah?" He raised an eyebrow.

Her eyes darted from me to him. "Help." A hoarse whisper. "Please."

His face was impassive, and he shifted back, giving us some space. He crossed his arms over his chest. "She's barely touching you. Stop acting."

"Cross!" Her voice sounded more normal there.

"Why the fuck are you talking to me?"

Her eyebrows shot up. "You're going to let her touch me like this?"

"Yeah." Jordan spoke this time, leaning on his elbow against the truck. His eyebrows wiggled. "You chicks need to learn that crews don't care about gender. Don't matter if the person has a dick or a vagina. Crew is crew." His gaze skirted to me. "She's my crew."

"Mine too."

Tabatha's eyes moved to Cross.

She gulped, then came back to look at me.

I removed my hand and stepped back. "I warned you earlier," I told her softly. "Fuck with me one more time, and you'll learn why I'm crew and you're not."

She laughed harshly. "What are you going to do—"

It wasn't my hand this time, it was Jordan's. He shifted so his hand was on the vehicle, but way too close to her. His finger pressed against her neck. His whole stance was meant for intimidation.

"Crew is crew. Our enemies are shared. Why don't you fucking get that?" Jordan loomed over her, twice her weight and probably three times her strength. No guy had ever dared treat her this way.

He didn't need to say anything else. Her eyes darted around the scene once more, and she gave the tiniest of nods. She'd gotten the message.

Jordan stepped back and flashed her a bright smile. "Hope this doesn't affect my chance of getting in your pants this weekend, but I'm glad you're sorted. Don't fuck with one of mine again." He began walking backward toward the house.

Taz remained frozen in place behind us, and she scooted to the side as he went past.

He glanced at me. "I know you had to."

Yeah. He'd asked me to be nice. "She insulted me."

"I know." There was no judgment in his eyes, just acceptance. With a wink, he opened the door and went inside.

"Cro—"

He cut her off. "Go inside, Taz."

Her mouth closed, but she didn't go.

"Go inside," he said again.

She bit the inside of her cheek, but did as he'd asked. Her shoulders hunched over as she went. Once the door closed behind her, Cross nodded to me. My turn now.

I stepped forward again, and Tabatha flinched, her upper back hitting the truck. She bounced off, steadying herself.

"You want to fuck him." I gestured to Cross.

Some of her color came back, pooling in her cheeks.

"And another of my crew members wants to fuck you." I folded my arms. I wasn't going to put hands on her again. "To say things are a little complicated is an understatement." I shook my head. "I have a feeling Taz has been telling you stories of how nice and kind I am, right?"

She gulped, but lifted her head. Just a bit.

"So she's talking to you and making me look like a pretty princess, right? And somewhere along the line, you forgot your first instinct about me—you forgot to stay the fuck away. You started remembering how much you like Cross. You started remembering how great a friend he is to me, and you heard all these stories from Taz about how close he and I are. But we can't be together, right? Because we're crew. So you started envisioning yourself with him. Am I getting this right?"

She looked down. "Yeah," she said.

I'd heard enough.

"My 'guys' aren't here to save the day," I told her. "My crew is—which includes me. I'm not just the girl in their guy group. I'm one of them. They bleed, I bleed. I am here to save the day, just like they are. You get it? You're talking to me like I'm one of *you*. Like I'm a fucking pretty princess who can't fight her own fight. I'm not. I'm crew. Are you following me?"

She refused to meet my eyes.

"I don't get what you intended just now," I told her. "Did you just forget how things work?"

Another wait. It wasn't as long this time.

"I forgot how things work."

Did I need to refresh her again?

Cross did it for me. "Don't fuck with *us*."

Her head had been so high in the beginning. Now she looked like we'd taken her favorite toy away. The transformation was remarkable. She could go cry to someone, say I'd put my hands on her. I had. I shouldn't have, but I did. I knew what we'd done was bad.

We did it anyway.

CHAPTER FORTY-EIGHT

THE DOOR OPENED behind us, and Jordan called, "We need your help with Race."

Cross and I moved at the same time, going for the house.

"They're hurting him?" Cross yelled.

"No." Jordan pushed the door wide for us. "It's the other way around. He's hurting *them*. It's all-out war out there."

We ran through the house and out onto the front lawn. He wasn't kidding.

The back half of the crowd was the jocks and their friends. The other half, their backs to the streets, was the Ryerson crew. I stopped to count them. Our crew went everywhere together, but Ryerson's crew was big—over thirty the last I knew—so they didn't always need everyone at a fight.

Tonight, however, I counted just under thirty, including the four on the ground.

Race stood in the middle of everything, throwing the crew members around. He wasn't letting them pin him down. That was his only saving grace. Once that happened, it would've been over. He was grabbing one and twisting his body around, evading and dodging, then hitting. It helped that the ones trying to grab him were a few of their older members, which was wrong in a whole other level. The high school guys should've waded in, but I saw some of them in the back.

Wait a minute.

They weren't just in the back. They were literally standing back, their hands in pockets, a few fisted at their sides, or their arms crossed over their chest.

They weren't okay with what they were doing.

They were actively stating it too, at least in crew language.

Alex, whether he realized it or not, was fucked. It was a matter of time.

Some of the jocks looked like they wanted in on the fight. A few waded in, but they pulled back if a Ryerson got too close. One threw a cup of something at them. It bounced off a Ryerson crew member like a fly.

Jordan moved through the crowd and gave the guy a look. "Nice," he sneered. "Real tough of you."

At the sound of his voice, everything changed.

The Ryersons all looked up, and the three surrounding Race fell back a couple feet. All eyes went to Jordan, then the rest of us. When the jocks realized Jordan was there, they moved aside. A path opened, and as one, we walked to stand in the center of it all.

Race's shirt had been torn off. Blood caked one side of him, and his chest heaved as he tried to catch his breath. His eyes were wild, panicked, and as he realized no one was advancing, he swung around. He almost raised a hand to Jordan, but caught himself.

His gaze jumped to me.

Alex moved forward, half his face bruised and his lip swollen. He wiped a hand over his face, smearing blood. He didn't notice, or he didn't care.

"What are you doing here?" he snarled at us. "He's not your crew."

Jordan looked to Cross, who stepped forward. "This is his house."

Alex's eyes narrowed. "Race isn't your crew."

Cross went rigid, then relaxed into a fighting stance. He was ready, and Alex knew all the signs. "This is *my house.*"

"So what?" Alex demanded. "You want us to move to the street?" He pointed to some of his crew. They started for his cousin, who jumped back. "We can do that. Believe me."

One reached for Race, who batted his arm away. He jogged backward, his arms up, ready to swing.

"What are you doing, Alex?" I'd had enough.

Alex shook his head. "Fuck, Bren. Really?"

"You're at Cross' house." I held his gaze. "If we singled someone out at your house?" I paused a beat. "If we didn't clear it with you first? It's about respect, Alex. You're not showing it."

Alex closed his eyes. He took a calming breath.

When he spoke, his voice was gravelly, like he was *just* clinging to his sanity. "Are you fucking kidding me? He's my cousin. This is a family thing."

"Bullshit." Jordan laughed in disbelief. "You have most your crew here. To beat up one guy?" He gestured to the jocks behind us. "These motherfuckers are too chicken shit to do anything except watch. Thirty to one isn't a fair fight."

"They're not all here, and he's a fighter!" Alex countered. "He can defend himself."

"You're making your family fight a crew issue. You think I have my crew back me up if I fight my sister?"

Cross indicated Taz, who held balled fists up to her face. She was trembling, and Tabatha pushed her way through the crowd to her side. She wrapped her arm around her, pulling her close.

Alex shook his head. "Why are you *involved*? We'll go to the street if that's the issue." He snapped his fingers at Race. "Come on. You heard him. We gotta move." He turned to go. So did his crew.

Race didn't.

His hands rested on his hips, and he seemed to be concentrating on steadying his breathing. Sweat trickled down his face. He wiped at it, almost angrily.

Alex stopped, looking back. "You're not coming?"

Race let his head fall back, his Adam's apple jutting out. "What do you think?"

"So you're saying it has to be here?"

Race didn't comment, still trying to breathe evenly.

Alex pointed to him. "You heard him," he told Cross. "It has to be here or nowhere."

Cross stepped forward again. He was fully in the fight now, almost side by side with Race. He held up a hand. "You back the fuck up or this definitely isn't a family fight anymore."

The tension doubled, sweeping through everyone.

Alex sputtered out a curse, raking his hands through his hair. "You're going to make this a crew thing? We outnumber you."

A smirk fluttered over Cross' face before his mask returned. "You know how we feel about a challenge." He grinned. "It's the shit we live for."

We all moved to stand with Race.

If Alex came, he was coming at us.

"This is bullshit!" Alex threw his arms wide. "This is a family thing."

"Thirty Ryerson crew to one Normal." My stomach churned with anger. "That's not a family fight. It's a massacre."

Alex started laughing. And then he couldn't stop. It reminded me of a hyena. He pointed at me. "That's funny coming from you. I've done a lot of things, but I've never stabbed my school principal."

We'd drawn the line.

He'd just crossed it.

I drew my knife out, flipping it open. Alex focused on it immediately

"This thing?" I murmured.

I was taunting him. He knew it.

His eyes went cold. "You're about to cross a line—"

"You already did. You insulted me. There's no going back after that."

I could see Tabatha from the corner of my eye. She was still comforting Taz, running a hand up and down her arm.

"People need to stop underestimating me," I said, turning her way for a moment. "It's getting old."

Her hand paused halfway up Taz's arm. She blinked, then kept rubbing. There was no other reaction from her.

"It's up to you, Alex. Stay and fight us, or leave."

We were all ready to go.

Race wiped a hand over his face, then assumed his fight position. He was still sweating and bleeding, but his shoulders rolled back.

"They interrupted round one," he said. "You ready for round two, cousin?"

Alex bit back a growl. He focused on me. "You cut us and what then? Cops will know. You'll get charged."

My mouth almost fell open. "Was that a joke?"

"He's desperate," Race said.

Alex gave his cousin a hostile look. "No joke, cuz. But anyway, you know how the cops are. They'll assume shit. They might assume it was Bren who sliced one of my crew open." He shrugged. "What about that? It's hard to tell who's doing what in a big brawl. You'll get charged, won't you? You might go away to juvie then? Maybe even prison."

I was having déjà vu.

This fucker was threatening me—same as Sunday, same as Tabatha. Same as all the other times Alex had forgotten his place.

But this time he'd really messed up.

A ripple was spreading through his crew. The first few couldn't believe what they'd heard. They looked at each other, shaking their heads.

Threatening what he had, implying they'd find out—that was snitching.

That was violation number one, of all crews.

No one narced, *no one*.

I shook my head. "You're no longer our problem, Alex." I glanced at his group. They were backing up, and he didn't even know. They had withdrawn to the street. He was almost alone. A few were already heading to their cars, though some lingered back.

I had no doubt one simple meeting would make up their minds.

Alex was out. And I was going to enjoy this.

"Tides turn real fucking quick, huh?" I gestured behind him.

He turned to look, and the fight drained from him.

"Guys?!" He started for them. "What are you doing? Come back here!"

They ignored him. The few that remained held up their hands. One by one, they turned to go.

It was quiet as we watched their vehicles leave.

The Ryerson crew had been led by a Ryerson for years. I wondered what their new name would be. It felt wrong not to have a Ryerson crew, but then I looked over at Race. He could lead them.

As if sensing my thoughts, he looked over at me, totally deflated. But I also saw the anger there, the darkness, the hatred burning. No, he wouldn't lead them.

I turned back toward Alex. "Threatening to be a narc is proclaiming you're a narc."

He roared, lunging for me.

I had my knife ready, but Cross and Jordan stepped in front of me.

They didn't hit him. They just shoved him back.

Jordan got in his face. "You touch one of us, you're dead. I'm goddamn sick of your shit." His waved to the street, dismissing him. "This fight is over. You're over. Get away from us."

Alex closed his eyes. The violence was still there, but he couldn't do a thing now. His hands were tied.

He looked right at his cousin. "Your mother is never going to find work here. She's over. It's been a long time coming."

"Goddamn!" Race exploded, surging past Cross and Jordan. They caught him and pushed him back, but he threw his arms over them, still trying to get at Alex. "Fuck you! Fuck your whole fucking family."

I was guessing someone had finally told his mom about her soon-to-be ex-sister-in-law.

Alex started moving toward his vehicle. "Yeah. Right. You'll learn what it's like to piss on a real Ryerson now, Race. Good luck with that." He opened his door.

"Good luck with being known as an informant!" Race yelled after him. "Hope you stay above ground longer than me!"

Alex started his truck, and extending a middle finger in the air, he drove off.

CREW

I would've liked to laugh off Race's last words, but I couldn't.

Narcs got killed.

A chill went through my body.

I'd never heard of a crew narc before now. I wished I still hadn't.

CHAPTER FORTY-NINE

"YOU OKAY?" JORDAN ASKED.

He was about to slap Race on the back, but he pulled the hit so it was more of a tap.

Race flashed him a grin before he doubled over, groaning. He rested his hands on his knees.

"Race!" Taz rushed to his side.

She slipped her head under one of his arms and straightened, helping him do the same. Race groaned again, grabbing at his side.

Two Normals stepped in, one replacing Taz and the other taking Race's free side. She followed, worry pulling her eyebrows together. She bit her lip as she reached out, her fingertips grazing over Race's back like she just needed to touch him. The guys led the way inside, and as soon as Race was seated in a chair at the kitchen table, Taz pulled out the first aid kit.

My crew stood around the table, ready to help. We knew our way around a first aid kit, but as Taz knelt in front of Race, I could see that wild horses weren't going to pull her away from him. Her mouth set in a determined line as she began to clean up his wounds.

Cross pulled out a chair close to Race and sat. "You going to live?"

Race started laughing, but the movement caused him pain, and he moaned. He cursed, shaking his head. "Goddamn Alex." He sighed. "Yeah, I'll live."

Jordan and Zellman sat at the table. I was content to rest against the wall. Tabatha and Sunday and a couple other girls were standing around in the kitchen, there if Taz needed something.

317

Some of the athlete guys lingered too, but no one said much of anything.

This was the aftermath of a crew fight—whether it had started as that or not. This was the time when we regrouped. We talked. We had our debriefing, sorting out the hows, whys, and what would happen next.

These meetings always tired me out. The goal was to protect ourselves against future threats, and that usually meant more fighting.

But these guys—the Normals in our world—did not seem tired. Awe, fear, and curiosity all mixed together in their eyes. They were hungry for more. Those of us around the table ignored them.

"You want to clue us in on what that fight was about?" Cross asked.

Race cringed.

Taz looked up. "Sorry." She went right back to cleaning.

Race let out a harsh laugh, hissing. "I might have a broken rib, Taz."

"I know." She didn't stop working though. "But you have a gushing cut here. I need to clean it up before we go to the hospital."

We all cringed at the mention of a hospital.

Hospitals meant questions, and those questions sometimes meant cops. No thanks.

I looked around. None of the people in the kitchen seemed concerned about going to the hospital. They didn't have reason. They weren't considered troubled.

My stomach rolled over.

I didn't want to be here. There were too many people, too many opinions, too many questions, too many of everything. I could feel the pressure pushing down on me.

The room was starting to suffocate me.

I slipped out, trying to go quietly. I didn't want the others to worry, but I had to exit. Once I stepped outside, I breathed in the night air and almost right away, it settled my stomach. I was moving toward the pool when I heard Cross' voice behind me.

"You want to talk now?"

I startled. I hadn't realized he followed me. I turned to find his face half in shadows.

I opened my mouth, about to answer, but then I just looked at him. I really looked at him. Like I had in my bedroom, I felt another veil falling from my eyes. He had stepped into a role he hadn't wanted until now, but I knew it was in him.

He was a leader.

He was just what everyone said he was. He was better than all of us.

And he was so goddamn gorgeous.

I reached up, touching his chin. "Why did it take me so long to accept this?"

He reached for me. "Because my good looks blinded you." He leaned forward, nuzzling my neck. He feathered kisses there, sending tingles through my body.

"You're only human," he added, his hand skimming up my back. "You couldn't see around the sun glare."

I barked out a laugh, which ended on a whimper as his lips continued to explore under my jaw, then down my throat.

I felt my legs actually weaken, and I reached for him—to steady myself and just to touch him.

His arm curved around my back, but then he pulled away. "Not here." His hand grabbed mine. "Come on."

Without a word, I followed him.

Without a word, I would've followed him anywhere.

He took me around the side of his house. Hopped up on their front porch deck, onto a small bannister outside the second floor, and finally through his bedroom window. I was almost moving with him, just a step behind. I knew this route like the back of my hand, having climbed in so many nights when his parents were still up and on the main level.

Moving silently and stealthily, he crossed to shut his door, flicking the lock.

I shut the window, and then it was just the two of us.

CREW

He wasted no time. An absolute look of need on his face, his hands tangled in my hair and his mouth came to mine.

I don't know if it was the image of thirty crew against one, or knowing that everyone in my crew knew my secret now, but I felt small. I needed to be reaffirmed of him, of us, of this between us, or maybe I just didn't want to feel small anymore.

Maybe I didn't want to feel like that could've been one of us. One against thirty. That's what happened in this town and this world—we survived. Either way, he was pushing everything away inside me, replacing it with *good*.

"Cross," I breathed, my fingers curling around his jeans waistband.

He sucked in his breath.

I leaned my head back, and his mouth moved to my throat.

I was throbbing for him, and as he pressed into me, I raised a leg. I hooked it around him and used it to bring him more snugly against me. He moved me back, pressing me against the wall and began to move, grinding into me.

I bit back another moan.

This guy—threading my fingers through his hair, I turned my head and his lips found mine. God. This guy.

Why had it taken me so long? Cross had his joke ready, but the question plagued me. Something had blocked me, something about *me*. It wasn't Cross.

His hand caught the back of my neck, and he held me, his lips moving over mine, making me shiver with need. But there was a nagging voice in the back of my mind. She wasn't talking—not yet—but I felt her. She wanted to say something, but I couldn't hear it. Or I didn't want to. Maybe I was scared to. There was something in me, like I was holding myself back...

As Cross' hand swept under my shirt and moved to my breast, I stopped trying to figure it out. Whatever it had been, my eyes were open now, and holy fuck, there was no going back.

"Hmm?" Cross pulled away, his eyes finding mine.

"Nothing." I pulled him close, fusing my lips to his.

I never wanted him to be away. Ever. It felt wrong.

"This feels too good." He lifted his head.

I wanted to stop him, but I didn't.

"Yeah?" I asked, panting a bit.

He nodded, his eyes darkening. He moved in for a kiss, and I surged up against him, meeting him.

It was a long while before he lifted his head again. His eyes were glazed, his face a little red, but I could feel the real evidence straining between my legs. If I reached down, if I unzipped my jeans, pulled my underwear aside... He'd be inside me in two seconds. One push, and we'd be one.

I bit my lip, trying to remember why that was a bad idea.

We heard Jordan call from below. "Anyone know where they went?"

We stilled. He was yelling, a full roar, so the crowd was loud beneath us.

A moment later, we heard the footsteps coming up.

A pause.

More footsteps, coming to his room.

I held my breath, feeling my pulse pounding in my ears, but Cross didn't move away. His arms didn't loosen, and neither did mine.

The footsteps stopped outside the door. "Dude!" Jordan pounded on it. "You guys in there?"

Cross stifled a curse, one hand anchored behind my neck, and he lifted his head toward the door. "We're talking."

"You serious?"

"Yeah. Go away."

I pressed my mouth into Cross' neck. He ran a hand down my back.

"A crew talk?" Jordan's voice sounded strained.

"A Bren talk." Cross' grin was wicked, looking down at me.

I shook my head, unable to keep from grinning back, and pressed a fist to his chest. He grabbed it, flattening my hand against his chest instead.

I sucked in some air. His heart was going just as fast as mine.

"Well. Okay. We're all taking off."

"We'll catch up with you later."

"Bren?"

Shit. I had to talk.

I tried smoothing out my voice so it came out normal. "Yeah?"

"You okay?"

"Yeah. I, uh..."

Cross put his lips to my ear, whispering, "What you said at Manny's, about your dad." Then he began nibbling.

I almost melted, my knees jerking.

"It's about what I said earlier. I just, I have to—best friend time, you know?"

"Yeah." Jordan sighed. "Taz wants to take Race to the hospital, so Z and I are going with the girls. They're shook up. We're going to comfort them, if you get my drift."

Cross snorted, tipping his head back. "Have fun getting laid."

Jordan laughed. "Yeah. Yeah. See you guys." He tapped the door once in his farewell, then started back down the hallway.

Cross dipped down, grabbed me around the legs and tossed me onto the bed.

He followed right after, dropping to the bed almost at the same second. His hands slid up my neck, his fingers moving through my hair, and he bent down, his lips meeting mine, taking mine.

He commanded, and I answered. I couldn't do anything else. This guy—I'd do anything for him.

It wasn't long until we heard everyone start to leave—footsteps traipsing outside, crossing the lawn. Voices outside, then car doors opening and closing. Headlights came on, some lighting up his room, until suddenly and so blissfully, everyone was gone.

It was just us. Us and his bed.

He paused, lifting his head. "Did you want to go to the hospital too?"

I smiled. "You're joking, right?"

He smiled back. "Yeah."

This was what I wanted. Him. Me. Alone. I just purely wanted him.

322

I wanted to let go of the armor I had to wear all the time. I could with him, and I was at that moment. I was merely a girl being held in the arms of the boy she was already in love with.

He'd been watching me and ran his hand down my hair again before moving to the side of my face. His thumb rested over my cheek. "I want you. God." He groaned, his lips coming to mine again. "I want you."

I whispered back, "Then have me, because I want you too."

His eyes blazed, burning into mine, dark and fierce and powerful, and he leaned down again. His lips touched mine as his hand slid inside my jeans.

My head fell back. Pleasure and ache surged inside of me. "Shit, Cross."

"Hmmm?" His lips moved down my throat. He touched right where my artery was, where the blood was pumping, and began to suckle there.

I felt his hand on my stomach, and he slid it upward, moving my shirt as he went. I stretched out, savoring this feeling as he explored my body, pulling my shirt up and off of me. I wore a sports bra, and that came off too. As soon as it did, his mouth was on me. He was kissing, licking, tasting. He was savoring me.

Every inch of me was in a frenzy. He added to it, making it richer, stronger, making it rise all over me until I was quivering in his arms.

"Cross." I grabbed for his shirt. I wanted it off. Now. Desperately.

Taking the end, I pulled it up and Cross pulled back, helping toss it off of him. He paused, right there, settled firmly between my legs, his jeans unbuckled, and his shirt off. I could see him in the street light. It cast a perfect glimmer through his curtains, just enough where I could see all the shadows over him. Rising up, I began to kiss him. I kissed his chest, moving down, lingering, exploring him the way he had done to me.

I made him shake, quiver, groan.

And when I couldn't wait any longer, when the throbbing was so strong that I swear he could feel it, my hands went to his jeans.

"Bren?"

I looked up. "Yes."

That was all he needed.

He pushed me back down, my head to his pillow, and he lay over me, his entire firm body molding to every inch of me.

I raised my leg and he caught it, curling it around his waist. One movement, and I was helpless to him. He held me in place as he continued to suck on my throat. His finger slipped inside, a second soon joining, and I couldn't do a thing except bite my lip. I was gone. I was beyond reality, lost in this ride.

In and out.

His fingers kept going.

"Cross," I moaned.

I found his mouth, and his lips pressed over mine. His fingers plunged in again. A gentle pressure from his lips, and then he cursed under his breath. His fingers came out of me, but he made quick work of pulling my other leg around his waist. I locked them around him, and he undid his zipper. He leaned over, opening his drawer, and I heard the crinkle of a condom wrapper.

He paused, holding himself above me, lined up at my entrance. "You sure?"

I opened my eyes and saw him hovering an inch from me. "Get the *fuck* inside me."

His eyes darkened, and he pushed inside. Sliding to the hilt.

I gasped. Finally.

He was inside.

He waited for me to adjust, stretching me, and with a low, guttural groan, he began moving in me. Slowly at first, his hands finding mine, our fingers lacing together, he pressed my hands to the side of my head. There was nowhere else I wanted to be.

In this moment, I felt more than I'd ever felt. Pleasure laced my insides as he thrust in, slid out, paused, and went back in.

My hips moved with him as he started to speed up. I strained to feel every inch of him. I wanted him as deep as possible. I felt him in my fucking stomach.

"Fuck, Bren." His hands moved to my hips, and he held me tight. He began going harder, a little rougher. My climax was building—whipping through me, making me feel feverish, but I couldn't do anything except go with him. I wanted it harder. I wanted it rougher. I wanted him to stay in me forever.

My hands went around his back, and he tipped my hips up, thrusting deep and pausing. He ground in there, and I groaned. I felt myself coming, but I wanted to hold off. I wanted to go with him.

As I raked my nails down his back, he let out a deep growl and began ramming into me.

"Cross!"

His mouth found mine again. His tongue was inside, and I opened for him, feeling him at both ends.

He pummeled into me, and when he slowed, I felt him coming just as my climax ripped through me. We surged together, our bodies straining to get closer than was possible.

Waves went through me, and Cross held me until my body stopped trembling. With a soft kiss to my lips, then forehead, he eased out of me.

I ran my hands over his chest, feeling him tremble above me.

This was unexpected, but so damned good.

It was hot. It was fast. It was—he lifted his eyes to gaze at me, and I reached to touch his mouth. God, that mouth. How could I crave him so soon? I already wanted to be kissing him, to be holding him again, to feel his hands all over my body.

"Holy shit," I breathed.

I pressed my forehead against his chest, and he laughed, running his hand down my arm.

He sounded just out of breath as I was. "You can say that again."

He pulled off the condom and tossed it into a garbage can in the corner, then moved to lie beside me. He curled around me, holding me tight.

He lifted his head to look down at me, his eyes darkening once more.

A lone finger touched my stomach as he murmured, "We're not moving from this bed."

I wanted that too. "Not arguing. I'm good with that."

"Good." He kissed my shoulder, tucking some of my hair behind my neck, gently.

I felt some stickiness between my legs, and as much as I didn't want to move, I needed to. "I should clean up."

Cross nodded, raking a hand over his head. "Okay." He sat up as I slid from the bed and crossed to his bathroom.

When I was coming back, after I'd pulled on one of his clean shirts, his phone buzzed from the floor. He bent to grab it, the screen lighting up his face.

"It's from Taz," he said. His finger scrolled down the phone. He tapped on another text. "Race is fine. She's staying with him. Everyone else went to Manny's." Another text, another tap on his screen. "Someone saw Alex there."

"We have to go."

"Wait." Cross grabbed my hand. He was reading more text messages. "Jordan said to hold off. They're partying with the Normals, but will watch Alex if he's there. They won't move on him." Then he started laughing, putting his phone on the nightstand.

"What?"

"He asked if I could keep you away. He's still hoping for a shot with Tabatha Sweets."

Typical Jordan. I laughed. "Of course."

Cross tugged me to him again, his hand sliding down my arm and curling around my waist. His fingers moved up under my shirt. "And that means we've got the whole night to ourselves."

And the whole house.

"Where are your parents?"

He grinned wolfishly. "Who the fuck cares?"

CHAPTER FIFTY

THE COUGH SHOULD'VE alarmed me.

Cross was never sick, and I hadn't coughed. But it didn't. It only woke me. I was too sleepy to process it all the way. I opened one eye to find Cross sleeping, his face turned toward me. He was half-curled in a ball, his head missing the pillow. His long eyelashes... I reached out to trace my hand down his face.

I'd always thought it, but it was only reinforced now: he had so much potential. He was smart. He was handsome. He was funny. He could follow, but he was a leader. He was my leader. I looked down over his strong jawline to the muscles that moved up and down with such ease as he breathed. He was a specimen, a perfect and masterful specimen.

He was mine. That's what he was.

"Are you done ogling Cross, Bren?"

Both Cross and I reacted at the same time. I flipped around, one hand going for the sheet and the other for my knife. Cross merely leaped over me.

It was Jordan sitting in Cross' desk chair, but Cross had lunged for him. He couldn't pull back, even after he saw who it was. They both fell to the floor, and Cross rolled away and to his knees. He'd had the foresight to put his boxer briefs on again, but not me. My underwear was on, but he'd talked me into letting my boobs breathe free.

"Jordan!" Cross scrambled to his feet, breathing harshly, which highlighted every single one of the muscles in his chest and stomach. He raised a hand, but stopped. He looked from me to Jordan. His hand lowered. "Shit."

Jordan wasn't smiling. His mouth was set in a firm line, and he looked worried.

"What happened?" I asked.

"Put your clothes on, Bren."

"Jordan—" Cross started, pointing to me.

Jordan cut him off, waving his hand briskly in the air. "I don't care about that."

I grabbed my tank and pulled it on. The same with my jeans. I couldn't find my bra, but at the moment, I didn't care. Something was wrong.

"What happened?" I asked again.

Jordan hesitated, glancing back to Cross. "Maybe you should sit for this?"

No one sat.

I rubbed a hand over my face. "Just tell us, Jordan." I looked to the open door.

"No one's here," Jordan said. "Zellman's at the hospital." He started to say more, but stopped. His eyes closed, and he seemed to shrink in size, becoming half the guy he usually was.

"Jordan." A low warning from Cross. "Just say it."

He opened his eyes, first finding me. An appealing look flared for a second, and I stepped toward him. I felt like he was asking me to draw near, but that wasn't like him at all.

"Race went to the hospital last night. He was there with your sister."

"Yeah. We knew that." Cross was frowning. He crossed his arms over his chest, his biceps bulging with the movement.

"And we all went to Manny's. We heard Alex was there."

"We knew that too."

A lump was in the back of my throat. "Why's Zellman at the hospital?" He wouldn't go to be there with Race. "Race would've been released last night. His injuries weren't that bad."

Jordan kept on as if I hadn't said a word. He was no longer looking at either of us. He stared at a spot on the wall. "Alex was at Manny's. At first."

"At first?" I prompted.

"He was drinking. Brandon wouldn't serve him, but he got a bottle of whiskey. He was drinking in the back. Heather looked for him a few times, but he hid from her. Brandon finally found him and kicked him out."

He looked at Cross then. His eyes were so strange, I almost gasped. They were bleak and stricken.

Hurting. They were hurting.

I felt a whisper inside me, a beckoning. He had the same darkness in him that I had felt, and as if on cue, I felt *her* wanting to come out. She wanted to rise and protect me.

I pushed her down.

Jordan took a breath, then spoke in a voice that was unnaturally soft. "I was making out with Sweets last night. Zellman was shooting pool. We were having fun, and we weren't watching. Everyone thought Alex would walk home, sleep it off."

But he didn't.

I could tell how this was going to play out.

I touched my forehead, feeling a headache forming. "Who did he hurt?"

"The hospital released Race last night, so Taz took him to the hotel in town. That one he's been staying at with his mom."

If Alex had been walking home, the hotel was right in the middle of his route.

"Oh no."

No, no, no.

I knew what he was going to say.

Race helped us, so many times.

We pushed him, not trusting. But he kept helping.

Now this...

I sank down on the bed. Alex had already hurt his cousin. Race would've been weak, or even drugged. The hospital would've given him painkillers. They would've made him fall asleep.

He was helpless.

I began to fear the worst.

Then Jordan looked at Cross. "He hurt Taz."

I looked up.

Taz.

He said Taz.

Not Race.

Taz.

I surged back to my feet. "Cross."

Cross was on his feet, a dark look clouding over him. He swallowed, and a look in his eyes I had never seen before flashed bright. "What did he do to her?"

Jordan spoke faster now, his hand out like he could soothe Cross. "I don't know the extent of it, but she's in the hospital. Z's with her." He paused. "So are your parents."

Cross nodded, like he knew that already.

Jordan kept on, "They were gone on some trip. The hospital called them. They got there an hour ago. I've been..." He gestured to the desk chair. "I waited as long as I could."

"For what?" Cross laughed, an edge of hysteria there. "To let me sleep in?"

Jordan straightened to his full height. "To let the cops talk to Alex first."

First.

I looked at Cross. He and Jordan stared at each other with a shared understanding.

Then Cross turned to me, and I felt it. It started in my toes, making them curl, but the trickle moved up my legs. It pooled between them—where he'd been not long ago before we fell asleep again—and now it filled my chest. It went down my arms, making my fingers twitch, and it continued its path upward. My neck. The back of my head. Finally everything was coated.

I was ready. I knew what Cross would do, and I held my knife out to him.

He looked at it and shook his head.

He dressed, pulling on a sleeveless black shirt and jeans.

He left the room.

I followed him. Jordan followed me.

Cross went to his father's office. The closet opened, I heard a series of beeps, and he appeared again—a 9mm in his hand.

CHAPTER FIFTY-ONE

WE WAITED THREE HOURS.

Three hours for Alex to be booked into police custody, to be processed, and then let out on bond. Three fucking hours, for hurting Taz.

In the meantime, we got the story.

Zellman was with Race at the hospital, and he relayed it on his way to the police station. He told us over the phone that Alex had shown up when Taz took him to the hotel. His mom had stayed back at the hospital to finish some additional paperwork, but Taz drove him, going ahead so he could sleep.

Alex showed up.

Drunk. High. In a rage.

He and Race started fighting, and he swung wide at one point, hitting Taz instead of Race.

He didn't realize it wasn't his cousin, and he hit her again and again.

Race shoved him off, but the damage was done.

Her left cheek was fractured. So was her lower jaw. All her teeth were intact, but she'd have to have her mouth wired shut for ten weeks.

Ten.

Weeks.

This wasn't supposed to happen.

Not to a Normal. To crew, yes. We ran that chance. We signed up for it. We signed up knowing the risks. But family. Friends? Fuck no. They didn't sign up for it.

It was wrong.

Alex needed to go.

That's what I thought as I was now sitting between the guys in Jordan's truck.

We were driving around Roussou. We were waiting to find out where Alex would be, and that was Zellman's job. He was following Alex to wherever he holed up. Once he did, once he told us, he was supposed to go back to Taz's side and not leave.

"Are you sure you don't want to check on your sister?" Jordan's voice was low in his cab, taking the same left he'd taken for the fiftieth time that morning.

We were on a continuous loop through Roussou, just waiting, just tense, just... There were no words to describe this morning.

Thinking about it, I stomped down the same shiver I'd been having since we left the house.

There'd been rage.

There'd been pain, inexplicable pain. Remorse. Rage again. A murderous rage. A quiet cold seeping out of my bones—a hunger to inflict what had been inflicted upon.

Cross had taken the gun out, but Jordan grabbed it, saying, "No way, man."

"Jordan." Cross had pushed him against the wall. He took it back. "Goddamn—you don't know!"

"Yes." He'd put hands on Cross, paused, looked at me, and then shoved him back. "My sister was almost raped, fucker. Raped! Yes. I do goddamn know, and Z took the gun out of my hands that night."

I had frowned.

Jordan had laughed, sounding almost as harsh as Cross. He looked between us. "You didn't know that, did you? You aren't the only ones with secrets in this crew." He extended his hand, holding it steady. "Z didn't trust me then, and I don't trust you now. Give me the fucking gun, Cross."

Cross didn't do anything. He stood glaring at Jordan, until—I was frozen in place for that moment—he finally held it out.

Jordan had snatched it, swiftly, and handed it behind his back to me.

I stepped forward, taking it, my eyes holding Cross' as I did. God.

My mouth dried.

She was in him too. *She* was blanketing him, protecting him, making him numb to feeling what had been in me for so long.

I paused, and without thinking, I pressed my palm to his chest. His heart lurched against it, pressing out to me, and it wasn't just him and me there. I swear I felt her. She really was in him. My insides split in half—someone was tearing me in two and doing it so slowly that I could hear every tendon breaking, feel the rip as every vessel burst open.

I choked up.

If that's what I felt, standing in front of him, looking into his eyes, and feeling his heart—I couldn't go there. I wouldn't. Not yet. Instead, I whispered, standing close until his forehead moved to rest against mine, "Just hold on."

His heart pounded three beats, all at once, and he jerked his head in a rough nod. Then his eyes closed, and his chest lifted as he filled his lungs. He was in control. For now.

Jordan tapped the back of my elbow, and I moved in response. We had to go fast.

He went with me, back into Cross' parents' closet.

Jordan grabbed the gun's lock-box, bringing it down. It was still open. I put the gun in. Jordan locked it again, and I headed back. Jordan was right behind me, almost breathing down my neck. I was scared, for a split second, that Cross had grabbed a different weapon and gone on his own, but he hadn't.

I had to stop, just the slightest of pauses, but enough where Jordan grunted so he didn't run into me, and then I was moving forward again.

Cross' eyes were dark and almost soulless, but he was focused on me. He was holding on.

I took his hand, lacing our fingers, and I was the one who'd led us outside. I was the one who'd taken us to Jordan's truck. I was the one who'd made the decision that instead of one in the back and two in front, all three of us would sit together. And I was the one who'd decided when Jordan got in and asked, "Where to?"

"Just drive."

Cross didn't want to go to Taz. Not until Alex was dealt with. We all knew that, so we never offered. That's why Zellman was tasked with staying there, until he got the call that Alex's lawyer was at the station. How he knew, who called him, I didn't know. I didn't ask. No one did.

My phone pinged now, bringing me back to the present as I sat between these two.

Durrant's house.

A second text: **Alex let himself in with a key.**

Mouth dry, hands sweaty, pulse pounding, I texted him back: 🐼 **No** 🎵 **till** 👀.

"He's at Durrant's house," I announced. "No one's there."

Jordan nodded once and swung around.

"You tell him to go back to Taz?" Cross asked.

I powered off my phone and put it in my pocket, feeling that locked gun box by my feet. "I coded it. He'll be radio silent till we see him."

Durrant was a Ryerson crew member, and apparently one of Alex's most loyal friends. Either that or...

Jordan grunted. "I think I remember Durrant's out of town. Someone in his family died. Sweets told me that last night. She was mentioning it because there's talk about having a party there."

I sucked in my breath for a second, but let it go almost as quick.

We were driving to let Cross shoot this guy.

Yes, we took the gun away from him at the house, but he'd released it only after Jordan promised to keep it in the box until we got to Alex. We were going with Cross because this was crew, this was having his back, but in this moment, knowing what he wanted to do, knowing what we were taking him to do—I didn't want it.

I didn't want any of it.

334

This was wrong.

This was a part of the crew life I didn't want.

I felt a punch at that, realizing I wasn't all-crew at that moment, but no. Fuck that. I was.

I *was*.

Cross stared straight ahead, locked down, an impassive expression on his face that sent shivers down my back.

I knew I had to speak up, or I was going to lose him.

I caught Jordan's gaze. He lifted his eyebrows, a message there for me. He made a face at me. It was brief, but I knew he was with me.

Fuck.

Okay.

Icy dread began trickling down to my stomach, but I had to try. I *had* to.

"I love you, Cross." My voice shook.

Jordan eased up on the pedal, his head turning toward us for an instant.

"Keep driving." Cross' voice didn't shake. He knew what I was going to say.

Jordan didn't, slowing the truck even more.

"Keep *fucking* driving, Jordan!"

Jordan was waiting for me, watching me. I gave him the slightest nod, and he pressed the pedal again. I had this time to talk. I would make it count.

"Mallory was nearly raped, and we didn't kill that guy."

"We should've," Cross bit out.

Jordan winced.

"No. That guy turned himself in. Alex already went in too."

"And he's out on bail." Cross was so rigid, so tense. His head whipped to mine. His eyes blazing. "What makes you think he'll do any goddamn time? He fucked up her head. He broke her jaw. He broke her cheek. She has a concussion. She could have permanent fucking damage. She might have problems for the rest of her life— we don't fucking know. What makes you think he shouldn't pay for what he did?" He was glaring at me.

I felt punched with every word he said.

"If anyone deserves to hurt him, it should be Taz then."

Jordan grimaced, and I ignored him.

Cross snorted. "Right. We should've let Mallory go up on that hill with us. Remember that night? I know you like to sit those beatdowns out, but fuck, Bren. I thought you were with us. I thought you were with *me*."

I heard his accusation.

Icy dread swirled through me.

I heard his pain.

"What do you think I'm doing?" I burst out, my voice cracking. My chest heaved. Every vein was stretching, trying to explode. "I am here for you, and you don't want to hear this, but you have to." I turned, and I faced him head-on. "You're going to kill someone. *You don't walk away from that!* You. Not him. Not that fucker. You, Cross!" I leaned forward, almost lunging at him. I grabbed his shirt, and I was right in his face. "My mom is gone. My dad is in prison. My brother was gone since I was fucking eight years old. It's been you. It's been goddamn *you* all my life."

I shook him with every word.

He went mute, but his eyes were on mine. He was listening.

He was giving me this time.

"Let's beat him up. Please," I rasped. "You want him to pay? Make him live with what he did. Beat him so bad he doesn't walk. Do that. Just don't kill him." My lungs rattled. My whole body was shuddering. I pressed my forehead to his. My lips grazed just over his. "You pull that trigger, and I lose everything. I lose you. I can't lose you."

The truck was turning. Slowing. We were on a gravel road.

"Taz loses you," Jordan added, his voice strained. "You're hurting your sister. Again."

Cross didn't move.

He didn't pull away.

He didn't reach for me. He didn't take my hands in his. He didn't move his face back.

He sat there, like a rock. He was cement, on the outside and inside.

I was going to lose him.

He wasn't going to change his mind, and realizing that, I did the only thing I could think of. I crawled onto his lap. I wrapped my arms around his neck and curled my legs in, and then—*then*—he moved. His arms pulled me the rest of the way.

He held me close, and I lifted my head. I put my lips to his ear and whispered, "Please don't leave me. I love you."

I was on repeat, saying nothing else.

But so was he.

He said nothing else.

He just held me, like he was saying goodbye.

Then we pulled up to Durrant's house.

CHAPTER FIFTY-TWO

I'D NEVER FORGET that house.

Every piece of chipped paint. Every crack in the sidewalk. Every step it would take to go up the patio and through that door. I'd never forget the yard, or the manmade lake it was on.

The temperature was burned in my memory.

It was hot. It was unnaturally hot. My shirt stuck to Cross' chest. There was a sweet smell in the air, mingling with our sweat. I remembered noticing that, and then feeling the goosebumps on my skin.

Everything was wrong that day.

I was usually the dark one. Cross was my light. We'd switched roles today. And that, somehow, was wrong too.

Jordan was the reasonable one.

Zellman wasn't even here.

All of it. All wrong.

I thought all of that before Cross opened the door. I hadn't moved from his lap, but it didn't matter.

Even the creak of the door was wrong. It was usually silent. Not a sound came from it. Jordan would've cursed about it. He was anal about the upkeep of his truck. And then that flashed from my mind too as Cross stepped out, carrying me with him. He set me on my feet, his eyes holding mine the whole time, just like always.

Then he reached around me.

His chest touched mine. His arm brushed against me before he stepped back, the gun box in his hand.

"Cross—"

"No!" He looked over my shoulder. "Both of you."

Jordan had stepped out on his side, his door still open.

"I mean it. This is my decision." Cross looked between us. "You're either with me or you're not. Which is it?"

"When you become one of us, you have to agree to three oaths."

"You made me promise to three oaths," I said.

He was ignoring me, getting the gun out.

"Hey!" I grabbed his shoulder, whipping him around. "Listen to me!"

"...will you treat us as family?"

I pushed up until my body was touching his. "Treat you as family." I cupped both sides of his face. "You're more family to me than anyone."

His eyes started to close.

"Don't!" I clipped out. "Look at me! You're going to do this, you're going to have to look at me before you walk away."

He shook, quivering, and he opened his eyes again.

A small amount of pressure lifted from inside of me. A small part of that icy dread warmed, just a tiny bit. But not enough. Not goddamn enough.

"Will you fight for us as you'd have us fight for you?"

"I'm supposed to fight for you like I'd want you to fight for me, and I *am* fighting for you. I'm fighting for you because you're me. We're a unit, whether we want it or not. I love you. I *love* you."

I was so close, my lips were grazing his, and I felt every word vibrate to my toes.

I couldn't stop cupping his face. I couldn't stop pressing against him, as if I could literally keep him from moving.

I felt him shifting, putting the gun in his pants, and then his hands came to my arms. They were gentle, but he moved me back.

"Bren." His hand touched the side of my face. "Let me do this. I have to. He touched Taz. He keeps touching you. I can't—this has to be done."

His body stiffened. His hands went to my shoulders again.

He was going to push me away, and then he was going to step away, and then he was going to go away.

"I want to die," I cried.

He stopped.

I'd pulled the last card I had.

"And the last, will you forgive as if we're one person?"

I felt her touch on my back. It was gentle and loving, and I felt her strength seep into me. I didn't care what anyone told me. I felt her presence as strongly as when she'd held me before I turned nine. I felt her heat. I smelled the rose perfume she wore.

I didn't feel her inside me anymore, not the way she used to be. It changed that second, that day. Searching Cross' eyes, seeing how stricken he was, I didn't see her in him anymore either.

"Bren?" he choked out, reading inside me.

"That's why I go to my house. I go to see her, but I go because I want a mom again."

A wall crumbled inside me. Everything was spilling out.

I needed to say it. I just knew I needed to.

"I want my dad back—the one he was before he drank, before she left, before Channing left. I want everything how it used to be, before I had to stab a guy to keep him from raping me."

My chest rose and held. "I can't have any of that again, so the only way is if I die too. You're keeping me from going down that road. You're keeping me here. I am fighting for you every goddamn day of my life! Don't you get that?!" Anger licked my insides, pushing everything aside. It rushed over all of it, and I was suddenly enraged. "I don't give a shit what's going on at your house. I don't give a shit how much you want to kill Alex. I don't give a shit how much you're hurting. You hurt more. You give a shit more. You deal with it more. You keep taking it, enduring it, fighting back, and you *goddamn* keep going, because that's what I'm doing!"

The edges blurred.

I wasn't seeing straight.

I grabbed for the gun.

Cross' hand closed around it, but I rotated my back into him, pulling the gun out and away. He couldn't keep his hold, and as soon as it was free, I flung it. As far as I could throw, as hard as I could throw.

Cross swore and started to go around me.

I hip-checked him, slamming him back. "No! NO!"

He shoved me away, getting in my face now. "This isn't your decision!"

"FUCK YOU!" I hit him. I hit him again. "It is because you're mine. You're MINE!" I started pummeling him, one fist after another to his chest.

I would fight him with everything in me.

I was crew. That was it for me.

I heard a crunch of gravel behind me. I heard Jordan's voice saying, "Here." And Cross bundled me up, shifting me to the side as he reached out.

He passed me to Jordan, as Jordan passed him the gun.

My mouth fell open. "Wha—"

Jordan's shoulders seemed to slump, and his eyes were bleak too. "It has to be his decision." He was resigned.

"Wha—"

"I'm sorry."

I didn't know who said that, but Jordan held me back, wrapping his arms around me.

It happened in slow motion after that.

My heart ripped out of my chest.

I struggled against Jordan's hold. I kicked at him, twisting, trying to fall out of his arms. None of it was working and he slumped to the ground with me, wrapping his legs around mine, keeping them in place and positioning his head next to mine so I couldn't hurt him that way either.

I was a pathetic, wiggling worm, and I watched Cross go into that house, the gun in his hand.

I waited.

Nothing.

I waited longer.

Still nothing.

Cross went into that house, and...nothing.

There was no yell, no gunshot, not even a struggle. Just the same silence that always accompanied me wherever I was, whoever I was with. It was always there.

I stilled and finally said, "Alex would've heard us."

His arms tightened around me. "Shit."

He let me go, and we both scrambled up, running for the house.

I got there first, bolting through the front door. "Cross!"

All the lights were off inside. There was a cold feeling to the house, like no one lived here. In that split second, I took in the pictures on the wall. The blankets folded over the couch. A pink little backpack on the floor, next to a larger black bag. The tennis shoes lined up by the wall. The little glittery sneakers next to them. A piano in one corner of the living room. A table that had mosaic tiles on the top of it. A kitchen counter with mail in a pile, a bag of bread with the end tucked under, a bowl of oranges next to it. A coffee machine in the corner. A tray of the little coffee cups that go inside it.

A cupboard of mugs.

There was a staleness in the air.

People lived in this house, but that wasn't the way it felt.

It felt cold—like death.

"In here!" Cross' voice came down the hallway.

We ran past doors until we found him, in a bathroom off the hallway.

Alex was slumped on the floor, a bottle of pills and whiskey next to him, his head hanging low. His body was already pale.

"Shit."

Jordan said that, but I didn't recognize his voice.

Cross wasn't standing over him with a gun. The gun was on the floor next to his foot as he knocked the pills and booze away and felt for Alex's pulse.

He yelled over his shoulder, "Back the truck up. We have to take him. Paramedics won't get here in time."

He wanted to save his life.

Both Jordan and I were paralyzed a second, letting the scene register.

Cross looked up and barked, "NOW!"

Jordan hit the doorframe next to me, using it to push himself around in a tight turn, and he was off.

Fuck.

Fuck.

Fuck.

My pulse was back to racing, but this was a different type of sprint.

Cross met my gaze. "He's barely breathing, but he's breathing. His pulse is slowing down."

I nodded, my throat swelling. I couldn't bring myself to talk, but I moved over him and jammed three fingers down Alex's throat.

His body jerked against me.

Cross moved back, giving me space.

I yelled at him, "Get rid of that. Now." I nodded to the gun.

He grabbed it, putting it in his pants again.

"HERE!"

Jordan pounded back inside, and with my fingers still trying to make Alex throw up, he and Cross picked him up. All three of us moved together, keeping Alex on his side as we ran through the house. We made sure his head didn't hit any walls or doorframes, and once we slid him onto the back of the truck, Cross and I jumped up.

Jordan sprinted back inside, coming out with his arms full of blankets. He slammed the tailgate shut behind me, throwing the blankets at us.

"Jordan." Cross held the gun out to him.

Jordan grabbed it, then leaped inside.

I had one second to grab one of those blankets, stuff it under Alex's head, and grab hold of the side. We were off. Jordan peeled out of there, spraying up dirt and half of Durrant's yard.

I didn't remember the drive to the hospital. I'm sure it was dangerous, and maddening, and wild. I'm sure there were times we might've been flung from the back because Jordan didn't slow down. He drove like he needed to save a life.

I didn't give a damn that my hand was inside Alex's throat half the time.

I remembered feeling such relief when finally he started throwing up.

I remembered looking up and meeting Cross' eyes over Alex's body and being so fucking grateful we were saving him and not burying him.

I remembered seeing my Cross once again.

Then we were at the hospital.

The doors to the ER slid open. A nurse came out, his eyes bulged, and he began screaming over his shoulder. He ran to the back with Jordan beside him, and all of us helped slide Alex to the edge just as a gurney appeared. I started to go with it until that same nurse touched my arm.

"We got this." He nodded to all of us. "Thank you. You probably saved his life."

There were two other nurses with him, and they pushed Alex inside, just as a doctor ran to meet them.

And I knew I would always remember that feeling—standing there, staring after them, with my guys right beside me.

I felt alive.

CHAPTER FIFTY-THREE

A NURSE SHOWED us to a room where we could shower and change into different clothes.

I was pretty sure it was a staff waiting room, and I was sitting on a bench between a bunch of lockers when the door opened.

"Bren?"

Cross walked inside. I didn't move.

An hour ago we'd been going to kill Alex. Thirty minutes ago we were racing to save him. And now, I didn't know. I just didn't know. It was all such a whirlwind.

"Hey." He kneeled at my feet, his hands on my legs, and he peered up at me. "Hey." He touched under my chin, raising my gaze to his. "You okay?"

"You were going to kill him."

He nodded. "Yeah. I was."

There was no remorse. He didn't regret it. There was no shame either.

"I would've, if he'd had an attitude, if he'd cussed me out, if he'd tried to fight me. I would've. I knew what I was going to do, and I'm not going to lie to you. I would've pulled that trigger."

"What made you not do it?" I raked my fingers through his hair.

"You." If possible, his eyes smiled at me. They warmed, and love shone through. "When I walked in there, he had no fight in him. He was trying to overdose."

"How do you know?"

He reached behind him and pulled out a folded-up piece of paper. It was wrecked, with blood on it. Cross unfolded it and gave it to me. "He left a note."

I know I have people coming for me, and I didn't mean to hurt her. I swear. An eye for an eye. I'm doing it so you don't have to. Peace out—Alex

I looked up, and Cross took the note. Folding it up, he put it back into his pocket. Then he stood. He grabbed my hand, pulling me up, and wrapped his arms around me, tugging me against him.

It was done. For now.

There'd be questions, probably suspicions about why we found him, but there was no evidence either way.

Cross dropped a kiss to my neck. "God, I love you." He laughed a second later, tightening his arms. "You realize we never did the whole 'I love you' moment, right? You said it at Durrant's house."

"I said it because I hoped it would make a difference."

He cupped the back of my neck and leaned away, just enough to see me. "It did. You have no idea how much. It did, Bren." Then he pulled me in, hugging me almost delicately now. I felt him brush his lips against my forehead, and he sighed. "Everything you said, it's the same for me. I'm saying it now. Everything, Bren. You hurt, I hurt. You bleed, I bleed. You smile, I smile. You're happy, I'm happy. It's almost ridiculous how much of you I am. It's been like that for a while. Now it's just official. You and me. We're a we, and I don't want anything to fuck that up. Anything."

I nudged him with my elbow. "Besides what you almost did?"

He paused, then his body relaxed. His head dropped to my shoulder. He peppered some kisses there, his hands slipping to my back, sliding under my shirt. "I might've killed him if you hadn't been there, and if you hadn't said all those words. I just might've." He paused, his lips on my skin. "You might've saved me."

Maybe.

I hoped.

I rested my head against his shoulder, reaching up to run my fingers through his hair.

I'd told him everything. Jordan knew everything.

This was... I didn't know how to feel. My walls were gone. I was exposed, but I didn't feel like freaking out. The opposite.

I felt strong.

"You okay?" He pulled back, asking again. A softness sparked in his eyes, and he rested his forehead to mine, his hands falling to my hips. "You still want to die?"

"I—" I shook my head. "I said all of that, and it didn't matter to you."

He lifted his head, frowning. "Bren?"

"You went in there anyway."

"It wasn't like that."

"It was." I started to pull away. I began to know how I was feeling. I was feeling that rage again, that betrayal again. "I peeled back all of my walls, and nothing. You still walked."

"You think if I'd killed him, I would be gone too. That's not what would've happened."

"You don't understand."

"Bren—"

"You don't!" I snapped, stepping back. "I was going to kill that guy in my bedroom. I was going to do it."

He tried to reach for me, but I twisted out of his reach, backing up until I hit the lockers behind me.

"Bren. Come on."

He lifted a hand, but I blocked him, hitting it away. "Stop!"

He fell back, his eyes darkening. He was quiet.

"My dad's in prison because he killed that guy, and he didn't do it because he wanted to. He did it so I wouldn't, because I was going to." I pressed my hands to the sides of my head, shaking from side to side. "I am messed up, Cross. I mean, holy shit. I'm fucked up, and that guy—my dad doing what he did is only half of it. If you had done what you wanted..."

I didn't know if I could finish that sentence. I didn't know if I wanted to put that on him, but it was the truth. My voice cracked. "I don't know if there would've been any coming back for me. If you'd killed him, if you'd gone to prison, I really don't know what I would've done."

I wasn't being dramatic. I wasn't crying. I was just speaking the truth.

Cross knew it. He understood how we needed each other.

I was fast realizing the depths of that—how fucked I would be if he wasn't here.

"You're my anchor," I told him. "You go, I go. It's as simple as that."

He didn't reply, just pulled me back in and wrapped his arms around my neck. Tucking his head right next to mine, he breathed, "It's the same for me."

This was how it was for us.

No pretty words. No happy ending. No lesson learned at the end of it all. It just was. We were us, Cross and Bren, and after we stayed in there for a while longer, he took my hand and led me outside.

It was time to face everyone else.

CHAPTER FIFTY-FOUR

TAZ LOST TWENTY POUNDS.

Her mouth had been wired for ten weeks, but she swore it was the best diet she'd ever been on. Race doted on her the entire time.

That part of his life was doing well. The rest, not so much.

The Ryerson fall-out was epic, and it happened in almost chronological order.

Race's dad moved to Roussou. Alex's parents divorced. Alex's dad moved out of town. Race's dad moved *into* Alex's house, to be with Alex's mother.

Race's mom sued Alex's family, and rumor was that most of the divorce settlement actually went to her.

That seemed like good karma, for once.

The two brothers were now mortal enemies.

The only other way to bring everything back around was if Alex's dad stayed and hooked up with Race's mom. The two brothers would've literally switched places.

Taz said the whole thing made her want to drink, which she couldn't because she was still on her meds. And she moaned longingly whenever Tabatha, Sunday, and Monica visited her. "They bring these Kahlua drinks, and I swear they do it to torture me." She sighed dramatically. "They know that's my favorite."

"Keep explaining the Ryersons," I told her. "Race's dad isn't marrying Alex's mom?"

"No." Taz settled back in her bed, her textbooks out in front of her.

We were supposed to be studying.

349

Taz itched under some of the wiring. She was finally getting it taken off tomorrow. "They're breaking ground between Fallen Crest and Frisco for a new Harley shop."

"So Race's dad is shacking up with Alex's mom?"

It was all confusing and all sorts of wrong.

She nodded. "Yep. It's fucked up. When Alex gets back from rehab, his uncle is going to be a different sort of uncle." She grinned.

"Lame joke."

She shrugged. "What can you do? It's a mess, all around."

"Are the two moms talking?"

"Not from what Race says. His mom is using the money from her settlement to buy a house in Fallen Crest. He told me he's worried she'll want him to move since they have a better school."

I grunted. "The rich one or the public one?"

"Either, honestly. She did good with the settlement." Pulling one of her pillows onto her lap, Taz began to pick at the edges. She didn't look back up.

"Race wants to stay?" I asked.

She raised a shoulder. "I don't know. I mean, I can't blame his mom, you know? Fallen Crest doesn't have crews."

"Yeah, but they have other problems."

"Besides." She put the pillow to the side. "It might not matter. If she buys a house in Fallen Crest, he can't go to Roussou anyway. Can he?"

"The district lines are weird. I know of someone who lived by Fallen Crest but went to school in Roussou. It could happen, I guess."

"Yeah. Maybe." She sounded dejected. "So." She seemed to force a lighter, happier tone. It made me cringe. "How about you? How's everyone treating the new Bren and Cross?" She laughed. "And I so saw that coming—for, like, ever."

I smiled. "It's going just fine."

Though it was great just to see her, I remembered the reasons I'd come. It must have shown on my face.

Taz laughed. "Out with it. I know my brother sent you to find out about Race's stuff. Everybody's been wondering. What else do you need to know?"

Alex was out as the Ryerson crew leader. He'd been kicked out months ago, and while everyone assumed Race would step into his role, he hadn't.

It was crew business. We had to know. "Is Race going to join the Ryerson crew?"

She shook her head. "No. He's trying to stay out of all of it."

That was good. But also not good.

"They've never not had a Ryerson lead." I was mostly talking to myself.

"They still do."

"What?" Was Alex coming back? Were they taking him back in? That was...surprising, if that was the case.

Taz shrugged, shaking her head. "I don't know who it is, but a couple of the members talked to Race. He was asked to join and lead. He turned them down, but then they came back and said they were going to be fine. There'd be a Ryerson leader after all. That was it. Race didn't ask. I don't think he wants to know."

Well. Shit. I didn't know if that was good or not.

A new Ryerson was stepping up to the plate. Problem with that was, there were no Ryersons left.

"Maybe a cousin or something?" Zellman wondered an hour later when I relayed the information to the guys at Jordan's warehouse.

"Maybe." Cross grabbed two beers and brought one over, sitting down next to me. "They have a big family, and douchebag seems to be in the genes. I wouldn't be surprised."

"We're not going to know until whoever it is makes his presence known. So..." Jordan put his drink on the table and focused on me. Or, no—he focused on Cross and me. "Let's talk rules. This has been put off for too long. You two broke ours."

Zellman broke out in a wide smile. "Yeah. No couples in crews."

CREW

"That's our rule, but it's not like we planned this." Cross put his beer on the table as well, taking point for us.

I was glad.

All the talking I'd done over the last couple months had tired me out. There'd been the whole professing at Durrant's house, then the police questions, my brother's own interrogation of me, Heather had her questions too. After that, once we went back to school, there was the community service. Taz had been out of school recovering, so I was stuck with Tabatha, Sunday, Monica, and all of their friends. Plus The Badger—for the committee and our counseling sessions, and I *just* started those.

I could go mute for the next six years to break even.

"Come on, Cross!" Jordan rolled his eyes.

"You come on." Cross pointed at him. "We put that rule in place to save ourselves from stupid drama, and it wasn't needed. We were in seventh grade, and be honest, you put it in place because you didn't want Bren and me kissing even back then. You wanted to be the one to kiss her."

"Wha—what?!" I surged to my feet.

Jordan's neck was getting red. He clenched his jaw, stiffening. "It's not like that. It wasn't like that, Bren."

Z shot his hand in the air, still grinning. "I always wanted to make out with you, B."

Well, that was... Okay then. I sat back down, still frowning. "Thanks?"

"But not anymore," Zellman added. "You're like my sister now. Crew family. But no lie, I'm hoping to see your tits someday. And it's probably going to happen, since we all scrap."

That was Zellman's new word for fighting. Scrapping. He thought it sounded better, less violent. Why he'd decided that, I'd never know. But we went with it.

"Fine," Jordan said. "I was young too, and I was stupid, and yes. Cross is right. I suggested that rule because I didn't want you and Cross to date, but even after I stopped caring, I thought it was a good rule. I *still* think it's a good idea."

I looked to the ceiling.

352

Cross groaned next to me.

Jordan spoke over us, raising his voice. "But I can see how serious you guys are, and I think it's a rule that's going to have an exception. The only crew couple we can have in this crew is Cross and Bren."

I wasn't the only one who snorted.

There were no other girls, and all the guys were straight. I had no intention of dating either of those two, but as far as Jordan, it was a win. He was conceding.

"Thank you," I said.

He nodded, a smile tugging at his mouth. "I'm fully aware you guys wouldn't have given a shit if we didn't make this amendment, but it means a lot that you're pretending to care."

"I want our crew to officially be a democracy," Cross added. "No more leader shit."

Jordan rolled his eyes this time. "Yeah, right. Things will get heated again. You'll take over, because you're better at that stuff than me, and when things loosen up, I'll step up like I'm doing right now. Let's call a spade a spade. We all know that's how it'll be." He picked up his beer, standing. Gesturing to Zellman and me, he added, "Bren will go rogue, start shit when she gets mad. Z will keep trying to get Sunday's pussy even though he does every other day—"

"And it's so good." Z moaned, closing his eyes and slumping back on the couch. "So warm and tight."

"—and that's how we're going to keep going." Jordan ignored Z. We all ignored Z. "Stand up, Wolf Crew, and beers up."

We stood, clinking our beers together and raising them, all pressed together.

Jordan's voice grew rough. He blinked a few times. "I wouldn't change our crew for anything. Never fucking change."

Z piped up, "On three! One, two—"

We all finished together, "Wolf Crew!"

EPILOGUE

TAZ SAT ON Race's lap in the middle of a field party—which was actually more of a woods party since we were in a clearing smack in the middle of a forest.

Alex remained away, going to a second and more intensive treatment facility after the first. The cynical side of me wondered if it was done at his lawyer's urging, as it would show "good faith" that he was trying to rehabilitate himself. The case against him for assaulting Taz hadn't gone before the judge yet for sentencing.

"And I told Tab it was a bad idea to date college guys. It's never going to work." Taz looped her arms around Race's neck, leaning back and looking up at him.

It wasn't even a subtle smile from girlfriend to boyfriend. It was a full beam. The girl was stupid in love. I shook my head, catching the pressed lips from the other girls sitting around Jordan's truck.

Yes. I'm as shocked as anyone, but somehow, Sunday, and even Monica had worn me down so I didn't immediately turn away when they approached.

But a few minutes was the longest I could last.

Taz was creating a target on herself, because while she might be happy and content, those girls weren't. After Cross, the next guy on the totem pole was Race, and they liked him. They liked him even more now than they had before. He was wealthy and still in Roussou, so those girls were plotting to break up the two of them.

"So, Bren—" Sunday began.

Nope. I was out. I recognized that smile on her face. She shared a look with Monica, who had been doing a whole lot of that with Cross over the last month.

Looking. Staring. Drooling.

Cross was the same, acting like he never saw it. If a girl stopped him, he kept moving.

But those girls didn't care about the hints. It was the same shit that had been going on at the beginning of the year. They were more and more hungry for him.

When it had come out that we were together, people stepped back. But it didn't last long. Some of that was because of us. Some was because of them.

We liked to keep things under wraps in public. Taz was on strict instructions to keep her mouth shut, and Race too. No one else would talk because the only other people on the up-and-up were Jordan and Z. But because Cross and I didn't act much different than we had before, the whispering had increased the last few weeks.

People were confused, wondering if maybe we weren't a couple. They *wanted* Cross to be single, so they were starting to buzz about it.

Cross was at this party, but he wasn't at my side. Only Jordan sat in this circle with me, right beside me. Z was off trying to get in someone else's pants because this was the "off" night or day or week, or whatever was happening between him and Sunday.

When she opened her mouth to ask me whatever she was going to ask, I decided not to stick around to see if she was asking for Monica, or for herself, or hell—for most of the female population at our school.

I stood, not giving a shit if that was rude, and tossed back the rest of my beer. It was my third, and I had a nice buzz going.

"I'm out." I looked at Taz and Race, then met Jordan's eyes.

He raised his eyebrows, a silent question if I'd come back.

I dipped my head, just the smallest of movements, but it was enough.

He settled back.

I had to come back. The new Ryerson leader was rumored to be showing up tonight. I almost laughed hearing a few guys speculating whether it was a girl, because it wasn't just our crew who was curious. Everyone was. But thinking back over the Ryerson family, there were only a couple cousins I thought could step up to the plate, but I didn't think they would. One was either in medical school or planning on attending. Another was in a state softball league for her high school. And there was a third, but I didn't know much about her. She lived up north. I'd met her once when she came down for a Ryerson family reunion, but it'd been brief. Alex's mom had said at the time that she was smart and driven.

Maybe her?

I had no idea.

The only thing I did have an idea about was getting some time with Cross, and I wanted him alone.

The rumors were starting to bother me, even though I told myself they shouldn't. But still, a girl could only hear so much about everyone's hopes and dreams of dating Cross before her claws came out.

And mine were sharp. I hadn't fought in a while, possibly too long.

I wandered around the party. Many watched me go past, falling silent. A few tried to draw me in for a conversation. I ignored all of them. They weren't as scared of me as before. Enough time had passed since they'd seen a fight break out, or *sorry, Z*—a scrap break out. That meant I hadn't been flashing my knife around.

I was following a path that led away from everyone when I heard Cross behind me.

"Looking for me?" He fell in step, glancing over his shoulder.

Only a couple people had seen us go. One guy nudged his buddy, and they started snickering.

I rotated swiftly and flicked both my middle fingers at them.

They shut up.

Cross was shaking his head, trying not to laugh.

"Shut it." I smacked his chest with the back of my hand.

He caught it, and I laced my fingers with his.

"God." He pulled me to him, dropping a kiss to my neck, running his free hand down my back. "You have no idea how hard it is to stay away sometimes."

The girlfriend in me melted. The best friend couldn't help but tease. "Weak sauce."

He barked a laugh, his lips nipping my shoulder, and his hands slipped inside my jeans. When they kept going, I moved to him, bringing us into perfect alignment. I lifted my mouth, and there he was.

His lips covered mine, opening and taking control.

A shiver ran down my spine, making my entire body tremble.

He grabbed a fistful of my ass before slipping around to the front. He pushed his hand in, not caring that my jeans weren't unbuckled, and I had a second's notice before he thrust two fingers inside of me.

"Fuck." I moaned.

Cross let go of my hand and banded his arm around my back. He pulled me off the trail, but we weren't far enough from the party. We could still hear their laughter, so groaning, he stepped away and tugged me ahead.

We moved farther off the path. Once we stopped hearing them, he pressed me up against a tree.

It was like we'd never touched each other. It was like he hadn't been moving inside me just this morning, but it didn't matter.

Fuck. This guy.

I would always hunger for him, now that I'd gotten a taste.

"I want you. Now." He panted against my mouth, unbuckling my jeans. His fingers pushed my underwear aside and were back in me, rotating, rolling, thrusting.

I fell back against the tree, my neck exposed, and his mouth latched there.

He was licking, tasting, taking what was his.

Everything in me shuddered. Pleasure coursed through me, electrifying me all the way to my toes.

He pulled out a condom, and then he was sliding inside of me.

I clamped onto him, winding my legs around his waist, and I moved my hips in rhythm.

It was hard, fast, and rough. It was a quickie snack, a fucking appetizer because when we were done, there was a rush inside of me. I knew this had been the foreplay for a long night before us.

"You're going to kill me one day." Cross groaned as he pulled out, his mouth dropping to mine.

I ran a hand down his back, savoring how he trembled under my touch. Even now. Even after we were done.

"I love you."

He pressed a hard kiss to my mouth. "I love you too."

He held me, standing against me as I lowered my legs to the ground. Still holding on with one hand, we adjusted our clothing back into place. I caught a whiff of hand sanitizer, and I didn't ask what he'd done with the condom.

After we were both breathing evenly again, we started back.

Cross put his arm around my shoulder, tucking me next to him. I held his hand in mine, and for a moment, we were lost in each other.

That lasted until we drew closer, near enough to hear someone calling, "Where are Bren and Cross?"

I stopped, my feet gluing in place.

No.

I recognized that voice, but it couldn't be right.

Cross' arm fell from my shoulder. He stepped forward. "Is that...?" He looked back at me.

He saw it was. It was written all over my face.

He swore, raking a hand through his hair. "You didn't know?"

"How would I?"

He wasn't the only one reeling. I was sucker-punched in the diaphragm.

I didn't want him here. Ever. But especially not now, not after I was with Cross, not after we'd just had a moment. I didn't want any of that shattered, and if I knew this guy, he'd sniff it out like a bloodhound.

"—until they get back. I have an announcement to make."

We had to go. I wasn't going to hide from this, whatever it was.

Jordan and Zellman were positioned just down our path, a few yards past the larger group. They knew we'd gone this way. They knew we'd return this way. As if sensing us, Jordan looked back. Z too.

Each of them wore a blank expression, but I could see their surprise. They were as shocked as us, just guarded.

"I know the Ryerson crew has only had a leader who's in high school—"

The crowd shifted.

When people saw us, they moved, opening an entire section of the ring so we had front row seats to the person standing in front. His arms were up, as if he were holding court or giving a sermon.

With his back to a truck's headlights, his crew lined up behind him like a backdrop, stood a Ryerson I hoped I'd never see again.

Drake Ryerson.

Alex's brother, and my ex. The same guy who'd quit, lived with Race for a summer, and talked all about how he hated the crew system. The same guy who'd wanted to mess with us by telling Race to push for a friendship with us. The same guy who knew we wouldn't take to that.

He still looked like Race, with the same round face, but he seemed to have aged. His face was scruffy, and he was more built, as if he'd been lifting weights in his time away. Dark hair. Dark eyes. A sneer I used to think was attractive, mixed with a twinkle in his eye, and a dimple in his cheek that he used as a weapon.

He was an asinine fucker. That's what he was.

He turned, mid-speech, and his eyes locked on mine. "I was approached earlier in the year by a member of Monroe's crew, and I thought long and hard about it. After finding out what my little brother had been up to, and how my cousin was now here but not joining, I decided to make an executive decision." He paused, a grin pulling at the corner of his lip. He finished as if he were speaking just to me. "I'm coming back, and I'm taking my old position. I'm taking over the Ryerson crew again. They're no longer without a leader."

Half the group was watching me instead of him.

He knew it, adding after a beat, "Hey, Bren."

He stepped toward us, but faltered when Jordan and Zellman closed ranks so they were standing in front of me.

Chuckling, he walked over.

The show was over. It was like he'd dropped an invisible cue, and everyone began talking at once. Or most did. The few who had eyes on us and were within hearing distance, tried to edge closer. A couple girls strained their necks. Some of the guy Normals were watching too, sipping their beers as if they weren't gawking like the rest.

He stopped right in front of Jordan and Z. "I'm not just here for her, you know. I'm here for all of you."

Jordan folded his arms over his chest. Z dropped his head lower, ready to fight.

"Cross."

Cross ignored that greeting from Drake, watching me instead. His hand touched mine, and he lowered his voice. "What do you want to do?"

"I come in peace," Drake said. "I have a gift for your crew. Your *entire* crew."

I hated it, but we had to hear him out.

Cross cleared his throat.

Jordan and Zellman shifted, presenting Cross to my ex.

Drake latched onto that movement, his gaze jumping from Cross to me and back again, then dropping and lingering on the hand that still brushed against mine. I felt singed, but Cross didn't move.

"What do you want, Drake?" Cross asked.

Drake flicked his eyes to Jordan, noting the change, but nodded. "Okay. Things have changed around here." Before anyone could respond—or growl in my case—he smiled the most fake smile I'd ever seen on his face. Then it was gone, along with any polite pretense. He stepped closer, right between Jordan and Z, and all amusement left his tone.

"I'm back for my crew, and to take care of my family." He looked over at me. "I don't need to tell any of you that, but I am, as a sign of good faith. I know my brother messed things up, and as a *further* sign of good faith, I left a present for you at the top of that cliff you guys love so much. It's there just for you, just to show you things will be different under my leadership. I hope you all appreciate it."

He looked at each of us in turn. He was wrapping this in a nice shiny paper, as if he truly meant what he was saying.

I grunted. "We'll see."

His eyes found mine and lingered. "Yes. You will." He stepped back. "Text me when you get there," he told Cross. "I have one more thing to add."

It took us ten minutes.

When we pulled up, Jordan's truck was first, pausing at the mouth of the clearing before pulling over and parking. Cross' truck lights lit the way, and we could see Drake's present.

"What the fuck?"

Cross texted Drake.

His phone buzzed back, almost right away.

He showed the screen to me. **Don't kill him. Don't cause any permanent damage. Beyond that, this is my crew sending their apologies for what happened to Taz.**

This was payback for her, payback we'd never collected.

In the middle of the lot, sitting cross-legged with his head hanging down, was Alex Ryerson.

Drake had left his brother for a beatdown.

This is the end of *Crew,* book one!
Visit http://www.tijansbooks.com/crew-princess.html to read
Crew Princess, book two!

Visit http://www.tijansbooks.com/the-boy-i-grew-up-with.html
to read Heather and Channing's book too.
More information and more reading
can be found at www.tijansbooks.com

If you enjoyed *Crew,* please leave a review!
They help so unbelievably much.

ACKNOWLEDGEMENTS

The idea of *Crew* started a long time ago. I wrote a few chapters. My agent shopped it around. No one wanted it, so I knew I was going to self-publish it, but it was set aside for other projects.

A few months after that, I started *Ryan's Bed*. I wrote eight chapters, and then set that aside. (That's all explained in the back of that book!) And then eight months later, a new beginning for *Crew* spoke to me and out came Bren's story.

Bren's life is similar to some of my other characters, but so not at the same time. She really is like a feral wolf at times. She yearns for family, for love, but she puts up a tough shield to break through. She snaps and snarls and she bites back, though not literally. But she's got a heart of gold for who she trusts not to hurt her, and that was the real story for me.

I want to thank all those publishers for passing on *Crew*, because this might've been a whole different book.

I want to thank my agent for always trusting me to do 'my thing.' Thank you to Nina for helping this book being seen everywhere it is! I want to thank Crystal for becoming someone I rely on so much. I want to thank Eileen, Heather, Autumn, Amanda, Christina, and Pam for helping me out anytime I popped in their private messages. I'd like to thank Elaine for always being so quick with a change in my books. And Jessica for being soooo flexible with me. I know I send you a lot and you're always amenable. It means A LOT! And thank you to Chris, Amy, Paige, and Kara. You guys catch the little details I'd never catch and your suggestions help mold my books every time. Your input is so golden.

Thank you to Katy Evans! Woman, you literally cheered me on with this book. That time we messaged, you have no idea how much I needed to hear some of the encouragement you were giving me.

And last, I want to thank the readers. You all have no idea how you're the rockstars. The support, the cheer, the kindness, the smiles, the happiness—it is so needed on those days where you're questioning everything. A simple post in the reader group might be a little thing to you, but not to us authors. We can't pay someone for that support, so thank YOU!

Okay. I'm wrapping up.

I'm beyond excited for Crew 2. (Not the title!) I hope you guys are too! I hope, hope, hope you enjoyed this one from me.

Tijan

CPSIA information can be obtained
at www.ICGtesting.com
Printed in the USA
LVHW030536030223
738516LV00002B/203